The Beach Hut called Alice

For Mum Dad and Kevin

4

Chapter 1

James arrived home after a long exhausting day's work in the city. Wearily closing the front door behind him he placed his briefcase on the floor, slipped off his overcoat and draped it over the banisters. Entering the kitchen he noticed the light flashing on his answerphone. It was bound to be his mother - she was the only person he knew who still persisted in using the landline. He pressed the play button.

Hello dear. Just checking that you're still on for roast on Sunday. It will just be the three of us. Your dad wants me to tell you that he's got some news. It's a bequest for you from Jem's estate. Dad will reveal all over lunch.

Pressing the delete button, James sat on the kitchen stool. 'Interesting!' he said to himself. 'I didn't expect that.' But in fact nothing about Jem's death had been at all predictable.

James had been as shocked as the rest of the family on hearing of his playboy Uncle's sudden death - apparently from natural causes. He'd been only 59 and had always appeared to be in robust health. James had never called him Uncle though – he was known to the whole family simply as 'Jem'. Sadly, they'd not communicated with each other for several years (apart from Christmas cards) and James just presumed that his Uncle was living the high life as usual, full of exotic holidays, lady friends and flashy cars. Jem had been well known for his bachelor lifestyle, particularly since taking early retirement some years back after making a fortune dealing on the stock market. Apparently nobody, including Jem himself, had any idea he was in anything less than perfect health. He simply went to bed one night as usual, and failed to wake up again the next morning.

A large crowd had gathered for the funeral. The family contingent was fairly small, and James had assumed that most of the bereaved were probably members of Jem's extensive social circle, including, he suspected, several grieving girlfriends.

Everyone was stunned by Jem's sudden departure. Understandably much of the conversation revolved around how shocked they had all been to hear the tragic news.

'I thought he had 30 more years of partying left in him yet ... We only saw him three weeks ago... He seemed in fantastic shape ...We were going to meet in Spain next month ... Scary isn't it – just goes to show you never know what's round the corner.'

On Sunday James visited his parents for lunch. His father was Jem's older brother and the executor of his will. James hadn't expected to inherit anything, assuming that most of the estate would go to his father because Jem didn't have any children (well none they knew of anyway), or maybe there was a special mistress somewhere.

Tucking into the delicious roast dinner that his mother had painstakingly prepared, it was obvious to James that his father was enjoying stretching out the suspense before revealing the details of the bequest, and he clearly wanted James to beg him to reveal all. But James had no intention of playing along, preferring to feign disinterest. Mind you, over the weekend James had amused himself remembering Jem's various eccentricities and all the hobbies with which he had briefly dabbled in before moving onto something new. Perhaps the bequest would be the Hornby model train-set? ... maybe the tandem? ... or what about his prized collection of original boxed Britains wargames figures? But then James was brought down to earth with a definite bump when he recalled the smelly old bearded collie Jem used to have. *No surely the dog must have passed away by now? That was donkey's years ago wasn't it?*

But, in fact, James was wrong about all of those possibilities. He couldn't have been more surprised when his father finally condescended to enlighten him. It turned out that Jem had left his nephew, 'The beach hut at Sebleigh Bay!' James laughed out loud.

'What? He's left *me* the beach hut? Gosh I had no idea he still owned it.'

'No we didn't either dear,' said his mother. 'We assumed he'd got rid of it years ago.'

'He hadn't mentioned it to either of us for decades,' added his father. James had a vague memory of visiting it as a child with his parents and sister, but had never been back to Sebleigh Bay since.

'It's a very generous gift James. You'll be surprised how much they're worth now!' His father pointed out.

'Jem was always very fond of you,' added his mother.

Three days later, his curiosity getting the better of him, James took a rare day off work, and set off in his car to visit his newly acquired beach hut. He had no intention of keeping it, seeing no use for a beach hut as he was recently divorced and had no children with whom to share sunny days at the coast. He hadn't picked a great day for his visit. It was a grey, cold, misty February morning when he took the two hour drive to the coast.

James drove through the old-fashioned seaside town of Sebleigh Bay, through the shopping centre and then turned left along the promenade. He noticed the well kept gardens along the seafront, and a few amusement arcades and fun fair rides.

At the very end of the promenade was Chalk Cliff Way car park where he left his car. Beyond the carpark was a slope leading down to Chalk Cliff Way which was a wide path that continued along the seafront with the chalk cliffs rising up on the left hand side and the pebbled beach with its long row of beach huts on the right. James walked along the path having a good look at all the pretty pastel coloured beach huts, noticing that some were in much better condition than others. Some of them had names and seemed to be well cared for, many of them decorated with bunting or fairy lights. Others looked neglected and in need of repair. He feared the worst for his hut, thinking that his uncle had probably not visited it for decades, preferring more exotic locations for his holidays.

The area was deserted, and it was a strange feeling to be walking at the bottom of the cliffs with an endless row of beach huts disappearing into the mist. There were no sounds except for his footsteps, the gentle waves breaking on the beach and a few haunting cries from seagulls. When James arrived at number eighteen he was pleasantly surprised to see that he had judged his uncle unfairly. His beach hut was painted in pale blue and white stripes and was in very good condition, although James thought it would be worth getting it freshly painted in order to fetch the best price when he sold it.

He walked all around the hut noticing a window on one side and a small veranda on the front facing the sea. Using the key he let himself in the door. He closed it behind him imagining it would keep the cold out.

The space inside was larger than he'd imagined. There was a table and two chairs folded up against the side wall, several deckchairs and an old settee at the back of the hut, covered in colourful blankets and some pretty cushions. A small ledge by the window held two glass jars, one containing a selection of sea shells, and the other, pieces of green and white glass. Loose on the shelf there were also a few smooth pebbles, a piece of driftwood and a small photo in a silver frame. James picked up the silver frame. The photo showed a very relaxed looking Jem lounging in a deckchair outside the hut on a summer's day. He was holding a large glass of wine and was smiling contentedly at whoever was behind the camera. James was moved by the photo. 'Thank you Jem,' he said quietly. 'Rest in peace.' In this cold dull weather it was hard to imagine a time when you could sit outside in shorts and t-shirt, sipping wine.

James wondered who had taken the photo – who was Jem smiling at? Possibly someone special judging by the twinkle in his uncle's eye.

A sound outside interrupted his thoughts. Someone walking on the beach – their feet crunching on the pebbles nearby. He might have a look in a moment – see who else would want to be here on this cold damp day in February. He continued to examine the interior of his hut. He noticed a colourful rug on the floor which looked brand new, and there was a copy of The Financial Times on the settee, which surprisingly was dated just a few weeks ago. *Interesting ... he obviously has been here recently.* James picked up the paper and leafed through it, recognising the recent news stories. References to share prices reminded him of the fact that Jem had bought James his first shares when he was just a young child, and which he still held now. James was then distracted from the newspaper by another sound outside. He moved towards the door and noticed that someone sounded distressed, sobbing even.

He opened the door and saw a young woman sitting on the beach just a few metres away looking out to sea. Her shoulders were shaking as she wept. She turned round and saw him. Her startled eyes full of tears were framed by dark curls of hair emerging from the woolly hat and scarf that she was wrapped up in.

'Sorry,' she said between sobs. 'No-one ever comes here in the winter. I thought I was on my own.' She wiped her eyes quickly and tried to compose herself.

'Are you okay?'

'Yes,' she sniffed. 'Thanks. I didn't see you there.' She was about to get up. James stretched his hand out to signal to her not to.

'No, please, don't get up. I apologise for disturbing you ... I ...'

'No, it's alright. I'm making a fool of myself – I was just feeling sorry for myself.'

9

James took a few steps towards her, his feet crunching on the pebbles.

'Are you sure you're alright?'

'Yes really. It's not as bad as it looks.'

'Can I do anything to help?' She shook her head. James felt she looked self-conscious so he switched the attention to himself.

'Well I've just been given a beach hut. I've come to see it for the first time. Was just wondering what to do with it?'

'You were *given* it? Lucky you! I wouldn't mind if someone gave me one,' she said as she pulled a tissue out from her coat pocket.

'Yes. My Uncle died recently and this is what he left me.'

'Oh – are you going to bring your family down here then?'

'Well no. To be honest, I don't really have anyone to bring. Divorced recently. No kids. My sister and her family live abroad.'

'Oh I see.' They both fell silent – neither of them sure how to proceed. He noticed that her eyes were actually very pretty despite the redness and tears. He didn't want their conversation to end there.

'Do you live round here?' he asked.

'Yes. Just on the other side of the town. What about you?'

'No, I live in Greysford, and work in the city. I haven't been here since I was a child. I don't remember much about the town to be honest. I think we visited the beach hut when I was small, but I only have vague memories. The town looks nice. I imagine it gets busy in the summer?'

'Yes the seafront really comes alive. I like seeing the tourists enjoying the beach. I go and join them when I get the chance and bring the kids down after school on a hot day for ice-creams and paddling.'

'That sounds good. Hard to imagine though, the way it looks at the moment.'

'There's not usually anyone around here at this time of year.'

10

'Yes sorry about that. You didn't expect a stranger to pop out of a beach hut and surprise you!' They both smiled.

'And you didn't expect to find a daft woman making a display of herself outside your newly acquired property. I feel a bit silly.'

'Oh please don't. Look – tell me to mind my own business if you like, but we're complete strangers. I don't come from round here. If you want to talk about anything – go ahead if it would help?'

'Well ... I don't know...'

'It wouldn't do any harm?'

'Hey! What the heck? Why not ... if you're sure? ... but ... I don't know ... it's probably just going to sound stupid.' She examined the large smooth pebble which she'd just picked up and explained thoughtfully, 'Let's just say that I've finally admitted to myself that I married the wrong man. It's been building up, and building up, and then it came to a head this weekend when he spent the whole time trying to persuade me that we should have another baby!'

'Ah. How many children have you got?'

'Two. They're five and six, and I've just recently returned to work part time. No way do I want to give it up – it's the only thing keeping me sane at the moment.'

'Do you mind if I sit down?' James asked tentatively pointing to the pebbles.

'No of course not.' James sat down on the pebbles, not too close, as he didn't want her to feel uncomfortable. The gentle sound of the waves added a calming back drop to their conversation.

'So what's wrong with hubby then? Why the big mistake?'

'Well nothing at all actually – it's me that's the problem. I suppose I just don't feel the right way about him.'

'Presumably you loved him once?'

Silence.

11

'Well ... if I'm completely honest ... no, not really.' She started looking tearful again. 'I've never admitted that before to anyone. I can't believe I'm actually saying it.'

'It's okay,' he said kindly.

'You see ... we hadn't been going out together long when I accidentally got pregnant. He proposed to me straight away, and before I knew it we were rushing into getting married and buying a place together before the baby arrived. I knew when I walked down the aisle that I was making a mistake, but I'm not the sort of person who could do an about turn in the church, leaving all the guests gaping, like a scene from a soap opera. Tim really is a nice man, and I just hoped my feelings would change ... grow stronger.'

'Hmm... doesn't tend to work like that does it?'

'No. I've really tried to make a go of it – for all our sakes. I didn't want my children growing up without their father like I did. I guess I was so determined to do things properly that I ignored my feelings. But, coming back to the present, I'm just not sure I can carry on living a lie like this.' She threw her pebble into the sea. 'What about you? You said you were recently divorced.'

'Yes. We were married eight years.' James paused. 'I guess we just didn't spend enough time together and grew in different directions. I was obsessed with my job. Stockbroker. I can see that now – we should have spent more time together. She got fed up with me never being around. Mind you, she was more than happy to spend the money I earned! We wanted children for a while, but that didn't happen. Most likely down to me! I think she resented me for that.'

'That's not fair.'

'Maybe not but I suppose she couldn't help the way she felt. But to be honest, now that we're divorced I'm really glad that I don't have children who I only see on alternate weekends. I have colleagues in that position, and it can be tough.' He suddenly felt self-conscious talking about himself and wanted to change the subject.

'Anyway …we're telling each other our life stories and I don't know your name.' He said with a big smile.

'I'm Alice.'

'Pleased to meet you Alice. I'm James.' He leaned towards her and stretched out his hand which she took in her small woolly gloved hand. They shook hands and laughed.

'Look Alice. It's freezing cold here, and these pebbles are not all that comfortable,' he said pulling a face and wriggling his bottom 'I couldn't buy you a cup of tea in a cafe somewhere could I?'

'Alright', she said cheerfully. 'Why not? There's a nice one just along here past the huts. I've heard it stays open in the winter.' They both got up and walked back to James's beach hut.

'I just need to lock up my mansion first.' They both laughed.

'I've noticed this hut before,' Alice said. 'I love the blue and white colour scheme – I think it's one of the prettiest ones here. I've always fancied owning one of these.'

'Have a look if you like.' Alice followed James onto the veranda and l in through the doorway.

'Oh I see someone's collected a jar of sea glass,' Alice said with interest. James picked up the jar on the window sill.

'This is sea glass is it?' he said examining the contents.

'Yes. You find it on the beach. It starts off as discarded bottles and after years and years of being broken and tumbled in the waves and the pebbles it turns into beautiful smooth pieces of glass – like little gems.'

'Fascinating. I didn't know such a thing existed.'

'Most people never notice them unless they're looking for them. Once I discovered them though I couldn't walk on the beach without collecting them. It's kind of addictive.' She put her hand in her pocket. 'There we are; there's even some in my pocket!" James looked puzzled.

'I find it hard to believe that my uncle would have collected those himself.'

13

'It might have been someone who visited him? Or maybe a previous owner of the hut left them there?'

'Maybe. This is my Uncle Jem,' James said handing Alice the framed photo. She smiled.

'Oh he looks so content there doesn't he.'

'Yes, that's what I thought – I really hope he was a happy man. As far as I know he seemed to lead a high old life. Had too much charm for his own good.' James placed the photo back on the window sill. 'Anyway – it's really chilly – let's go and find that cafe.'

James locked up and they walked along the path between the bottom of the cliffs and the long row of beach huts. They were looking at the huts and comparing the different colours and conditions of them and commenting on which ones they liked best. As the huts finally came to an end they saw the welcome sight of the Beachcomber Cafe with a warm glow coming from the lights inside. It was the only building at the end of the path. It was an old building which had been modernised with huge windows all the way around. An 'A' board sign on the path outside said 'open' and welcomed them to the cafe. They walked across the forecourt of the cafe to the entrance which was round the far side.

As they entered, a friendly attractive woman walked past the door cheerfully saying 'Good morning' to them, and they both noticed her carrying a tray with two delicious looking mugs of hot chocolate, with cream and marshmallows piled high on top. The mugs were on plates with chocolate buttons. James and Alice's eyes lit up they smiled at each other.

'Mmm, they look good,' said James. 'Shall we have what they're having?'

'Oh I think so!' Alice said enthusiastically.

'Do you want to go and choose a table, and I'll order them? My treat.'

'Thank you.' Alice chose a table by the window, looking out to sea, while James was having a joke with the man serving behind the counter. The huge windows allowed plenty of light to pour inside even on a dull day like today. There were only a few customers there this morning. James came over and sat down opposite Alice.

'They're bringing the drinks in a minute,' he said. 'In the meantime we have these to keep us going.' He was holding two small plates containing large chocolate buttons in three different colours.

'Oh wow! What a treat. I'd heard this was a great place for chocolate lovers, but I haven't been here for years. Thank you for this James. It's kind of you.'

'You're welcome,' he said cheerfully, giving her a big smile, making her feel at ease. They both tucked into the chocolate buttons. Alice looked around at the surroundings.

'This cafe is lovely isn't it,' she said. 'It's been modernised since I last came in.'

'Yes. I was just thinking how nice the ambience is. Did you see those photographs on the wall over there – they've got some of your pieces of glass on them.'

'Really? Oh yes. They're obviously beachcombing themed pictures. I'll have to have a proper look sometime. I'll definitely come down here again soon. So, now that you've seen your beach hut ...any more thoughts about what you're going to do with it?'

'Sell it I guess.'

'That's a shame.'

'Do you think I should keep it then, and come and visit it every year, treat it a bit like an elderly aunt or grannie who lives at the seaside?' Alice laughed.

'Well maybe you should just think about it for a while and not rush into making a decision just yet.'

'Hmm, very sensible. Ah – here are our drinks. Thank you,' James said to the man who brought them over.

'Wow! These look incredible. Thank you'.

'You're very welcome.'

They laughed at each other as they tried to sip their drinks without getting cream round their faces.

'Did you say you were a stock broker?' Alice asked.

'Yes that's right.'

'Hmm …You don't look like one.' James pretended to look himself up and down.

'Why not? What *do* I look like then?' He was very slim, with longish dark floppy hair. He was wearing black jeans and an expensive looking but well worn leather jacket.

'Well ... I think you look quite creative. Like an artist or a designer maybe? Or an actor?' James burst out laughing, nearly spilling his hot chocolate which he was about to sip.

'But nothing at all like a stockbroker? Perhaps I'd better change profession then? Only ... I can't draw, I can't design things and I certainly can't act!'

'Well I guess appearances can be deceptive,' she giggled. James loved it when Alice smiled and laughed. He was feeling pleased with himself for cheering her up so much. He was enjoying her company hugely and didn't want their time together to end.

'So where do you work Alice?'

'I have a part time job. What kind of work do you think I might do?' Alice asked with a smile.

'No honestly, I really couldn't guess. I wouldn't dare.'

'At least try – go on.'

'Oh I don't know. You work with children?" Alice shook her head as she sipped her hot chocolate.

'Is it ... anything to do with the holiday or tourist industry?'

'No.'

'You work in an office?'

'Yes I do actually.'

'Aha. You tell me which office you work in?'

'Okay. I work at the garden centre.'

'Oh right. So you work in the office rather than the greenhouses.'

'Yes. My work's more to do with the gift department – I'm a buyer - I order candles, ornaments, gifts, books ...things like that. I do a job share with another

16

woman. We work the hours out between us. As long as one of us is there everyone's happy. She's very helpful about me fitting my work round the children too, so it works out well.'

Alice and James passed away a very pleasant hour or so sipping their hot chocolates and talking about their jobs and some of the colourful characters they each worked with. James noticed Alice glancing up at the clock on the wall a couple of times.

'You've got to go haven't you,' he said, trying not to sound as disappointed as he felt.

'Yes. I'm picking my daughter up early today to take her to the dentist.' James got the feeling that she didn't really want to go and that she was delaying her departure as long as possible, so it gave him the confidence to pull a pen out from inside his jacket, and he grabbed a paper napkin and scribbled his mobile phone number on it. He passed it to her.

'It's been so nice to meet you. If you fancy a chat or a text sometime, here's my number.'

'Thanks.' She folded the napkin and put it in her pocket. Despite the beautiful smile she gave him, he had no idea if he would hear from her. Alice stood up and put on her coat and scarf.

'Did you come by car?' asked James.

'Yes – it's in the car park just past the beach huts,' she said leaning her head in that direction.

James made a point of calling out 'Thank you' to the cafe owners and followed Alice out the door and they walked back along Chalk Cliff Way together. He thought she seemed a little quiet, slightly self-conscious perhaps. He wondered if he'd done the right thing giving her – a married woman – his phone number. But it wasn't every day he met someone as lovely as her, and he just couldn't bear the thought of not speaking to her again. They were making polite conversation about the town and the weather. James was intending to walk all the way to the car park with her, but as

17

they approached James's beach hut, Alice slowed down and said firmly,

'I'll leave you here at your property!' She turned towards him with a big smile. 'Thank you so much for cheering me up.'

'It's been lovely to meet you. Take care and good luck with everything.' He put his hand gently on her arm and bent forwards and kissed her on the cheek.

'Thanks James. And thank you for the drink. It was kind of you.'

'You're welcome. Bye.' As he watched her walking off briskly towards the car park, he wondered if he'd ever see her again.

Chapter 2

James spent the following days on tenterhooks, jumping every time his mobile phone rang, or a message came through, followed by disappointment when he discovered it wasn't from Alice. He really couldn't guess if she would contact him or not. He'd always considered married women as strictly off limits, but when he thought of Alice, all he could think of was the girl with the most beautiful smile who he'd met on the beach. He was shocked by how much their meeting had affected him.

A week after the day at the beach, he was travelling home from work on a crowded train, when a text message came through. Caller unknown.

Hi James, Thanks for the delicious hot chocolate with all the works. I'm still very embarrassed about the state I was in when we met. You really cheered me up though. I realised afterwards that I never said sorry about your Uncle. Apologies. Were you close? How's your hut? Alice x

Dear Embarrassed-Alice, I haven't been back to see my Hut again yet (I've decided She deserves a capital letter!), but am thinking of returning soon with a tin of paint. I'm ashamed to say I hadn't seen my Uncle for many years. I don't deserve my inheritance. How are things with you? James x

Hello Ashamed-James, I think you'll find you need 2 tins of paint - pale blue and white. So she's a 'She' your beach Hut is she? I'm OK thanks – the job's good this week – discovered some fantastic new lines. How are you? Embarrassed Alice x

And so their light hearted texts continued for a couple of weeks, until ...

Hi Alice, I'm thinking of taking a couple of days off to decorate my Hut. Maybe next week. Would you be free for another hot chocolate with all the works – or lunch maybe? If so, which day would best suit you? James x

Hi James, I don't work Fridays, and the children do after school clubs, so I'll be free during the day until about 4.30. I can be quite handy with a paint brush. Alice x

James decided to take the Thursday off work as well and go along and paint his hut the day before he saw Alice on Friday. He was swayed by the weather forecasters who were predicting a good day for Thursday and a stormy one for Friday. He didn't tell Alice what he was doing – wanting to surprise her when she turned up on Friday. He hadn't done any DIY for many years and didn't realise just how long it would take to paint a small hut. It was made much harder by the alternate blue and white panels. After accidentally dripping white paint on to the blue panels for the umpteenth time, he had been quite tempted to paint the whole hut one colour but he knew Alice would be disappointed, as she'd loved the striped colour scheme, and if he was honest with himself, he wanted to impress her.

It was indeed, as the forecasters had predicted, a lovely sunny day when James arrived on the Thursday. He was enjoying the fresh air, and as he painted he thought about how much his life had changed over the last few weeks. Instead of his usual overwhelming

20

obsession with share prices, his thoughts now tended to revolve around Alice; a little blue and white beach hut; and his many regrets about not keeping in touch with Jem.

The sunny weather brought more people to the beach today, and James stopped several times to enjoy brief chats with dog walkers and other beach hut owners who'd taken advantage of the good weather to come and inspect their huts before the Spring. Others had come simply to enjoy the sunshine. He liked the way people seemed so friendly and laid back here on the coast – in contrast to his usual city life. The tide was high up the beach when he arrived, but as the day went on he observed the sea's gradual retreat, revealing large stretches of sand as well as areas of pebbles and rock pools. By lunchtime the tide was far out. That along with the clear blue sky and sunshine made it feel like quite a different place to the one where he'd first met Alice on that cold misty morning, with the gentle waves only yards from James's hut. The more that James thought about Alice coming to meet him here tomorrow, the more determined he became to finish his painting and show off his gleaming hut.

By 3:30 James had just about covered all the panels of his hut with a fresh layer of paint. He'd hardly stopped all day, so after clearing up and admiring his work, he set off for the Beachcomber Cafe. As he opened the cafe door he was hit with the enticing aroma of fish and chips! However, it was late in the day and the cafe was almost empty. He was starving hungry and wondered if they might have stopped serving. He went to the counter and was greeted by the same man who he remembered had served him and Alice with the lovely chocolate button selection.

'Hello there,' he smiled warmly at James. 'Been a lovely day hasn't it.'

'Yes. Can't complain. Am I too late to order some food?'

'No, it's fine, we're open for a while longer.' James had a quick glance at the menu.

'Brilliant. I'll have plaice and chips please, and a cup of tea,' James said putting his money on the counter.

'Thank you. One plaice and chips,' he said. Then he turned round and called out, 'Did you get that Carmen?'

'Yep.' Carmen called out from the kitchen. James could see her through the door shaking the chip frier.

'Take a seat, and Carmen will bring it all over when it's ready.'

'Thanks.' James then heard the man saying to Carmen, 'I'll be off then. Won't be long.'

The cafe was nearly empty – there was only one couple with a toddler sitting by the window at the table where James had sat with Alice. He chose another table with a sea view. Carmen soon brought over James's meal. She was a nice looking woman in her 40s, James guessed.

'Plaice, chips and tea?'

'Thanks. That's great.'

'Enjoy your meal.'

James was so hungry he ate his meal quickly – hardly noticing what he was eating. He was thinking about coming down here again tomorrow and meeting Alice. His mind drifted to Jem as well. He wondered if his uncle ever came into this cafe, and what else he did to amuse himself in Sebleigh Bay?

When James had finished his meal he carried his plate and cup over to the counter. Carmen was busy clearing up behind the counter. She looked up at James and smiled.

'Oh thank you, you didn't have to do that. Would you like something else?'

'I'd love another cup of tea if it's not too late.'

'No problem. I've seen you in here before haven't I?' she said grabbing a large mug off of the shelf.

'Yes, that's right – I was in here with a friend a couple of weeks ago. You've got a good memory – you must have so many customers in and out of here.' She smiled at the compliment.

'Are you local?'

'No. Just visiting ... visiting my beach hut in fact,' James replied, aware of the fact that he sounded rather proud.

'Just bought one have you?' She poured the tea and put it down on the counter in front of James.

'Well, no, it was given to me actually – well I inherited it from my uncle.'

'Oh. He died recently did he?'

'Yes, in January.'

'Oh I'm sorry.'

'Thanks.' He passed her the money for the tea.

'Thanks love. Nice to be given the hut though – they're quite hard to get hold of apparently.'

'Yes it was a real surprise actually because we didn't know he still owned it – we all assumed he'd got rid of it years ago.'

'What's the condition like?'

'Surprisingly good actually, but I've just been giving it a lick of paint anyway.'

'How did I guess?' she said looking at the paint all over his hands. 'Blue is it?' They both laughed.

'Blue *and* white actually!' She looked slightly puzzled.

'Not striped is it?' she asked, looking slightly worried.

'Yes that's right – makes it really fiddly to paint – I was considering doing it all one ...'

'What number?' Carmen interrupted.

'Eighteen.'

23

'*Number eighteen?!*' Carmen said sounding absolutely horrified, '*Jem's hut?!*' she shrieked!

'Yes that's right. You knew Jem did you?'

'He's died?... Jem has?'

'Yes ... '

'Oh God!' She leaned on the counter to steady herself.

'Oh gosh – I'm sorry. You're really shocked ... and you didn't know ...'

'I can't believe this.' She looked distraught.

'Oh, I'm so sorry ... look ... I think you'd better come and sit down.' She walked round to the front of the counter in a daze. James pulled a chair out for her and she sat down.

'I'm really sorry about this ... finding out this way ... he obviously meant a lot to you,' he said as he sat down opposite her.

'What happened to him?'

'Well, if it's any consolation, he didn't appear to have suffered at all. They reckon he just passed away in his sleep one night. It was a complete shock to everyone. His cleaner found him in the morning. He'd died just a few hours before ... natural causes they said.' She buried her face in her hands and started crying. James put his hand on her arm.

'I didn't know he was ill,' she sobbed.

'No-one did. I don't think he knew himself – there were no medical records of heart problems or anything serious at all. It just seemed to happen out of the blue.'

'I had no idea,' she sniffed. 'I wondered why I hadn't heard from him... all this time I've been wondering ... I just can't believe it.' The family who were sitting by the window got up and left quickly and quietly. James and Carmen were alone now.

'Would you mind changing the sign round?' Carmen said pointing to the door.

'Yes of course.' James leapt up and rushed over to the door to flip over the sign to say CLOSED. It was starting to get dark outside.

'When did you last hear from him?   Can you remember?' James asked kindly as he came and sat down again.

'Yes. It was the 4th of January. He was here. We had some time together ... really special... it was so good – I couldn't understand why he hadn't contacted me since.'

'He died just three days after that.' Carmen stared at the table, shaking her head slowly in disbelief.

'You must have had the funeral by now then?' she asked.

'Yes. I'm sorry. My father contacted as many people as possible. Emails were forwarded all over the place but we didn't really know that much about Jem's life. If we'd known about you we would have told you of course.' James remembered all the grieving women at the funeral and thought it was probably a good job that Carmen *wasn't* there.

'So you're his nephew are you?'

'Yes. I'm James.'

'Oh yes. He talked about you. Said you work too hard – like he used to. You're a stock broker as well aren't you.'

'Yes. That's right.'

'He thought the world of you though. Was glad you had the same name.'

'Really? I never knew that. I prefer James to Jem though for myself.'

'Well yes. You would do these days.'

'I'm Carmen. He never mentioned me then?'

'I feel really bad saying this Carmen, but I hadn't spoken to him for years.   We hadn't communicated except for a few Christmas cards. I don't think my Dad spoke to him that often either, so we had little idea who his current friends were. We didn't even know he still came down here.'

'Oh thank God Clive isn't here - my husband – he doesn't know about me and Jem – *obviously*.' She glanced up at the clock. 'He'll be back in half an hour or so though. I don't think I can put on an act...'. Carmen kept wiping tears from her haunted looking eyes. James felt terrible for inflicting this pain on her. As if she heard his thoughts, she said, 'Thank goodness you told me ... I could have gone for months waiting to hear from him.'

'Did he come down here often Carmen?'

'Yes he did. He loved his beach hut. I used to pop in and see him there. He usually stayed in The Grand Hotel. I used to visit him there as well ... whenever I could get away.' She shook her head again. 'I love him... I just can't believe I won't see him again.' James held her hand as she cried.

'Do you know James?' Carmen sobbed. 'I've never talked about this to anyone before? You're the only person I've ever told. I've kept it to myself all the time. I couldn't risk Clive finding out. He would've killed Jem if he'd known. Me too probably.'

'How long had you been ... seeing Jem?'

'It's been going on for years – about six.'

'That's a long time to keep a secret.'

'I know. Promise me you won't tell *anyone* James, please,' she said with desperation in her voice. 'It would be terrible if Clive ever found out. He doesn't deserve it. He's been good to me. We have a good life here.'

'I promise. Well I don't live round here anyway and I might be selling the beach hut.'

'You married?'

'Not any more.' James noticed Carmen glancing up at the clock again. He was aware that she needed to somehow try and pull herself together before her husband came back.

'Look Carmen, I'll give you my phone number. If you want to talk about things any time ... I mean now that you've told me about you and Jem.' He was aware of history repeating itself as he once more grabbed a napkin and wrote his phone number on it and gave it to Carmen. She quickly stuffed it in her apron pocket. 'It might be that I'll find out more about my Uncle too – I can let you know if I do.'

'Thanks. You'd better go James.' They both stood up.

'I'm so sorry that you had to find out this way.'

'I'll ring you.'

'Will you be alright?'

'I don't have any choice. I've got to pull myself together before Clive gets back.'

'Look after yourself,' James said giving her a hug before he left. He glanced back at her as he went out through the door. She looked so distressed – haunted even – he felt unhappy leaving her in that state. He could see why his Uncle Jem liked her. She was very attractive, and probably only a few years older than James – quite a bit younger than Jem – the old rascal!

Chapter 3

The moment Alice was rudely awoken by Tim's alarm clock she remembered there was something special about today. Normally she hated the early morning rush to get herself and the children washed, dressed, fed and off to school. She would lie in bed trying not to slip back to sleep as she heard the sounds of Tim getting himself showered and dressed. She would hear his steady walk down the stairs, the click of the kitchen light switch, the kettle being emptied and refilled, the opening of the bread bin and the clunk of the bread in the toaster. He went through exactly the same routine every day, at exactly the same steady speed, in exactly the same order, finishing with the cup of tea he brought her just before he kissed her on the forehead and left for work.

Was it his predictability which explained her lack of contentment with their marriage? Same actions, same words every day. 'Bye love, see you this evening'. She often felt guilty for her critical thoughts. How was he supposed to make life more interesting for her at 6.30 in the morning? And anyway she shouldn't blame him for the way her life had turned out. She had agreed to go out with him. They were both equally responsible for the accidental pregnancy. He hadn't forced her to marry him and buy a house together. She'd been a willing partner in all of this. And, after all, without Tim she wouldn't have had her two beautiful children. Her mind would be flooded with a further rush of guilt when she thought of Mollie and Sam. How could she possibly even think of a scenario in which they wouldn't have been born?

Five year old Sam was an early riser and occasionally he would hear his dad getting up and follow him downstairs and join him in the kitchen.   On those occasions, Alice enjoyed listening to his endless chatter and questions...

'Daaaad, you know you said I'm too young to have my own lizard, well can I have one when I'm six?' .... 'Daaaad, at school yesterday Mrs Jones told me that I had ants in my pants. Well I had a look and I couldn't find any and she just laughed at me. Then the whole class started laughing too!'

Tim would do his best to engage in Sam's conversations and answer his endless questions, yet always managed to leave the house dead on 7am without getting stressed or impatient, as he patiently explained that he had a train to catch. Alice couldn't work out how he managed to do that - she wasn't nearly as good at keeping her cool when she was trying to get the kids ready and rush them off to school, or to mini-tennis or wherever else it was that they were running late for.

Today, when the alarm clock buzzed and Tim crept out quietly to the bathroom, she didn't even notice the usual sounds of the shower, the stairs, the kitchen light, the kettle and the toaster.   All she could think about was meeting James. In fact it was practically all she'd thought about ever since that day at the beach. She was thrilled when he gave her his phone number – thrilled and then scared. She'd loved the impulsive way he just grabbed the napkin and scribbled his number on it, without asking her first. And there was the kiss on the cheek. She'd replayed that unexpected moment in her mind so many times. She'd been shocked by how much it had affected her. The split second touch of his soft lips on her cheek … the earthy scent of his aftershave.

Since they'd arranged to get together again, she'd told herself repeatedly that there was nothing wrong with meeting up with a friend. Nothing was going to happen. It couldn't, could it? So how come she hadn't mentioned this to anyone? Not even her closest friends? And why did she have butterflies inside her the moment she woke up this morning?

29

'Bye love. See you this evening.' Tim interrupted her thoughts as he put her mug of tea down on her bedside table, kissed her on the forehead and left for work.

'Bye,' she mumbled, pretending she wasn't really awake. She decided to get the kids up and off to school a little earlier today so she had chance to compose herself before she went down to the beach. She tried to put James out of her mind as she woke up Mollie and Sam and gave them each a big cuddle.

'Will you both get yourselves dressed quickly please while I get myself ready?'

'Yes Mummy,' they groaned sleepily in unison. Alice rushed into the bathroom for a quick shower and then headed downstairs to make the children's breakfast. The children staggered downstairs sleepily.

'Mummy,' asked Mollie 'Why did you have a shower today? You normally only have them at night time?'

'I just needed it today to wake me up Poppet – I still felt half asleep when I got out of bed.' *Crumbs, nothing gets passed Mollie!* They sat at the kitchen table as usual and Alice served up breakfast for the three of them of toast and cereal. Her heart sank when she got up and opened the kitchen blind to see the torrential rain outside. It wasn't going to be the fine day on the beach which she'd hoped for – and definitely not a day for painting the hut.

'Oh what a horrid day. I think you'll have wet play today.'

'I don't like wet play,' Mollie moaned. 'The boys are always so noisy in the classroom. They run round shouting their heads off and then Miss Ellis shouts at them to be quiet, and it goes on like that all through break, with everyone getting louder and louder.' Sam leapt up from the breakfast table and launched into his aeroplane impersonation, arms outstretched, zooming around the kitchen yelling 'neeeeeooooooow' as loud as possible upsetting his sister. Alice couldn't help laughing. Then she half-heartedly told him to sit down and eat his breakfast, but Sam carried on a good while longer, enjoying making his Mum laugh, while Mollie shut her eyes tightly and put her hands over her ears.

'Mummy, why aren't you stopping him? You usually do!' she said angrily. 'You normally hate it when he's noisy.'

Half an hour later the three of them were running across the school playground, as fast as possible through the heavy rain, with Sam deliberately stamping in the puddles, and Molly holding her red book bag over her head. Because of the bad weather the children were allowed to go straight to their classrooms, rather than playing outside until the bell rang. Alice called out 'Bye' to them as they disappeared down the corridor, and she headed back towards her car, saying hello to a couple of her friends who were rushing across the wet playground with their children.

Remembering the red eyed, tearful, and very unglamorous state she had been in the first time she met James, Alice had intended to put on some nice clothes and make up today to try and surprise him by looking her best this time. However, the weather had truly conspired against her and her main priority now seemed to be simply to keep as dry as possible and avoid arriving at the beach hut looking like a drowned rat. Her unflattering see-through raincoat with the hood was her only option, and her only hope of keeping her carefully selected trousers and jumper dry.

When she parked in Chalk Cliff Way car park, the sky was very dark. Not only was the rain as heavy as ever, but it was accompanied by strong gusts of wind and sea spray. Alice battled with the elements as she made her way past the beach huts. She gave up on her umbrella after it blew inside out and pulled her hood down to try and keep her hair dry. She could barely see more than a few steps in front of her. The tide was high up the beach and the waves were spectacularly crashing on the pebbles only a few yards away. As Alice reached James's hut and walked round to the front the door opened immediately and James pulled her inside and shut the door. Alice saw that his hair was soaked too. They both looked at each other and laughed. Alice pulled off her hood knowing that her hair which she had styled carefully this morning, was now a wet straggly mess.

'Welcome,' said James, smiling warmly at her.

'It's nice to see you again,' Alice replied.

James once again bent over and kissed her wet cheek.

'Ready for some beach combing then?' James joked.

'Oh yes. After we've painted your hut that is. Doesn't look like we're going to get much done today though does it?'

'Alice, if it wasn't for the fact that I'm not a complete sadist, I would make you go outside in the rain and take a good look at my hut.'

'Oh... why? You haven't done it already have you?'

'You'll have to wait and see?'

'Oh. You didn't tell me. When did you do that?'

'Well, it was a *lovely* day yesterday.'

'You came here yesterday? Oh I can't wait to have a proper look.'

'So may I offer you a cup of tea? I brought a flask.'

'Thank you. I should have brought something too.'

'Well hopefully if the rain dies down in a while we can go along to the cafe.'

'Sorry it's so dark in here. It's a shame there's no electricity.'

'That's okay. We couldn't have picked a worse day could we?' Alice laughed.

'No. It's pretty noisy isn't it?' James said as the rain hammered on the roof and the waves crashed on the beach just outside the door.'

'It's quite exciting actually! I was just wondering if it's high tide, because if it comes in any further I think the waves will be crashing against the door.'

As James poured two cups of tea from the flask Alice sat down on the settee. She was impressed that he had gone to the trouble of bringing two china mugs with him rather than using the plastic cups attached to the flask.

'The weather is the complete opposite to yesterday – it was a beautiful spring day,' James said.

'How did you get on with the painting?' Alice asked, thinking that while she was in the garden centre just up the hill, she hadn't known that James was so nearby.

'Quite well. It took me pretty well all day and then I went along to the cafe for fish and chips. Had a good chat with Carmen. She and her husband are the owners.' Alice noticed a thoughtful look on James' face as he mentioned Carmen. He quickly smiled and said,

'We could have lunch there if you like? The food seemed good.'

'I love fish and chips.'

'And chocolate buttons.'

'You didn't exactly turn your nose up at them either!'

'Too right. So … fish, chips, hot chocolate and buttons it is then!'

'Mmm lovely,' Alice said, looking at James and thinking how lovely *he* was. There was a flash of lightning which lit up the dark inside of the beach hut.

'Wow!' James exclaimed. 'That was spectacular. I think you could feel a little vulnerable being in a shed on the beach in a thunderstorm.' Before Alice had chance to answer there was the loudest crash of thunder she'd ever heard. They both nearly jumped out of their skins, laughing nervously.

'Crumbs that was quite shocking,' Alice said. 'Lucky we'd put our cups of tea down.'

'Yes it must have only been about three seconds after the lightning.'

'Must be directly over head.' There was another flash. 'Oh dear – here we go again,' Alice said, doing her best to smile instead of revealing how nervous she was beginning to feel. James instinctively leaned forwards and grabbed her hand. She held it tightly and they both hunched their shoulders waiting for the next bang, hoping it would be further away this time. It wasn't!

'Good grief!' James said quietly. 'I've never heard anything like it.' Then as if nature was mocking him, the loudest wave yet crashed right outside throwing a shower of pebbles against the front of the beach hut. They both jumped again.

'Oh God,' Alice said. 'Do you think we should escape?'

'You live round here Alice – do you ever hear of beach huts getting blown away in storms or anything like that?' James said looking quite concerned.

'No. Never.'

'Well I'm sure there weren't any major weather warnings on the forecast last night, so hopefully this is just a normal storm as opposed to one of those hurricanes where trees get blown down and rooves fly off.'

'Or beach huts get washed out to sea,' Alice said pulling a face.

Another flash. By now they were both leaning forward and holding both hands. Alice looked at James and in an attempt to distract them both from the impending thunder said cheerfully,

'I was really looking forward to today but I have to say I didn't imagine it would be quite like this.'

'Well if I have to be in the middle of the scariest thunder storm on earth I can't think of anyone ....

BANG!

..... I'd rather share it with.' His voice tailed off quietly. Alice was surprised James said that. She hadn't expected him to be quite so forward. She realised it must have shown on her face because James quickly leaned back and let go of her hands. She felt a sense of disappointment.

'It must ease off soon,' James said. 'Move along the coast a bit.'

'Yes hopefully.' Another huge wave with a shower of pebbles hammering on the front of the beach hut, made them both jump again. Alice instinctively grabbed James's hand.

'Yikes!' James said. 'This is quite scary isn't it? Are you alright?' he asked her kindly.

34

'Yes. It will pass soon hopefully. It's so dark isn't it –
like night time.'

Another flash.

'Here we go,' said James. 'One, two, three, four, five,
six, seven.....'

BANG!

'That was definitely a bit longer,' he said.

'Not so loud either. Phew!'

To their relief the storm soon passed by and the tide was
receding. As soon as James and Alice felt safe enough to do
so they tried to open the door only to find the pebbles were
piled up against it. They managed to get the door open a
little and throw the stones back onto the beach one by one,
gradually clearing the veranda. On a bit of a high after
surviving the scary storm, they chatted away happily as they
walked along to the Beachcomber Cafe. They were relieved
to find that it was open and once again the warm atmosphere
and inviting aroma of coffee and cooked breakfasts,
welcomed them in. There were several customers in the cafe
already, but plenty of free tables so they both queued at the
counter.

'Could we have two cappuccinos please?' James asked
Clive when it was his turn.

'Two cappuccinos, coming up. You're Jem's nephew aren't
you? Carmen was telling me.'

'Yes, that's right.'

'Sorry to hear the bad news,' he said matter of factly, as
he got to work on the coffee machine.

'Thanks.'

'I hear you've been painting the hut.'

'Yes I did it yesterday. Came down again this morning
and we got trapped in there during the storm.'

'Don't tell me you were in the beach hut during that
storm?' Clive looked up in surprise.

'Oh yes!' James and Alice said in unison.

'Good grief! The tide was right up wasn't it? Rather you than me. It was bad enough being in here!'

'It was pretty exciting. Waves and stones crashing against the door. Some of the new paintwork got damaged too!'

'Not surprised. Back in the eighties when there was that huge storm – gale force ten or whatever – some of the beach huts actually got smashed up and washed away apparently.'

'Crumbs' Alice said, 'I'm glad we didn't know that this morning.' Clive stopped what he was doing and looked at James.

'Yes, I can see you're related to Jem. There's a definite resemblance.'

'Can't see it myself, but I have had that said to me once or twice. Thanks,' James said, taking the drinks as he handed over the money.

'Morning Clive.' A loud jolly female voice called out as James and Alice turned away to find a table.

'Hello Joy – the usual for you?'

'Yes. The usual ... as usual!' she said with a giggle. 'Is Carmen around today?'

'No she's not well. I think it's a migraine.'

'Oh I didn't know she has migraines. Wish her better won't you.'

'Thanks Joy.'

Alice and James enjoyed the warmth and comfort of the cafe. They chatted quietly as they watched the tide receding and, thankfully, the weather very much improving. Now that they were feeling safe and warm they were able to laugh about the drama in the beach hut earlier on.

'Oh, I nearly forgot ... I've got something for you,' James said.

'Really? What's that?'

'Guess.'

'I've no idea.'

'No, go on, have a guess.'

'Oh I couldn't.'

'You made me play the guessing game last time.'

'Oh yes I did didn't I. Sorry about that. Obviously been spending too much time with the little ones. I forget how to be an adult sometimes,' Alice laughed. 'Well give me a clue then.'

'It's in my pocket.'

'Sooo … it's not very big then.'

'Correct.'

'What colour is it?'

'Greeny blue?'

'And what's it made of?' Alice said with a smile. James laughed realising that would give the game away.

'Hold out your hand and shut your eyes.'

'O … kay …'. James placed something in Alice's outstretched hand, and he closed her fingers around it. Alice opened her eyes and her fingers …

'Seaglass!   Oh that's a lovely piece,' she said enthusiastically.

'I thought you'd like it.'

'I do, thank you. Where did you find it?'

'Right next to my beach hut when I was painting it.'

After finishing their coffees Alice and James took a long walk on the beach away from the town and past the cliffs.

'So how well do you know Sebleigh Bay?' Alice asked James.

'Oh, I don't really know it at all. I only have a very vague memory of coming here as a child. I don't even recognise the place to be honest. I do have an image in my mind of my sister and I playing outside the beach hut and the adults sitting in deckchairs – probably the same ones that are in the hut now. My mum thinks we only came here once. When my Uncle died my parents were amazed that he still owned the beach hut. He hadn't mentioned it for donkey's years apparently. They just assumed it was some passing phase he'd gone through a long time ago, a bit like some of his other hobbies.   But now I've discovered that he'd been coming here regularly and quite recently.

'Yes the cafe owners sounded like they knew him well didn't they?'

'Yes I think so,' James said thoughtfully.

Alice bent over and picked something up.

'What have you got there?' Alice showed James a tiny yellow shell.

'These are my favourites. I collect them and put keep them aside for craft projects. They add a nice bright splash of colour.'

'You are very good at spotting them. I wouldn't have noticed any of these pieces of glass or shells if you hadn't shown me.'

'It's quite addictive. Once you get into beachcombing you just can't stop looking. Let's take a look at these rock pools here. I bring the children here sometimes. Once we saw a stunning starfish. You can go crabbing here as well.'

'I'm ashamed to say that I don't think I've ever been crabbing, and probably never picked up any seashells off the beach either. We always went on holiday abroad. I'm beginning to think I've really missed out on the good old English beach holiday.'

'I think you should have these then,' Alice said as she handed James a small collection of shells and glass from her pocket. 'Take them back to the city with you to remind you of a different life here in sunny Sebleigh Bay.'

'Thank you. I will treasure them forever,' James said with a smile as he studied Alice's gift with interest. 'Strange to think these pretty shells each used to house a little creature isn't it? Do the spirals always go the same way?'

'Yes I think they do! It took me a while to realise that though.'

'Fascinating! Do you know I can't help wondering if my uncle gave me the beach hut because he knew that I never did things like this and he wanted me to discover a different lifestyle away from the intensity of city life. He was always telling me I should expand my horizons and get out of town.'

38

After a long walk on the beach, James and Alice returned to the cafe for fish and chips. James noted that Carmen still hadn't turned up today. After lunch the weather was much improved and the sun was shining so they returned to the beach hut and got the paint and brushes out so that they could touch up some of the damaged paintwork from the storm.

'Your painting is so much better than mine,' James said looking at Alice's very neat brushwork. 'I could have done with you here yesterday. I think you're quite an artist.'

'No way. But I've done a fair bit of decorating in my time. To be fair though, you had the whole thing to paint yesterday so you had to get on with it, but I'm just touching up a few little patches.'

'Mm. Even so. A woman's touch I think.'

Sadly, their day together was coming to an end. Seeing Alice glancing at her watch, James realised that it was time for her to leave and collect her children from school. Together they put all the painting gear back inside the hut. They both became a little self conscious, knowing it was time to say goodbye, but not sure what was going to happen.

'I'd better let you go hadn't I?' James said as he took hold of Alice's hand. They looked at each other. 'Thank you for your help. It's been quite a day hasnt it! Thunderstorm and all.'

'Yes! That's not something I'm going to forget in a hurry. Thank *you* for a lovely day.' James bent over and kissed her on the cheek. Alice didn't want him to stop there. She caught sight of the photo of Jem.

'Oh, I meant to look at the photo of your uncle again.' She picked it up. 'Yes, I *can* see the resemblance ... in the eyes.' She looked up at James' eyes.

'Really?'

'Yes, definitely.' They both looked into each other's eyes, feeling shy but not wanting to look away. James took the photo from her and placed it back on the windowsill. He looked intensely into Alice's eyes and she returned his gaze unhesitatingly. He bent forward and their lips met. This time they kissed properly. Then they stood and held each other tightly, reluctant to let each other go.

'You're beautiful Alice,' he whispered.

'James ... today has been ... really special.' They kissed again.

'When can I see you again?' he asked.

Chapter 4

Two weeks, numerous text messages and a couple of phone calls later, James took another day off work and once again travelled to Sebleigh Bay to his little beach hut on a glorious Friday morning. Alice arrived soon afterwards, walking along the path at the bottom of the cliffs looking simply beautiful wearing a camel coloured coat with her dark wavy hair tumbling over the collar. Her delight at seeing him was obvious. Neither of them could stop smiling.

'You look amazing ... come here,' James said as he took her hand and lead her around to the other side of the hut. He took her inside, closed the door, and then pulled her to him. They kissed passionately and hugged each other tightly, reluctant to let each other go.

'Do you know James? This strange thing keeps happening to me.'

'Oh really?' he asked, brushing his lips lightly against hers again. 'What's that?'

'Well, sometimes I find myself walking along here, just minding my own business, when I suddenly get grabbed and pulled inside this nice little blue and white hut ... and then who knows what happens next?'

'This strange thing you're talking about ... is it *bad* strange? ... or *nice* strange?'

'Oh, it's *very* nice.' They kissed again, and then James led her over to the settee and they sat down holding hands.

'I've missed you so much,' he said.

'I know. It's been a long fortnight.'

'You look so lovely. When I saw you approaching ... I was bowled over.'

'Well it had to be an improvement on the other times you saw me – the first time I'd been crying my eyes out - *so* embarrassing - and the second time I was like a drowned rat.'

41

'Mm. A very tasty drowned rat though. What would you like to do today?'

'The weather's so warm for February I suppose we could go for a walk.'

'Where do you recommend?'

'It's lovely up on top of the cliffs if you fancy it up there.'

'I definitely fancy it ...' James started kissing Alice again. 'Quiet up there is it?' He asked mischievously.

'We'll have to see,' she replied giggling.

Alice and James took a relaxed walk along the beach, past the Beachcomber Cafe and towards the cliffs until they came to a steep pathway, which they climbed to reach the top of the cliffs. They stopped to catch their breath and admire the stunning views. They looked back at Sebleigh Bay with its long stretch of seafront with the damaged pier in the far distance and the funfair rides in the foreground just beyond the car park. They continued walking along the cliffs leaving Sebleigh behind them. The sea was sparkling down below and there was nothing but green fields around them, and the occasional group of old cottages in the distance. There was no one around apart from an elderly man with a small white dog running ahead of him. As he approached he called out,

'Morning. Beautiful day isn't it.'

'It certainly is,' James replied.

'Good morning,' Alice replied happily.

Shortly afterwards without another human being in sight, James held Alice's hand as they continued walking.

'I love the way people are so friendly in Sebleigh,' James said thoughtfully. 'There's a different attitude here. Strangers just don't make conversation with each other very often in the city. Things are so much more relaxed here ... and all this space ... it's breathtaking.'

'I know. This *is* a lovely area. You've got the beaches and you're never very far away from the countryside either. I've never wanted to move away.'

'I'm not surprised. I envy you living here. Do you know? It's making me wonder about the reasons why my uncle left me the beach hut.'

'Oh, why is that?'

'Well I hadn't seen him for some time as you know, but when I did see him he was always saying to me *Don't work too hard James! Don't make the mistake I did. There's more to life than just long hours in the office.* I never really took much notice to be honest – I didn't know why he was saying that or what the mistake was that he made.'

'That's interesting – so are you saying that you think he left you the beach hut so that you might discover another way of life?'

'Maybe? Who knows? I'm probably reading too much into it. But then he couldn't have predicted that he was going to die so soon.'

'True, but then you write your will just in case don't you? I can see this must be quite a contrast to your normal life.'

'Mm… never mind contrast - it's like being on a different planet.'

'Planet Sebleigh!'

'Yes – and only an hour or two's drive away ... You know those shells you gave me? Well I've put them on the kitchen table at home, and I often pick them up and look at them, and I remember the things you told me about them and it's made me realise how out of touch I am with things like nature and beautiful scenery... and ... well out of touch with everything really …except the city, my daily commute, my job, my house, my cat, the pub ... oh and the squash club! My only form of exercise!' Alice laughed and then looked at James and said sternly.

'You need to get out more!'

'I really do! Also, I just can't remember the last time I went for a walk in the countryside, or looked at a lovely view like this.' James looked over to the cliff edge. 'Actually I'm surprised there isn't a fence along the edge

43

there. Health and Safety obviously doesn't reach as far as Sebleigh Bay.' Alice laughed.

'Well I must admit I've not brought the kids up here much for that reason. It's not very relaxing constantly keeping them away from the edge. It's easier to just let them run around on the beach.'

'Shall we go and have a look?' Walking towards the cliff edge they noticed a convenient bench with a fantastic view.

'Shall we sit and look at the sea?' asked James.

'Okay.' They sat on the bench and huddled up together.

'This is beautiful.' James said admiring the view all around them.

'Yes I haven't looked at this view for ages. Tim and I always tended to go along the coast to Smallchurch for long ...' her voice trailed off. 'Oh I'm sorry ... I don't know why I said that.' Neither of them said anything for a moment. James broke the silence,

'No. Don't apologise. Its okay,' he said, noticing how upset Alice looked. 'Are you alright?' James asked.

'Yes. Oh its just that this is all so lovely ... being here ... with you ... I didn't mean to mention …' her voice trailed off. 'Talk about being brought down to earth with a bump.

'I know. But look ... we can't bury our heads in the sand forever ... but, just for now ... for today at least ... let's just focus on you and me okay? No-one else ... just us and this beautiful place ... what do you think?" Alice smiled.

'Agreed. Just you and me ... and a cute beach hut!'

'You love that little hut don't you?'

'Yes. It seems such a shame to sell her. Are you reconsidering at all?'

'Mm ... Maybe? Who knows? But right now, I've got other things on my mind.' They started kissing and then Alice said,

'Maybe you should give her a name?' James laughed.

'A name? Well I'd never be able to sell her then would I? That would be like naming your pet chickens or piglets, and then you wouldn't be able to eat Henrietta or Percy for dinner!' Alice giggled and tried to see the connection between the farm animals and the beach hut.'

'Oh, and by the way,' James said, 'talking of names, I was thinking Ms Alice, I don't actually know your name ... well apart from Alice I mean.'

'No, and I don't know yours either *Mr* James ...'

'Right – you first then.'

'No you. Guess!'

'Guess? Oh here we go! How can I possibly guess? I mean there's millions of names to choose from.'

'No go on. Have a guess. I mean what do you think I look like?'

'Good grief! Well there's a question ... what do you look like? Where do I start? Pretty, luscious, small ...'

'No, silly! What name do you think I look like I might have?' she said with a giggle.

'Well I don't know, and anyway, presumably you've changed your name?'

'Well either name will do – so that narrows it down slightly.' Alice was really laughing now – acknowledging that this was the most ridiculous conversation ever.

'How can you possibly guess a name? And how would you go about guessing mine?' James laughed.

'Well ... I'd use my imagination ... and I'd ask for clues. Or I might ask if it begins with a B ... or an H ... or an X maybe?'

'What like Xylophone?'

'No that would be silly.'

'Oh and this guessing game isn't silly? This is all too much for me ... I think we should just go back to kissing ... in fact I insist,' James said masterfully and started kissing Alice again.

'Alright Mr X. Just have one guess first.'

'Is that a promise?'

'Yes.'

'Alice Appletree?' Alice burst out laughing, but James silenced her with his kiss.

'So was I right then?'

'Just kiss me Mr Xylophone.'

'I think I love you Alice Appletree... despite the daft games you play.' Alice looked a little startled. Neither of them said anything – they just looked at each other, considering what James had just said.

'I think I love you too,' Alice added quietly.

They started kissing again before they were interrupted by the sounds of voices. They stopped and listened. Adults and children were heard getting nearer.

'I want to be on my own with you. Come on,' James said. They both stood up. They smiled at the family who were walking by. A man was carrying a giggling toddler on his shoulders, and a mother was holding hands with a girl who was skipping along beside her.

'Morning,' the man said. Alice said 'hello' and waved and pulled a funny face at the toddler who was grinning at her from his high vantage point.

Alice and James walked back down the cliffs to the beach, past the Beachcomber Cafe and along the path by the huts. They didn't talk much - both feeling a little stunned by what they'd just said to each other. When they reached James' beach hut they locked themselves in and pulled the curtain.

Chapter 5

Alice Appletree, last time we met up ... Well, it was beautiful ... But I don't want you to think I'm only after one thing. I want to take you out somewhere special. How about a nice meal? Do you know a really good restaurant we could go to? My treat. Xx

Mr Xylophone, that sounds nice. I'm giving it some thought. Xx

On their next date, James met Alice at the Lynchester Golf Club and Hotel. For obvious reasons they hadn't wanted to dine in Sebleigh Bay so Alice suggested the golf club which was known for its outstanding restaurant. She had only ever been there for drinks in the lounge bar with colleagues from work on special occasions, but didn't expect to see anyone she knew there today.

They enjoyed a delicious meal in the Spring Court restaurant. Alice felt thoroughly spoilt and she noted to herself how special James always made her feel. He was so attentive towards her and always remembered everything that she'd told him. They were never short of anything to talk about. Conversation just flowed so easily.

The weather was perfect and after their leisurely three course meal they decided to have coffee in the garden outside. Tables and chairs were arranged on the patio in between huge pots containing flowers and bushes, and the whole area was surrounded by magnificent tall trees which must have been growing there for hundreds of years. In the far distance golfers could be seen enjoying their game. Alice and James brought their coffees out from the restaurant and settled down at a table on the edge of the garden. Alice loved the way James looked at her. She thought to herself that no-one had ever made her feel the way he did.

Her thoughts were rudely interrupted by the sound of a black Labrador running in through the gardens followed by its frantic owner.

'Cedric! Come here!! Cedric!' a stout woman with a walking stick, called to her dog.

'Oh no!' Alice said between clenched teeth, as she recognised her as a friend of her mother-in-law's. The dog charged over towards Alice.

'Oh hello Alice! Cedric was coming to see you – he recognised you.'

'Hello.'

'I should really have him on a lead here, but he's usually very good. You two taken a nice day off work have you? – oh it's not Tim!' She said with an air of surprise. 'Cedric! Come here **now**!! Don't jump up will you,' she said as the dog approached Alice.

'I'm just here with colleagues from work,' Alice said quickly as the dog put one of it's paws on her lap.

'Cedric! No! Come here I'll put you on your lead. We can't have you putting your dirty feet on Alice's clothes. I'd better take him away before I get into trouble! Send my love to Margaret won't you!' Cedric's owner called over her shoulder as she walked away.

'Yes of course. Bye,' Alice said with a look of relief. 'Oh no! She's a friend of my mother-in-law. I didn't think I'd see anyone I knew here. We don't know any golfers.'

'Don't worry. She doesn't know who I am. You said you were with work people. She won't think anything of it.'

'I suppose so. But Tim knows I'm not at work today. I suppose I could have gone to meet them though. Oh dear.'

'Alice it's fine. Really. We weren't doing anything. She was so busy shouting demands at that dog, I doubt she would have thought much about it anyway. Could you tell Tim you went for a drink with people from work?'

'Yes I guess so. I'll have to. It should be okay.' Alice looked anything but okay though. As they sipped their coffees, James tried to change the subject and talk about other things, and Alice did try to lighten up, but he could see that she was uncomfortable.

'Are you alright?' James asked her kindly.

'Yes. Oh I'm sorry. This has all been so lovely coming here with you, but I've let that incident spoil it.'

'Don't worry. No harm done.'

'Sorry – I'm just not used to this sort of thing. I've never done anything like this before.'

'Me neither! Believe me this is not something I ever thought I would do.'

'I know. Oh I'm sorry James. Its difficult for you as well. It's just frustrating that the first time we come somewhere like this we get spotted.'

'Spotted having a cup of coffee … with someone from work.' They looked at each other and laughed.

'Look, Alice, I shouldn't be saying this because I was sworn to secrecy, so this must never go any further, but, you know Carmen at the Beachcomber ...'

'The owner? Yes.'

'Well I found out that she was having an affair with my Uncle.'

'Really? Your Uncle Jem?'

'Yes. For six years no less!'

'You're joking! Was that up until he died?'

'Yes. The whole thing was pretty awful actually, because on the day that I painted the beach hut, I went into the cafe afterwards and I got talking to Carmen. I was innocently telling her about how my uncle had just died and left me the beach hut, and she suddenly realised that it was Jem – her lover – that I was talking about. She'd been having a secret relationship with him and she didn't even know he'd died.'

'Oh God! That's terrible!'

'It was. She nearly collapsed, she was so shocked.'

49

'I'm not surprised. So what happened? Was her husband there?'

'No he wasn't thank goodness. The cafe was just closing so I sat down with her and we had a talk. She was in a terrible state. I think she was really in love with him, but she said she'd never told anyone except me.'

'In six years? No one knew?'

'Apparenty not.'

'And we've just been spotted already!'

'She didn't see anything – it was no big deal.'

'Maybe not. It's just that it brings home the reality of the situation though, doesn't it.   I can't believe that about Carmen though. Imagine finding out like that.'

'I know. I felt really bad for causing her so much pain. I couldn't stay with her long either as her husband was due back and she needed to try and compose herself. I gave her my phone number and told her to phone me if she wanted to.'

'That was nice ... oh talking of which ...' Alice's mobile was ringing in her bag. 'Sorry, I'd better just see who this is. Oh dear, it's the school.'   James waited patiently as Alice talked to the teacher. He realised from the conversation that her son had obviously had an accident.

'Oh dear, Sam's hurt himself,' she explained as she put her phone back in her bag. 'He managed to get hit with a tennis ball in his eye. Mrs Parks thinks he's alright, but she just said she doesn't take any chances with head injuries, and she wants me to come and get him.'

'Yes of course you must. It's fine.'

'Oh James, I'm so sorry to cut this short.' He squeezed her hand and said kindly,

'Nothing to apologise for.'

They abandoned their coffees and walked to the car park. Alice looked all around to make sure no one was watching, and then she kissed James.

'Thank you so much for the lunch. It was wonderful. And thank you for being so understanding about Sam.'

'You're welcome. Let me know how he is won't you.'

'I will. I've got to go ... sorry. She kissed him again and rushed off, as James said quietly, knowing she probably didn't hear,

'Love you ...'

James could see Alice wasn't happy at all. It made him realise just how badly he wanted to make her happy. He hated leaving her like that, and he hated the fact that she was so uncomfortable being seen by the woman with the dog. He could tell that had really thrown her. He wanted to hold her and tell her everything would be alright and that he loved her and nothing else mattered. He sat in his car, suddenly feeling really lousy. *So this is what it's like being in love with a married woman - beautiful and exciting one minute, and then you hit complete rock bottom the next.* He suddenly felt really scared. *What on earth are we doing? And where is this going to lead?*

Chapter 6

James arrived at the beach hut, took a parcel from a carrier bag and removed the wooden sign from it's wrapping. He took some tools out of the box he'd brought with him. He had twenty minutes to fix the sign on to his beach hut before Alice arrived.

It had been a difficult fortnight since they last saw each other at the golf club. They had communicated with each other through numerous text messages and a couple of phone calls made during their respective lunch hours from work. Alice kept apologising for ending their date so abruptly after the wonderful meal he'd bought her. James wasn't bothered about that, but he was worried about how panicked she was about being spotted by her mother-in-law's friend. Alice had become almost paranoid about the conclusions her family might jump to, and she told James that every time Tim or his mother spoke to her she was a nervous wreck expecting them to have found out what she'd been up to.

James was determined to cheer her up today and he thought he knew just how to do it. Alice had tried many times to persuade him not to sell the beach hut. He felt that by giving it a name it would be his subtle way of showing her that he'd decided to keep it. As he worked with his drill he imagined the hopefully happy surprise that Alice would get when she saw the new name sign. He wasn't going to point it out to her – he would just wait for her to notice. He also had a present for her in his pocket – a silver bracelet. He would understand if she didn't want to take it home with her, but he thought that if she wanted to she could pass it off as something she'd bought for herself.

As with all DIY jobs, fixing the name sign on to the beach hut took longer than expected, and James had only just finished it and put the tools away in the hut before Alice was due. He couldn't see her walking along Chalk Cliff Way yet, so he wandered down to the sea. It was roughly half way in – or was it half way out? When he reached the water he glanced back towards the cliffs, but he still couldn't see Alice on the beach or on the path between the gaps in the beach huts. He could clearly see his name sign from this distance and wondered how long it would take for Alice to spot it. She was pretty observant – he felt sure she would notice it straight away. His mobile phone made a noise in his pocket. *I'd better check in case Alice has been delayed for some reason. Oh it is from her.*

> *James, I'm so so sorry. I can't come today. I can't do this. I meant it when I said I love you, but I have to put my family – my children – first. I have no choice. This hurts so much, but I can't see you again. I'm so sorry. Please forgive me. Alice x*

James' heart sank ... to depths he'd never experienced before. He read the text again – struggling to see the words through the tears that were forming in this eyes, not wanting to believe what he was seeing. He hit reply, and was about to text her back, but he knew she wouldn't have written that if she didn't mean it. He felt like throwing his phone into the sea. He never wanted to see those painful words again Should he ring her? He couldn't. That wouldn't be fair – he didn't know where she was or who she was with. He had no choice but to respect her wishes. She was married and she had children. He'd always known that. He put the phone back in his pocket. As he did so, he felt the wrapped bracelet he'd bought for Alice. He'd put so much thought into that present. He spent ages choosing it for her. Never had the act of buying a present for someone been so significant to him. Without thinking he found himself swinging his arm right back and throwing the bracelet as far out to sea as he could.

Chapter 7

Carmen would never forget that sunny afternoon when the attractive dark haired man with the blue paint all over his hands had come into her cafe and inadvertently given her the shock of her life.

During the weeks leading up to that awful day, she'd been wondering what had happened to Jem. Why wasn't he answering the phone when she rang? They had an agreement between them that he never rang her, so she would phone him when Clive wasn't around. But as the days and weeks had gone by without him answering any of her calls, she'd lost count of the times she'd listened to his loud and jolly voice on the answer phone asking her to leave a message. Her frustration grew and she finally left a message asking him to text her just to let her know what was going on.

But still she heard nothing and her concern for him and their relationship grew. There had been other times when he'd gone incommunicado for a while, but he'd always turned up eventually, usually with an excuse or other about some exotic foreign trip he'd been on. 'You don't need to worry about me my dear – you know I always turn up eventually - just like a bad penny!' However, he'd never been off the radar for this long. It wasn't just the length of time though that was bugging her; there was something else – the way he'd behaved when they last met up. Something was different. She replayed in her mind the events of the last day she'd seen him, and the more she thought about it, the more oddly she felt he'd behaved. Did that have something to do with his recent silence?

Jem had been staying in Sebleigh Bay for a few days – spending a long weekend at The Grand Hotel. He hadn't warned her of his arrival – surprising her by just turning up unexpectedly in the cafe one day. On the one hand she wished he wouldn't do that – catching her out unawares like that – on the other she was always just so pleased to see him. He never took any notice of her when she begged him not to embarrass her like that, and she always forgave him much too easily for putting her on the spot. He would sail into the cafe – his big personality filling the whole room – always managing to be the centre of attention wherever he was. That was Jem for you. He would shake Clive's hand warmly across the counter, and kiss her briefly – whispering something flirty if he thought he could get away with it. She would then do her best to appear normal as she busied herself in the cafe, serving customers or preparing food.

On this particular visit she had only managed to snatch the odd hour or so on her own with Jem which included a quick drink in one of the less salubrious pubs in the back streets of the town, which they knew none of their acquaintances would be likely to visit, and also a brief romantic interlude in Jem's beach hut on a freezing cold morning when she was supposed to be on an errand for the cafe. The things they got up to in that hut! Sometimes they had just a few minutes to themselves, but they always made the most of them. She couldn't think about those moments without blushing. Whenever Jem was in town she would hope that Clive would receive a call from a friend with an invite out for a drink – usually at the golf club – and then she could go along to The Grand Hotel for an evening and spend some quality time with Jem, but frustratingly, it hadn't happened yet on this visit.

On the last day of Jem's stay in Sebleigh Bay he and Clive met up at lunch time for a drinking session in the Golden Bell in town. Carmen didn't like it when her two men went out together. It always made her feel anxious. She'd asked Jem to stop doing it, but he said it would look odd if he didn't meet Clive any more, and besides they were old friends! 'Hardly friends when you're sleeping with his wife', she'd told him. On this occasion Clive returned to the cafe afterwards on his own surprisingly early. They would normally come back to the Beachcomber together for some strong coffees. Carmen was disappointed by Jem's absence this time, but she didn't like to ask Clive why he wasn't there. She noticed that Clive was in a strange mood and she couldn't work why. He was unusually quiet, as opposed to his normally buoyant mood which he'd be in after a few whiskeys. She was overwhelmed by a feeling of disappointment as she realised Jem would be leaving Sebleigh Bay in the morning and it didn't look like she would be seeing him again today, and Clive's mood was decidedly disturbing.

Later that afternoon, she and Clive cleaned up the cafe and closed a little early as it was a quiet winter's day. When they returned to their home, which was a couple of miles inland, there was a message on the answer phone for Clive from an ex colleague who was on a lads' golfing holiday in nearby Lynchester. He invited Clive to go and join them that evening for a catch up session at the Nineteenth Hole. Carmen was relieved when Clive left pretty well straight away and told her not to expect him back until late. Her thoughts switched immediately to Jem, and she seized the unexpected opportunity to phone him on his mobile.

'I'm free this evening if you are.'

'Good. Good,' he said, hesitantly. He asked her a few questions about where Clive was and then told her to come to The Grand Hotel. He promised he would order a fabulous meal for them to have in his suite. She was excited that they would be spending an evening together at last.

Carmen and Jem had a wonderful time in the very luxurious Albany Suite but Jem was unusually quiet and thoughtful. Carmen thought he seemed, on the one hand distracted, but on the other very attentive towards her. After a delicious three course meal which Jem had ordered from room service, they reclined on the lavish maroon velvet settee together. She had her legs lying across his lap as they sipped expensive vintage champagne.

'You know I only love you for your money Jem,' she joked as she looked around the impressive hotel suite. Jem laughed.

'I'm heartbroken Carmen – I thought it was my magnetic personality, charm and handsome figure that you'd fallen for,' he said as he tried in an exaggerated manner to hold his ample stomach in.

'Nope! It's definitely the money! I mean look at this champagne - you've really pushed the boat out this time.'

'Only the best for you my love,' he said looking lovingly into her eyes, his expression changing suddenly from jovial to serious. He took her glass and placed it on the table and started kissing her, very gently and tenderly at first and then with gradually more and more passion. They kissed for a long time, which Carmen thought was unusual for Jem. He normally had her on the bed within seconds of their lips meeting. Eventually he took her hand and led her to the ornate four poster bed. He undressed her slowly, pausing several times to kiss her and then he made love to her with exceptional tenderness. At one point she asked him if he was alright, but didn't keep asking because she didn't want to spoil the moment. Afterwards, they were lying in the candlelit room with their arms around each other. Jem stroked Carmen's hair.

'Love you Carmen. Whatever happens in the future, don't forget that.'

'You know I love you Jem.'

Carmen found it a huge wrench to pull herself away, but somehow she managed to get dressed and leave before 11 o'clock. She always did this, preferring to slip out while the hotel bars and restaurants were still busy, hoping that no-one would notice her presence there.

As she left his room and walked to the lift, she was aware that Jem was standing in the doorway watching her. He didn't normally do that. She glanced back just before she stepped into the lift and caught a quick glimpse of sadness in his eyes. She went home with her mind full of confusion. It had been the most beautiful perfect evening with him – and yet at the back of her mind she was worried that something was wrong. Looking back, it was almost as if he'd known he wouldn't be seeing her ever again.

Over the next few days she had tried to call him on his mobile at every opportunity. After a while she became concerned as he wasn't answering at all, and she started taking slight risks and phoning when Clive wasn't far away, but Jem still never picked up. Sometimes she was convinced that something bad had happened, and then other times she'd tell herself, don't be silly, he'll be fine – he always is. He's probably abroad somewhere and forgotten his phone. It's not the first time he's gone AWOL. He will turn up eventually.

On that beautiful winter's day when the cafe and the beach suddenly came alive after the long grey months, the unexpected sunshine and blue skies were making Carmen feel good. She was in an optimistic mood and told herself everything would be alright. The beach hut owners were turning up to inspect their huts, clean them up and make repairs, and she had an enjoyably busy day in the cafe. At the end of the day she saw the good looking man come in and give his order just before Clive popped out to the supermarket. She was glad when he came up to the counter for another cup of tea. He was a few years younger than her and looked strangely familiar. She remembered she'd seen him before. She was enjoying a brief chat with him – commenting on the blue paint all over his hands. It was a nice end to a good day's work - nice, that is, until the bombshell hit when she discovered that this man's uncle who had recently died, was none other than her darling Jem.

She didn't remember much about the conversation that followed. She must have been in shock. James was kind to her – she remembered that. She could see he felt terrible for unintentionally delivering such devastating news to her. After he'd gone, she clung to the phone number he'd given her, managing to save it to her phone. She began to treasure

James - as a connection to her Jem. She could see the family resemblance clearly. His facial features reminded her of Jem but he was slimmer and much quieter and more modest and sensitive.

Carmen didn't know how she'd managed to find such strength and, it has to be said, an unknown acting ability, to hold it together when Clive came back to the cafe to lock up and take her home. As soon as he walked in the cafe he could see something was wrong.

'Are you alright? What's the matter?'

'I've just had a bit of a shock. You know that man who came in when you were leaving? Well it turned out he was Jem's nephew – he's called James. He's inherited Jem's beach hut because he's died.'

'Died?!' Clive almost shouted. 'Jem has? Are you serious?'

'Yes. I'd hardly joke about one of our friends dying would I?'

'Good God. What happened?'

'Natural causes I think he said. To be honest I was so shocked I don't think I took it all in.'

'Bloody hell!' Clive said quietly.

'It happened a few weeks ago – just a few days after we last saw him here.'

'Shit!'

They locked up the cafe and drove home in virtual silence – both overwhelmed by the unexpected news, and deep in their own thoughts.

Over the next few weeks Carmen went about her life on auto-pilot – putting on a fixed smile for the customers, and trying not to show her feelings in front of Clive. She had got into the habit of bursting into tears every time Clive went out of the house and left her on her own, enabling her to be herself. Sometimes she would sob uncontrollably hoping that at some point the pain would begin to leave her. Then she would pull herself together before Clive came home. Her tears weren't just for Jem. They were also for the guilt

59

she felt for cheating on Clive. For some reason, now that Jem was gone and her affair was finished, she found herself flooded with guilt for the years of deception.

She told Clive she kept getting migraines, allowing her to take time away from work when she needed it, and also so that she could retreat to the bedroom at home when she couldn't hold her sorrow in any longer. They'd recently employed young Ellie to help out in the cafe, and she was keen to work as much as possible, so Carmen kept calling her in when she had one of her "migraines."

She phoned James a couple of times and found enormous comfort in their conversations. He seemed like a lovely man – so kind and thoughtful. He filled her in as much as he knew about Jem's family, and she was amused by some of the childhood stories about Jem which had been passed down to James by his father, Jem's older brother.

In some ways it felt so good to be able to at last talk about her relationship with Jem, as she'd kept it a complete secret for so long. How ironic though that it was only after his death that she was now able to confide in someone. James admitted that the family had always viewed Jem as a bit of a ladies man. Despite her strong feelings for him Carmen had never deluded herself. She knew she was unlikely to be the only lover in his life, but she found his charm and energy irresistible.

Carmen was very disappointed when James told her he was going to sell the beach hut. Unfortunately his own relationship hadn't worked out and he wasn't likely to be using it.

For several months Carmen couldn't bring herself to walk along Chalk Cliff Way past the beach huts. That would be far too painful. She didn't even know if Jem's hut would look the same after James had painted it. He told her he'd left all the contents inside. He had offered to let her retrieve anything she wanted to keep, but she declined as Clive might think it odd.

60

Eventually on a dull rainy day when the cafe wasn't too busy she told Clive she needed some air and she found herself walking along the beach past the huts. She nervously approached number eighteen and noticed the new name sign on the front door which said 'Alice'. That was a surprise. *Strange name for a beach hut.* She didn't realise James had named it. She was pleased to see that he had painted it well though – matching the colours exactly – smartening it up a bit. A pain stabbed at her heart as she remembered the pale blue paint on James's hands that afternoon in the cafe, and the horrific shock that followed.

She walked round to the side window and was moved to tears by the familiar items on the window sill. The jar of seaglass which she and Jem had collected over the years, and the pebbles and driftwood, and most importantly the familiar photo frame with the lovely picture of Jem in it which she'd taken herself several summers ago. The same furniture remained inside including the orange rug which she'd helped Jem to choose just a few months back. She wondered if James would remove everything before he sold it. She looked at the the old settee. Tears poured from her eyes and she couldn't bear to dwell too much at the moment on the memories of what she and Jem had got up to on there! She briefly recalled some of the snatched hours of pleasure and passion, sometimes with the sound of the waves breaking on the beach just outside, and often in pitch darkness.

As she walked away she thought about the name 'Alice.' She was pretty sure that she was James' friend – the girl he'd come into the cafe with. Gosh she hadn't realised how serious he must have been about her. She wondered what the story was there? Poor James. She suspected he'd had his heart broken too. She felt a little guilty. He'd been so supportive to her and yet he'd hardly talked about his own situation.

Carmen walked slowly back to the cafe, delaying the moment when she had to face Clive. She found herself doing that an awful lot these days. Her emotions weren't yet under control so she walked further down the beach on to the sandy part, out towards the sea. Thank God Clive never found out about her and Jem. She didn't want to lose him too. Sometimes she had been worried that he might have suspected something but she felt that if he had found out, it would have been immediate divorce. He would never forgive her. She'd taken a terrible risk. Why had she fallen for Jem when she already had a decent loyal husband who treated her so well? Carmen asked herself that many times, but couldn't find the answer, and doubted that she ever would.

She was surprised how much Clive was affected by Jem's death. He'd been quite snappy and moody. She didn't really know what was going on inside his head. He'd always tended to keep his feelings hidden. She noticed he was avoiding talking about Jem. Maybe his death had scared him – reminded him of his own mortality? The two of them had been friends though. They had shared many whiskies together, and if Jem was in town when Clive had one of his daft wargames evenings in the cafe, he would go along and join in. This bugged Carmen as she would rather Jem had spent those evenings with her while Clive was fully occupied with his mates. Still, no-one could compete with the boys and their toys.

As she reached the sea's edge she glanced back at the cafe and saw several people going inside. She thought she'd better go back and serve some customers. As usual she tried to snap out of her melancholy thoughts and switch them back to her day to day tasks.

When she put her apron on and joined Clive round behind the counter, he glanced at her as if to say 'About time!'

'Well, sorry, but it was almost empty when I went out. Anyway, I'm back now.' She put on her professional smile and charm, and greeted a family who had just entered.

'You've brought the sunshine with you - it was pouring with rain yesterday.'

'Yes. We were just wondering if you allow dogs in here? Our son's outside with him at the moment.'

'No, I'm sorry we don't,' Carmen said kindly.

'Okay. We'll sit outside then.' After they'd placed their orders and joined the rest of the family outside, Carmen said quietly to Clive,

'Blooming cheek! Does this look like the sort of place that has dogs? I don't really like them outside, let alone in here.'

'Oh don't be silly Carmen. What harm can they do?'

'It's unhygienic having dogs indoors.'

'No it isn't. Everyone has them in their houses and that's not considered to be unhygienic is it? Anyway, lots of cafes allow dogs these days. Actually I've been seriously thinking that we ought to consider it? We'd get a lot more customers especially in the winter.'

'You're joking! Anyway very few people walk their dogs along here in the winter.'

'Yes *exactly*, but that's the whole point. There might be a lot more dog walkers down here if they were allowed to bring them in the cafe.' Carmen raised her eyebrows in disgust as Clive carried a tray of fish and chip dinners over to the family sitting by the window. He returned to the counter and didn't let the subject drop.

'We could talk to the local paper, get some publicity. Have a special day to launch our new arrangement – give out free dog biscuits or sausages or whatever to get people in here with their dogs?'

'I can't believe I'm hearing this! You're not serious are you? ... My God, you are!'

'Yes I am actually. I keep telling you it's hardly worth staying open in the winter the way things are at the moment. We're running a business and we need to face facts and make changes.'

'I don't like change Clive. You know that. Especially when it involves having four legged creatures in our cafe!'

she said raising her voice in exasperation. 'Don't even think about it Clive, it's a definite NO!'

Chapter 8

Poppy Dancey moved to Sebleigh Bay after the breakup of her relationship with her partner Darren, and more significantly, the loss of her beloved dog Pluto. These sad events caused her to rethink her life and make a fresh start on the coast, not far from where her parents lived.

She and Darren had been living together for four years with her much treasured companion Pluto, her mad and lively red setter cross with the huge black eyes and a big shaggy coat. Darren had never been overly keen on dogs but when they decided to get a place together, it was simply a case of 'love me, love my dog.'

In time Darren did appear to grow fond of Pluto and even enjoyed occasional country walks with him, but Poppy knew deep down though that Darren wouldn't want her to get another dog when Pluto finally passed away. He dropped several hints along the lines of, 'We can renovate the kitchen when we haven't got Pluto anymore,' and 'we can go on more exotic holidays when we don't have a dog to worry about.' Poppy found these comments hurtful and always felt that Darren was just tolerating Pluto, knowing that he was unlikely to be around for much more than another year or two. She even felt that he was looking forward to a time when he'd have her to himself rather than having to share her with her lovable, but demanding, rusty coloured hound.

Ironically though, it was Pluto's eventual death which brought about the beginning of the end of Poppy and Darren's relationship. Poppy was naturally devastated when Pluto had to be put to sleep because of his old age and deteriorating health. She was overwhelmed by the feelings of pain and emptiness that followed. Pluto wasn't 'just a dog' – he'd meant everything to her, and been her constant companion for the last twelve years. She felt she couldn't have loved him more if he'd been her own child.

For several days Poppy hardly slept or ate, and she couldn't bear coming home to an empty house. Each time she came in the front door the silence and the lack of her beloved Pluto bounding up to her brought tears to her eyes. She hated waking up in the morning remembering he was no longer there, and she dreaded going to bed at night without a lovely walk with Pluto to look forward to the next morning.

Initially Darren did his best to be supportive. He was shocked by the extent of Poppy's sorrow and he allowed her to cry on his shoulder every day for the first week or more. He treated her to some meals out and took a day off work to keep her company. Poppy appreciated his efforts and even told her friends how marvellous he'd been.

After a few weeks Poppy had reached a point where she was just beginning to realise that the phrase 'time is a good healer' may indeed be true ... to a certain extent! Her well meaning parents had repeated those words to her so many times and eventually her sadness lessened a little. She at last felt able to remove Pluto's toys and his lead from the hall, and to put them out of sight in the garage. In fact it was at the very moment that she'd completed this small but significant task and come back indoors, that Darren arrived home from work.

'Hello Honey – oh you look better today ... That's great! ... Guess where I've just been?' He snapped open his brief case before he'd even taken off his overcoat, and thrust a pile of travel brochures in her hand. 'What do you think? We've always wanted to travel haven't we? Where do you fancy? Australia? New Zealand? An African Safari perhaps? We're free to go at last.' Over the coming months Darren often wondered whether those two words 'at last' were the biggest mistake he'd ever made. Poppy stared at the brochures in her hand, and stared at Darren.

'Well ... I'm not sure I'm ready for a holiday ...'

'We won't be going yet – but we can make a booking - something to look forward to,' he said with enthusiasm.

'I don't know ... I mean, this is a bit sudden ... I can't think about this now ...' and then her expression changed from confused to angry. 'What do you mean *at last?!*'

'I didn't mean anything. I just ...'

'At last? *At last?* You mean you've just been dying for us to be without Pluto so that we can go on holiday? ... *At last*!'

'No, of course not ...'

'Do you really think I'm in the mood to be planning a holiday?'

'Well maybe not ...'

'I feel so utterly empty at the moment – it's like ... I've lost the most important thing in the world to me.'

'Gee thanks Pops. You really know how to make a guy feel good. For goodness sake, this has gone on long enough*! He was a dog!*' At this point Poppy threw the holiday brochures on the floor, and Darren knew he'd messed up big time.

'Sorry Poppy – I didn't mean that okay. Look, I was fond of him too ...'

Poppy had already stomped off. They didn't speak much for the rest of the evening. However on the following day they both apologised and agreed to start again. Darren promised he wouldn't mention the holiday for a while and Poppy said she realised he hadn't meant to hurt her. But the truth of the matter was that she had been shocked by her own words. As she began to examine her feelings she discovered that Pluto had indeed meant more to her than Darren had. What did that say about their relationship? She also felt resentment growing inside her because Darren just couldn't accept that she was still heartbroken several weeks after Pluto had gone.

They split up exactly four months after Pluto's passing. Although Poppy's spirits were at rock bottom for a while she didn't have any doubts that she'd done the right thing letting Darren go, simply because she knew that she missed Pluto far more than she would miss him.

After much soul searching she decided that a clean break and a new start was necessary. She needed to get her own place; somewhere where every little detail of her surroundings didn't constantly remind her of Pluto and bring tears to her eyes. Her parents had moved to Sebleigh Bay when they retired, and she and Pluto had always enjoyed visiting them there. She loved the seaside, and amongst the many estate agent particulars she received were the details of a small but stunning flat which was available to rent right on the seafront. An old Victorian house had recently been converted into four beautiful flats, each with their own enormous living room windows providing impressive sea views. She wouldn't be allowed to have a dog there, but that didn't worry her because she couldn't imagine ever being able to replace Pluto.

Poppy felt tremendously proud of her new home - Flat Number 4, on the first floor of Anchor House. She and her parents loved being near to each other again – she was only about fifteen minutes walk from their bungalow. She couldn't stop admiring the beautiful sea views from her windows. She positioned her favourite arm chair next to the large lounge windows facing out to sea, and she put her favourite photo of herself and Pluto, in it's gold frame, on the window sill. She loved that photo. Whenever any of her friends and family had seen it for the first time, they'd always quoted the old saying about people growing to look like their pets. Her auburn hair was indeed the same colour as Pluto's fur, and she kept it in a long shaggy style. She and Pluto had even won a competition once in a dog show in the category of 'the owner who most looked like their dog.' Mind you, she attributed their win very much down to the fact that when the judge came by, Pluto rolled on to his back and waved his legs in the air, so Poppy followed suit and did exactly the same thing. She was not only awarded with laughter and applause from the other entrants, but first prize in the category, for herself and Pluto.

Poppy was excited about her new life in Sebleigh Bay, but she had two things uppermost on her mind which she needed to sort out. Firstly she needed to find a job, and secondly she needed to make some local friends. Poppy took these two tasks very seriously, and spent time every day searching the local papers and the internet for a new job and new social activities. As far as her career was concerned her previous experience lay in the areas of hotel receptionist (which wasn't her thing at all), primary school teaching assistant, and children's party entertainer – in a previous life she'd been known as Cleo the Clown! Despite the hours she put into her job search she was concerned to find that there were so few suitable positions to apply for locally, but she registered with all the right places and got to work on improving her CV. She was convinced that the right job would come up eventually.

The local papers were also a good source of information on leisure activities and hobbies. Poppy drew rings around the adverts for Beginners Jive Dancing Classes, Sebleigh Ramblers, and a book group at the library. She made up her mind to try all three over the next few weeks.

The jive class at the Ballroom in The Grand Hotel was great fun, despite Poppy discovering that she was the proud owner of two left feet! She struggled with the dance steps but enjoyed chatting to several different people and vowed to give it another go the following week.

The Book Group wasn't so successful. She had to sit through an hour and a half analysis about a book that she hadn't read. The discussion was dominated by two of the twelve members, who Poppy felt were rather too fond of the sound of their own voices. Despite being bored and unimpressed she found it difficult to get out of buying a copy of next month's book. Unfortunately it wasn't her cup of tea and she couldn't get beyond the first chapter, so the Book Group was firmly crossed off of her list of activities.

The Rambling Club was okay except that it reminded her how much she missed Pluto. On the day she participated, the group did a long coastal walk where they enjoyed exploring parts of Sebleigh which she hadn't previously visited. She couldn't remember the last time she had walked on a beach without Pluto for company though. The other walkers were friendly and welcoming – she enjoyed some interesting conversations – but they were more her parent's age than her own. One very positive point though was that she discovered a lovely stretch of beach beyond the main town, where you could walk past a long line of attractive old fashioned beach huts, and end up in the Beachcomber Cafe for a drink. Poppy was a big fan of cappuccinos, of which the Beachcomber did an excellent one, and she really liked the atmosphere there. She would definitely be taking more walks down that end of the promenade in future.

When the next local paper came out Poppy turned immediately to the job section, and was once more disappointed by the lack of any suitable positions for her to apply for. She also looked at the hobby section, but there wasn't anything new on this week. She sunk back in her armchair and looked out to sea. *Well it's all very well having a beautiful flat at the seaside with a stunning view, but I won't be able to afford it much longer if I don't get a job!* Not knowing what to do next she flicked through the rest of the paper, not expecting to see anything of interest, but a photo of the lovely Beachcomber Cafe caught her eye. She vaguely recognised the faces of the smiling cafe owners who were standing outside next to a huge dog – the woman with her hand on his big furry brown head. The headline of the article read, 'Beachcomber Cafe welcomes dogs.' It went on to say, 'From this weekend onwards, dog lovers Carmen and Clive Collier are welcoming all well behaved dogs into the Beachcomber Cafe, at the end of Chalk Cliff Way. They will be holding a special open day on Saturday where all dogs attending will be given free treats.'

'Oh this I must see.' Poppy said out loud. 'It's tomorrow! Brilliant.'

70

Chapter 9

Poppy arrived at the Beachcomber Cafe after a brisk walk along the promenade and past the beach huts.   She was really looking forward to this – the thought of lots of lovely dogs and their owners all congregating at the cafe was so appealing.   She noted that extra tables and chairs had been placed outside and there were about six blue doggy water bowls at regular intervals along the edge of the forecourt. There were several families sitting at the outside tables with their much loved pets – possibly enjoying the cafe for the first time.   A huge cream coloured Pyrenean Mountain Dog was sniffing a miniscule Chihuahua which was seated on the lap of a young woman on the next table.   Both owners looked on in amusement.

As Poppy entered the cafe she was hit with the buzz of companiable conversation.   People were turning round and talking to their neighbours on nearby tables – sharing dog stories and exclaiming with oohs and aahs as they admired each other's treasured pets.   Every table was occupied with humans and dogs – a wonderful array of mixed sizes, colours and breeds.   She couldn't contain her excitement at seeing so many beautiful animals in one place.   She was desperate to get to know some of those gorgeous animals.

As she approached the counter Carmen and Clive had just finished serving a customer and were having a chat.

'Clive, what's wrong with that one?' Carmen asked as she looked down at a dog just nearby.   Poppy looked round expecting to see an animal with some sort of injury, but couldn't see one.   Carmen appeared to be looking at two black spaniels.

'Which one?' asked Clive.

'That black one. It's legs are too short.'

'How can they be? They reach the ground.'

'Very funny!' Carmen groaned.

'It's just the way it is I guess – it looks like a spaniel ... with short legs.'

'Well the other one doesn't look like that.   It's not supposed to be like that is it?'

'Perhaps it's a cross?'

'Cross? I'd be cross if my legs were that short.'

Poppy couldn't help laughing at the woman, who smiled at her and asked,

'What can I get you love?'

'Just a cappuccino please.' Carmen leaned forward and looked over the counter down towards Poppy's feet.

'Oh I was just looking to see if you had a dog.'

'No, I haven't unfortunately. I lost my dog Pluto. I had him for twelve years. He was a red setter cross. I still miss him terribly.'

'Nice name. Are you going to get another one?' Carmen asked kindly as she prepared the cappuccino.

'No. Well I couldn't even if I wanted to because I live in a flat now – no pets allowed.'

'There you are – one cappuccino. Thanks love.'

'Thank you.' Poppy picked up her cappuccino and turned round to look for somewhere to sit in the packed cafe. The couple nearby with the two black spaniels saw that she was looking for somewhere to sit, and the woman caught Poppy's eye and said,

'There's a spare chair here, if you don't mind sharing with us?'

'Thank you very much. I thought I was going to have to sit on the beach.'

'You're brave – coming in here today when you haven't got a dog with you.'

'Well, I couldn't resist it to be honest. I was intrigued when I read about it in the paper.' Poppy then went on to explain once more all about her beloved Pluto. The couple listened sympathetically to her every word. Poppy was enjoying having someone to talk to as she had spent so much time in her own company since she'd moved to Sebleigh Bay away from her friends. However, after a while she noticed that the eyes of the man and woman were looking so full of sadness and sympathy, that she suddenly snapped out of her story.

'Anyway, sorry, I didn't mean to be a misery,' she said cheerfully, 'this is such a fun occasion.'

'Oh it's alright dear,' said the woman. 'We know what it's like to lose a dog – it takes time to get over it.'

'When we lost our previous dog, Worzel,' the husband said kindly, 'we found it very hard to cope with the bereavement. I think we only really started to cheer up when we got these two.'

'They're lovely aren't they,' Poppy said as she stroked 'short legs'. 'What breed are they exactly?'

'They're working spaniels,' said the wife, 'but you're probably wondering why Jet's legs are a bit short? It's because they're a quarter dachshund. You can't see it at all in Dusty, he looks just like a spaniel doesn't he?' The spaniels' owners appeared to be in their 40s and were wearing identical fleeces, and sported matching brightly coloured short haircuts. Even the man had highlights and colours added, Poppy noticed. They kept giving each other loving glances, and touching each other's hands.

'Oh it's so lovely to be cuddling some dogs again,' Poppy said. 'It makes me realise how much I miss my Pluto. I didn't think I'd ever be able to replace him, so when I came here to Sebleigh Bay I moved into a flat which doesn't allow dogs, but just recently I've been changing my mind a bit. Maybe I could have considered having another dog after all?'

'That's a shame,' said the man, 'I don't suppose there's much you can do about it now. You won't want to move again yet.'

'Mm. Maybe I should find an elderly person who can't manage their dog very well, and I could offer to walk it for them. I've got plenty of time on my hands at the moment.'

'You can borrow these two if you like?' he suggested enthusiastically.

'Yes,' said his wife 'I was thinking that. We both work full time and they don't get walked properly until the evening. We feel a bit guilty about it actually.'

'Really?' said Poppy 'Yes I could take them out for you. I'd love to. Where do you live?'

'Do you know the Stardust Hair Salon in Dooley Street? It's painted purple.'

'Oh yes. I've seen it.'

'Well it's ours, and we live in the apartment upstairs.'

'Oh right. I noticed your fabulous hairstyles – that would explain it. I'll have to come in sometime. I haven't had my hair done since I moved here.'

'Oh please do,' the man said as he rummaged in his pocket, 'I'll give you a card if you like so you can book an appointment if you want to.'

'Thanks,' said Poppy as she took the card and read it. 'So you're Selina and Simon are you?'

'That's right.'

'And I'm Poppy.'

At that moment they were interrupted by some very loud barking which was coming from a small black dog underneath a table in the corner.

'Quiet Raymond! Stop it!' his owner said angrily, as if she was addressing a naughty child.

'Raymond!' her voice got louder, 'If you don't stop you'll have to go outside.' Poppy glanced up at the counter to see how Carmen was reacting to the commotion.

'Horrible little thing,' Carmen said quietly to Clive.

'Shush!' said Clive.

'I didn't like the look of that one when it came in – it was staring at me with those beady little eyes it's got.'

'Carmen – we're supposed to be welcoming the dogs, not telling them their legs are too short or their eyes are beady!'

'Well we made it quite clear in the newspaper that they're supposed to be well behaved dogs.'

'He only barked Carmen. It's not as if he's been going round biting people's ankles or stealing their sausages.'

Poppy was trying not to laugh too much at the conversation behind the counter. It was becoming very clear that Carmen wasn't the doggy fan that she'd appeared to be when she was photographed for the newspaper. Selina and Simon were distracted by a little girl on the next table who was showing off her Alsatian, which was bigger than she was. As they talked to her, Poppy carried on stroking the soft silky fur of the two black spaniels as she listened to Carmen and Clive's amusing conversation at the counter.

'This is going really well isn't it?' said Clive as he nudged his wife, 'Go on you've got to admit it, it's been a great success so far.'

'Well ... yes ... if you call filling a cafe with four legged creatures a success?'

'Oh come on – you've enjoyed yourself when you've made the effort.'

'What do you mean when I've made the effort? I've made a big effort from start to finish. I've been the perfect host, welcoming every person who's come through that door – like I always do – and I've shown an interest in every one of their furry little friends – asking what breed they are and everything. I've learnt a lot actually. Do you know Clive, I reckon I could name the breeds of all the dogs in here.'

'Really?' Clive said sounding surprised, 'Go on then.'

'Well that big one over there with the little girl is a German Shepherd. The two little white ones by the window are Jack Russels. That woolly one there is a mixture – it's called a cockerpoodledo or something.' Clive fell about laughing.

'I think you'll find it's a cockadoodle – a cross between a cockerspaniel and a poodle.'

'Yeah yeah, and apparently they cross everything with a poodle these days to produce dogs whose hair doesn't fall out and make a mess.'

'Oh, you really have been taking it all in haven't you,' Clive said – thoroughly amused by his wife's interest in the dogs.

'I haven't finished yet. I don't know what the noisy little one with the beady eyes is because his owner doesn't know either – some sort of mongrel by the look of it.' Then Poppy saw Carmen turn to the two spaniels who she was still stroking. She smiled at Carmen, who leaned over the counter and asked Poppy,

'What type are they? Are they spaniels?'

'They're working spaniels with a quarter dachshund.'

'Dachshund? That's a sausage dog isn't it? That explains it.' Selina and Simon turned round when they realised that their dogs were being discussed.

'You must be talking about Jet and Dusty,' Selina said.
'Yes their grandmother was got at by a dachshund – tiny little thing – no-one knows how he managed to do it!' she said giggling.

'Did you say working spaniel?' asked Carmen, 'What does that mean? What work do they do?'

'Well these don't work,' said Simon 'It's the name of the breed, but they can work as gun dogs.'

Poppy suddenly looked towards the door and gasped with excitement! Selina, Simon and Carmen all turned to see what had caught her eye. A family with two young children and a red setter came through the door. Poppy couldn't resist making a fuss of the dog as the family stood by the counter and studied the menu.

'Oh you're so beautiful, aren't you ... you remind me very much of my Pluto,' she said to the dog as he enjoyed the attention and wagged his tail excitedly. When the mum had finished choosing drinks for the children she turned to Poppy and smiled,

'He can't get enough of that - he'll let you carry on stroking him all day given the chance.'

'Oh I don't mind – you're so lovely,' she said to the dog in her soppy doggy voice. Then she turned to the owner and asked,

'What's his name?'

'You'll probably laugh, but he's called Turnip.'

76

'Turnip! Oh that's so cute.'

'Little Jade here insisted on calling him that when he was a puppy, and it stuck.' Poppy turned to Jade and said,

'I do like your dog, he's gorgeous, and what a lovely name he's got.'

'I called him Turnip,' she said pointing to herself.

Well this was the beginning of a long and cheerful conversation with Turnip's family. They sat down at a nearby table when it became free and Poppy spent a happy half hour or so tickling and stroking Turnip as she heard all about the family's weekend away in Sebleigh Bay in their campervan. Of course Poppy recounted the sad tale of her Pluto once again. Simon and Selina politely interrupted to say goodbye to her when they left and Poppy said she'd see them in the salon very soon for a haircut.

She finally left the Beachcomber Cafe after spending a good couple of hours there, and not before she'd stopped to chat to several more wonderful dogs and their owners. She was on a tremendous high as she strolled back along the seafront towards Anchor House, recalling all the fabulous dogs she'd met and the great conversations she'd had. She suddenly felt very positive about her new life in Sebleigh Bay. She knew she'd be back at the Beachcomber Cafe very soon, and that she'd be along to the hairdressers to see Selina and Simon again. It had been a thoroughly successful afternoon!

Chapter 10

Just three days after the doggie day at the Beachcomber Cafe Poppy found herself seated in front of a huge purple edged mirror in the Stardust Hairdressing Salon. She'd just had her hair washed and was sipping a cup of tea as she waited for Selina. The interior of the salon was luxurious and trendy with all the fixtures in black and purple. There were six stylists hard at work, all wearing black outfits with the Stardust logo spread artistically across their backs in glittery purple. Selina came breezing over.

'Poppy, I'm sorry to keep you my dear. I hope you've been well looked after.'

'Yes, very well thanks.' Poppy was surprised by the contrast in Selina's appearance from the comfy dog walking trackies and fleece she'd been in at the Beachcomber to the sophisticated image she presented today.

'Now, what are we going to have done today?'

'Well I'm not sure. I think I need a fair bit chopped off as it's long overdue.' Selina ran her hands through Poppy's hair and experimented by holding it in different positions.

'Do you think I can persuade you to have a complete change? You know, new town, new flat, new hairstyle?' she said gathering it all up on the top of her head to get an idea of how it would look short. Poppy quite liked that look.

'I'll tell you what Selina, do whatever you want. You can have free reign.'

'Oh, wonderful! That's just what I like to hear.'

Poppy enjoyed chatting to Selina as she snipped away. Large chunks of auburn hair were dropping to the floor as her long floppy hairstyle was rapidly disappearing in front of her eyes. The conversation soon came round to Poppy's favourite subject – dogs! She was keen to offer to take out the two black spaniels for walks while Selina and Simon were working. She wasn't sure if they'd been serious though when they suggested it.

'Would you like me to take Jet and Dusty out for you sometime?'

'Would you seriously like to do that?'

'Yes definitely. Well certainly until I get a job. I go for a long walk every day anyway – I might as well take Dusty and Jet with me if it would help you – I'd love it to be honest. I haven't walked a dog since I lost Pluto.'

'That would be brilliant. Thank you. What sort of work are you looking for?' The two women continued their discussion as Selina carefully created Poppy's new image.

Their conversation flowed effortlessly and Poppy was so engrossed in it that she hardly noticed the transformation that was happening.

'Well I think that's just about it.' Selina said, stepping back.

'Wow!' Poppy said, taking in the sleek and very short new style.

'Is that a good wow?' Poppy wasn't too sure. But she wouldn't have dreamt of upsetting Selina.

'It's so different. I've never looked like that before. Actually it's very smart – I think I'd better put on some decent clothes and get out there and do some serious job hunting.'

'Good idea. I was just thinking ... you're my last appointment, and if you're not in a rush now I could take you up to the flat to talk about the dogs.'

'Yes I can do that. I can't wait to see them again.'

'Ahh,' Selina said sympathetically. 'You love dogs so much don't you. It's a shame you haven't got one.' Poppy pulled a worried face.

'I'm trying not to think about that. Anyway let me settle up with you first.'

Half an hour later Poppy was settled upstairs in a comfortable armchair in Selina and Simon's apartment just finishing a cup of tea, with Dusty and Jet at her feet. Jet had his sleepy head on her lap and was loving the attention that Poppy was giving him.

'Well they've certainly taken to you. They just won't believe their luck when you come and take them out.'

'I can't wait. I'll come tomorrow if you like.'

'That would be wonderful. You can just turn up at the salon any time you like and I'll let you through.'

The two women swapped phone numbers and discussed a few details about their arrangement and off Poppy went – as happy as Larry. Not only did she have two beautiful dogs to take out, but she hoped that she and Selina would become good friends. Today had been her best day in Sebleigh Bay so far – with the doggie day in the Beachcomber on Saturday a close second. If she was honest with herself, she wasn't too sure about the new hairstyle yet – it would take some getting used to – but if the worst came to the worst, it would grow again wouldn't it?

Chapter 11

Poppy couldn't wait to do her first dog walk, so she turned up bright and early at the Stardust Hairdressing Salon in the morning – simply raring to go. Selina was busy rolling up a perm and Simon was painting colour onto a young woman's foiled head, so they told Poppy to see herself through. As she entered the lounge upstairs Dusty and Jet charged at her excitedly, yelping and wagging their tails furiously.

'Okay you gorgeous guys, let's get your leads on and off we go.' The three of them hurtled down the stairs and left by the back door which lead into an alley way down the back of the shops.

Poppy had a wonderful time. She took Jet and Dusty straight down to the beach and they all headed off in the direction of the beach huts, and then along to the Beachcomber Cafe. Poppy decided to keep the dogs on the leads for their first walk, so that they could get used to each other. Carmen greeted them as they entered the cafe and looked at her as if to say 'I've seen you before somewhere?'

'Hello,' Poppy said, feeling pleased to see a familiar face, 'I came along to your doggie open day on Saturday, and I found myself these two lovelies to take for walks.'

'Oh, it's short legs isn't it, they belonged to the couple with the matching spiky hair didn't they?'

'Yes that's right – Selina and Simon. I went into their salon yesterday to have my hair done – you probably don't recognise me as I had lots of long hair beforehand. Selina gave me quite a transformation!'

'Oh right! Everything's clicked into place now. They're the owners of that purple place aren't they? Oh you got off lightly – no coloured spikes then. They've got a reputation for sending everyone home with the same hairstyle – short, spiky and coloured!'

'Really? Well I certainly got the short bit.'

'That's funny actually, because when I saw those two in here I thought "I bet they've been to Stardust" – I didn't realise that they *were* Stardust. Oh yes I remember you now – you had long hair before didn't you. And ...' she changed her voice to a kinder tone, 'you recently lost your dog ... Neptune wasn't it?'

'Pluto.'

'Oh yes! Pluto!'

'Well you've got a good memory.'

'So you're walking their dogs for them now?'

'Yes. It's great. We're having a lovely time aren't we guys. Selina and Simon don't have much time because of the salon. They said I could take the boys any time I like.'

'That's interesting. Do you know, I reckon you could make a full time job of that round here. There must be lots of people who'd pay someone to walk their dogs because they're infirm, or busy working or whatever. There's a lot of elderly people in Sebleigh Bay too.'

That evening Selina phoned Poppy to thank her for walking the dogs.

'I'm sorry I didn't get much chance to talk to you when you brought them back, my dear.'

'Oh that's fine. I could see you were busy. I just wanted you to know we were all back safely.'

'And another thing ... Simon and I have been discussing things and we'd like to pay you the going hourly rate.'

'Oh there's no need Selina. That's not why I offered to walk them.'

'No, Simon insists – especially as you haven't got a job.'

'That's kind of you, but if you pay me, we'd have to formalise times and days etc, and there's really no need.'

'No you don't need to worry about that. Our arrangement can remain exactly the same. You turn up whenever you like – we don't mind if it's one day or five days a week, and we'll keep a note of the hours you do and pay you accordingly.

You're doing us a big favour and we'll be very happy to pay you.'

And so although Poppy didn't realise it at the time … that was the start of her new business venture. She couldn't believe her luck, that she was being paid simply for taking lovely dogs out for walks. It hardly seemed like work.

The next time Poppy turned up at The Beachcomber Cafe with Dusty and Jet, Carmen greeted her.

'Oh I was hoping to see you. I was talking to an elderly friend who's got a monstrous great fluffy thing, and she is no longer up to walking it, and the neighbour who has been helping her is not available any more. Anyway I thought of you. I didn't know if you wanted to take on any more work, but I told her about you and she asked me to give you her phone number if you're interested.' And so, Carmen's friend with the 'monstrous great fluffy thing', who turned out to be a Saint Bernard called Philip, became Poppy's second client.

So she now had two dog walks to do each day, one with Jet and Dusty, and another later on with Philip. This usually meant two trips to the Beachcomber for cappuccinos and a chat with Carmen and Clive if they weren't too busy.

One rainy afternoon Poppy found herself sheltering in the Beachcomber for ages with Philip at her feet. While she waited hoping the rain would ease off a little she was chatting to Carmen as she went round wiping the tables of the almost empty cafe.

'Do you know, I really am beginning to think I could make a proper business of this?"

'I'm sure you could. You can put a poster up in here for nothing. That would be a start wouldn't it. We get so many dogs in here now. Get some business cards done too, so I can give them out. We'll recommend you to people, won't we Clive?' She said turning to Clive who was sweeping the floor behind her.

'Yes of course.' He came over and bent down to talk to Philip. 'You're a lovely old chap aren't you?' he said stroking his head. Then he whispered to Carmen as if it were a child he was talking about. 'Shall we offer him one of those left over sausages?' He looked up to Poppy 'Would that be alright?' The dog's ears perked up and he looked up excitedly.

'Did you see that?' asked Carmen. 'He knows what sausages are.'

'I think it would be okay for a treat,' Poppy said laughing. 'His owner obviously gives him them because he knows what they are.' Clive went off to get the sausage and Carmen raised her eyebrows.

'Clive will be wanting to put adverts in the paper next telling everyone we're giving out free sausages for their dogs.'

'He loves dogs doesn't he. Wouldn't he like to have his own.'

'Yes he does, and no he wouldn't – well I wouldn't. It's bad enough we've filled this place with them. I'm quite happy to keep our home as an animal free zone thanks!' Poppy wasn't bothered by Carmen's stern tone. The more she got to know her, the more she liked her.

It wasn't long before Poppy's advertisement was up on the wall in the Beachcomber, and Carmen and Clive were telling everyone about her services and giving out her business cards on a regular basis.

Poppy very much enjoyed her regular chats in the Beachcomber with Carmen and Clive. They were becoming quite friendly, and Carmen's PR exercise on Poppy's behalf was paying off well. Poppy was soon picking up more regular customers, as well as continuing to walk Philip, Jet and Dusty every day. Selina and Simon continued to be flexible and didn't mind what time their dogs were walked so Poppy could fit them in easily around her newer clients. Selina would often invite Poppy in for a cup of tea if she had the time.

Poppy's business built up nicely over the next few months. There seemed to be no shortage of dogs who needed walking and she was pleased with her increasing fitness brought about by the many miles that she covered each day. She fitted in regular visits to her parents too, often bringing her furry clients round to their bungalow to meet them. She also found herself being asked to feed other pets like cats, hamsters and rabbits, for owners who were going away, so she adjusted her advertisements to include holiday cover for small animals.

Despite all the exercise she was getting Poppy continued with her jive dancing classes, and was happy with the social side of her life which was gradually developing in Sebleigh Bay. She never tired of her trips to the Beachcomber, and Carmen would usually greet her with, 'And who have we got today then?" as she looked over the counter to see which of Poppy's four legged clients were accompanying her. Carmen always insisted on calling Jet 'Short Legs' and came up with a few other amusing nicknames for some of the other more distinctive looking dogs.

Poppy was very satisfied with the way her business and indeed her life in general was going – and none more so than the day that Selina and Simon asked her if she would be prepared to look after Dusty and Jet while they went on holiday for two weeks.

'We haven't been abroad for years because we couldn't put them in kennels ... they would never forgive us ... we couldn't enjoy ourselves. But now that we've found you, my dear Poppy ... we'd like to ask you to do proper holiday cover for us. In addition to the daily walks, we wondered if you might consider staying over with them.'

'Yes, of course. I could do that, and I can keep an eye on everything while I'm there.'

Simon interrupted, 'Well we were thinking perhaps you could fit in a few perms and sets inbetween dog walking.' Poppy's jaw dropped.

'Don't be silly darling,' Selina giggled, as she prodded Simon with her elbow.

'Oh you had me going there for a second Simon,' Poppy said with a look of relief on her face.

'So would you really be happy to take all this on for a fortnight? We'll pay generously of course. You can go out and do all your normal activities in the day time but the dogs are used to having us there with them at night.'

'Yep! Consider it done. I suggest you get straight on to the travel agent and get that holiday booked right away.'

'Oh darling, you're such a treasure. We're so glad we met you aren't we my little chaps,' Selina said bending over and kissing Jet and Dusty on the top of each of their velvety black heads. 'Mummy and Daddy can have a wonderful holiday in the sun while Auntie Poppy looks after you.'

And so, that's what happened. Everything went well for the first week of Selina and Simon's holiday and Poppy was enjoying staying with Jet and Dusty. She loved being so busy with all her dog walking and being able to spend so much time with the spaniels. It was like having her own dogs again.

'How are things going at the purple place Poppy?' Clive asked when Poppy turned up at the cafe, one cold foggy morning, with Jet and Dusty.

'Oh it's great. I love doing holiday cover. I get to know the dogs so well. I think I'll push that side of things more when I redo my adverts as it brings in a bit more money too.'

'I'm surprised you need to advertise at all with my lovely wife being your unofficial PR manager,' he said, raising his voice, so that Carmen, who was serving a customer, would hear over the sound of the coffee machine. 'I tell you, she missed a vocation there.'

'Oh, she's just brilliant – I owe her so much. And you Clive,' Poppy said raising her voice too.

'Gosh look at the mist – it's very thick today.' Clive wiped the counter and then wandered over to the window, followed by Poppy.

'I know. That's why I came in here before I let the dogs off. I'm hoping it will lift a bit while I have my cappuccino.'

'Cappucino Poppy?' Carmen called out.

'Yes please. I'll have a piece of Victoria sponge too. I need to wait a bit before I go out again.

'I wouldn't bother unless it improves. You can't see a thing out there.' Clive said with concern in his voice.

'Oh, it should be okay. I know the beach pretty well now – and the tide's out – you can just about hear it in the distance. We'll be fine won't we guys?' Poppy said to the dogs as she sat herself down.

As it happened the thick mist didn't lift at all – if anything it got worse – but Poppy ignored Clive's warnings, and, determined to give Jet and Dusty their daily exercise she set off along the beach towards the cliffs. As soon as she let them off their leads they shot off into the mist and Poppy was shocked to realise she couldn't see them at all. She could barely see the white cliffs to the side of her and the sound of the gentle waves in the distance was the only thing that stopped her becoming completely disorientated. She could hear the jingle of the dogs' collars but became concerned as she really didn't know where they were.

'Jet! Dusty!' she called, 'I don't like this guys - I've changed my mind. Let's have you back here. Come on you two.' As she expected the dogs were reluctant to return having only just been let off their leads.

'Jet! Dusty! Here please. It's too foggy – I can't see you. Come on guys, you're worrying me now.' After calling them several more times the jingling got louder and Poppy was very relieved to see Dusty running towards her. She grabbed his collar quickly and fastened his lead.

'Where's Jet?' she asked him. It was unusual for him not to be following closely behind Dusty. Then Poppy became alarmed when she realised she couldn't hear Jet's collar jingling. That didn't help.

'Dusty, show me where Jet is.' She held Dusty's lead firmly and they walked further into the mist.

'Jet!' she called, 'Come on mate, it's time to go – this wasn't a good idea. Dusty where is Jet? I'm sure you must know.' Dusty started pulling towards the cliffs. Poppy followed and she saw the steps which lead up the cliffs emerging through the mist.

'Are you telling me he's gone up there? Oh if only this mist would go away – we could surely see him then. Come on let's climb the steps.'

'Poppy and Dusty briskly climbed the steps following the steep path which lead to the top of the cliffs, while she constantly called out to Jet. She hoped he'd be waiting at the top, but there was no sign of him. She was very anxious now and decided to head back to the cafe. Maybe he'd lost them and gone back there. As she and Dusty walked along the cliff top path she was amazed by the lack of visibility. She couldn't see the beach down below at all, in fact she could only just see a few yards in any direction. Poppy had a horrible thought. What if Jet had fallen down the cliff? But surely she would have heard something if he had?

When she and Dusty arrived at the Beachcomber she rushed in the door looking for Carmen and Clive.

'What on earth's the matter Poppy?' asked Clive as he came out from behind the counter. 'You look terrible.' Poppy noted the customers in the cafe and spoke quietly, 'You haven't seen Jet have you? I lost him in the mist. I was hoping he might have returned here.'

'No, sorry. Oh dear ... let me think ... well let's have a look outside and call him.'

'There's no point – I've been calling him constantly for ages – there's no sign of him at all.' Poppy was now close to tears.

'When did you last see him?'

'Soon after I left here. We were just outside and I let them off their leads and they shot off straight into the mist along by the cliffs. I didn't see Jet again after that.'

'Look, sit down and have a cup of tea and we'll think about what to do.'

'I can't. I've got to do something. I can't rest until I've found him.'

Clive put his hand on her shoulder and guided her towards a chair. 'Sit down. I insist,' he said firmly but kindly, 'and we'll see if the mist clears a bit.'

Carmen, realising something must be wrong, finished serving a customer and then came over to see what was going on. Seeing the distressed look on Poppy's face she sat down with her while Clive explained the situation. He then went to fetch some tea.

'When do Selina and Simon come home?' Carmen asked.

'In a week's time. I've got exactly seven days to find Jet.'

'Well don't panic my love. He's only been gone a short while and we've got every reason to be optimistic. We'll probably have him back much sooner than that. If only this rotten mist would clear off it would help a lot. Clive and I were saying earlier that we'd never seen anything like it.'

'I was so stupid to let them off the leads. What was I thinking? If only I'd listened to Clive.'

'Don't blame yourself Poppy. You weren't to know.' Clive put two mugs of tea down on the table. Carmen had an idea.

'Clive, why don't you give your policeman friend a call? Someone could find Short ... err Jet any time, and if they did they might go to the police station.

'Good idea. I'll do that straight away.' After Clive had made his phone call he spoke quietly to anyone who came in with a dog and asked them to keep an eye out for Jet. Poppy hung around all afternoon at the Beachcomber and she and Clive went outside many times in the mist to call Jet. Clive insisted that she didn't wander off though and stayed close to the Beachcomber. The customers were all chatting to each other about the thick sea mist and showing concern for the lost spaniel. Everyone was aware that the tide was nearly in, but they didn't voice their fears about Jet being trapped against the cliffs. By the time it was dark there was no let up from the mist so there wasn't a lot that could be done. Clive tried to reassure Poppy many times with optimistic comments.

89

'There's every chance he'll turn up somewhere. He won't get lost – he knows the beach like the back of his ... paw.'

'He's got Simon and Selina's phone number on his collar so I'll take Dusty back and check the answer phone.' Carmen gave Poppy a big hug as she left and asked her to phone if she heard anything. She scribbled her home phone number down for Poppy.

'Ring us any time.' As soon as Poppy left the cafe with Dusty, the cheerful looks on Carmen and Clive's faces dropped and they looked at each other with concern.

Poppy arrived at the salon which was now closed and let herself in the back alley entrance. She dashed straight over to Simon and Selina's answer phone. The red light was flashing with the number 3. Surely one of those messages must be about Jet? She pressed the PLAY button and prayed.

'Please, please *please* ...'

The first message was from a friend asking for a haircut, the second was blank, and the third was from a friend of Simon's asking him out for a drink. None of the messages were about Jet. She saved them all and reset the answerphone. She sank into the chair and sobbed. *How on earth could I have lost my favourite clients' dog? Why did this have to happen? Everything was going so well. If someone had lost my Pluto I would never have forgiven them. If I don't find Jet, Selina and Simon will hate me and my reputation and business will go down the tube. And my poor darling Jet ... Where is he?*

Poppy spent the whole evening, willing the phone to ring with news of Jet.

'This is no good Dusty – feeling sorry for myself won't help me find Jet. I've just got to make sure I do.' Poppy switched on her laptop and started creating a Lost Dog poster. Luckily she had enjoyed photographing all of the gorgeous dogs she'd taken out for walks, and she had a good clear picture of Jet to use.

That night she hardly slept at all, and when she did she kept being woken by scary nightmares about Jet being trapped on the cliffs by the incoming tide, and other horrible scenarios. At around 6 am she realised she hadn't eaten since yesterday lunch time, so she gave up on her sleep and made some breakfast. As she ate it she switched her laptop back on and did a final check on the poster. As soon as the shops were open she walked along to a print shop and got thirty posters printed. She could hardly look at Jet's photo on it now without bursting into tears. She had five different dogs to walk today, including Dusty, so instead of taking them on the beach she would walk them around the town and put up posters everywhere.

Poppy soon used up her thirty posters, and her reel of tape. By the end of the day Jet's face was attached to numerous lamp posts, fences, noticeboards, and shop windows. She hoped that by the time she returned home there might be some news for her on the answerphone. Unfortunately there wasn't.

Over the next few days, every time she returned to Selina and Simon's place she would rush inside without closing the front door and would make a dive for the answerphone button. A friend of Carmen and Clive's heard about the lost dog and shared one of Poppy's posters onto local social media groups for her.

As the days went on and there was no news of Jet at all – not a single phonecall or sighting – she became more and more depressed, and she was now worrying constantly about how she was going to break the news to Simon and Selina that she had lost Jet. The only other time she'd ever felt this miserable in her whole life was when Pluto died. *If only I hadn't let Jet and Dusty off the leads in that mist.*

One rainy afternoon she was on her way back to her flat to check her own answerphone and post, and she paused across the road standing by the sea wall opposite Anchor House. The tide was up high and the sea was rough. Many times she'd enjoyed watching the exhilarating view of the waves crashing on the rocks and told herself that living in Sebleigh Bay was like being on a permanent holiday. *But now, it's turned into a nightmare. How will I ever feel that way about this place again? I might even have to move and start off again somewhere else. Shame. I won't find another stunning flat like mine.* She glanced back over her shoulder at Anchor House. She vaguely noticed a removal van outside. *Oh, it must be today that someone new moves into the empty flat next door. I hope they have better luck here than me. I'd go and introduce myself if I wasn't feeling so miserable.*

The rest of the week passed by in a horrible grey blur – her mood reflecting the dismal weather. She felt now that she wasn't going to find Jet because too much time had passed. Selina and Simon were coming home tomorrow. Poppy once again called in at her flat to collect a few supplies for her last night at Selina and Simon's. She wearily climbed the stairs feeling devastated. Poor darling Jet. I'll probably never know what happened to him. I just have to hope he didn't suffer too much.

She entered her flat and kicked off her shoes, and headed for the loo. As she passed the radio she pressed the button. A moment later she emerged from the bathroom to hear the news reader announcing the last piece of local news in a cheerful voice that gave the impression that it was going to be something nice, in order to end on a positive note.

... And it's been an eventful day today for Sebleigh Bay's lifeboat crew. They were out on a training exercise along the coast, when one of them thought they spotted a black dog on the lower cliff face in a remote spot close to Frincoln's point. They turned in land to take a closer look and sure enough there was indeed a black spaniel barely visible against the dark rocks. The dog must have fallen down from the top of the cliffs and could have been stranded there for some time...

Poppy didn't realise it, but she screamed! 'Jet! Jet! It must be mustn't it?' She dived on to the settee next to the radio and listened to the rest of the story the ending of which explained that the dog had been taken to Sebleigh Bay Police Station and the owner was being sought.

In a split second she grabbed her car keys and charged out on the landing and shut the door. She was just about to hurtle down the stairs when a young man stepped out from the door opposite her own, and said politely,

'Err ... Hi, I'm David ... I just wondered ... are you okay, only I heard a scream?'

'Yes, yes, I'm fine,' Poppy said frantically, 'Couldn't be better. It's Jet! It's Jet! I think they've found him – I've got to go. Oh ... I'm Poppy.' As she ran down the stairs she yelled, 'Welcome to Anchor House!' and disappeared out the door.

Within minutes Poppy was entering the police station. She charged over to the desk where a young WPC was talking to an elderly woman who'd locked herself out of her house and had no means to get in. Poppy had to wait patiently, well very impatiently in fact, while the old lady told her story in the most minute detail. She paced up and down; she sat down, she stood up, and paced some more. Finally a policeman was called to assist the old lady. Poppy charged in.

'It's my dog. I'm Poppy Dancey. My dog Jet ... you've found him ... the lifeboat men ... well I hope it's him. Well he's not mine – he belongs to Selina and Simon Collier, but I was looking after him when he disappeared.' The police woman looked at her as if she was completely mad and calmly asked her to sit down a minute. She spoke to someone on the phone,

'Poppy Dancey is here. She says she's come to pick up the dog called Jet ... no she's not the owner – the dog belongs to Mr and Mrs Collier ...' Poppy started panicking – what if they wouldn't let her take him and they insisted on waiting until Selina and Simon could collect him? She must have him back home before they come back from their holiday.

'Someone will come and talk to you in a minute.' That minute seemed like ages but eventually a tall policeman came out and addressed her. '

'Poppy Dancey?'

'Yes!' *Where is Jet? I thought he'd bring him out.* He sat down next to her.

'Can you just show me some ID please? Driving licence?' She rummaged around in her bag and found her driving licence. 'That's fine thanks.'

'I heard about him on the radio ... I couldn't believe it! I'd nearly given up hope!'

'Would you just give me a description of the dog please?'

'Of course. He's a black working spaniel. He was wearing a purple collar with his owner's phone number and he has unusually short legs, because he's a quarter dachshound.' The policeman smiled.

'That's fine.' The policeman relaxed and showed his more human side. 'Let me go and get the dog for you and then I'll tell you what happened to him. I think he's quite famous now.'

'Is he alright?'

'Yes I think so - he seems fine. He was extremely hungry and thirsty, but we've just fed him and he drank a lot of water. Just wait there a second.' A few moments later the policeman was back with Jet on a lead. When the dog saw Poppy he charged at her and jumped into her arms yelping excitedly. Poppy was crying with emotion and Jet frantically licked her face.

'Oh you lovely, lovely boy. I've missed you so much. Let me look at you.' Poppy burst into tears and she said between sobs, 'He looks alright doesn't he? I can't believe what happened to him.'

'Well I think we can be sure that he knows you very well,' the policeman said with a big smile.

'Oh I can't believe it. Those wonderful men on the lifeboat. I must go and thank them.'

'Yes they did a great job. I think they really enjoyed it actually. They were so glad they rescued him in time. He couldn't have eaten for a while.'

'I know. Oh Jet. This is SO wonderful. Oh thank you so much,' she said to the policeman.

'Anyway, you'll probably want to get him checked with the vet. We were about to hand him over to them. It looks like he must have fallen down part of the cliff.' Poppy carried on chatting excitedly to the policeman who turned out to be Clive's friend PC Plaistow. She resisted the urge to fling her arms around him and kiss him, but thanked him over and over again instead.

She put Jet in her car and drove straight to the vet's who confirmed that nothing was broken and that Jet seemed alright, but to keep an eye on him, and then she took him home to Selina and Simon's flat to be reunited with Dusty. She had a good look at Jet and cleaned him and gave him a brush and she fed him again. She then just sat her for ages cuddling him and feeling so thankful.

Poppy was so hyped up that night she couldn't sleep. What a week it had been! She eventually dropped off and had all sorts of strange and confusing dreams about lost dogs, Jet and Dusty, and even Pluto. She woke up at 4 am and immediately checked on Jet again who seemed fine. Then a sudden thought occurred to her, *The posters! I need to get them down. They're all over the place.* She felt like getting up there and then and making a start, but she came to her senses and eventually managed to get back to sleep instead.

Chapter 12

Poppy woke early, got up quickly, fed the dogs and gave them lots of cuddles. She tidied up a bit and ran the vacuum cleaner round the flat. She only gave the dogs a five minute walk as she thought it would be better for Jet to have a quiet time after his ordeal.

Poppy had a couple of hours to go before she was due on her first dog walk of the day so she returned to her flat, bringing home most of her clothes and possessions from Simon and Selina's, and she wanted to pick up the list she had made of where she'd put up all the posters. She pulled out a notebook from the book shelf and as she did she glimpsed her set of well read Harry Potter books. Harry Potter? Why was that switching on a light bulb in her mind? Oh, of course! The lad next door. She'd forgotten all about him. They met for the first time last night – just for a few seconds when she was rushing off to get Jet from the police station. He looked so much like Harry Potter. Gosh, he must have thought she was a bit rude the way she rushed off. Perhaps she'd better go and introduce herself properly. Before Jet disappeared she'd been eagerly waiting to see who the neighbour would be.

She rang his bell. The young man answered the door with a camera in his hand.

'Oh hello,' said Poppy. 'I just thought I'd come and introduce myself properly – I was in such a state when I saw you last night.'

'That's okay. No probs.'

'Well I didn't want you to think I'm crazy. I'm Poppy by the way.'

'Pleased to meet you again Poppy.' He reached out and shook her hand. 'David.'

'Hi David.'

'You seemed quite err ... panicked. Was everything alright?'

'Well it is now. Couldn't be better. I walk other people's dogs you see. It's my job. Anyway, earlier in the week I lost my best client's spaniel in the mist.'

'Jet?'

'Yes that's right,' she said enthusiastically – and then her expression changed to confusion. 'How did you know?'

David screeched playfully, 'It's Jet! It's Jet – I've found Jet!' – mocking Poppy's excited voice. And then he added quietly 'Bit of a clue?' Poppy laughed, feeling rather silly.

'So you found him then?'

'Yes – when I saw you I'd just heard the news story on the radio saying a black spaniel had been rescued from the cliffs by the RNLI, and I was rushing off to the police station to get him.'

'Aha!'

'That must have been when I screamed? Did I really scream?'

'Well I'd say someone in your flat did.'

'I honestly didn't realise. I was just so thrilled.'

'So, no murder or anything then?'

'No. Just a lost dog ... which had been found.' Poppy was finding David quite amusing. He had a strange manner, but not in a bad way – the opposite in fact. He was younger than her – in his mid 20s she guessed, with a slightly old fashioned look wearing round black rimmed glasses. He seemed quite shy in some ways as he found it hard to look her directly in the eyes, and he kept looking downwards, but she was amused by his witty manner and the way he was teasing her, even though they'd only just met.

'Actually I think I saw that story on the TV news this morning – they showed the rescue – it was quite heroic. I was only half listening and I didn't realise it was your dog.'

'On the TV news?' Poppy was shocked. 'Good grief. I didn't see it. I hope they didn't mention me?'

97

'I don't think so. They showed a video taken by one of the lifeboat crew - it was great – and I think they just said the dog was being taken to the police station.   Err,' he said looking very thoughtful, 'would you like to come in for a cup of tea and I'll see if I can find the news item on the laptop?'

'Gosh, yes! Thank you. Just a quick one before I go and pick up Lucky.'

'Lucky?'

'Mrs Griffiths' large silver poodle. I'm due to pick him up in a while for his walk, and we're going to go round together and take down all the lost dog posters which I put up all over the town and the seafront.'

'Do come in," he beckoned. 'Lucky's good at taking down posters is he?' Poppy giggled as she walked into his flat. The layout was a mirror reflection of her own. As she entered his living room she was struck by two huge photographs on the wall.   They each showed close ups of breaking waves. Brilliant blues and greens swirled around with splashes of white spray, pulling the viewer into the picture.

'What gorgeous pictures!'   Then she spotted a tripod standing in the corner of the room with a professional looking camera attached, and she added, 'Oh don't tell me you took them yourself.'

'Guilty.'

'Wow. Are you a professional?'

'Guilty.'

'Gosh. What else do you photograph?'

'Well anything that anyone's willing to pay me for really.'

'I'd pay you to photograph my dog any day.' Then seeing David's puzzled expression, she added almost as an aside, '... if I had one.'

'You seem to have your hands full with dogs. How do you like your tea?'

'Just white please.'

'I'll ... just switch the laptop on and while its waking up I'll put the kettle on.'

When David disappeared into the kitchen, Poppy continued to study the huge photos – wondering if she could put something similar on her walls, or maybe some large photos of her favourite dogs. Then she looked at a smaller, but no less impressive image on the end wall which looked familiar – some driftwood and shells lying in the sand – it looked just like the photos she'd seen on the walls in the Beachcomber Cafe. When David reappeared, carrying two mugs of tea, she asked him,

'You didn't take the photos in the Beachcomber Cafe did you?'

'Yep!'

'Guilty of that as well then!'

'You go in there then do you?'

'Do I ever? At least twice a day – I take the dogs in there.'

'Every day? That is keen. I haven't been down there for awhile. Well you'll know Carmen and Clive then?'

'Oh yes – they're great aren't they. So how come you took the photos for the cafe?'

'Well Carmen's been really good to me. She knew my mum very well, and, um, well my mum died ... when I was at University.'

Poppy gasped, 'Oh gosh ... sorry ...'

'Well, Carmen and Clive helped me out an awful lot – I mean Carmen's been like a second mother to me. To be honest I probably owe my career as a photographer to her. And Clive as well.'

'Really?'

'Yes, she encouraged me to complete my degree – I could have easily dropped out when mum died – and then she commissioned me to take the photos in the Beachcomber. Well you probably know what Carmen's like, but she didn't stop there - she started getting me all sorts of commissions to do for her friends and customers – portraits etc. My business really took off because of her.'

'Brilliant. Is that what you do mainly – portraits?'

'No, I do all sorts actually. I do a lot of work for local businesses, just about anything that needs photographing. Actually Clive helped me with that side a lot. He's got so many business contacts and he recommended me to everyone. I've got a website as well where I sell prints,' he said, looking at the photos on his wall. 'This kind of thing.'

'Fantastic. Actually that's really interesting about Carmen because my dog walking business was mainly down to her as well – she's found quite a few clients for me, and she let me advertise in her cafe.'

'Oh, and I thought it was just me that she took an interest in,' he said pretending to be put out.

Poppy laughed, 'Not just you then!'

'My illusion is shattered. Would you like to sit down?' Poppy settled into an armchair with her mug of tea.

'Carmen's really kind isn't she,' Poppy said. 'To go to so much trouble to encourage us – I mean she hardly knew me at the time.'

'Yes, she's lovely,' David replied. 'A real people person. I mean I've watched her in the cafe – she shows an interest in everyone that walks through the door.   She really loves people.'

'Mmm, not so sure about the dogs though!'

David burst out laughing. 'Oh the dogs!' he slapped his hand on his leg. 'When that picture appeared in the local rag of her cuddling that ginormous beast, I nearly fell off the chair laughing.   So misleading.   I don't know how Clive managed to talk her into that. She must have owed him one big time – or maybe she was feeling guilty about something!?'   David then put on one of his silly voices, 'Clive, I am not having any smelly mutts in my cafe! No, no, no!' Poppy was in stitches now. David was so funny. She said,

'I went along to the doggie open day and I could tell Carmen wasn't keen, but to give her her due, she showed real interest in every one of the dogs who came in the door.'

'I heard lots of dogs turned up?'

'There were dogs *everywhere*! It was wonderful!'

'Oh I was so disappointed that I couldn't go to that – I was working – I would love to have seen Carmen trying to cover up her disdain for all those creatures in her beautiful cafe, whilst all the time being the perfect host. I know what she's like.'

'Yes. Mind you ...' Poppy hesitated and looked puzzled, 'I sometimes think that behind it all there's a slight sadness about her ... something she doesn't talk about.'

'You know, that is so interesting, because I've often thought that too. Well more so in recent months, now I come to think about it.'

'Oh, do you know what's happened to her then? In her past maybe?'

'No. I'm not aware of anything awful. She's been with Clive a long time. They haven't got children of course.'

'I wondered about that – whether they'd ever had any?'

'Not that I'm aware of. I don't think that's an issue – I've never got that impression. But what do I know? Of course ... we're going on about Carmen, but Clive's been brilliant too. I owe a lot to him.'

'Oh I know. It's just that Carmen is the one with the big personality and Clive's more the steady rock who carries on quietly in the background. He's a really nice man.'

'He is. Oh and then there's Oswald. Have you met him?'

'No? Who's Oswald?'

'Carmen's dad. Oh you're in for a treat sometime then. He's quite a character too. I didn't know what to make of him when I first met him. He was really taciturn and kind of ... gruff ... the way he talks. But as you get to know him, he's got a heart of gold. I've had lots of meals with the three of them. They're kind of like my replacement family really. Oswald takes a lot of interest in my photography. I've taken him along on a few jobs just to get him out and about. Carmen's always worried about him being lonely. Since he retired he does some driving job for the hospital. He keeps busy. You'll see him at the cafe sometime.'

'Oh I'll look forward to that. Hey! I was just thinking - what a coincidence that we're next door neighbours and they've helped to set us both up.'

'Yes. Actually, I think Carmen has mentioned you and your dog walking business, but I didn't know who you were until now. So when did you move in here?'

'Just last year. I used to live near Bincaster with my dog Pluto.' Like everyone David beamed when he heard that name. 'Oh, and my partner ... ex partner ... Darren,' she added dismissively. It was very obvious to David who had been more important to Poppy.

'Oh so what happened to Pluto?'

'He passed away,' she said pulling a miserable face. 'I miss him terribly so I decided to move away to a different area where everything didn't remind me of him. My parents live in Sebleigh Bay – they moved here when they retired – so I already knew it quite well.'

'Sorry about Pluto. We can't have pets here though can we? Wouldn't you rather have moved somewhere that allows pets?'

'Mmm, well, at the time I didn't think I'd ever be able to replace Pluto, and I was bowled over by these stunning flats ... but I must admit I was just starting to regret not being able to have a dog when I met Selina and Simon from the Stardust Hair Salon, and their dogs Jet and Dusty ...'

'Jet! Jet!...'

'Stop it you! I'll ignore that. Anyway, they became my first clients. I walk them every weekday, so they're kind of like my own part-time dogs. Mind you if they find out what happened to Jet it might be the end of our arrangement.'

'Oh talking of Jet, the laptop should have stirred itself by now. Let's have a look.' David wandered over to his desk. 'Right let's google it. Sebleigh Bay ... Lifeboat ... dog rescue ...? Ah here we are. A video. Brilliant.' Poppy jumped up and went over to the desk and David tilted the screen and pressed play. They were both intrigued as the lifeboat drew as close to the rocks as possible in the choppy water and

102

some of the crew jumped into the sea and scrambled up the rocks. And there was Jet perched on a ledge waiting to be rescued. "Quick!' yelled one of the men. 'Just grab him and get him on the boat.'

Poppy was crying with emotion as she watched the heroic rescue of her beloved spaniel.

'Oh I'm sorry,' she spluttered.

'Don't worry,' David smiled reassuringly. 'It's incredible to watch, especially for you when he's your dog ... well kind of.'

'Oh, I'm going to have to go and buy some presents for those lifeboat crew. I owe them so much. Crumbs! I've just realised the time. I've got to go and get Lucky.'

'The big silver poodle?'

'That's right.'

Lucky was treated to a very long walk taking in all the places where Poppy had put up her Lost Dog posters. They went along the promenade, passed the beach huts, and into the Beachcomber for a coffee and catch up with Carmen and Clive.

'Oh Poppy – I was so thrilled for you when you phoned last night. I was in tears. And just in the nick of time. Oh, and I can tell you Clive had tears in his eyes as well. Not something you see often.'

Poppy and Lucky then walked all through the town, removing posters from shop windows, lamp posts and noticeboards. When Poppy returned home to her flat the phone was ringing as she came in the door. As she picked it up the display told her it was Selina & Simon. *Oh dear – I haven't prepared for this – I didn't think they'd be back yet. Here goes ...*

'Hello, Selina?'

'Darling! Hello. We've just got back.' Selina greeted her with great excitement in her voice.

'How are you? Was it a lovely holiday?'

'Oh it was fabulous! So relaxing. But it's wonderful to see our lovely boys again ... isn't it sweety ... oh I'm just talking to Dusty, he's just here, aren't you my gorgeous. How have they been my dear?'

'Well ... actually ...'

'Oh! I must tell you, there was a spaniel just like these two staying near us. Every time I saw him I kept thinking of my two boys back home ... didn't I gorgeous. Oh I just wanted to thank you Poppy – we couldn't have gone without you to look after them. We didn't have to worry about them at all. We're so grateful my darling ... Simon, just put the cases in the bedroom would you darling, we'll sort them out later ... yes I'm talking to Poppy ... oh and I see you put some supplies in the fridge for us. That's so sweet of you my dear.'

'Oh it was nothing ... I hope everything at the flat's okay.'

'Absolutely! You've done a wonderful job, hasn't she Simon? We've just realised the Carnival's on today – Sebleigh Bay's packed, so we're going to give the supermarkets a miss, but we'll just pop out to the Corner Shop in a minute and get something for dinner, then we can settle down with our boys for the rest of the day. Look I won't keep you my dear, but I just wanted to let you know we were back and say thank you. We'll be in touch tomorrow though if that's okay.'

'Yes – I'll be at home tomorrow – in between walks of course.'

'Okay my dear, lots of love for now. Mwah!'

'Bye Selina.'

Poppy put the phone down and realised how exhausted she was. *I didn't tell her. Oh dear. I thought she'd notice how thin Jet looks ... but she's only just come in the door.* Poppy got up and paced up and down. *I don't know what to do. I'm going to have to go and tell her. She'll probably find out about the news story. Maybe I should just go and see them right now? Tell them everything. But they're going to The Corner Shop ...**The Corner Shop!!** There's a poster there which I didn't take down! Oh no! How could I have forgotten?* Poppy grabbed her car keys and bag, shot out the door, hurtled down the stairs and ran to her car. She could hear vibrant festival music with loud drums, and as she drove along the seafront the traffic came to a halt. The music got louder and she spotted the Carnival floats up ahead. *Oh no! Why did this have to happen now? I could have walked there quicker.* There was nowhere to park the car or turn around. She just had to sit it out in the queue of traffic and wait for the Carnival to pass up ahead.

It was a good half an hour or more before Poppy arrived at The Corner Shop. All of the parking spaces were taken so she had no choice but to park on a yellow line and be as quick as she could. As she got out of the car she looked up and saw Simon and Selina looking brown as berries, coming out of the shop. Simon, looking very well in a pale yellow shirt was carrying bags full of shopping, while Selina, wearing a stunning white dress had a serious expression on her face as she was studying the piece of paper she was holding. Poppy rushed forward and blurted out,

'Selina! I'm so sorry. I feel awful. I was going to tell you. I was on my way to see you ...'

'Oh hello Poppy,' she said as warmly as ever. But then her expression changed to one of concern. 'Whatever is the matter dear? Actually you don't look very well, you look terribly tired. Have you been ill?'

'No, I'm alright, but ... I'm so sorry. I was going to tell you on the phone, but somehow it just didn't come out.' Poppy gabbled away desperately as Selina and Simon listened with puzzled expressions on their faces, 'I couldn't spoil things – you sounded so relaxed after your holiday. There was this terrible sea mist. Clive ... you know, at the Beachcomber ... he said he'd never seen anything like it in all his years at the coast ... I shouldn't have let them off the leads, but I just didn't realise the danger, and Jet just disappeared by the cliffs. We all searched for ages and ages. I was so relieved when he was found though. Apparently I screamed! I didn't realise but my next door neighbour – David his name is - he's just moved in - he came rushing out thinking there'd been a murder ...'

'Poppy!' Simon said firmly, 'Poppy, stop! We've got no idea what you're talking about. It sounds like something happened to Jet, but unless I'm seriously mistaken, I'm pretty sure he was at home this afternoon, complete with his four little legs and a contented expression on his face ...'

'But ...' Poppy interrupted ... 'You've got the poster,' she said pointing to the piece of paper Selina was holding, 'You've ...'. Selina, looking more puzzled than ever, held out the piece of paper far enough for Poppy to see that it was a sheet of The Corner Shop's Special Offers.

'Oh! You mean ... you didn't know ... you didn't know I lost Jet ... I thought you'd seen the poster ... I put up loads you see and I forgot to take that one down...'

'Poppy,' Simon said kindly, 'Is that your car over there?' He pointed towards the road. Poppy nodded. 'Well I think you'd better go and use your charm on that parking warden who's about to issue you with a ticket, and then you can come back to the flat with us and calm down with a cup of tea and explain everything.'

'Oh no!' Poppy rushed over to the parking warden, a tall stern looking man in his 50s. 'Please ... don't give me a ticket. I was just leaving. I was only here for a moment. It was an emergency.'

'Emergency?'

'Yes. I lost a dog you see. I was worried sick, and I put up posters everywhere hoping someone would find him. Anyway he was found last night. Did you see it on the news? The RNLI rescued him from the cliffs. They were amazing. I collected him from the police station and I took all the posters down this morning, but I forgot the one in The Corner Shop. I had to get here double quick before his owners saw the poster.

'His owners?'

'Oh yes. Didn't I say? It wasn't my dog you see. I walk other people's dogs – it's my job. I don't have a dog of my own ...'

'You don't?'

106

'No, well I used to. He was a red setter cross called Pluto …'

Chapter 13

David paced up and down in his flat with his phone tucked under his chin, leaving his hands free to scribble down notes on the pad he was holding. He couldn't believe the assignment he'd just been offered, let alone the fantastic pay, but he was trying to keep calm and sound cool, as if it was no big deal to be commissioned to take photos for a national newspaper's Sunday magazine. Having agreed the details, accepted the job and said goodbye, he switched the phone off, put it down and punched the air.

'Yes, yes, *yes*!!' he shouted, 'Brilliant.' He paced about some more and admired his own huge panoramic photos of the sea which nearly filled the whole wall, and then he visualised the framed copy on his wall above the fireplace, of the magazine containing his beach hut photos. Undoubtedly this was his most exciting commission to date. He picked up the phone again. Who could he share his good news with? It was at times like this that he really missed his Mum. He would have loved her to see his latest photos and share his success. She would have been so proud.

I hope you're watching Mum. He often talked to her, and imagined her response. *I always said you had talent David. Never give up on your dreams. If you believe them – you can make them happen.* Wise words indeed, David thought, but he never felt that life had gone that great for his Mum so he didn't always find it easy to believe in what she said. He asked her about this once, as tactfully as he could, and she said that being able to adopt David when he was a baby was all she'd ever wanted. It was a dream come true. Unfortunately her husband had left soon afterwards so as far as David could remember it had always been just the two of them. After his Mum died, when he was at University, he had to get used to standing on his own two feet, although he still missed her terribly. He generally enjoyed his own company though. But on this occasion he just wanted to share his news with someone who cared. It was a bit late to go and see Carmen and Clive now. They'd probably be closing up the cafe. He could phone them later but he had a feeling they were going out this evening. He'd rather wait until tomorrow and go and tell them in the cafe. Carmen would be so thrilled for him and would be telling all her customers. He could ring one of his mates from Uni but it would be good to chat to someone face to face.

He wondered if the nutty dog woman next door would appreciate his news. She seemed nice and she laughed at his jokes. She'd admired his photos too. They had chatted on the stairs a few times since he'd invited her in for a cup of tea, and she always seemed to be pleased to see him. He was pretty sure she was at home now – he'd heard her coming up the stairs a little while ago, no doubt returning home from one of her numerous dog walking sessions. He grabbed his keys and went and knocked on her door.

Poppy opened the door with a plate of sandwiches in her hand, and a mouthful of food. Despite the fact that she was eating, she seemed pleased to see him.

'Oh hello David,' she managed with her mouth full.

'Err hi ... it ... doesn't look like a good time?' He said looking at her sandwiches.

'No it's fine,' she said cheerfully. 'No problem. Come in and talk to me while I'm finishing these. I'm off to see Wallace and Gromit soon.' She beckoned him into the lounge and moved some magazines off the chair so he could sit down.

'Thanks.' David tipped his head to the side and patted his ear. 'I think my hearing must be going. For a moment there I thought you said you were going to see ... Wallace and Gromit? Is the film on somewhere?'

'Mrs Wilson's two lionhead bunnies.'

'Bunnies? Oh of course! Obvious isn't it. Silly me.'

'They're Lucky's neighbours.'

'Lucky? The big silver poodle?'

'Yes. You've got a good memory. They're so sweet actually ... the bunnies. You could take some great photos of them. They're very fluffy – well especially their heads – that's why the breed is called Lionheads.'

'Actually, it was photography I came to talk to you about ... I wanted to share some good news.'

'Oh yes?' she said eagerly.

'I've been commissioned to take some photos for the Sunday Times magazine. An article about beach huts.'

'That's fantastic! Gosh it must have a huge circulation. Think how many people will get to see your work.'

'I know. That's what I was thinking. I was dead chuffed. I just got the confirmation phone call. Wanted to tell someone.'

'Shame I'm going out – we could have cracked open a bottle. I'm off to my jive class too after seeing to the bunnies.'

'Jive? As in dancing?'

'Yes. A dance class down at The Grand Hotel. Actually I'm terrible at it. Two left feet. The teacher despairs of me. Mind you ...' she said looking thoughtful, 'I think maybe the others actually like me because I'm so bad that it makes them look good!' She put her plate down on the coffee table. 'So when are you going to photograph the beach huts?'

'Oh I've got a few months to take the photos in all different weather and lighting conditions. Trying to make the humble beach hut look spectacular ... and arty. Some snow would be good? I hope we get some.'

'Oh well done David! How did you get the job?'

'The writer who's doing the article searched for beach hut photos on line and he came across my website.'

'Oh I looked at your website by the way. I'm not surprised he was impressed. I love your photos, especially the seaside ones.'

'You're too kind.'

'No I'm not being kind – I mean it. You know how to make a pile of grey pebbles look interesting. Oh and I loved the rainbows too. Can't wait to see your beach hut photographs.'

'I've also got to travel around and visit some other types of beach huts – you know, the really posh all singing all dancing ones that sleep six, with running water, and mod cons! And apparently there's some kind of modern capsule or pod type things. They're sending me a written brief.'

'Interesting.'

'The writer also said that if it goes well he could be putting more work my way.'

'Brilliant David. You're doing so well with your business. It's not easy setting up on your own – I know that from my days as Cleo the Clown!' David's mouth opened and he stared like a goldfish.

'Now don't start.' Poppy laughed.

'This I must hear about, but it will have to wait till another time. I must leave you to get on with Wallace and Gromit and your hijinks at The Grand Hotel.' As he said this he got up and did a few dance steps vaguely resembling a Highland Fling.

'Yes, sorry,' Poppy said as she laughed at David, 'I would have offered you a drink otherwise.' As David reached the door he turned back round.

'Oh ... Poppy ... if you see Carmen and Clive before me ... could you not mention my news to them ... it's just that I'd like to tell them myself ... you know ... face to face. I'll be down there in the morning.'

'Oh of course. I understand.' She pretended to zip her mouth. 'Won't say a word!'

The following morning David was walking along the seafront to the Beachcomber Cafe. His enthusiasm to tell Carmen and Clive his news made him realise just how much they had come to mean to him. As he walked down the slope from the promenade on to the beach he started thinking about all the kind things they had done for him.

111

David's mum had known them for many years and she used to work part-time in the cafe before she became ill. David knew he would feel guilty for the rest of his life for not realising how ill his mum was until he received the news that she had suddenly died. When he was home for Christmas after his first term away at University, she mentioned casually that a slight heart problem had been detected and that she was on medication. He was concerned, and he noticed that she seemed to get tired easily, but he hoped that the medication would do it's job. She had always seemed so light-hearted about it that he didn't give it much more thought. He would always regret this despite Carmen telling him over and over again,

'No-one realised how serious it was David – I don't think she did herself – and there was nothing any of us could have done.'

She died early the following summer. David's memories of the next few months were a blur. He had wandered around in a daze trying to come to terms with the fact that his mum wouldn't be there anymore. He'd never considered a life without her. During this time Carmen and Clive had supported him in so many ways. Carmen became like a second mother to him. She was always ringing him up, cooking him meals and, most importantly, giving him as much emotional support as she could. Clive was also a tower of strength to David, advising him on all sorts of practical and financial matters and giving him much assistance in sorting out his mother's estate. Not that she had very much to leave to him.

Towards the end of the summer holidays David felt he couldn't face going back to university. As soon as he uttered the merest suggestion of this to Carmen she sprang into action in the way that only Carmen could.

'Oh no, David ... Oh no, no, no ... don't even think about dropping out. Do you think your mum would have wanted this? Going back to uni and throwing yourself into your studies is exactly what you need. I just won't hear of you giving it up. Look, we'll be on the other end of the phone. Call us any time – in the middle of the night if you need to - and you can come and stay with us in the holidays if you like – can't he Clive?'

'Yes, I ...'

'That's sorted then.'

So, David went back to university and for the duration of his course. He returned to Sebleigh Bay in the holidays and stayed with Carmen and Clive. When he'd completed his degree he found some digs not far from Sebleigh Bay in a shared house with some old school friends. He visited Carmen and Clive regularly, often popping into the cafe, or having meals with them in the evenings at home. He would never forget how much they had done for him.

When David started looking for ways to make a living as a photographer, Carmen once again worked her magic and told all her local customers about his wonderful photography. What a saleswoman! The portrait sessions started flowing in whether David wanted them or not! As his confidence grew he started contacting local businesses - many of them Clive's contacts - and taking on commercial work.

David was enjoying living with his friends, but some of his clients were assuming he had a studio, and if he needed to bring home products to photograph, he just didn't have the room in his digs. Clive and Carmen let him keep his evergrowing collection of photographic equipment at their house and use their large conservatory as a studio whenever he needed it.

It was around this time that Clive and Carmen decided to give the cafe a makeover. It was previously called Pebbles. After years of moaning about the shabby state of it, Carmen finally persuaded Clive that they should splash out and considerably smarten it up. When the cafe closed for a month for the renovations, Carmen asked David to take some beautiful photographs to go on the walls. David knew that Carmen was envisaging sunsets or something similar

113

but he wanted to do something different and came up with the idea of a beachcombing theme. When he suggested this to Carmen he could tell she wasn't that keen but he asked her to trust him and wait until she'd seen the photos.

When he arrived at the sparkling newly renovated cafe carrying some large canvasses, he could see Carmen looked a little concerned.

'Oh! I thought you were bringing us a range of small prints to make a selection from.' David pretended not to hear her and stood the four pictures up against the counter.

'Da daa!' he said, sounding more confident than he felt.

Carmen gasped as she looked at the pictures and then beamed with delight.

'Oh David! They're amazing! When you said beachcombing I imagined a few shells and some seaweed – nothing like these beautiful pictures. Did you really find all those things on the beach?' she asked, scrutinising the photos close up. 'It makes me want to get straight out there myself and start collecting. The customers will love them won't they Clive!' Clive was clearly impressed too.

'Phew!' David was hugely relieved. 'Actually Carmen ...' he said nervously, 'err ... if you don't mind me making a suggestion ... I was wondering ... you said vaguely you might consider a name change ... well how about calling the cafe The Beachcomber?'

'Oh brilliant idea David! The Beachcomber. A new name for our new cafe. What do you think Clive?'

'Whatever you say my love,' he said with playful sarcasm. As if she really wanted his opinion when it was obvious her mind was already made up.

With some publicity in the local press the new look cafe became very popular. Several customers commented on David's amazing photos and said they'd like greetings cards with them on, so he created a whole range of cards which Carmen and Clive sold in the cafe. Carmen never missed an opportunity to sing David's praises to anyone who was prepared to listen. If a customer so much as glanced at one of David's pictures, or picked up one of the greetings cards, they would hear all about how Carmen had commissioned David to take those stunning photos and how he was a really successful professional photographer – the best she'd ever come across - and how he was like a son to them. David would get very embarrassed if he was in the cafe and Carmen pointed him out to people or introduced him to them. And after this had happened a couple of times he asked her not to do that anymore. So now, instead, if he was within earshot she would give him a wink when the customer wasn't looking and then recently she'd taken to saying something funny about him to wind him up.

As David had almost reached the cafe and was walking past the last few beach huts, he was remembering one of these occasions when his thoughts were interrupted.

'And what are you smiling about David?' He looked up to see Poppy walking towards him with a shiny brown dachshund wearing a red tartan coat, tucked under her arm.

'Oh nothing. I was miles away,' he said shaking himself and returning to the present. 'So - who's this little ... chipolata of an excuse for a dog then?'

'This is Chip.'

'No! You're having me on.'

'No really. That's her name ... honest.'

'Hello Chip,' he said as he stroked the little dog's head, 'Very smart coat Chip ... and you Poppy.' He pretended that he was about to stroke her head too.

'You're in a good mood. Off to tell Carmen your news?'

'Guilty!'

'I didn't say anything.'

'Thanks. Does little Chippy actually have any legs? I mean does she walk, or is she just a carrying sort of dog?'

'She doesn't like the shiny floor in the cafe, do you my sweet, so I pick her up in there.'

'Good job she's not a Saint Bernard then!'

Poppy giggled as she put Chip on the ground. 'Actually I think Carmen could do with some good news – she didn't seem very happy today.'

'Mm – she's been like that a lot lately.' David looked concerned. 'Oh well ... see what I can do.'

'Good luck. Bye David.'

David put on a silly voice, 'Bye bye Chippy. Bye bye Poppy.'

As he entered the cafe, he noticed that Carmen was deep in thought as she wiped the tables. As the door banged closed she looked up and saw David and her face and her mood changed completely.

'David.' She smiled warmly, 'How are you my love?'

'In good shape. I've got some news to tell you.'

'I can tell it's good,' she said studying David's face with intrigue. 'You look pleased with yourself.'

'Well – I've been commissioned to take photos for the Sunday Times magazine – an article about the popularity of beach huts. They spotted my photos on the website.'

'Oh David! That sounds brilliant.' She turned to Clive who was behind the counter, 'Clive did you hear that?'

'No, what's that?'

'David's only doing photos for a national newspaper.'

'Really? Oh I think this calls for a celebration. Take a seat David and I'll bring some drinks over and you can tell us all about it.'

Chapter 14

Over the next few weeks Poppy and David became quite friendly. Their paths crossed many times not just at Anchor House where they lived in their adjacent flats, but down at the beach as well. Poppy was often to be found walking her various clients' dogs down there, while David, whenever he had some spare time in between other jobs, would be photographing the beach huts for the magazine article.

There were many times that they ended up in the Beachcomber Cafe together, much to Carmen's delight.

One cold winter's morning David was catching up on some sleep following a fun night out with some old school friends. He didn't have any specific photographic commissions lined up today so he'd stayed out late, and had a few beers knowing he could lie in until lunch time if necessary. But he was woken by loud knocking on his front door. *Strange ... that can only be someone from the building as my door bell wasn't rung. Or maybe I'm hearing things? Or perhaps it was a dream?* He was just about to roll over and ignore the interruption when the knocking started up again, this time accompanied by Poppy's voice.

'David – are you there? David ...'

'Oh ...' he groaned to himself ...'Coming ...' He literally fell out of bed on to the floor, and glanced at himself in the mirror as he got up to make sure he was wearing pyjamas. He staggered sleepily to the front door and unlocked it. There stood Poppy looking all bright eyed and bushy tailed and raring to go.

'Is something wrong?' he asked her.

'Oh dear ... Have I woken you up? I'm fine but I wanted to ask you if you'd looked out of the window?' she said enthusiastically.

117

'The window? Why? What's happened? ... Come in ...'
He staggered into the living room rubbing his head, while Poppy followed. 'Has the sky fallen in? Or has there been a tsunami? ... Only ... since I moved to the seafront I often have dreams about tsunamis ...' he mumbled.   Poppy watched as he opened the lounge curtains and looked down to see the road and pavement covered in thick snow. The cars were driving slowly and a child and his mum were building a snowman on the sea wall.

'Fabulous! Wow! ... camera ... memory card ... battery ...'

'Clothes might be an idea!'

'Yeah yeah ... whatever. Hey! The beach huts! I can get them in the snow!'

'Exactly! That's what I thought!'

'Brilliant. You coming with me?'

'I'll tell you what – I've got to go and pick up Philip, but I'll meet you down there.'

'Right I'll see you in a bit. Oh ... and thanks Poppy. Really wouldn't have wanted to miss this. It could be melted by lunch time.'

David had probably never got himself up and dressed and out onto the seafront so quickly. He had rarely ever seen snow on the beach here, but today it had actually settled. The scene was quite surreal with the calm deep blue-grey coloured sea contrasting with the pure white snowy beach. Mindful of the fact that the tide was slowly creeping in David took as many photos as he could before the incoming sea would wash the snow away. Using his longest zoom lens, he managed to get some quick shots of the pier in the distance with the carpet of snow beneath it before he hurried along to the other end of the promenade towards the beach huts which were his priority today.

The snow had stopped falling and Sebleigh Bay was alive with people excited to witness the beautiful scene. The happy sounds of people chattering and playing in the newly laid snow could be heard all along the seafront. As the sun emerged between the thick yellowy snowclouds the sea and the icy beach both sparkled magically. David walked towards the beach huts with his feet crunching on the snow covered pebbles. A young woman was playing with her two small children who were wrapped up warm with brightly coloured scarves and hats. They were excitedly building castles out of snow and sand. The mum looked at David walking by.

'Isn't it lovely?' she called out.

'Yes it's incredible!' David agreed.

He scanned the beach huts looking for the most photogenic views. The huts even had coatings of snow on the rooves. He photographed them from various different angles sometimes showing several huts, as well as picking out the most pretty ones to feature on their own. The blue and white one which he noticed had been named Alice was one of his favourites and looked particularly photogenic with the addition of the blanket of snow. 'Ah that's the money shot!' David said to himself, as he reviewed the images on his digital screen.

After exhausting all of his photographic ideas David approached the Beachcomber Cafe and noticed Poppy sitting on some rocks nearby.

'Ah there you are! … Hello Philip.'

'It was too noisy and crowded in there today. Philip doesn't like it when it's like that - he'd rather stay outside.' David sat himself down on a rock next to Poppy. She asked him how his photography had gone.

'Really great thanks. I'm pleased with what I got. Would you like to have a quick look?'

'Love to.' David flicked through a few photos on his camera to give Poppy a quick viewing. She was very impressed. 'Oh I love these. It's such a special day isn't it? I might have to buy one of your photos to put on my wall sometime.' Philip kept nuzzling David's knee looking for attention. David stroked Philip's brown shaggy head.

'I wonder why someone calls a dog Philip?' David asked. 'I mean don't dogs normally have dog names ... like Lassie, or Blackie, or ... Fido?'

'Not necessarily. I've never given it much thought. Philip suits him though doesn't it.'

'Does it? You wouldn't exactly call a dog David or Poppy though would you? David! Come here boy ... David! Or, come on Poppy ... walkies!' He said in one of his silly voices.

'Well, I don't think I've ever known a dog called Poppy or David, but I don't see why not though. Actually, I'll let you into a secret, my first name is not actually Poppy.'

'Really? So is Poppy your middle name?'

'Yes. I much prefer it to my first name.'

'Go on... spill the beans then ... what's your first name?' David said gently nudging her with his elbow.

'Well, I'm probably going to regret telling you this, but it's actually Georgia. I hate to say it, but I think I was conceived there.' David smiled and looked thoughtful, trying to imagine Poppy as a Georgia. 'Georgia's quite a nice name. Why don't you like it?'

'It dates back to when I was at junior school. Some horrible boy called me Ginger Georgia, which made me angry because I had a complex about my auburn hair. You know what kids are like... once they've discovered your weakness they don't stop. I used to lose my temper when they kept poking fun at me, which just made them do it all the more. They used to chant Ginger Georgia at me. It may not sound anything terrible now, but honestly, I still have nightmares about it. I had a reputation for being really stroppy and losing my temper quickly. But when I look back on it, I realise I'm not actually like that. It was just down to the provocation and bullying.'

'That must've been horrible. Because I know you as Poppy I just can't imagine you as Georgia really.'

'You won't tell anyone will you? I always use Poppy now. Even my parents do.'

'What's it worth? … Joke!! Of course I won't.'

'What were your school days like?'

'Not too bad really, but actually I was always worried that they'd find out I was adopted in case they gave me a hard time over it. I never told anyone. The funny thing was that literally in my last few days at school, I did mention it to my best friend. I thought I didn't have anything to lose as I was about to leave school. Anyway it turned out he'd known all along – he said his mother knew, and had told him years ago. I thanked him like mad for never telling anyone and he said that he hadn't purposely kept it quiet – it was just no big deal and he never thought to mention it.'

'Wow. It's funny how we can get things so out of proportion isn't it – especially our fears. When I was at school I just assumed that whenever I walked down the corridors *everyone* was staring at my auburn hair, but I can see now how ridiculous that was. Actually talking of hair, I'd better make a move soon and take Philip back, because I've got an appointment with Selina to have my hair cut.'

'Oh yes! Mr and Mrs Short & Spiky down at the purple parlour!' Poppy laughed, while David continued, 'Actually,' he pondered, studying her hair thoughtfully, 'how come you haven't gone short and spiky yet? Well, short maybe, but you haven't got the spikes ... that's very unusual for that place apparently.'

'Yes, so I've heard. But that's just not my image! Actually, I'm growing it out a bit now, but I'm just going to get my fringe cut.'

'Well if you keep going there you're guaranteed to succumb to the spikes eventually – everyone does.'

'No *way*!'

'Just you wait and see – I bet you anything that by ... say first of July... you'll have spikes.'

'Absolutely not. Selina always asks me what I want. She doesn't tie people up and force them to have spikes you know.'

121

'Maybe not, but she'll just get you one day when you're not concentrating. You'll be busy recounting some doggy tale or other about Shortlegs, or Longlegs, or Chip or Fish or some other little canine, and before you know it she'll have sculpted your curls into sharp little spikes!' He pressed his finger on to an imaginary spike on Poppy's head and said 'Ouch!'

'Mm, I must admit you've got a point. The first time I went there I had a full mop of long hair. Selina and I got engrossed in conversation and before I knew it, there was a huge pile of my locks on the floor and this short haired imposter was staring back at me in the mirror,' Poppy said laughing.

'Aha! Told you so.'

'I'll tell you what ... we *will* have a bet on it.'

'O ... kay ...' David said feeling intrigued, 'If you do get spikes you have to let me take a portrait of you.'

'And if I don't ... you come dancing with me!'

'Yeah right,' he said sarcastically, completely dismissing the idea.

'No, I mean it.' She grabbed his hand and shook it. 'It's a bet. Right I'm off now.' She leapt up quickly leaving David unusually lost for words. 'First of July!' she called back at him – leaving him with his mouth gaping open.

Chapter 15

George Treforth was conscious of his unusually cheerful state of mind. In fact he felt quite smug as he drove down to Sebleigh Bay. He knew he was becoming increasingly grumpy in his old age, especially since his dear wife Evelyn had sadly died three years ago leaving him to live on his own for the first time in his life.

But he also appreciated that even though he often awoke in a negative mood, he could often turn things around if he really tried – usually by giving himself a severe kick up the proverbial backside. Today was one of those days. On this particular Saturday morning, instead of slumping into his favourite armchair immediately after breakfast, with only his copy of The Times for company, he got up and made a phone call. As it turned out, he was very glad he did.

As the mist lifted and gave way to bright sunshine, George turned left at the traffic lights, along the road which lead him away from the busy town where he lived, and towards the coast. He smiled to himself as he thought of his very special gift which he had placed in the boot of his car that morning, and more importantly, of his favourite companion seated next to him for the journey.

George thought back to his recent birthday. He hadn't wanted any fuss, so he thought it was all a bit much when his family insisted on descending on him. He didn't want a party, and definitely no surprises. But, as his daughter Miriam pointed out to him,

'You wouldn't want us to ignore your birthday Dad, would you?' He begrudgingly admitted to himself that this was true. So on his birthday, his three daughters, their husbands and his eight grandchildren dutifully (or so he imagined) took him out for a special meal at a smart restaurant in town.

'We can't buy you a present Dad ... we wouldn't know what to get you ... you can buy yourself anything you need ... so we thought a family meal ... somewhere nice ... we'll book a table.'

Actually, George had thought, somewhat sulkily, that a present would be nice for once. Something wrapped, a complete surprise, a gift that he would be thrilled to receive. He couldn't ever recall a single time in his life when he had received such a present. Why did everyone assume that he wouldn't like one?

Most of his childhood birthdays were spent at boarding school, where he would generally receive money from his relations, and maybe a small gift from his parents which he had probably chosen himself. There were certainly never any surprises. Funnily enough the best part he remembered of his childhood birthdays was the standard cake which was provided by the school cook on every boy's special day. That was quite a treat.

During the many years that he was married to dear Evelyn, she always bought him smart clothes, ties or cufflinks for his birthdays – all part of her continual campaign to mould him into what she wanted him to be. He never complained about this – preferring to opt for the easier life and just accept things to keep Evelyn happy.

George and Evelyn had three daughters, so George had little involvement in choosing presents for them, but when their grandchildren started arriving, he looked forward to being able to buy toys for their birthdays, especially for the three boys. On their birthdays he spoiled them with expensive trainsets and Lego, not without more than a little self interest of course, as he was always on the lookout for an opportunity to play with them himself.

Unfortunately the years flew past all too quickly and before he knew it the boys were abandoning their toys in favour of computer games.

George always had a soft spot for his youngest grandson, who was also called George, not just because he was his namesake, but also because he was the only one of the four boys who continued to play with "real" toys after the age of about ten. The other boys were, in George's opinion, too obsessed with their Xboxes and Playstations, leaving very little space for anything else in their lives at all.

Luckily for George, Young George shared his Grandad's love of model trains, so his help was enlisted in building a wonderful layout in his spare room. Young George who was only twelve years old when his Grandma Evelyn died, started dropping in regularly on his way home from school to play with the trains for an hour or so before he went on his way home for tea and homework. George never knew whether Young George did this off his own back or whether he was being press ganged by the family to pop in and keep Grandad company and cheer him up a bit. George often felt he should say to his grandson 'oh you must have better things to do than spend your time with an old man like me'. He never actually said this aloud though because, if he was honest, young George's visits were all that kept him going in the months after Evelyn's death, and he dreaded the time when the young lad would lose interest and stop calling round.

Young George really did seem to enjoy visiting him though, and would always be thrilled when his Grandad had purchased a new engine or an extra set of points, or sometimes a kit which they would sit down and build together at the dining table. They would create a lovely old-fashioned station or farmhouse building to add to the ever-expanding layout. After a year or two the impressive layout even boasted attractive scenery and hills handmade from papier mache by the two Georges, and many little human figures, dogs and farm animals which they had bought and painstakingly painted. By this time young George's homework and after school clubs were taking up more of his time, but he always made a point of visiting his Grandad every Friday on his way home from school.

George always loved the moment when Young George came crashing in the front door, saying 'Hi Grandad' in his usual cheerful manner as he threw his school bag on the floor and dived straight into the kitchen for a snack. George would keep his larder stocked with plenty of lemonade and whatever Young George's favourite crisps or snacks happened to be at the time. He would have a cup of tea and biscuits ready for himself too and they'd both take their refreshments into the spare room and switch on the trains!

George recognised that the precious hours spent with his grandson building their railways were among the happiest times of his life. Every minute was treasured.

When the family arrived at the restaurant for the birthday celebration, it seemed only natural that the two Georges – having such a close bond – would sit together. After the waiter had taken everyone's order, Young George announced enthusiastically,

'Grandad, I've got a present for you – a surprise! You'll never guess what it is.'

'He bought it with his own money Dad. He saved up and chose it himself,' Miriam explained. Young George bent down under the table and pulled out a surprisingly large rectangular gift wrapped in colourful birthday paper and placed it down across the table on top of his and his Grandad's place setting.

'There you are. I hope you like it.' The whole family's attention had turned to George and his birthday gift now.

'What is it?' some of them were whispering.

'It's obviously a train,' said one of Young George's cousins smugly.

'It's a complete surprise Grandad – you'll never guess what it is,' repeated Young George.

George started unwrapping the parcel. At last! He thought. At this grand old age he was finally receiving a surprise birthday present, and there was no-one who he'd rather have buy it for him than Young George.

126

As he pulled the paper off, he was expecting it to be something for the railway layout, so it was rather a shock when the words "Metal Detector" were revealed on the box.

'Oh goodness me! I've never used one of those before – I can go and seek some treasure.'

'Yes and I'm coming with you Grandad – I thought we could go down to the coast together.'

'Oh how marvellous! Thank you George. That really is a splendid present. Look everyone. A metal detector!'

When George phoned Young George first thing this morning he didn't hold up much hope of him being available at short notice to go to Sebleigh Bay to try out the metal detector, but to his delight Young George was free and raring to go. They enjoyed the peaceful car journey together down to the coast, chatting happily about trains and metal detecting – wondering what they might discover together on the beach.

Chapter 16

'Here we are,' Rose said to her two friends. It's the pretty blue and white one just there, number eighteen. When you walk round the other side you'll see she's called Alice.'

'Hello Alice. Pleased to meet you,' said Doris patting the side of the beach hut. The three elderly ladies stepped down on to the pebbles and walked enthusiastically round to the other side of the beach hut. Rose had the key ready and she unlocked the door.

'Do you want to come in and help yourselves to a deckchair each?'

'Oh it's nice isn't it,' Doris said looking around inside. She's been well looked after I must say.'

'Who are you talking about dear?' asked Ivy, looking a little puzzled.

'Alice. This lovely beach hut. She is called Alice,' Doris explained slowly. 'Do you remember? Rose's niece Caroline owns the hut and she's let us borrow it for the day.'

'Oh that's nice of her isn't it,' Ivy said.

'There you are Ivy,' said Rose 'Would you like to take this one?' Rose handed Ivy a deck chair. Rose noticed Ivy looking worried, so she added, 'Hold on a moment Ivy, I'll help you put it up. They're tricky things deckchairs aren't they? You can get in quite a muddle if you're not careful.' Rose carried the deckchair outside and put it up – wedging the legs firmly into the pebbles. 'There you are Ivy. Sit yourself down now.'

'Thank you dear. It's very comfortable isn't it. Did you say Alice is coming? I can't remember who Alice is.'

'That's alright Ivy. Alice is the name of the beach hut. Look – if you turn around you'll see the name sign on the hut. Look up there – it says Alice.'

'Alice. That's nice ... Alice,' Ivy said thoughtfully.

'Here you are Doris, you sit next to Ivy and I'll sit here,' Rose said. 'Ladies, let me know if your legs get cold and I'll fetch you a blanket from the hut.'

'Well this is nice isn't it,' Doris said as she sank herself into the deckchair, 'I can't remember how long it must be since we three sat down on the beach together.' She patted Rose and Ivy's knees.

'No I don't know either,' Rose said. 'But we did it an awful lot when we were youngsters didn't we? Do you remember Ivy?' Rose leaned across towards Ivy and said slowly and clearly, 'Do you remember the three of us having picnics on the beach?'

'Oh yes. I remember the boys too. They used to chase us,' Ivy said with a wicked look in her eyes, which amused the others. 'They used to catch us too, and then who knows what would happen?' The three ladies all giggled together.

'Oh that's right Ivy,' said Doris enthusiastically, 'and then there was that time when Samuel Harper stole all our sandwiches. Do you remember?'

'Oh I do,' said Rose. 'He was a right little rascal wasn't he. He took rather a shine to you didn't he Doris. I remember you saying once that he would never leave you alone.'

'Well he used to tease me a lot and poke fun at me.'

'It was more than that. He fancied you like mad Doris.'

'He never had the nerve to ask me out though. Just used to follow me around like a lovesick puppy.'

'Mm. He did that for years,' Rose said, ' ... until you met Albert of course.'

'Yes, and when Albert and I got married Samuel said he couldn't come to the wedding because he was going away, but someone told me he hadn't gone on holiday at all. I always suspected he just didn't want to see me getting married.'

'Aah. Poor thing. He got married himself eventually though didn't he ... to his friend's sister if I remember rightly.'

129

'Yes, Isaac Milton's sister, Lily.'

'I wonder what happened to them?' I haven't heard anything of them for years.'

'I don't know about Samuel and Lily, but funnily enough I heard recently that Isaac and his wife got divorced.'

'Really? Isaac and Cynthia? After all those years together'

'Yes. Forty odd years I should think. He used to hit her you know!' Doris said dramatically.

'Goodness! I can't imagine that.'

'Well you didn't know Cynthia like I did. I mean, I would never condone a man raising a hand to a woman, but Cynthia ... honestly! ... I'm sure there were lots who'd like to give her a slap ... the most annoying woman I ever met.'

'Oh yes, I remember she was rather tactless.'

'Tactless? That's putting it mildly! I certainly wouldn't want to be married to her.'

'Isaac and Lily Milton ...' Ivy said thoughtfully. Rose and Doris turned to her attentively, glad that she was joining in. 'Isaac and Lily Milton ...They lived next door to Ernest Wright.' The sound of Ernest's name made Rose blush. She was wondering if he was going to come up in the conversation.

'That's right,' Doris said to Ivy. 'They lived in Honey Street didn't they. I remember them all walking to school together every day, and of course Rose and Ernest had quite a history together. Do you remember Ivy? Rose and Ernest were an item for a long time.' Ivy looked blank. She started watching a man and a boy walking on the beach in the distance. Rose and Doris knew they'd lost her for a while. Doris turned to Rose.

'Have you ever heard anything of Ernest or his family Rose?'

'No, not at all. We lost touch as you know, after they moved away.' Rose said sadly, feeling silly that memories of Ernest still affected her after all this time. 'I've never heard mention of his family since. They probably didn't keep in

130

touch with anyone from Sebleigh.' Ivy suddenly stretched her arm out and pointed to the ruins of Sebleigh Pier. Rose and Doris turned towards her and waited to see if she would say anything about it.

'Doris and Ernest were kissing under the pier!' Ivy stated, with her arm still outstretched towards the pier. Rose tried to make sense of Ivy's statement, and then she said gently,

'No Ivy. I think you must be mistaken. It was me who was going out with Ernest.' Rose laughed nervously. 'I don't think I ever walked under the pier with him because I had a strange phobia about going underneath it in those days. Anyway - it was a long time ago.'

'I remember it!' insisted Ivy. 'Doris was kissing Ernest under the pier. It was dark.'

'It's easy to remember things wrong,' said Doris, looking a little embarrassed. 'Anyway, I wonder what's going to happen to the poor old pier? It's a shame they can't get the money together to fix it. Mind you ... it's a shame that boat had to crash into it in the first place...'

'I saw them you know,' Ivy interrupted. 'Doris and Ernest. They didn't know I saw them, but I did. They were kissing. His hands were all over her white dress.' Doris patted Ivy's arm, and smiled awkwardly.

'We were just talking about the pier Ivy. Do you remember when the boat crashed into it?' Doris asked. Ivy didn't answer.

'Well, there is a campaign going on,' Rose said with a shaky voice, trying to ignore what Ivy had been saying. 'There's a local group trying to organise fund raising to rebuild the damaged part. I expect it could take a long time to get that sort of money together though.' Ivy stretched her arm out and pointed – this time directly in front of them towards the sea.

'What are those two doing over there?' she asked.

'Which two?' Doris replied, relieved that Ivy wasn't looking at the pier this time.

'That man with the young lad - they're hoovering the beach!'

'Oh ...I think they've got a metal detector,' said Rose, sounding intrigued.

'Well I wonder what they'd want with that?' said Doris.

'You use it to look for treasure, or maybe coins that people have dropped. I expect it makes a noise when it detects something made of metal.'

'Yes the young lad's got a spade to dig the treasure up with,' Doris noticed.

'It looks like they've found something. The boy's started digging,' Rose said.

'I wonder what it could be?   Ooo look!' Doris said excitedly, 'They've pulled something out. I wonder what it is?'

'The young lad's giving it a clean by the looks of it,' Rose said. 'Oh that's funny – I think he's pointing up here. He's not pointing at us is he?'

'Well I shouldn't think so,' Doris said.

'Oh they seem to be coming this way,' said Rose. 'They look rather pleased with themselves I must say.'

'They *are* looking at us,' Doris said. 'Perhaps they've come to chat us up.'

'That would be nice,' Rose giggled, 'He looks quite distinguished doesn't he.'

'Good afternoon ladies,' said the elderly man addressing the three giggling ladies, 'I don't know if this is of any interest to you, but my grandson and I have just been doing some metal detecting, and we dug up this bracelet. It looks like silver. But what's interesting is that it's got the name Alice engraved on it. Young George here is very observant and he noticed that your beach hut is named Alice as well. It seems quite a coincidence that we found it so nearby.'

'Yes - it was just down there,' said grandson George pointing down the beach, 'directly in line with your beach hut - it was buried quite deep too.'

132

'Oh how fascinating,' Rose said as she examined the bracelet. 'We were just watching you digging it up.'

'Well, that's a coincidence,' Doris said as she bent over to look at the bracelet. 'The bracelet and the beach hut are both called Alice.'

'Did you give your beach hut its name?' asked George.

'No. It actually belongs to my niece, Caroline,' Rose explained, 'but she only bought it recently. We're just borrowing it for the day. But Caroline didn't name it. The hut was already called Alice when she bought it. To be honest we thought it was rather strange at first, but we've all got used to it now and I think we rather like the name.'

'So you don't know the history behind it then?' asked George.

'No - but I'll tell Caroline about the bracelet though. I think she'll find that quite intriguing. In fact, people who've owned the hut in the past have collected bits and bobs off the beach and left them here in the hut. Come and have a look,' Rose said as she got up and beckoned the man and the boy inside the hut. She showed them the little display on the windowsill with the jars of sea glass and seashells, the pieces of driftwood, the stripey pebbles and the old black and white photo of the man in the deckchair outside the beach hut, enjoying a glass of wine.

'What a splendid collection,' he said. 'Well how about we give you the bracelet to add to these other treasures?'

'Oh that would be lovely,' Rose said. 'But are you sure you want to part with it? You might want to check it first and see if it has any value?'

'No I don't think so. It's a little scratched and damaged. It's obviously spent some time being tumbled in the sea. It's a lovely piece of jewellery though. I think it belongs here in the beach hut called Alice,' he said as he draped it over a piece of driftwood on the windowsill. 'There. It looks good like that.'

'Thank you. That's very kind of you. Do you often come here with your metal detector?' Rose asked looking up into the distinguished gentleman's face.

'This is the first time actually. Young George here gave me this splendid gadget for my birthday and today is it's maiden voyage,' he said proudly.

'Oh how lovely. Well if you come again and see my niece and her family here – do call in and say hello won't you.'

'Yes of course we will,' George said as he turned and walked out the door.

'I'll tell her about you – and the bracelet of course. Can I tell her your names?'

'Yes, I'm George and my grandson is also called George.'

'Oh how nice,' said Rose. 'Was he named after you?

'Well I rather like to think so. Well it's been lovely to meet you ladies,' he said turning round politely to address all three of them. 'Right Young George – shall we go and find some ice creams before we search for some more treasure?'

The two Georges said their goodbyes and headed off towards the cafe.

'Oooh he was very charming wasn't he?' said Rose feeling quite bowled over as she sat back down in her deckchair.

'Yes - nice. I wonder if he's taken?' Doris said with a wink.

'Mmm .....' wondered Rose. 'Actually I don't think so – well not anymore.'

'How can you possibly know that Rose?' asked Doris.

'Well I don't know for certain, but did you see how much pride there was in his eyes and in his voice when he talked about his grandson?'

'Yeeeesss?' replied Doris.

'Well I may be wrong but I would guess that his grandson is by far the most important person in his life. I just have a feeling that he doesn't have a wife anymore.'

'You always were the clever one Rose. I would never have thought of that.'

134

'Posh and clever,' piped up Ivy. 'Posh and clever our Rose.'

'Oh don't be silly,' Rose said, looking embarrassed.

'Ivy's right,' Doris said 'We always called you the posh and clever one. And beautiful. You outshone us all, there's no doubt about that. And you're still so tall, slim and elegant. I mean look at me, squeezed into this deckchair like a sack of potatos.'

'Don't be silly,' Rose said laughing at Doris. 'Goodness me. Did you really used to say those things about me?'

'Yes we all did. And I'm sure you would have been snapped up by some lovely eligible man if you hadn't been so busy keeping an eye on little Caroline.'

'I can't believe you used to say that about me,' Rose said, very flattered by the compliments.

'Anyway, how is Lillian these days?' Doris asked. 'Still as wayward as ever?'

Rose groaned, 'Nothing changes with my sister. She never grew up. Still as selfish as ever. Her latest thing is that she complains that Caroline doesn't visit her very often! Honestly she was such a bad mother it's a wonder Caroline bothers to stay in touch with her at all. She's a very kind and forgiving girl though.'

'Yes she is. That's your influence on her Rose. She takes after you rather than her mother.'

'Thank goodness.'

'So have Caroline and her family been down to the beach hut a lot then?'

'No. In fact they haven't brought the family here at all yet. They're planning a holiday here soon though. To be honest I was very surprised when they bought the hut in the first place, because they've always been a bit short of money, and these aren't cheap.'

'Yes, everyone says that. The most expensive sheds in the country!'

'I know. I couldn't believe it when Caroline told me. She often comes down here to see me, but I was surprised she'd want to spend holidays here, because of all the bad childhood memories associated with Lillian. Actually I'm almost wondering if she did it for my sake, because she was so keen to tell me that she'd got me a key and I could use it whenever I wanted and bring my friends here. I hope she doesn't feel she owes me anything. It's been a privilege to have her in my life.'

'Well it's nice she appreciates you so much. I wonder where she got the money from? Did someone die and leave her some?'

'Not that I know of. Certainly not in our family.'

'Is Alice here yet?' asked Ivy.

'No dear,' Doris said kindly, putting her hand on Ivy's arm again. 'Alice is the name of this lovely beach hut. Look – do you see the sign there? It says Alice.'

'Alice. Oh yes.' Ivy said looking puzzled.

'Rose's niece Caroline bought the beach hut for her and her family, and for Rose to use too. That's why she's brought us here today.'

Chapter 17

'Are we nearly there yet Dad?' Daniel moaned from the back of the car.

'Oh stop it Daniel. You're being silly now,' replied his Dad, Richard.

Daniel's younger brother Harry joined in.

'But Dad …when *will* we be there? It's been ages since you said we would be there soon.'

'Yes,' Daniel added, 'It was at least half an hour ago.'

'*Mummy! Mummy!*!' Daniel and Harry's little sister Mary-Ann, suddenly shrieked at the top of her voice, making them all jump. '*Mummy*! I just saw a fairy!!'

'Did you darling?' her Mum, Caroline, answered, relieved by the change of subject.

'Yes, she was so pretty.'

'Amazing imagination,' Caroline whispered to Richard, not expecting Mary-Ann to hear her over the noise of the boys who were still complaining.

'It's not my *im-a-gin-a-tion* Mummy, I did see a fairy.'

'Oops!' Caroline said quietly to Richard. She twisted her head round towards her three children who were in the back of the car. 'Really darling? Did she have wings?'

'Of course she did,' Mary-Ann said grumpily. 'That's how I knew she was a fairy.'

'What colour were they darling?'

'Pink.'

'Oh how nice.' Caroline then added thoughtfully 'How big was this fairy then?'

'About the same height as you Mummy,' Mary-Ann paused before she added, 'but thinner.'

'I guess she would be. Where was she exactly?'

'Just walking in the woods back there.'

Dad laughed. 'Not flying through the trees then?'

'No. She was walking along with a friend. I don't know if her friend was a fairy too because her back was facing the other way and I couldn't see if she had wings or not,' Mary-Ann replied matter of factly.

'Ah ha!' Dad said, sounding very pleased with himself, 'What does that sign say?' The three children replied in unison,

'Welcome to Sebleigh Bay.'

'Well where's the sea then?' challenged Harry.

'Be patient,' said Mum calmly, 'you'll see it any minute now.'

'So we'll be at the beach hut in few minutes then?' asked Daniel.

'No' Mum said, 'Don't you remember? Dad told us earlier, we're going to the hotel first to unload, before we do anything else.'

Harry moaned, 'I still don't see why Dan and I can't just live in the beach hut - that would be so cool.'

'You don't really sleep in them Harry,' Dad explained, 'They're quite small, and they're just for using when you're enjoying the ...'

'Look!' Mum interrupted. 'Rosewater Drive! That's where Auntie Rose lives. I spent a lot of time there ...'

' ... When you were a little girl,' the three children groaned together.

'Yes you told us Mum.'

'About a million times.'

'And it's not as if we haven't visited Auntie Rose ourselves.'

'Not for a long time though - I'm surprised you can remember, and there's no need to be so cheeky, thank you.'

'Is Auntie Rose coming to the hotel with us?' Harry asked.

'No stupid,' Mary-Ann said rudely, 'Don't you ever listen? I'm only seven and I know Auntie Rose is away in ... err ... that place with the clouds - where is it Mum?'

'The Isle of Skye. It's in Scotland.'

138

'Well why are we coming to Sebleigh Bay where Auntie Rose lives if she's away in Scotland?' asked Daniel.

'I booked the holiday without telling her, because I wanted to surprise her, and when I rang her up she had already arranged her trip.'

'It doesn't matter,' Dad added. 'We can come again another time when Auntie Rose is here. Anyway, your Mum's given her the spare key for the beach hut, so she can use it any time. She's already been there with her friends.'

'What, before us?' said Mary-Ann sounding horrified, 'But I wanted to be the first to go to our new beach hut, and I wanted to show Auntie Rose around it myself.'

'It's only small you know,' Daniel said, 'I don't think you can exactly show people round it!'

'Do you mind Daniel?' Mum said indignantly, 'It's very special. We were lucky to get it. They don't come on the market very often.'

'Yeah, with a very special price tag too!' muttered Dad.

'Look! The sea! At last!' said Daniel.

'It's lovely and sparkly,' said Mary-Ann. 'Mummy, I think the fairies will like it here very much.'

'Yeah right,' said Daniel sarcastically.

'There are fairies here, I just saw some more going into a shop.'

'Actually, I hate to admit it,' Harry said begrudgingly, 'but I saw them too.'

'Really?' asked the others.

'Never mind fairies,' said Dad dismissively. 'It looks like we've arrived.' Then he stated dramatically,

'The Grand Hotel!' They drove into the hotel grounds between two huge pillars each with a lion seated on top. The children gasped with excitement as they saw the imposing Victorian hotel building in front of them. It must have been the largest and most impressive building on the seafront.

'Are we staying in *that*?' Harry asked, with his eyes almost popping out of his head.

'Oh yes! Nothing but the best for the Nightingale family!' Dad said smugly.

'Wow! It's huge!' said Daniel.

'I think it looks like the sort of place where Kings and Queens would stay,' said Mary-Ann.

'Wait till you see our suite!' Mum said with a glint in her eyes, 'You won't believe your eyes.'

'Sweets? ... Do they give us sweets too? ... Extra nice ones?' the children asked.

Chapter 18

'Oh that's good – there's a signal here,' Richard said as he checked his mobile phone.

'What do you need that thing for on the beach?' asked Caroline as she stretched herself luxuriously on her sun bed just outside the beach hut called Alice.

'I'm just browsing the internet. Thought I'd look at a few cars.'

'I thought we'd agreed that the one we've got is fine?'

'Well it's pretty old. With the money we've got we could afford something much better and more reliable too.'

'I really don't want us buying anything flashy – people will wonder how we got the money.'

'Oh for heaven's sake Caroline! Look, I didn't want to have a row on holiday, but this is just ridiculous. We need to have a serious talk about all this.'

'Please don't lecture me now Richard. I was so looking forward to coming here today.'

'I don't care Caroline. Sorry – but it's got to be said. I don't know why you've been buying the tickets every week if you didn't want to actually win. We could have bought a villa in the South of France, but instead we buy a shed in Sebleigh Bay...'

'It's not ...'

'Let me finish!' Richard interrupted. 'We're driving around in a knackered out old banger, but we can't buy a new one because you're worried what the neighbours might think. I'm surprised you let me pay the mortgage off in case the bank manager thought we'd done a robbery or something....'

'Stop it Richard! No one's going to think that. I just don't want people to know we're wealthy.'

'Well why not?'

'I don't know.' Caroline paused. 'It's embarrassing.'

'Why is it? No don't answer that. I'll tell you why. It's your upbringing ... your religion! It's all about guilt isn't it. You don't think you deserve to be happy or to enjoy yourself or to have some spare money to be frivolous with.'

'I can't help my lousy mother; I didn't choose my upbringing; and please don't insult my beliefs. Anyway ... it's not that...'

'Well what is it then?'

'Well ...' Caroline took her sunglasses off and rubbed her eyes. 'if our friends and family knew how much money we've got now they'd expect us to share it with them.'

'You mean you would feel you'd have to share it with them. Look, I told you I don't mind treating your mother to a holiday (even though she definitely doesn't deserve it), or buying something nice for your Aunt Rose, or helping Linda with her wedding ...'

'But I do. I know it might sound mean, but I don't want to give our money away. I want to keep it for us and the children – to provide security for their futures and for ours. When they're grown up we could buy them each a house so they never have to worry about mortgages for instance.'

'Ah! So that's what this is about – you don't *want* to share our money. You don't *want* to tell anyone we've got it because you would then feel that you would have to give it away ... otherwise you are worried that they'd think we're mean!' Richard burst out laughing, and he leaned over and hugged Caroline, 'Oh you're so funny! I do love you.' He gave her a big kiss on the cheek.

'You may laugh but don't you think that providing security for the children's future is more important than anything else?'

'Yes of course I do,' he said kindly.

'It's okay for you Richard – you had a stable upbringing, and you never had to worry about much ...'

'Oh that's not true,' he said mischievously, 'I'm sure I used to worry about all sorts of things.'

142

'Like what?'

'Like ... going to the dentist ... or what I would spend my pocket money on ... or my mum finding out I'd spilt red paint on the new bedroom carpet. Did I tell you I rearranged my room so she wouldn't see it, and she never did until we moved house?'

'Exactly!' she laughed, 'If that's all you had to worry about, you didn't know you were born. You can't imagine what it was like for me.'

'Okay, okay. I'm sorry – honestly – I mean it. I'm not laughing at you. I'm actually laughing at myself because it's taken me this long to work out what this is all about. We should have talked about this before and got everything out in the open.'

'Actually – thinking about it – I *would* like to buy something for Aunt Rose – I owe her so much.'

'Well you've already given her a key to the beach hut, which was a nice thought, but I don't mind if you want to do more than that. You're so fond of her aren't you?'

'I am. Well as you know she's always been there for me my whole life and I'll always be grateful to her. And anyway – the fact that she lives here in Sebleigh Bay it's ideal – she can come here as much as she likes.'

'She *is* nice isn't she. I'm surprised she's never married actually – she's very good looking. I can imagine she would have been really pretty when she was young.'

'Do you think so? I've never thought about it really. She's just my lovely Aunt Rose.'

'Well she's got that classic bone structure hasn't she, and she always looks so elegant.'

'Oh you *are* taken with her. I'll have to dig out some old photos of her sometime to show you. Anyway, it's probably lucky for me that she wasn't married or she may not have been around to keep an eye on my irresponsible mother and to look out for me. Do you know – when I was Mary-Ann's age I actually used to wish that Rose *was* my mother? I went and stayed with her sometimes and I never wanted to

143

go home afterwards. And another thing ... I used to fantasise that she somehow turned out to actually *be* my mother and she claimed me back.'

'That is bad. Hey, I know how you feel about your mother, obviously, but you've never told me any of that before about Rose.

'I know. I suppose it's because we're here in Sebleigh Bay where it all happened. It's bringing it back to me. The thing is, it would kill me if our kids felt like that about me.'

'Well there's no reason why they ever will is there? As I've told you a million times before – you're nothing like your mother, so that will never happen.'

'You do realise you'll have to tell me that another million times before I stop worrying about it.'

'I know. I have to say that apart from the connection with lovely Aunt Rose, I've not really been able to understand why you actually wanted to buy a beach hut here when everything must remind you of your unhappy upbringing.'

'Mm ... I think it's because when I was an unhappy child going through all that trauma with my mum, one of my very best memories was of spending time with my friend Sharon and her family at their beach hut.'

'Oh yes. You pointed it out to me. ... number 35.'

'That's right. Well, I guess it was my safe happy place. I have such brilliant memories associated with my time there. I've thought about it a lot over the years. The hut looks very different now, by the way. I wouldn't have recognised it. Anyway... let's focus on the present. It's nice here and the children are really enjoying being outside on the beach.'

'Yes! Let's just enjoy the holiday. The hotel's amazing. The beach hut's fun, and we might even get some sunshine if we're lucky!'

'Well I can't see us going back with much of a tan but as long as it's not raining too much the kids can still enjoy themselves.'

'Look Caroline ... about the money. When we're back home we need to sit down and work out exactly what we want to do with it. We've been skating around the subject, but we need to make some serious decisions like how much to put away for the kids, how much to invest, and decide what both of us want to spend. We don't have to tell anyone how much we've got. That's our business. We'll get some professional advice and set up proper trust funds for the children – that sort of thing.'

'Oh can we? That would be good.'

'But honestly Caroline,' he lowered his voice to a whisper, 'I can still hardly believe I'm saying this, but, we're loaded! We can afford to do all those things and more.'

'Okay. I believe you.'

'Look, we're not going to fritter all of the money away obviously, but I do think you should treat yourself to something special. Have a think about it. Something just for you like a really nice piece of jewellery perhaps? Or maybe something completely different.'

'I'll tell you what I would *really* like to do. I've always fancied going to an auction. There was a film I watched when I was a youngster… I can't remember the title, but there was this auction scene which has always stayed in my mind. This mysterious sophisticated woman had everybody enthralled as she kept bidding higher and higher and purchased a valuable painting. I'd love to do something like that.'

'Really? That's a great idea. We'll have to have a look and find a local auction to visit.'

Caroline visibly relaxed and stretched out on the sun bed again.

'I like that idea. But right now let's just enjoy all this. I love the beach.'

'Yes you're right. It *is* nice. Tell you what – I'll put my phone away.'

'Hallelujah!' Caroline closed her eyes and relaxed for a moment. Then, keeping her eyes shut she said, 'By the way Richard ... I didn't know you fancied mature ladies.' Richard closed his eyes and relaxed onto his sunbed.

145

'Do you think Rose might like a toy boy?' Caroline gasped. 'Well you'd better be a good wife or I might swap you for your Aunt.'

'What a cheek! Swap me for an older model?' She giggled and leaned across and playfully hit Richard. He grabbed her arm and pulled her to him and kissed her full on the lips.

'No it's OK. You'll do. I like the way you kiss,' Richard said. They were just about to kiss again when they were interrupted by Daniel's young voice.

'Eww *yuk*! Not in public *please*!!' Then Harry joined in.

'Oh, do you have to? That's *disgusting*!'

'Mummy! Daddy!' said Mary-Ann. There's a really nice cafe down there. Can we buy an ice cream? We can get some for you too.'

'No,' Daniel said with disgust in his voice, 'they're too busy doing other things to want an ice cream.'

'Yes – like eating each other – eww!' said Harry. Mary-Ann looked shocked.

'I don't think I want to know about that thank you very much!' she said. Richard looked at his watch.

'Actually it's time for lunch. Shall we all go down to the cafe? Apparently they do excellent fish and chips.'

'But I don't like fish and chips ... I want a pizza ... But what about the ice creams?' the children all complained together.

'That's enough!' Richard said firmly. Let's put everything in the beach hut and lock up, then we'll all go along to the cafe for lunch. You can have your ice creams afterwards.'

'Cool,' Daniel said.

The children ran on ahead and reached the Beachcomber Cafe first. Then Mary-Ann came running back to meet Caroline and Richard, who were walking along Chalk Cliff Way. She looked so excited she could hardly speak.

'Mummy! Daddy! The cafe is full of fairies! They're everywhere. I *love* this place!'

146

'Caroline looked ahead and could see two young women sitting at a table outside the cafe. They wore pretty multicoloured dresses, blue tights, big clompy boots, and they had the most stunning fairy wings on their backs.

'Goodness me, Mary-Ann! How ... magical! Don't they look beautiful.'

'Yes, and look at their dog!'

'Wow! A fairy dog!'

A small white terrier with pretty pink wings on its back was on a rainbow coloured lead attached to the chair which one of the fairies were sitting on. Mary-Ann was jumping up and down with excitement.

'Do you think they'd let me stroke it?'

Richard replied with amusement in his voice,

'Yes. Just treat it like any other dog Mary-Ann ... always ask the owner first.'

'You mean, go and ask one of the fairies?' she said, hardly able to contain her excitement.

'Yes, of course.'

Mary-Ann went up to the two fairies who were sipping their hot chocolates drinks. They also had little plates of chocolate buttons and marshmallows.

'Excuse me, could I stroke your fairy dog please?'

'Yes of course you can,' one of the fairies replied with a big smile. Mary-Ann was mesmerised by her striking face which was intricately painted with a myriad of swirling colours. Her eyelids were decorated with pink and blue glitter, set off beautifully with gold eyelashes. As Mary-Ann crouched down to talk to the fairy dog, the fairy looked up at Caroline and Richard and gave them an exaggerated wink. Then she turned to Mary-Ann and spoke in a slow and mystical manner.

'So, you're Mary-Ann aren't you?' the fairy asked.

'Yes ... how did you know my name?' The fairy continued mysteriously,

'Us fairies just know these things.' Caroline and Richard looked at each other with puzzled expressions.

'What do you think of my little fairy dog then?' asked the fairy.

'He's really cute. What's his name?'

'He's called Bruce.'

Mary-Ann giggled. 'That's a funny name ... especially for a fairy dog.'

'It's a very normal name for a dog where we come from.'

'Where do you come from?'

'Ahh ... that would be telling ... let's just say ... we're not from this world.'

'I saw some other fairies on the journey down here.'

'Oh yes. You will see us all over the town this week. We are having a special fairy convention in Sebleigh Bay. Why don't you see how many of us you can spot?'

As Mary-Ann chatted away and stroked the dog, Richard pulled out his phone and held it up, catching the eye of one of the fairies, as if to ask if it was alright for him to take photos. She nodded happily, so Richard took photos of Mary-Ann and the fairy dog, while the fairies struck a number of poses behind her – looking mystically at the camera and turning sideways so their wings were in full view.

The boys were already inside the cafe looking up at the board above the counter, and arguing over what they would have for lunch. The cafe was indeed full of fairies who were munching at their pizzas as they compared wings and admired each other's outfits and make-up. Richard came in on his own and spoke quietly to the boys.

'I think Mary-Ann actually believes that the fairies are real. Let's keep it that way shall we?' Harry raised his eyebrows and pulled a face.

'Are you serious?'

'Yes. Just do it for me please – it will make the holiday really special for her ... and ... you can have any pizza you choose.'

'Cool. Large pepperoni for me!'

'How about, large pepperoni for me *please Dad?*'

148

'*Please Dad*!'

'Cheese pizza for me *please Dad*! Large! *Please Dad*!' added Daniel. Richard shook his head, raised his eyebrows and told the boys to go and find a table outside. When he reached the front of the queue Carmen took his order.

'You're not part of the fairy convention then?'

'No,' he laughed. 'Left my wings at home today. Never seen anything like it.'

'Yes, it's quite a sight isn't it. Fairies everywhere. They come here every year.'

'My daughter's bowled over – she's only seven – she's outside now stroking a little dog with wings on.'

'Sweet. They camp over at Hillthorpe Farm – we saw them there at night time once, dancing round a fire – it was quite magical actually – and sometimes they have a barbeque on the beach at night. You're outside are you? We'll bring your meals out when they're ready.

'Thank you. You'll spot us easily – the ones without the wings!'

The Beachcomber pizzas and fish and chips went down very well with the Nightingale family although Mary-Ann was too excited to eat much and she was distracted by her task of counting all the fairies who were milling around at the cafe or on the beach.

'Ooh look! Those two fairies are going to have a paddle – they're taking their boots off. That's another two. That makes 35 altogether. 35 fairies plus two fairy dogs.'

'You've seen those two before!' protested Harry, 'they were in the cafe earlier ... you can't count them again.'

'No they weren't. I haven't seen fairies with those rainbow coloured wings before.'

'Yes you have ...'

'Oh stop it you two. It doesn't matter Harry does it ...' Caroline was interrupted by Carmen.

'How were your meals – everything alright?'

'Yes thank you.' Caroline replied, 'Lovely fish and chips, but I think the kids eyes were a bit too big for their tummies

149

– the boys can't finish their pizzas, and Mary-Ann's too excited by the fairies to eat.'

'No problem – I'll bring you a box to put the leftovers in. You can have them later.'

'Oh would you? That's kind.'

'You like the fairies I hear?' Carmen asked Mary-Ann.

'Oh yes! I wish I lived here all the time.'

'Well they're only here for a little holiday – just for a few days. They come every year.'

'We're here for a holiday too.'

'Are you? Where are you staying.'

'We're in the big hotel ...'

'The Grand Hotel she means,' Daniel added.

'Yes we're in The Grand Hotel and we own a beach hut too.'

'Oh how lovely ... best of both worlds.' Carmen said smiling at the parents.

'Yes and our beach hut is special because it's got a name ... it's called Alice.'

'Oh I know. That's the blue and white one isn't it ... I heard it had changed hands.' Carmen hoped the pain didn't show on her face. She changed the subject by talking about the weather.

'You've picked a great week for your holiday – it's going to warm up tomorrow apparently - we're due for a heatwave.'

'Oh lovely!' replied Caroline, 'We can make the most of the beach hut then.'

'And it's a great week for our holiday because the fairies are here too,' added Mary-Ann.

Over the next couple of days the heatwave materialised so the Nightingale family spent their days on the beach, making the most of Alice. Richard and Caroline relaxed on their sun beds while the three children built sand castles, buried each other, swam in the sea and searched the rock pools. They all made regular trips to the Beachcomber for

150

ice creams and lunches, getting to know Carmen and Clive a little more each time, and they would all return to The Grand Hotel in the evenings, and get dressed up and dine in style in the hotel's restaurant.

As expected the children had been thrilled with the luxurious hotel suite, although Mary-Ann did complain once or twice that none of the fairies seemed to be staying at the hotel. The boys were keener than usual to wash themselves as they loved the luxury bathroom with its marble surfaces and it's large round spa bath.

Their initial introduction to the beach hut called Alice had been met with mixed reactions. Mary-Ann thought it was sweet, Caroline loved it, Daniel wished it was bigger, Richard would have clearly preferred a villa in France, and Harry wasn't happy that it still had the previous owner's belongings in it.

'Don't worry,' Richard said, 'When we get chance we'll throw out this furniture and buy some new things, and all that stuff on the window sill looks like it's been collected from the beach ... we can put it back where it came from and choose some things of our own instead.'

'Oh I quite like those things,' Mary-Ann said. 'Can I play with them before we put them back on the beach?'

'Yes of course – there's no hurry.' Mary-Ann had a lovely time spreading all the pieces of seaglass and driftwood over the floor of the beach hut – making various different mosaic pictures with them, such as faces and butterflies, and getting her Dad to photograph them.

One day whilst lunching in the Beachcomber Cafe, Carmen was chatting to them all and the boys mentioned how they loved rockpools and were going to go and look for some after lunch when the tide had gone out. Carmen told them about some particularly deep rock pools.

'They are by those big rocks where the trees have fallen down the cliffs. I used to go there when I was a child, and they're still there. You get some very interesting creatures

151

and you can sometimes see starfish. Do you know where I mean?'

'Oh yes,' Daniel and Harry said in unison. 'Can we all go there Dad?'

'Actually ...' Caroline said, 'I'd really like a coffee before we go.' So after some discussion it was decided that Caroline and Richard would have their coffees and then go back to the beach hut to pick up the fishing nets and buckets to take down to the rock pools. The children would be allowed to go ahead with their mother's warning ringing in their ears, 'Promise me you will all stick together ... and keep away from the cliffs in case any bits drop off!'

'We will.'

The children set off together enthusiastically and soon spotted the big rocks that Carmen had mentioned.

'Let's race!' Daniel said. The boys were just about to sprint off when Mary-Ann squealed,

'That's not fair – I'm much smaller than you two.'

'And you're a girl!' said Harry.

'So what!? Girls are just as fast as boys but I'm younger than you.'

'Alright,' said Daniel, 'you can have a head start Mary-Ann. Off you go.'

Mary-Ann shot off along the sand towards the rocks as quickly as she could and when she was about half way there the boys began to run. Mary-Ann was the first one to reach the rocks.

'I won!' she said as she started climbing up them. As the boys arrived, Daniel said,

'We misjudged it. We gave you too much of a lead.' They followed Mary-Ann up on top of the rocks, where a beautiful deep pool was revealed.

'It's brilliant! ...Cool ...' the boys said.

'Look!' yelled Mary-Ann, 'A star fish. Carmen said we might see some. And look – I think that's an enemy – we learnt about them at school.'

'Enemy?' Harry said sarcastically. 'What's she on about?'

152

'I think you mean anemone, Mary-Ann.' Daniel said. 'Wow there's some fish in here. I hope Mum and Dad hurry up with the nets and buckets. We can try and catch some.'

'Can we take some home to live with our goldfish?' asked Mary-Ann.

'No, silly,' said Harry rudely. 'These fish live in sea water with salt in it.'

'This is brilliant!' Daniel exclaimed. 'It's even better than computer games, and that's saying something.'

Harry stood up on top of a big rock and pointed in front of him.

'There's another pool over there. I'm going to look in that one.' As Harry moved forwards, his foot slipped on some green algae. He tried to regain his balance but he fell backwards. A sickening crack was heard as Harry's head hit the rock. Daniel and Mary-Ann gasped in unison as they took in the shocking image of Harry's seemingly lifeless body sprawled on the rocks with his blood rapidly appearing in a puddle on the rock where his head lay.

'Harry! Harry!' Daniel spoke to him hopelessly. 'Oh no. I think he's unconscious.' Daniel nearly burst into tears but in a split second he knew he had to take responsibility to save his younger brother and to keep his little sister calm. Mary-Ann stood like a statue with her mouth and eyes wide open. Daniel crouched down to her level, looked her straight in the eyes and spoke in a very adult manner.

'Mary-Ann ... Listen to me. I need you to be a really clever and brave girl. Okay?'

'Yes.'

'Good girl. Right ... I want you to climb down the rocks very carefully, and then run as fast as you can back to the cafe and find Mum and Dad. I need to stay here and look after Harry. Now, if Mum and Dad aren't at the cafe any more, I want you to talk to the man or lady who run the cafe - you know the nice lady we were talking to earlier ...?'

'Carmen?'

'Yes Carmen! Thats right. Good girl! Or her husband. Now, listen carefully ... I want you to say that Harry's hurt his head on the rocks. We need an ambulance. He's unconscious ... asleep, okay? Right what are you going to say.'

'He's hurt his head bad ... We need an ambulance ... Harry's asleep.'

'Brilliant. You must remember all of that okay? Now off you go as quick as you can ... careful on the rocks now ... oh, and Mary-Ann, tell them where we are ... on the big rocks by the fallen trees.'   Daniel kept an eye on Mary-Ann as she climbed down the rocks with ease. When she reached the sand, he glimpsed down at Harry's head and pleaded desperately,

'Go as fast as you can Mary-Ann ... we need help...'

Mary-Ann was very bright. Daniel knew that even though she was the youngest she would normally be the most likely of the three of them to recall instructions accurately. But she looked so shocked that he was worried that she would get confused and forget something important. He watched her running like a gazelle across the sand into the distance, then he sat down and held Harry's hand.

'Please be alright Harry, *please*!'

Mary-Ann had been too frightened to ask Daniel if Harry was going to be alright, but she knew he looked really bad. She'd never seen blood pouring like that before and the fear in Daniel's eyes wasn't lost on her. *I'm going to run faster than I've ever run in my life*, she thought. *If only I had a pair of wings like those fairies. I could do with some of their magic at the moment too.*

Clive was clearing up the remains of fish and chip dinners from the outside tables. He stopped to stroke a sleepy Bassett Hound which was lying in the shade by the wall, while the owners enjoyed a coffee. He was interrupted by a polite young couple who were just leaving and made a point of thanking him for their meal.

'That was excellent. We're here for the week, so I'm sure we'll be back again,' the young man enthused. Clive smiled. He always appreciated compliments however many times he heard them.

'Where are you staying?'

As they explained about their guest house he noticed a familiar young girl approaching the cafe running like the clappers. She rushed into the cafe and came straight out again. He noticed the look of alarm on her face as she came towards him ...

'Hello there, are you alright?' he asked her kindly.

'My brother Harry ... he's hurt his head badly on the rocks ...he fell ...' she pointed over towards the rocks. 'Daniel said we need an ambulance urgently... I don't know where Mum and Dad are ...'

Clive bent down and put his hands on Mary-Ann's shoulder. 'Now ... you are Mary-Ann, aren't you?'

'Yes, Mary-Ann Nightingale.' Clive pulled out his mobile phone.

'Right Mary-Ann, I'm going to phone my friend in the police - he'll know exactly what to do. Now what's your brother's name?'

'Harry Nightingale.'

'And how old is Harry?'

'He's 10.'

'And he's on the rocks ...?'

'Yes. By the fallen trees.'

'Good. I know exactly where that is.' Clive's phone was dialling PC Plaistows number.

'Is he alone?'

'No, my brother Daniel is with him.'

'And how does Harry's head look?'

'It was bleeding a lot and he was asleep ...'

Clive started walking into the cafe holding his phone to his ear, with his other hand leading Mary-Ann in beside him, just as Carmen emerged from the kitchen.

'Carmen, we've got an emergency. Can you get someone to cover for you? This is Mary-Ann... Ah Peter, it's Clive Collier,' he spoke down his phone. 'We've got a medical emergency here on the beach ...' Carmen took Mary-Ann's hand as she listened to Clive's conversation with PC Plaistow.

'Do you know where your parents are Mary-Ann?' asked Carmen.

'I think they've gone back to the beach hut to get the fishing nets - they said they would - but Daniel told me to look in here first, and if they had gone to speak to you.'

'That was a very good idea. My Clive knows all the right people when it comes to a situation like this. Your parents only left a few minutes ago - we'll soon find them.'

Clive bent down and spoke to Mary-Ann.

'Right. This is what we're going to do. I'm going to head straight down the beach to find Harry, and I'll be talking to the emergency people on my phone until they get there, and Carmen will look after you Mary-Ann.'

'Alright my dear,' Carmen said to Mary-Ann, 'I think we'll go along to your beach hut and see if we can find your parents. I'll tell you what ... you look very hot. Let's quickly get you a lolly to cool you down. You can eat it on the way.' Carmen opened the freezer and told Mary-Ann to choose whatever she fancied.

They walked quickly along Chalk Cliff Way by the beach huts. Carmen was trying to stay cheerful and positive, but at the same time she was dreading breaking the news to Mary-Ann's parents.

Richard and Caroline had enjoyed a leisurely walk back along the beach, and before they collected the nets from the beach hut had walked down to the sea for a paddle, enjoying their fifteen minutes of quiet time without the kids.

'I must admit Caroline, this holiday's working out very well, much better than I expected.'

156

'I know. The heatwave has been a real bonus, and it's wonderful to see the children playing outside all the time.'

'Mm ... I thought Daniel might be unbearable without his gadgets!'

'So my whole beach hut plan wasn't as ludicrous as you thought then?'

'Yeah, yeah ... you were right and I was wrong ... come here wife!' Richard grabbed Caroline around the waist and kissed her.

'You're only doing that to shut me up! To stop me bragging about organising such a great holiday.'

'Whatever – it's as good a reason as any! Nice to be able to kiss you in a public place without traumatising the kids too.'

'Eww, that's disgusting, stop it ...' Caroline giggled, mimicking the children. 'We'd better not leave them long.'

'It's good for them to have a bit of freedom. I shouldn't think Mary-Ann's ever been anywhere without an adult with her.'

'I know. They're all pretty sensible, but we'd better go and find them.'

'That sounds like a helicopter.' They both looked up and saw a helicopter above the cliffs in the far distance. 'That's something I'd like to do – take a ride in one of those. The boys would love it too – especially Harry. He's always been fascinated by them.' Richard pulled his phone out of his pocket. 'If it comes a bit nearer I'll take a photo.'

'Well maybe when we've taken a look at our finances we could put some money aside for a ride in one. I assume it's expensive.'

'Yes, but I think we could afford it in the circumstances. Gosh, I think it might be landing on the cliffs or the beach – it's hovering.' Caroline was distracted by a woman and child over by their beach hut. They were coming towards them. She stood and watched them for a moment.

'That's not Mary-Ann is it?' Caroline sounded puzzled.
'Where?'

'Over there.'

'It can't be. She wouldn't have left the boys. We told them to stick together.'

'It is Mary-Ann, and she's with Carmen from the cafe. That's strange.'

'Mum, Dad ...' yelled Mary-Ann as she broke into a run. Both couples started rushing towards each other .

'Something's wrong ...' Caroline said.

Mary-Ann ran into her mother's arms looking very panicked,

'Mum, Mum ..'

Carmen spoke gently,

'Mary-Ann my love, let me explain to Mum and Dad – it's important.'

'What's wrong?' asked Caroline and Richard.

'Now, try not to worry, but your Harry has had an accident on the rocks. I think he's hurt his head. It's ok - my Clive is with him and he's called the emergency services straight away.'

'Oh God.' Caroline looked distraught.

'The helicopter,' Richard mumbled. 'It's the air ambulance. Oh my God. It's not for Harry is it?'

'It wouldn't surprise me. Come on.' Carmen said, 'Let's go.' The four of them set off in a run towards the rocks and the helicopter.

Chapter 19

Caroline, Richard, Daniel and Mary-Ann were huddled together on a big settee in the relatives room in hospital, waiting anxiously to hear news of Harry who was in the operating theatre.

'Ironic isn't it,' Richard said sadly. 'Harry's always wanted a ride in a helicopter and now that he gets one he won't remember it?'

'Was he awake at all dad?' Mary-Ann asked. 'I mean, since he hurt his head?'

'No I don't think so love – he stayed asleep.'

'I'd like to fly in a helicopter too one day,' Daniel added. 'but not in these circumstances.' Caroline looked up through tear stained eyes.

'Are you alright Daniel? I've been so worried about Harry I haven't thought about what it must have been like for you. And for you Mary-Ann.'

'I'm a bit shaken up that's all,' Daniel said sadly. 'I just want Harry to be alright.'

'I just want Harry to be alright too,' Mary-Ann added. Richard turned to the children doing his best to sound positive, which he didn't feel at all,

'I'll tell you what ... when Harry is better, we'll all have a lovely treat. We'll see if we can go for a helicopter ride together, and have the time of our lives.'

Caroline thought that time had never gone as slowly as it had this last hour or two. Richard had travelled in the helicopter with Harry and the paramedics, while Carmen had given Caroline, Daniel and Mary-Ann a lift to the hospital. By the time Caroline was dropped off at the hospital with the children, Harry was being rushed into theatre for a potentially life saving operation. The doctors looked concerned. There were no reassuring words - just a kind nurse directing them into the relatives room while the operation was in progress.   A few others were waiting anxiously for news of their loved ones.   Harry's skull was fractured and until the surgeons investigated further, they couldn't tell what damage he may have sustained.

Carmen tried to help. She wrote down her phone number and told Caroline to ring her any time and she'd come and pick them up or look after the children. For the time being the Nightingale family clung together. With Harry in danger, Caroline and Richard didn't want to let the other two children out of their sight.

A man who was sitting nearby went over to the drinks machine, leaving his jacket and phone on the chair. He got himself a cup of tea.

'Shall we have a drink?' asked Daniel.   Richard rummaged in his pockets and pulled out a handful of coins.

'Here - get whatever you want.'

'I'll help,' Mary-Ann said getting up. 'Let me see what drinks there are.' As the children studied the drinks machine, Caroline spoke quietly to Richard.

'I knew no good could come out of this.'

'What do you mean? Staying in Sebleigh Bay?'

'No, the lottery win. It didn't feel right somehow.'

'What's that got to do with anything?   That's ridiculous. You can't think like that.   It's just a horrible accident ... a twist of fate.   Harry falling on the rocks has no connection with the money we won.'

'It was too much though – we didn't deserve to be given that huge amount,' she whispered. 'I knew it was too good to be true. I'd happily give every penny back now if it would mean Harry would be ok.'

'Yes, I do know what you mean about that.   I'd gladly hand it all back in exchange for a healthy Harry.   It puts everything into perspective when something like this happens doesn't it.'

The man sat nearby was sipping his tea and checking with his phone. He looked up from his mobile and caught Caroline's eye and smiled.

160

'Is it your son you're waiting for?'

'Yes. He's having an operation. Had a nasty accident on the beach.'

'I'm sorry. Was he badly hurt?'

Richard replied to the man, 'Bad enough to be airlifted in a helicopter and rushed straight into theatre.'

'Oh I heard about an air rescue from the beach. Was it your son who fell on the rocks?'

'Yes that's right,' Richard said. 'We were lucky the helicopter arrived so swiftly – the cafe owner had a contact in the police I believe.'

'That was fortuitous. Which cafe was that?'

'The Beachcomber, the one past the beach huts. He was brilliant. He looked after Harry until we arrived.'

'Well I hope your son is alright. Hopefully you'll get some news soon. How did he hurt himself?

'We're not sure exactly,' Caroline replied. 'I feel awful because we let the children go off on their own, and Harry somehow fell on the rocks…What about you? Are you waiting for someone?'

'Don't worry about me, you've got more than enough to think about …' At that moment, a nurse came in and turned to Caroline and Richard.

'Mr and Mrs Nightingale, would you like to come through and we can explain everything to you?'

'How is he?' Caroline asked anxiously.

'Please come through …and bring the children …and your drinks,' she said glancing at the children. The nurse then glimpsed across at the other man, looked slightly puzzled and said,

'Are you together? On no, you're not are you?' The man shook his head and looked down at his phone, and as the Nightingale family nervously followed the nurse down the corridor, the man got up, grabbed his things and slipped outside into the corridor and quickly walked off in the opposite direction. He found his way out of the hospital and back to his car. Once he was inside he got out his phone,

161

listened to the recording he'd made and tapped out a message.

> *Got it!! And from the horse's mouth!! Boy Harry Nightingale (don't know age) fell on rocks - Sebleigh Beach. Unconscious. Just been operated on. I had to leave – nurse noticed me. Mother feels guilty – let children go off on their own. And there's a bonus! They've just won the lottery!!! Mum feels guilty about that too. Recorded it all. Off to Beachcomber Cafe now. Owner helped them and called helicopter via friend in police.*

Half an hour later the man entered the Beachcomber Cafe feeling hot, sweaty and irritated at having to walk all the way there past the many beach huts and holiday makers. He bought a cup of tea from a young girl at the counter. He decided not to start asking questions yet but to sit inconspicuously by himself at the nearest table and to do his best to look like he was engrossed in his newspaper and his phone - something he'd got off to a fine art after twenty years in the business. He hoped nobody would notice that he was looking at yesterday's paper. Bad mistake to make, but he hadn't had time to buy a new one today when he'd been diverted to Sebleigh Bay to see if he could find out anything about this beach rescue.

Caroline, Richard and the two children huddled around Harry as he lay in the hospital bed. They hardly noticed the tubes which were attached to him and all the equipment and gadgets that he was wired up to. They focused anxiously on his little sleeping face peeping out from his bandaged head, waiting hopefully for some sign of movement. The surgeon had explained that they had done what they could to repair Harry's wound and it was now simply a case of waiting. He was suffering from concussion, and there was a small amount of direct damage to his brain, but only time would tell if he would be alright. Caroline stroked Harry's hand and

162

they all talked quietly, trying to cover up how nervous they really were.

The man was getting bored in the Beachcomber Cafe, and was considering trying to get into conversation with the girl at the counter ... He could mention that he saw the rescue helicopter on the beach earlier. He saw an attractive woman rushing into the cafe carrying some bags of shopping. She spoke to the girl behind the counter.

'Hi Ellie ... What a day! Those poor parents ... I can't imagine what they're going through.'

'What's happened to the little boy?'

'They took him straight into theatre for surgery. It wasn't looking great. I left while he was still being operated on. His poor mum and dad – they looked so scared. I did a quick bit of shopping while I was in town. Is Clive in the kitchen?' She didn't wait for an answer but went straight in there to find her husband. The man watched through the open kitchen door as the cafe owners hugged each other, and talked. The man was irritated that he couldn't hear what they were saying over the noise of the coffee grinder. He wished that girl would turn it off. Finally she did, but it was too late to hear anything as the couple in the kitchen had finished their conversation. He went up to the counter to order another cup of tea. While the girl made it for him, he decided to ask some questions.

'I hear there was a dramatic rescue on the beach today.'

'Yes. Not every day we have a helicopter land down here,' Ellie said as Carmen came out of the kitchen putting her apron on. 'Carmen here helped to get the family to the hospital while the boy was air lifted in the helicopter.'

'Boy? Gosh, how old was he?'

'Quite young, about 8 or 10,' Carmen answered. 'Maybe older. Awful it was. He fell on the rocks down there by the big rock pools. Injured his head. Actually Ellie, I'm just thinking - I'm worrying that the children went down there because of me – it was me who told them about those rock

163

pools – you know, the really deep ones - and apparently they set off there after having lunch here. Oh I do hope that poor little lad will be alright.'

'How rotten.' The man replied, trying to sound sincere. It was many years since he had actually felt any guilt for intruding on other people's grief and taking advantage of the situation. 'So who called for help? Did the kids have a mobile?'

'No,' Carmen said. 'The little girl, the sister, she's the youngest – she ran all the way back here and spoke to my Clive. He went and helped and called the emergency services. Is that just a tea you're having? Thanks.' She took his money and put it in the till.

'So where were the parents?' the man asked.

'Oh they were just along the beach.' Carmen explained, tilting her head in the direction of the beach huts – I went and found them. Lovely family … they've just bought a beach hut, it was their first holiday here … excuse me.' Carmen said with a smile, turning to serve another customer.

Caroline thought she sensed some movement in Harry's hand. She glanced down, opening up her hand to look at Harry's little hand lying in hers.

'What is it?' Richard asked with a shaky voice.

'I think Harry moved his hand.' Caroline closed her hand gently around Harry's and he squeezed it.

'He squeezed my hand! Harry …' she said quietly, watching his face, 'It's Mummy … darling … we're all here …'

Harry's eyes flickered and opened slowly. He was looking at Mary-Ann directly in front of him.

'Hello Harry,' she gave him her biggest smile. 'It's me! Mary-Ann!' They all waited with baited breath to see if Harry would respond. A few seconds passed, which felt an age for the anxious family. Then, with his lips barely moving, Harry mumbled 'My head hurts...' Caroline and Richard had never been so relieved to hear Harry's voice.

'Oh Harry!' Caroline said as she burst into tears.

'Welcome back Harry,' Richard said trying to hold himself together. He took Harry's other hand. 'You're going to be just fine Harry … I know you are. I'm just going to fetch a nurse.'

'Why are you crying Mummy?' Harry said quietly, as he turned his head slightly and looked at Caroline.

The man in the cafe sipped his tea and considered his next move. Should he stir things up further? The cafe owners and staff were kept busy so there wasn't much chance to talk to them. However a family sat down at the table behind him. They'd just ordered a meal. The two young boys were squabbling over the seating – they both wanted to sit on the same chair. One of them accidentally bumped the chair against the man's chair, giving him an excuse to look round at them. The mother apologised.

'Oh I'm so sorry. Boys! Will you please sit down now. You've just crashed into this poor man's chair.'

'Sorry,' the two boys in unison.

'Oh don't worry,' the man said jovially with a big smile for the children. Then he turned to the parents and lied, 'Got two of my own. I know what they're like.'

Carmen had a brief lull inbetween customers and for some reason the man sitting on his own who was twisting round and talking to the family, caught her eye. He didn't look like a holidaymaker, or a local. There was something about the way he was dressed… It was a boiling hot day and he wasn't wearing appropriate clothing for the weather or for the beach. People who worked in the town didn't often walk down this far in their breaks – it was too far out of the way. Maybe he'd finished early for the day? Even so…he seemed to be hanging around. She didn't know why but something just didn't add up. He was now chatting to the family. Perhaps they knew each other? No, it didn't look like it. They were all being too polite. You could tell if people were friends or family by the way they reacted to each other. He's still chatting to them. *I hope he's not some weirdo. I'm keeping an eye on you mister.*

The surgeon was sitting with Harry and talking to him very quietly, and carefully checking to see if his reactions seemed normal.

'I think you're going to be fine Harry. I'm going to turn some of the lights off now. I can see they're hurting your eyes a bit.' He then turned to Richard and Caroline and said in a reassuring manner: 'That often happens after a knock on the head – Harry might be a little noise and light sensitive for a while. We'll have to keep him in for a few days to keep an eye on things, but everything seems very positive so far.' Caroline became tearful again. 'Oh thank you so much. You've been brilliant.'

'Yes, thank you,' Richard said - with enormous relief obvious in his voice.

'You're very welcome.' He turned to Harry, 'And thank you young man for letting me check you over. No more rock climbing today I'm afraid!'

Harry managed a small smile. 'No, I'm a bit tired. Maybe tomorrow?' Harry yawned, and he was struggling to keep his eyes open. 'Did I really fly in a helicopter Dad?'

'Yes you certainly did!'

Daniel joined in, 'And Dad says we can all go for a helicopter ride another time when you're better.'

'Cool.'

A bed was organised so that Caroline and Richard could take it in turns to stay the night in hospital with Harry.

Carmen was just taking a customer's money when her mobile phone buzzed in her pocket. She took the order over to the kitchen and handed it to Clive as she pulled out her phone.

'I've got a message. I wonder if it's about that little lad? Yes it is.' She read it out *Carmen and Clive, thank you both so much for your help. Harry is awake and talking. We've*

166

got every reason to be optimistic. Love Caroline. X Oh Clive that's fantastic news. I was so worried there....'

'Oh thank goodness. I must admit I really feared for him - it didn't look good.' Clive had tears of relief in his eyes. Carmen turned to Ellie.

'Ellie – the little lad Harry is awake and talking. It's looking good his mum said.'

'That's fantastic!'

The man approached the counter.

'Excuse me overhearing, but was that the little boy who was hurt that you were talking about?'

Ellie started to answer excitedly, 'Yes he's ...'

but Carmen interrupted, 'Yes. He's much better thank you.' She said firmly.

'Oh that's marvellous. Is he going to be alright?'

'We don't know anymore. Did you want some more tea?'

'Err, no thank you, I was just about to leave, but I was concerned about the boy...'

'Do you know the family then?'

'Well no but I heard about the rescue.'

Carmen turned to Clive and walked him into the kitchen, calling behind her,

'Ellie, would you go and clean the tables by the window now please.'

'Crumbs, Carmen! What was that about?' Clive asked quietly.

'I don't trust him - there's something about him.'

'What do you mean?'

'He doesn't look right. Why's he been hanging around in here?'

'Well the same reason as everybody else I should think – it's a hot day he wants some tea and a sit down.'

'I don't trust him, I mean what's he doing here? He's not on holiday... he's not local.'

'That's ridiculous – you don't know everyone who lives in Sebleigh Bay. He could be anyone.'

167

'Is he going? Get rid of him Clive. I don't want him hanging around here any longer.'

'What do you mean get rid of him? I think he's just saying goodbye to the family there. What's the problem anyway?'

'I don't know - it's just a feeling. Call it female intuition if you like?'

'Good grief! We're now chucking our customers out because you have a feeling!' Clive laughed.

'He was asking a lot of questions. I answered them without thinking ... I mean I was quite shaken up. I didn't think, but maybe I shouldn't have said so much. I'm normally careful Clive – you know I am. I don't gossip.'

'That was hardly gossip. I expect that incident was the talk of Sebleigh today. It's not every day a helicopter lands on the beach. And there were loads of people around to see. I don't know what you're worried about.'

'I just think there might have been something dodgy about that bloke.'

'Ahem ... ' Clive coughed. 'He's coming over.'

The man had gathered up his newspaper and jacket and brought his empty cup to the counter, where he faced a hostile looking Carmen, and Clive who was trying to compensate for her frostiness.

'Thank you sir – very kind of you,' Clive said as he took the cup.

'Thanks. Nice cup of tea.'

'You're welcome. Work in the town do you?' asked Clive nonchalantly as he wiped the counter. Carmen disappeared into the kitchen.

'No, just in the area for the day. I got caught up watching the helicopter rescue. I hope that young boy is alright.'

'Yes we all do. Nasty business.' The man hesitated.. should he just leave now? He had his story. But ... no ... he just couldn't resist stirring things up a little further while he had the opportunity ...

'Poor family. Actually someone was telling me that they've just won the lottery – hit the jackpot apparently?'

168

Clive immediately stopped cleaning the counter and froze. Carmen might be right about this man after all.

'I don't know anything about that. Who told you?' Clive said sounding irritated.

'Oh someone mentioned it to me …'

'Well I'm sure that money is the last thing on their minds with their little boy in hospital! Anyway - I've got a cafe to run, so if you'll excuse me …' Clive turned away and marched into the kitchen.

'Carmen,' he whispered. 'I think you're right about him… he was asking questions … that was definitely weird.'

'I know. I heard what he said to you. Something about a lottery win. Oh God, I hope he isn't a reporter.'

Chapter 20

Caroline sat on the edge of Harry's hospital bed encouraging him to eat some of his breakfast cereal. She'd slept very little in the bed which they provided for her in Harry's room, but she didn't care about the tiredness – she was just so happy to be listening to Harry chattering away, and to watch him pushing his food reluctantly around the bowl. She noted to herself that he looked pretty normal apart from his bandaged head. The doctors had said that they would probably need to keep an eye on Harry until at least the end of the week.

Carmen and Clive were opening up the Beachcomber Cafe.

'God Clive, I'm knackered today. Could have done with a lie-in.'

'Me too. It's not surprising after yesterday. It was quite an ordeal.'

'It was. I hope Caroline will get in touch and let us know how Harry's doing.'

'Oh! It's Poppy,' Clive said. 'She's early. No dog either.'

'Hello my dear,' Carmen smiled as Poppy strode in. 'Did you hear what happened yesterday?'

'Yes, David told me everything last night. I've brought the newspaper to show you – have you seen it? Your interview?'

'Did you say interview? What interview?' Carmen exclaimed.

'Well it's in here. You're famous now! I haven't read it properly yet. I just wanted to rush it round for you before I collect Matilda.'

'Let me see that,' Clive said crossly. 'It's in there? Why on earth would yesterday's incident be in a national newspaper? Why did you think we'd given an interview?'

'Hold on I'll find the page for you … There's a photo of you both …'

'A photo?!! Good grief!' Clive was getting more and more angry.

'Yes and I think there was something about Carmen feeling guilty, so I just assumed ... here it is.' Poppy pushed the paper across the table for Clive to see.

'Good God!' Clive said fuming. '*8 year old son of lottery winners in a dramatic helicopter rescue... fighting for his life.* Harry isn't eight is he? I thought he was older than that. Oh no! Carmen we know where this came from don't we? You were so right about that vile man. I wish I'd listened to you and slung him out the cafe when I had chance.' Clive read some more of the article.

'*Eight year old Harry Nightingale was seriously injured as he played in the rock pools on Sebleigh Bay beach and was only saved by the quick thinking of his six year old sister who ran for help.*' Clive scanned through the article getting more and more angry. 'What's this? *Mother felt guilty for letting the 6 and 8 year olds play on their own ....* They weren't on their own. What about the older brother? There were three of them and I'm sure they're older than six and eight ...Where did they get this nonsense from? *Clive Collyer* – spelt wrong! – *from the Beachcomber Cafe, called the police for help while his wife Carmen fretted over having advised the youngsters to go to the deep rock pools about a mile away from the cafe* A mile? It's a few hundred yards! This is outrageous!! How dare they tell these lies?!...' Clive carried on reading. '*It was touch and go whether Harry would survive the life-saving operation. Harry's parents, Caroline and Richard Nightingale, had recently won millions of pounds on the lottery and their first major purchase was a beach hut in Sebleigh Bay. Caroline found it hard to come to terms with winning so much money. She felt she didn't deserve it and she was convinced that Harry's accident was a form of punishment. What a load of utter bull...*'

171

'This is terrible!' Carmen was almost in tears. 'How could those bastards write that? And where did they get that photo of us? It's really old.'

'The photo's the least of our worries. Actually I remember that picture – I think it was taken when I was on the council – I don't know how they got hold of it though. Maybe it's on the Internet. Scumbags.'

'Oh my God Clive – Caroline is going to think that we spoke to the press!! Oh no!! We've got to talk to them.'

Richard lead Daniel and Mary Ann through the hospital building. They had really missed their mum and Harry and couldn't wait to see them again. They passed through a coffee shop area and a newsagents.

'Hang on a minute…' Daniel said. He walked over to the newspapers and picked one up. 'Dad!… Look!… it's about the Sebleigh Bay helicopter rescue.'

'Really? Has it made the local paper? That was quick. We'd better buy it then.' Richard said as he rummaged in his pocket for some change. 'Here you are. Do you want to go and get it?'

'Oh can I?' Mary-Ann asked excitedly. Daniel raised his eyebrows as he allowed Mary Ann to take the money and go and buy the paper.

A minute later Mary Ann came walking over studying the newspaper carefully. 'Dad, is this about Harry? And if it is… What does lott-er-y winner mean?' Richard's heart sank. He stopped in his tracks.

'Mary Ann – give it to me now!' Richard vaguely registered Mary Ann's shocked little face as he uncharacteristically snapped at her. But he couldn't help himself. He grabbed the paper and then marched forward towards the lift, as if snatching and folding one copy was going to stop the whole world finding out their secret. And how did the newspaper know? How did anyone know? They hadn't told a soul. He knew he could trust Caroline not to say anything because she was the one who desperately wanted to

172

keep it quiet. *Oh hold on a minute...it's not the local paper ... it's a national! Mind you, just because Mary-Ann saw the words lottery winner it's not necessarily to do with us. Perhaps it's just another headline on the front page? Perhaps I'm just being paranoid.* Richard hardly noticed the children's questions. 'Are we famous now Dad? ... Will there be a picture of Harry?... Am I in it?... Can we see it Dad?'

'Patience, patience... It may not even be about us. I'll have a look in a minute.' They all got in the lift and Richard told the children to push the button for the third floor. As the lift went up he quickly glimpsed the newspaper above the children's head.

Oh no... This is a nightmare ... How on earth am I going to break this to Caroline?

'I was right!' Carmen ranted. 'That nasty bastard...I knew he was a creep. I can always tell Clive. I know you don't take me seriously, but my intuition was correct.'

'Yes, yes you were right all along Carmen. Did you actually say something about feeling bad that you sent the children down to the big rock pools?'

'I'm not sure ...I might have done... I certainly didn't say they were a mile away though. Clive, does it actually say that they interviewed us? What will that family think? We help them out and then go to the newspaper.'

'Well what about the lottery win? If that's true it certainly didn't come from us. We didn't know about it. That must've come from somewhere else.'

'*Dad*!!' Harry said with excitement as Richard, Daniel and Mary-Ann came in. Harry had his arms out and Richard came over and held him and hugged him tightly with the newspaper folded in his hand.

'How are you feeling Harry?'

'I think I'm all right Dad – but I wouldn't want to stay here too long.'

'You're looking good – much better than yesterday. Mummy looks a bit tired though.'

'Nothing a good night's sleep won't fix,' Caroline said yawning. ' – or maybe make that a week of good night sleeps.' She and Richard kissed each other while Daniel and Mary-Ann settled on the bed on the other side of Harry. Richard spoke to the children,

'You two just catch up with Harry for a few minutes while Mum and I just need to go outside quickly. Talk very quietly to Harry.' Caroline looked confused but followed Richard outside noticing how concerned he looked. Once outside the room he held her hands.

'Darling, I'm really sorry but there is something I've got to tell you. You won't like it one bit, but I've got to tell you now before you hear it from someone else.'

'What is it? The doctors haven't said anything to you about Harry have they?'

'No no, it's nothing like that. I really think he's going to be fine, don't you? He's looking good – much more like his old self already.'

'Yes and I haven't had chance to tell you that the doctor looked at him this morning and was very happy with his progress.'

'Oh that's brilliant!'

'What's wrong then? Are you okay?'

'We are in the gutter press … a national newspaper … they reported Harry's accident and helicopter rescue. I haven't actually read it yet but I do know that somehow they've found out about our lottery win and told the whole world!' Caroline gasped and burst into tears. She cried on Richard's shoulder, while they hugged each other. Richard started welling up as well, but once he'd managed to compose himself he looked into Caroline's eyes, 'Do you know darling – it really doesn't matter what any stupid newspaper says, or if everyone knows. What happened to Harry yesterday was the worst thing I've ever experienced, and seeing his face just now and having him throw his arms

174

around me, and knowing he's going to be okay, was the best thing that's ever happened to me.'

'I know! I completely agree with you. I'm just so tired. I don't care about any of that any more. I just want to gather up the children and go home and sleep for about a week. But I'm just so happy that Harry is alright. Nothing else really matters does it?'

'Of course not. I'm so relieved to hear you say that. Love you.'

Chapter 21

Carmen was so upset about unknowingly contributing to the newspaper report about Harry's accident. She desperately wanted to apologise to Caroline and Richard but was just too distraught to phone them. Clive called Caroline's mobile instead and admitted to them how they had been tricked by the reporter. To his relief, Caroline said that they didn't care at all what had happened or what was in the newspaper, and explained that they had also been conned, probably by the same man, so she completely understood. She said that Harry was on the mend and that was all that mattered. Clive invited them all to come into the cafe any time and have a meal on the house.

Richard encouraged Caroline to take up the offer as she had been the one who had stayed in hospital most of the time with Harry and could do with a break and a treat.

A couple of days later Caroline arrived at the Beachcomber Cafe, after going back to the hotel for a luxurious soak in the enormous jacuzzi in their suite. Richard was at the hospital with the three children, playing a game of cards to keep Harry occupied.

When Caroline walked in through the door of the Beachcomber Cafe, Carmen caught sight of her and rushed over to give her a hug and promptly burst into tears.

'Please don't feel bad, Carmen. We are just so grateful the way you and Clive helped us on the day. The doctors actually told us that if the air ambulance hadn't arrived so quickly, things could've been much worse.'

'It's so brilliant that Harry is doing well,' Carmen said as she pulled herself together. 'What a relief. Come in and sit down and we'll get you something. What would you like? Anything at all?'

It was late in the day and the cafe was quiet so Carmen and Clive were able to sit down with Caroline while she had fish and chips and they all shared a bottle of prosecco. Caroline told them both all about how well they had been looked after in the hospital - receiving exemplary care.

'We've been thinking...' Clive explained, 'that we'd like to organise some sort of charity fundraising event for the air ambulance and possibly for the children's ward at the hospital as well. I'm part of the local Rotary club, and I've been on the council in the past, so I have a lot of useful contacts - local businesses – that sort of thing. I was considering an auction maybe? I reckon I could persuade quite a few businesses to give generous donations. I've already put out a few feelers and I'm keeping everything crossed that I might even be able to get a helicopter ride donated.'

'That would be amazing!' Caroline explained enthusiastically. 'Do you know I've always wanted to attend an auction? I was saying that to Richard just the other day. We've both been talking about it and saying how we really want to give something back. We are so grateful for the help we received. As you know - well as the whole world knows now - we won some lottery money, so there's nothing we'd like more than to put some of it to good use.'

'That's great!' Clive said smiling enthusiastically. 'We will keep in touch with you obviously and let you know what we organise. And of course we'd love to be kept up-to-date on how Harry is doing.'

Chapter 22

Richard was driving through the countryside with Daniel beside him and Mary-Ann in the back of the car. It was a warm evening and the sun was slowly setting. They had received the most wonderful news that Harry was being allowed to return home from hospital tomorrow, following one last check up with the doctor in the morning. Richard had explained to Mary-Ann that he had a surprise for her - a special treat lined up for her this evening - and that Daniel could come along too. Despite lots of excitement and questions from the children, he refused to tell them where they were going.

After a drive down a long narrow country lane, they pulled into a car park in the woods. As they got out of the car, they could hear gentle music in the distance. There was a pathway lit with lanterns and fairy lights and a large sign hanging from a tree saying "Welcome to the Enchanted Glade".

'Are we going down there Dad?' asked Mary Ann.

'Looks like it!' Dad replied taking Mary Ann's hand. Daniel held his Dad's other hand and the three of them set off enthusiastically along the winding path.

As they walked through the woods they could hear wind chimes amongst the rustling leaves. The music got a little louder as they approached a gathering. The instruments sounded like a lute, some flutes and some hand drums which were mingling with the inviting sounds of happy chatter and singing. A warm glow appeared in front of them as they began to make out the shapes of people adorned with all sorts of incredible costumes. Delicious aromas were wafting towards them from the food and drinks.

'Look! There are fairies there!' Mary Ann said with a huge smile on her face.

178

'Wow!' Daniel joined in. 'Look at that man's antlers!'

There was a large crackling fire in the clearing in front of them creating a golden light which lit up the faces of fairies with their gossamer wings of all different colours. The men wore beautiful velvet cloaks and antlers made from driftwood. Children were running around wearing beautiful headdresses made of flowers and leaves and everyone had the most incredible make up highlighted with stars and glitter.

A lady fairy wearing a deep green velvet dress came over to greet Richard, Mary-Ann and Daniel.

'Welcome my lovelies ... I'm Fae.' She reached out and shook hands with each of them, asking their names.

'Oh yes ... Mary Ann, Daniel and Richard... We've been expecting you. We heard you were coming to join us.'

Mary Ann could hardly contain her excitement.

'We're going to join you?' she asked.

'Oh yes!' replied Fae. 'Of course. Come with me and we'll find you some costumes.'

Within a short time, Richard and Daniel were sporting sumptuous velvet cloaks of rich green woodland shades. Daniel wore a golden crown while Richard had a headdress of driftwood and ivy. Mary-Ann was wearing a beautiful pair of sparkling wings which seemed to change colours in the flickering light of the fire. She was sitting on a wooden stool having her makeup expertly applied by a stunning fairy. The clearing in the woods was marked with hundreds of glowing lanterns hanging in the trees all around them. A long table made from reclaimed wood was laid out with an enticing feast, along with gold goblets and bowls of fruit. The whole table was scattered with rose petals.

An elderly storyteller with a long grey beard and big pointy ears was entertaining a group of children who were gathered around him sitting on blankets, enthralled by the magical tale he was reading from a large book with an engraved wooden cover.

Nearby a lady fairy sat on a tree stump at a small wooden table laying out tarot cards for a man dressed as a fawn who sat opposite her.

When Mary Ann's makeup was complete she, Daniel and Richard were fitted with pixie ears to complete their makeovers. They were then invited to join in with everyone and immerse themselves in the life of the enchanted glade.

They made their way over to the group of musicians in the corner. The music stopped briefly, and the children were invited to play the drums. They were shown how to tap out a simple but effective rhythm, which they continued in time with the other musicians.

Throughout the evening they joined in with many of the different activities including making friendship bracelets from grasses and flowers, creating stories with the others, dancing around the fire, chatting to everyone, and joining in with the sumptuous fairy feast.

As the sun finally set completely, giving way to the night sky with a bright full moon shining amongst the stars, Mary-Ann chatted happily to another small fairy-girl sitting next to her - both of them too excited to eat much. Daniel who had just finished his strawberries and cream turned to Richard.

'I'm surprised to say this Dad, but I've had the *best* time tonight. Perhaps we could come back again next year with Mum and Harry?'

'Yes that's a nice thought. It really has been very magical, hasn't it? And Mary-Ann of course is in her element. I don't think we will ever forget this evening.'

Chapter 23

After a full day of photography, starting with an early morning shoot of a milking session at the local dairy, David climbed the stairs to his flat carrying his heavy camera bag and tripod. He'd really enjoyed the day but was looking forward to kicking his shoes off and relaxing with a cold beer and a sandwich. As he put the key in his front door he noticed a handwritten note stuck in his letter box. He unfolded it.

It's July!
No Spikes in my hair!
I won the bet.
You're coming dancing.
I'm calling for you tonight at 7 o'clock sharp.

Px

'I can't believe you talked me into this,' David said to Poppy on their arrival at The Grand Hotel for David's first, and only, he assumed, jive class.'
'You'll enjoy it. Anyway I didn't talk you into it – it was a bet.'
'Well that's alright then,' he said sarcastically. 'Do we go in at the main entrance at the front?'
'No, round here, there's a side entrance for the classes.' They found their way round to the side of the vast Victorian building where crowds of people from the previous dancing class were just leaving.

'Those people have just done the ballroom class,' Poppy explained to David. 'I tried it once but I much prefer the jive.' As they approached the entrance which had a large board outside marked 'Jive and Ballroom Dancing', David suddenly called out,

'Poppy! Look over there.' David pointed towards the grounds behind the hotel.

'Where? What?' As Poppy looked puzzled, David sped off in a sprint in the opposite direction, back towards the road.

'David!' Poppy called, exasperated. His feet slid to a halt on the gravel. 'Honestly! It's like dealing with a badly trained dog!' They both giggled as David came back and Poppy pushed him in through the side door. David pretended to stumble, making it look like Poppy had shoved him really hard into the corridor. Poppy tried not to laugh as they walked along the corridor.

'Everyone will be so pleased to see another man here tonight. There's never enough to go round. Remember what I said – you don't have to dance with me – just share yourself around.'

'But I keep telling you I can't dance at all!'

'You're here to learn. That's the whole point.' A thin stern looking middle-aged woman was walking towards them – her dark hair tied back severely in a bun.

'Good evening Poppy,' she said in an intimidating voice which matched her appearance.

'Hello Margaret. May I introduce you to David? David, this is Margaret, our teacher.'

'Good evening,' he said as he shook her hand awkwardly thinking that Margaret seemed to look down her nose at him.

'So you've come to join us have you David?'

'For my sins, yes.'

'Very good,' she replied without amusement. 'Do go into the ballroom – Poppy will show you the ropes.'

'Bloody hell Poppy,' David whispered as they went through the door. 'She looks more like some harsh Russian ballet mistress. I thought this was supposed to be fun!'

'Relax,' Poppy said, unphased by his negative attitude. 'She comes across a bit scary but she's fine really ... well ... sort of...'

They paid their money to a young girl who was sitting at a table by the door, and then walked across the ballroom towards some seats.

'Did you see the way she looked at you?' asked Poppy.

'Yes, like something she'd just scraped off the bottom of her shoe!'

'No, not Margaret, the girl at the table – she couldn't keep her eyes off you – obviously fancies you.' David pretended to look smug and cocky. Then he looked around at the other people who were arriving and said,

'It's probably just a novelty for her to see a bloke who's not drawing a pension in this place. Either that or she's amused because she thinks I look like Harry Potter ... yawn yawn.'

'Don't be silly – plenty of young people come here as well, you'll see.' Poppy lightened her voice, 'It's a beautiful ballroom though isn't it – you must admit.'

'Yes it is actually.' He said begrudgingly. 'Those chandeliers are pretty impressive – mind you, I hope they're fixed on well,' he said as he pretended to duck. Poppy led them to some chairs along the side of the room and took off her jacket and hung it over the back of a chair.

'Nice frock!' David observed. 'Didn't know you had a pair of legs.'

'No, well they don't see daylight very often. Thought I'd at least try and look the part tonight. Mind you, I usually end up dancing as a man!'

'Professional looking dance shoes you've got on as well. The same as Miss Stiff and Starchy's in the corridor.'

'I only bought them a couple of weeks ago – not sure they've helped my dancing much.' They sat down and watched the other participants arriving and chatted to a few people who Poppy knew. About sixty people had arrived by the time Margaret returned. She took to the platform along the other side of the room and spoke through her microphone. She welcomed everyone to The Grand Hotel Ballroom and asked them to get into pairs. Despite Poppy encouraging David to share himself around he insisted on staying firmly by her side. Margaret explained that as there were quite a few new faces tonight they would start with some basic steps. A young couple stood on the platform with her and demonstrated the moves. When it was their turn to have a go Poppy took David's hand and was surprised to see that he had no trouble following the steps.

'Well done,' she whispered, 'It took me six weeks to get the hang of that. You're not having me on are you? Did you learn to dance at university?'

'No. I swear I've never done this before. Well it's hardly difficult so far is it? ... Just a step here and step there, and a ...'

'Poppy!' said Margaret sternly, making her jump. 'Have you and your partner mastered the sequence?'

'Yes thank you Margaret.'

'Perhaps you'd like to demonstrate?'

'Oh ... err.'

'Yes sure,' said David taking Poppy's hand and leading her into the sequence they'd just learnt.

'Thank you,' Margaret said with slight sarcasm, 'It's quite helpful if people don't chatter, so that everyone can concentrate.' David pulled a face of mock terror and Poppy was trying not to laugh – she didn't dare! Poppy found herself wondering why it hadn't occurred to her before now how hilarious this could turn out to be with David in tow.

'We'll try that with the music now. Thank you Adele.' Margaret said nodding to the young woman who had been taking the money. The music started up and Margaret's voice was heard, 'and five, six, seven, eight, step back, step ...'. Poppy always felt a huge thrill as the music began

184

and everyone in the ballroom began to move in unison, however simple the steps might be. She and David managed the sequence surprisingly well.

'Well done everyone. Gentlemen, remember to lift your arms high enough for your partner to turn underneath. Let's begin again. Ready? And five, six, seven, eight, step, step ...'. Once this section was practised several times some new steps were introduced and repeated without the music several times.

'I can't believe how easily you're picking this up David,' Poppy whispered, glancing round to make sure Margaret wouldn't hear.

'Bring on the music,' David said smugly, taking Poppy's hand and waiting enthusiastically for the track to begin.

'And five six seven eight ...' Once David had swirled Poppy round, he continued straight into the second sequence. However, Poppy unfortunately thought that they were going to repeat the first one, so as they moved in different directions she stumbled and somehow managed to plant the thin heal of her dance shoe straight into David's ankle.

'Arghhh!' he yelled. David let go of Poppy and grabbed his foot – hopping round in a circle holding it.

'Oh David, I'm sorry ... are you okay? ... I got confused and went the wrong way.' Several nearby couples had stopped dancing and were asking David if he was alright.

'I'm a nurse,' a friendly smiling middle aged lady said to David, 'Let me take a look at that foot.' Margaret noticed the interruption.

'Carry on everyone,' she said as she walked over towards the group of people surrounding David. When she realised that it was Poppy and David at the centre of the commotion she raised her eyebrows as if to say 'I might have guessed.'

'Is there a problem?' she asked unsympathetically as she watched the nurse who had sat David down on the floor and was now lifting up his trouser leg and pulling his sock down. She examined his ankle and foot carefully and said,

'It feels okay. I think it will be pretty bruised, but I don't think anything's broken. Let's see if you can walk on it shall we.' David stood up and limped around in a circle - his walking gradually returning to normal. He spotted Poppy's distraught face, and suddenly felt guilty for making such a fuss.

'It's okay. Err ... it's fine. Just a bit of a shock that's all ... having my ankle speared.'

Margaret came forward. 'David isn't it? Are you alright?'

'Yes ... thank you. Sorry about that. Right! Where were we?'

The class continued and David did his best to ignore his sore ankle. After a while everyone was divided up into three groups according to their level of experience, so that they could practise different dance moves. At the end of the evening each group had the whole floor to themselves to show what they'd learnt while the other groups sat and watched. When David and Poppy were sitting out, David whispered,

'Have you noticed that lady outside the window over there, looking in from the gardens?'

'Oh yes. People often do that. I think they take a walk in the hotel grounds, hear the music, and then like to watch us making fools of ourselves.'

'She's been there a while. I feel like beckoning her to come in a join us.'

'No don't! She'd be embarrassed. Probably doesn't realise we can see her.'

'The class must be nearly finished now isn't it?'

'Yes pretty well. How's the foot?'

'Oh it's fine. We just need to call in at the hospital on the way back ...' Poppy elbowed him playfully in the ribs and giggled,

'I was just going to ask you if you'd like to go for a drink in the Seaview Bar afterwards? I think I owe you one,' Poppy asked hoping to change the subject.

'Is that the one upstairs?'

186

'Yes. Some of the others go in there as well after the class.'

'Okay, thanks. If I can make it up the stairs. I'll have to see how I get on with one leg.' Poppy shook her head in despair, but David hadn't finished teasing her. 'Will the nurse be coming? Perhaps she can give me some treatment while we have a drink?'

'Oh goodness, I'm never going to hear the last of this.'

'Watch out! The dragon's about to make an announcement.' As the music finished and the last group of dancers – the more advanced people – relaxed and smiled at each other, having obviously thoroughly enjoyed themselves, Margaret addressed everyone.

'Thank you very much ladies and gentlemen. You've all done very well indeed. I'm sure you're all pleased with what you've learnt tonight. The new people danced particularly well. I'll see you all next week. Give yourselves a round of applause.' Everyone clapped.

'Oh she seemed almost human then,' David said.

'I think she's okay actually – just a bit old fashioned and takes her dancing rather seriously.'

'You're telling me!'

Poppy and David made their way to the bar upstairs with David of course fooling around on the stairs pretending to struggle with his injured ankle and Poppy pretending she wasn't with him. They entered the Seaview Bar and went to get some drinks. David leaned on the bar and said quietly to Poppy,

'Don't make it obvious, but do you see that bloke standing at the end of the bar?'

'The one with the brown shirt?'

'Yes. Let's go and sit down and I'll tell you something about him.' They made their way to a table at the opposite end of the room and sat down.

'He wasn't at dancing was he?' Poppy asked.

'No, definitely not. I would have noticed him. He's been in the cafe and few times recently, and Carmen can't stand him.'

'That's not like her.'

'Exactly. His name's Seamus Booth. He's a local politician. She says she doesn't trust him, and that he acts suspiciously.'

'Really? What does he do?'

'She says she can't put a finger on it, but he's not the usual type to come in the cafe. He's brought different people in with him and they always sit there talking quietly and having a good look round. She's convinced he's got an agenda.'

'Oh – intriguing. Well Carmen is very perceptive about things like that. She's good at sussing people out.'

'Yes I agree.'

'Does she know him then?'

'Oh yes – I should have said – they go back a long way. He's well known in the town. He's very involved with the Chamber of Trade and he's also on the local council, and he owns half the businesses in the town.'

'Really?'

'Well – I exaggerated a bit. He owns the big arcade on the seafront, a hotel, several shops in the town - and probably others that I can't remember. There's been a lot of criticism of him for making important decisions on the council which benefit his own businesses a bit too much. I don't take much notice of politics to be honest, but I know he went to great lengths to stop another arcade opening on the seafront because he didn't want the competition.

'Oh, so has he been in the cafe lately?'

'Yes he has, and Carmen's convinced he's up to something. She really hates him though – I've noticed a couple of times that she even avoids serving him. I saw her make an excuse to go to the kitchen and she got Ellie to serve so that she didn't have to talk to him.'

'Strange. Why would she do that?'

188

'I know. It's odd isn't it. But, can you keep quiet about this conversation though? Strictly between you and me.'

Yes of course. I'll keep an eye out for him. I'm always in the cafe – as you know!'

'Yes. You should ask Carmen to introduce a loyalty card system. You'd do well. You'd soon fill your card up with stamps!'

'I know. Mind you, Carmen and Clive are really sweet... they often give me a free one. Poppy looked along the bar and saw Seamus Booth still standing there. 'He looks quite arrogant doesn't he? Showing off to his friends.'

'Oh he is. Definitely. He always plays to the audience – likes to be the centre of attention. I guess that might be one reason why Carmen is suspicious, because he's been talking unusually quietly in the cafe. He normally likes to make himself heard. Another thing … he apparently badgers all his friends into standing for council. The councillors are not allowed to vote on matters which they have a vested interest in. You know Seamus owns the arcade on the seafront, well he's probably not allowed to vote on issues relating to the seafront, but to get round that he instructs his council chums to vote his way. Mind you he came a cropper recently because his mate disagreed with him and voted against him. They fell out badly over it and don't talk to each other now. I don't think he's got quite so many people on his side any more. People are beginning to realise what he's like.'

'Watch out – I think he's on the move. Change the subject.'

At that moment the nurse who had helped David with his foot happened to walk by and spotted David and Poppy.

'How's your foot?' she asked David. He pulled a very over the top face pretending to be in excruciating pain.

'Oh here we go!' Poppy said raising her eyes to the ceiling, '*Again*!'

'Has he been giving you a hard time Poppy?'

'Just a bit!' she said sarcastically.

189

'Oh it's not *all* that bad,' David finally conceded, 'I think I'll live. Seriously I must apologise for inflicting my feet on you. It's not really what you came here for.'

'Oh not at all,' she said with a generous smile. 'If it troubles you go and get it checked out, but I think it's alright because you seemed to be dancing on it alright. Actually, I noticed you seemed to be doing very well for your first time here – just wait and see what you can achieve next week.'

'Next week? Why? What's happening next week?'

'Is he always like this?' she asked Poppy.

'Yes,' Poppy replied. 'Worse!'

Chapter 24

Rose was sitting in the striped deckchair on the veranda of the beach hut called Alice with her foil covered sandwiches in her lap. The beach hut was sheltering her from the gentle breeze as she looked out at the distant sea. She'd been waiting for a nice day like today to come down here again and take advantage of her niece Caroline's kind offer to visit 'Alice' whenever she felt like it.

Rose often marvelled at what a thoughtful woman Caroline was, unlike her mother Lillian – Rose's sister. It gave her so much pleasure to see Caroline happily settled with her husband Richard and their three delightful children. Caroline deserved all the happiness in the world after Lillian had brought her up so badly. Rose lost count of the times she'd had to pick up the pieces of Lillian's dreadful parenting. She would have given anything to have a beautiful daughter like Caroline, and she hated the way her sister had treated her precious child.

When Rose heard about dear little Harry's accident on the rocks at Sebleigh Bay she prayed and prayed that he would be alright. She couldn't bear to think of Caroline going through any more suffering. Rose thanked God when Harry recovered from his head injury. She wondered whether Caroline and her family would actually want to have any more holidays down here after that horrifying incident, so she decided to make the most of the delightful little beach hut in case Caroline and Richard decided to sell it in the near future.

Rose turned her foil-wrapped sandwiches over but didn't get round to unwrapping them. Once again her thoughts drifted to the day she spent here with Ivy and Doris. Yes ... *that* day. It would have been such fun if only dear Ivy hadn't made that revealing comment about the past. When Rose first heard those horrible words 'I saw Doris kissing Ernest under the pier,' she didn't realise just how much they were going to affect her over the coming weeks. At first she told herself Ivy had got it wrong. It must be down to her dementia. Of course she couldn't have seen Ernest kissing Doris under the pier. It was Rose who Ernest was in love with – and who had courted for several years, and who said he would always love her. They were besotted with each other and would surely have got married had not his parents decided to move the family away. That's what she had believed throughout her life. She had never considered that he might have been disloyal to her. *Never*! Surely Ivy must have remembered incorrectly or got muddled. Rose had been so looking forward to meeting up with Ivy and Doris at the beach that day, even though there was a heavy sadness hanging over them because they were slowly losing Ivy to her dementia. She and Doris felt it would be so good for Ivy to come out and enjoy herself.

For a couple of days after their meeting at the beach, Rose had tried to convince herself that Ivy had made a mistake, but as time went on she was unable to block out that split second of awkwardness and embarrassment she noticed on Doris's face as Ivy made that revelation. That look said everything. It was then followed by several attempts by Doris to change the topic of conversation as quickly as possible.

Rose had spent most of her life yearning for Ernest. Even in recent years she would sometimes dream that he would return to Sebleigh Bay and sweep her off her feet once again. Of course deep down she didn't really believe that they would be reunited, but it was just a dream she liked to have to distract herself from life's ups and downs, and she'd been dreaming it for so long it had become a habit that she couldn't break – or maybe, didn't want to break. What woman didn't like the idea of a happy ending with the perfect man?

There had of course been other boyfriends over the years, but no one had measured up to Ernest. No one had stolen her heart the way he had when they were both so young. There were so many happy memories: walks down the pier, picnics on the beach, and dancing together in the beautiful ballroom at The Grand Hotel. She went for a walk in the grounds there last night and looked in the window at the jive class. What splendid fun they were all having!

When Ernest had moved away with his parents, they wrote to each other for a while, but the letters gradually petered out as he became more and more settled in his new life.

Now – more than 50 years later – she'd found out that her boyfriend and her best friend had betrayed her and she had to accept that her relationship with him maybe hadn't been quite as perfect as she'd always thought. How stupid she'd been. He was an adult when he'd moved away with his parents – a young man. Of course if he'd chosen to he could have found a way to stay in Sebleigh Bay and be with her, or he could have returned at a later date. But until now she'd chosen not to see it that way.

And how did she feel now about her lifelong friend? Doris had always been there for her – they'd never lost touch. Surely their friendship shouldn't go wrong now over some silly incident that happened when they were so young. *We all did daft things when we were young didn't we? But was it just one incident? Or had their betrayal gone on for some time?* That was a truly painful thought. Rose felt such a fool now as she'd never hidden the fact that she'd always held a special place in her heart for Ernest. Oh how she wished now that she hadn't confided in Doris.

Tears filled her eyes, and not for the first time since that day at the beach hut with Doris and Ivy, but as her vision blurred and she started to reach for a tissue she suddenly found herself involuntarily jumping to her feet.

No! I shan't cry. I won't! I've wasted enough of my life on a silly dream and I'm not going to waste another minute.

193

Feeling a sudden inner strength, she picked up her bundle of sandwiches and marched over to a nearby rubbish bin. She ceremoniously threw the sandwiches into the bin. *I do NOT want a miserable pile of squashed sandwiches for my lunch! I deserve better than that. I'm going to go along to that cafe down the end and treat myself to the best hot meal they have and the tastiest piece of cake I can find. From now on, everything changes. Chin up Rose!*

'Hello there. What takes your fancy?' Carmen asked the tall elegant lady who was standing at the counter studying the menu.

'Hello,' Rose answered. 'Well, I was considering the curry but I think the fish and chips just smell too good to resist, so I think I'll have ... plaice and chips please.'

'Plaice and chips it is then. And would you like a drink to go with that?'

'A cup of tea ...' Rose paused mid sentence as she caught sight of a waitress bringing out some glasses of red wine on a tray, 'Actually, no. I'll have a glass of red wine please,' she stated decisively.

'Plaice, chips and red wine then.'

'Lovely combination,' giggled Rose.

'You won't regret it,' Carmen smiled warmly.

'I can't wait.' Rose handed over her money.

'Thank you my love. I don't think I know you. Are you on holiday?'

'No, I live just up the hill actually, but I'm ashamed to say I've never been in here before. What a lovely place you have though,' she said as she looked around. 'I had no idea. I've really been missing out. My niece has one of the beach huts and she lets me use it, so I'll be popping down here more often now hopefully.'

'The huts are nice aren't they. Where abouts is yours?'

'It's number eighteen.'

'Oh I know.' Carmen's heart lurched. 'That must be your family with the boy who had the accident on the rocks?'

194

'Yes. Oh you must have a good memory to know who owns all the huts.'

'No, I just remember that one ... because of the accident,' she added quickly. 'The little girl, Mary-Ann, she came running into the cafe to ask for help, and it was my Clive who called the rescue services and went down to the rocks to help out, while I took Mary-Ann to break the news to her parents.' Carmen pulled a face, remembering what a horrible task that had been.

'Oh, it's all falling into place now. Yes Caroline told me all about you. She said you were both wonderful.'

'Not at all. Anyone would have done the same. How is the little lad now?'

'Oh he's really well now thank goodness. He didn't remember much about it, and I think the other children actually suffered more because they were a bit traumatised by it all, you know, seeing him like that – and his parents of course.'

'Oh the parents must have gone through hell. They did keep in touch with us afterwards and let us know he was doing well.'

'Good. Anyway, I'd better get out of the way and let you serve some more customers. But I'm so pleased I've met you.' Rose smiled and went over to an empty table by the window and sat down. Shortly afterwards Clive came over with her glass of red wine.

'One red wine?'

'Thank you.'

'Carmen was just telling me that you're from the family of the lad Harry who hurt himself on the rocks.'

'Yes, that's right, I'm his great Aunt. Caroline told me how wonderful you and your wife were.'

'Oh we just called for help that's all. We were just so glad he was alright – that's all that matters. And the kids were brilliant – little Mary-Ann who came and got us – she's only about seven isn't she?'

'Mary Ann, yes. Oh I'm so proud of them all – they're a lovely family, and they're very kind to their old Aunt!' Clive laughed.

'Not so much of the old now! Well, I expect you know all about the a charity auction I've been organising?' he said glancing over at the kitchen.

'Oh yes. Caroline and Richard are thrilled. I think they are hoping to attend. I know they are also keen to give something back after what happened.'

'Yes, I'm buzzing about the whole thing to be honest. I've got some really excellent lots lined up. I've been able to persuade some local businesses to make some fantastic donations. Oh, I'm sorry. I'm going to have to go… bit busy in the kitchen.'

'Of course. I'm so pleased to meet you though. Thank you for what you did for my family.'

'You're very welcome.' Clive picked up some empties from a nearby table and rushed off to the kitchen. Rose sipped her red wine as she looked out to sea. Well this is pleasant. A change of scene, and some friendly chatter with that delightful couple who run the cafe. Life seems a whole lot better already.

As she put her glass of wine down, a familiar face appeared on the forecourt outside the cafe. Rose recognised him as the charming man with the metal detector who had been with his grandson and brought the bracelet with 'Alice' engraved on it to the hut. She thought once again how distinguished he looked. *I bet Ernest doesn't look that good now. No! I'm not thinking about him anymore.* She watched the man come into the cafe holding his metal detector. *George! That was his name. The same as his grandson who he was obviously so proud of.* When it was his turn to be served, Rose watched him having a chat at the counter with Carmen about metal detecting. *There's something very nice about him - I'll have to say hello to him and ask him what he's found lately.*

196

A small table became available close to the counter by the door just as George paid for his meal. He carefully leaned his metal detector and spade up against the wall and then sat down and read his newspaper. She decided that she would say hello to him on the way out. Rose tucked into her delicious plaice and chips when it was delivered to her table, and she felt warm and confident as the wine slipped down nicely. As she finished her meal Carmen was clearing some tables and she came over to Rose.

'Did you enjoy that?'

'Oh yes. Very good thank you. I don't know when I've ever had such nice plaice.'

'Yes, it's all locally sourced – our customers are rarely disappointed.'

'I'm not surprised.'

'Send our love to your family won't you.'

'Oh yes of course I will.'

'We were quite taken with little Mary-Ann. Bright kid. Loved the fairies from the festival.'

'Oh I heard all about the fairies. They really caught her imagination didn't they. She has her own wings and outfits now.'

'I expect you know that Clive is in the process of organising a charity auction to raise money for the air ambulance and the children's ward.'

'Oh yes. That will be marvellous. Caroline and Richard are very interested.'

As Rose chatted to Carmen, to her disappointment, she noticed George in the background getting up and leaving. She wanted to go too so she could catch up with him outside, but Carmen was in full flow.

'Well I expect we'll see them again sometime when they next come to the beach hut.' Rose saw George out of the window walking back in the direction of the carpark.

'Well I'm so pleased I've met you and your husband.' Rose said, trying to wind things up quickly, just in case there

197

was a chance that George was still around. 'I'll remember you to Caroline, and I'll see you again soon no doubt.'

'Take care my love.'

'And you.'

Rose left as quickly as she could and looked for George. As she suspected he and his metal detector were way in the distance, on their way back to the car park. Oh well. She'd still had a nice time. She loved the cafe and the owners were so welcoming. She'd have to come back again soon. What a tonic it had been.

Well that turned out to be the start of many regular trips to the Beachcomber Cafe for Rose. At least once a week she would walk down to the coast and pay a visit to 'Alice' to check that everything was in order. If the weather was good she would get a deckchair out and spend some time there. She would then walk along to the Beachcomber Cafe and enjoy lunch or a cup of tea and some friendly conversation with Carmen and Clive. She soon began to notice that several of the locals visited regularly as well. She was amused by the young woman with the auburn hair who kept turning up with different dogs, and also the young photographer lad who Carmen seemed very fond of. He always seemed to make everybody laugh.

Rose often wished that George would turn up again but unfortunately after several weeks she hadn't seen him since the day she first came in for her fish and chips. After a while she came to the conclusion that he probably wasn't local, and that she wouldn't see him again.

Chapter 25

One Monday morning Rose was in a very cheerful mood after spending a delightful weekend visiting Caroline and her family. She had taken some photos of the children and got them printed at the photographic shop and she decided she would go and show them to Carmen and Clive, as they were always asking about the family, and she thought it would be particularly nice for them to see a picture of Harry looking fit and well. As usual she visited the beach hut first. She loved looking after the hut and keeping it nice for Caroline. The weather was good today and Rose enjoyed watching the people and dogs who were milling about on the beach.

She entered the cafe clutching her envelope full of photos and was quite thrown when she noticed George sitting by the window with his metal detector and spade propped up against the wall. It was fairly quiet in the cafe so she felt it wouldn't be difficult to go up to him and re-introduce herself. He was engrossed in his newspaper and his lunch and didn't appear to notice her. Carmen welcomed her as usual.

'Rose my love – how are you today?'

'I'm very well thank you Carmen. Actually I brought some photos to show you if you'd like to see them. I visited Caroline at the weekend - they all send you their love by the way. I took some pictures of the children and I told them I would show them to you.'

'Oh lovely – I'll come and have a look in a minute. What would you like? Your usual tea?'

'Yes please.'

'Okay love. Take a seat and I'll bring it over.' Rose paid for her tea and walked over towards the window holding her bag and packet of photographs and she placed them down on the table behind George's. He had just finished his meal and was reading his newspaper. She had butterflies in her tummy – a feeling she'd not felt for many years. She knew she must speak to him straight away before she lost her nerve and changed her mind. She was just about to say hello when a huge commotion broke out as two large, shaggy, grey and white dogs entered the cafe and shot across the room followed by the young dog walking lady with the auburn hair who looked absolutely distraught.

'Bobby! Bounce! Come here. Now! Oh Carmen I'm so sorry - I accidentally let go of the leads when I opened the door. I shouldn't have brought them in.' One of the big fluffy dogs had its front paws up on George's table – big sandy feet which were all over his newspaper. Poppy was there in a flash. She grabbed his collar as she held on to him.

'Bounce! Bounce!' she yelled at the other dog. 'Come here now!' She was trying to apologise to George at the same time. 'Oh I am so so sorry. They're not my dogs – I walk them - It's my job you see. I don't know how I managed to let go of their leads. I'm just going to take them outside and tie them up and then I will come and apologise some more.' George brushed the sand from his newspaper, recovering from the surprise of the intrusion.

'Don't worry - no harm done. Look why don't you give me that dog while you go and grab the other one.' Poppy passed the lead to George, thanked him and rushed off to grab Bounce. Rose was impressed by how tolerant and helpful George was. Many people wouldn't have taken things so calmly. Clive came out from the kitchen and looked around the cafe.

'Everything under control there?' he asked.

'It is now,' Poppy said breathlessly. 'I'm so sorry Clive. We've caused havoc. I'm just taking them outside.' George lead Bounce outside following Poppy. Carmen calmly walked around the cafe apologising to people and then she brought Rose's tea over.

'Sorry, I nearly forgot in all the kafuffle! I do apologise for the disturbance.'

'Yes, it's all happening round here today,' Rose smiled. She was aware of George standing outside for quite awhile chatting to Poppy who was desperately trying to cling onto the two big dogs. Eventually, George came back into the cafe, but just at that moment Carmen came over to look at Rose's photos. *Oh dear - another opportunity missed to speak to George.* As she showed Carmen her photos she noticed Clive in the background offering George another cup of coffee on the house. George thanked him and said there was no need. As he gathered up his metal detector to leave he looked over at Carmen and thanked her for the meal. Rose caught his eye just for a second and gave him her best smile, and he smiled back.

As Carmen finished looking at Rose's photos, the cafe door opened and she looked over towards the door with a big grin.

'Oh it's David. How are you?' She got up and walked towards him.

'In good shape. Very good shape in fact.' David thrust his arm forward, with a magazine in his hand. 'Da daaaa!'

'What's that? Oh!' Carmen stood stock still open mouthed. 'Not the beach huts already?'

'Yep!'

'The Sunday magazine? You didn't tell me it was out this soon. Was it yesterday?'

'It was!'

'Oh David! I could hit you sometimes ... it's too late for me to go and buy a copy now.'

'No need. Present.' He said handing over the magazine to Carmen.

'Oh look! It's on the cover too! Oh David, this is fantastic.'

'And if you go to page 43 ...' David said waving his arm with the air of a magician. Carmen put the magazine on a table and carefully leafed through it and found the beach hut article with David's photos. She gasped:

'David! All these photos ... they're wonderful.' She gasped again. 'It's Jem's hut in the snow! Number eighteen ... Alice ... oh you've made it look so beautiful. Oh well done David. Can I keep this?'

'Of course.'

'Clive, come and look at this!'

'I was wondering what all the fuss was about? I thought perhaps one of Poppy's dogs was giving birth in the cafe.'

'It's David's beach huts in the Sunday magazine. Are your hands clean?'

'Oh excellent. No they're not. You show me.'

'Oh look!' he said. 'Jem's hut – trust him to have a starring role even after he's gone, how typical is that?' Carmen and David looked surprised and embarrassed by Clive's outburst. Clive, realising what he'd said, and not wanting to spoil David's good news, added quickly, 'Just kidding – it's a stunning photo - in the snow no less. Well done David. I had no idea you'd make the huts look so good.' David took the opportunity to change the subject.

'Actually ... there's more good news. As a result of this, I've already got another interesting commission – I've been asked to take photos of the wreckage of the damaged pier.'

'Really?' asked Carmen excitedly. 'Who's that for?'

'You know the organisation that's trying to raise funds to rebuild it, well they've asked for some arty looking shots to use for their publicity.'

'Oh yes,' Clive said. 'They keep having articles in the free sheet – they're completely deluded - they'll never raise that sort of money though – it'll cost millions.'

'Clive, you're in a very cynical mood today.' Carmen said quietly, wishing he'd keep his views to himself. Clive clapped his hands together.

'Right! Celebration! Let's get David a drink. Well done you! Splendid job.' Carmen sat down and looked at the magazine again.

'These really are lovely David – I don't know where you get the ideas for such interesting angles – I mean look at that one – who'd have thought of doing it like that?'

'Well to be fair, I did take an awful lot of photos and it took me ages to whittle them down to these few, not to mention the little touches of computer jiggery pokery.'

'I'm going to have to put one on my wall,' Carmen said looking around the cafe for a suitable space. 'Also David, if you've got loads more photos, why don't you hold an exhibition – sell framed pictures – that sort of thing.'

'Mm,' David said thoughtfully, 'I have been vaguely considering something like that.'

'Well there you are then – they have art exhibitions in The Grand Hotel.'

'Food for thought. Has Poppy been in yet today?'

'Has she *ever*?!'

'Crumbs, what's she done? Only I thought I just saw her disappearing into the distance being dragged along by those two monstrous Old English Sheepdogs.'

'Hot chocolate for David?' Clive interrupted.

'Oh get him a beer Clive,' Carmen said dismissively. 'Yes Poppy caused quite a commotion today, bless her, well her dogs did – nearly ransacked the cafe. Some poor man – the one with the metal detector – had a dog on his table … sand all over his newspaper!' David looked thoroughly amused.

'Shame I missed it. Still there'll be chance for me to give her some stick later.'

'You're so naughty the way you tease that poor girl.'

'She doesn't mind – she loves it. Anyway, I owe her big time for forcing me along to those infernal dancing classes of hers and for treading on my feet about a million times! I think I'll have to get some hobnail boots for next time.' Carmen laughed and then added thoughtfully,

'You two get on really well don't you.' Clive turned up with the drinks.

'One beer for David. Well done lad!' and he handed Carmen a glass of wine. She looked around the cafe.

203

'I shouldn't really, but it's so quiet, I guess I can relax for five minutes.'

'Yes it has been quiet lately,' said Clive, 'probably just as well today with Poppy's drama, but it's normally much busier at this time of year.'

'Yes, I've been thinking that. It might get worse too because there's that new cafe open down by the arcade. You know the one that used to be The Fudge Shop?' Carmen said looking quite worried. 'Anyway, cheers David, bottoms up!'

'Cheers!'

Chapter 26

Caroline arrived in style at The Grand Hotel in a taxi. It was a strange feeling returning to the impressive hotel under such different circumstances from the recent family holiday which had turned into a nightmare following Harry's accident.

Could she really keep a straight face and pull this off - hopefully without being recognised? She thanked the driver and stepped out onto the gravel path being mindful of the alien high heeled shoes she was wearing to which she was not accustomed. She straightened out her smart close fitting skirt and jacket, which reminded her of her younger days commuting to the city before she was married and had children. She'd had her hair cut from its normal longer length into a shorter bob which had been expertly styled and coloured for the occasion, giving her quite a different look to her usual one. Her makeup and her glasses which she rarely wore added to her altered appearance.

She entered the building following closely behind two older couples. They walked along the corridor to the ballroom which was buzzing with loud chatter. The enormous room with its lavish chandeliers made a perfect backdrop for the eagerly anticipated Grand Charity Auction. Large banners on the walls reminded everyone of the charities which they would be supporting enthusiastically today - none more so than Caroline and Richard for obvious reasons. They were thrilled that Clive had organised this auction giving them such a great opportunity to fulfil their plan.

A man in a suit at the door was welcoming everyone into the room and giving them each a paddle with a number and a sheet of paper listing the different lots, and another sheet explaining how to pay afterwards. Caroline thanked him and made her way towards the front of the room and took a seat at the end of the row on the far side next to the enormous windows with the view out into the beautifully laid hotel gardens. An older couple sat down next to her and briefly made small talk.

She looked down at the list. The helicopter ride as expected was the star of the show and would be the final lot of the auction. She took her phone from her bag and typed three words in a text message to Richard. *I'm in place.* Caroline waited anxiously for the buzz of her phone, which happened at the very last minute just before the auction started. *So am I.* She didn't look round, but assumed that Richard had, as agreed, arrived and positioned himself as far away from her as possible towards the back on the other side of the room. She switched her phone off and left it in her bag. She was relieved that so far she had not seen anyone she recognised. All of the seats were now taken, with additional people standing at the back and round the sides of the room, many of them holding drinks which they'd brought in from the bar. The ballroom buzzed with excitement. This was going to be quite an occasion! Caroline really wanted to send Richard another text saying how nervous she was, but instead she thought of Harry, and how lucky she was that he was almost fully recovered, thanks to the amazing help they had received. It was now time to pay something back. She took a deep breath and prepared herself for the action.

Finally, the room quietened as Clive from the Beachcomber Cafe walked up onto the platform at the front. Speaking into the microphone he introduced himself and thanked everyone for coming along. He explained that each item in the auction had been donated by local people and businesses for which he was extremely grateful, and The Grand Hotel had not made a charge for using the ballroom today. He then talked about the two charities which were to benefit from the proceeds - the local air ambulance and the children's ward at Lynchester Hospital - and he asked everyone to please dig deep and give generously to these worthwhile causes.   Finally he introduced the professional auctioneer who was giving his time for free.

The auctioneer received an enthusiastic round of applause as he climbed up onto the platform. He took his place and picking up the gavel announced dramatically,

'Good afternoon ladies and gentlemen and welcome to this beautiful ballroom. Without further ado, let's get off to a start shall we with lot number one ... a spa day for two, which has kindly been donated by the Lynchester Health Club. Will someone start me off with twenty pounds? ...Do I see twenty pounds? ..."

Very quickly, the auction was in full swing with extremely generous amounts of money being pledged for each item - everything from works of art to funfair tickets. The atmosphere in the room was exciting, with the enthusiastic audience having a brilliant time - with everyone determined to make bids and win something.

The auctioneer worked through the list briskly and professionally and didn't take long to reach the final lot.

'And now for the grand finale ... the moment which I'm sure many of you have been waiting for ...a unique opportunity for a family helicopter ride along our beautiful coast - generously donated by Sky Surveys. Will someone start me off at one thousand pounds?'   A few gasps were heard from the audience.   Caroline prepared herself to hold up her number but immediately someone just in front of her lifted theirs.

'Thank you. One thousand pounds from the gentleman at the front.   Do I see two thousand? Yes!   Two thousand pounds from the gentleman at the back'.   Caroline couldn't resist a quick look over towards the back and sure enough she saw Richard holding his number 108 in the air. *We are off!*

'How about five thousand pounds? Do I see five thousand pounds?' This was Caroline's turn. She raised her number into the air.

'Thank you. Five thousand pounds from the lady over by the window. Would anybody like to raise the bid to ten thousand pounds?' To Caroline's surprise the man in front held up his number again. A gasp from the audience was heard.

'Ten thousand pounds at the front here. I have ten thousand pounds for these two wonderful charities. Do I see fifteen thousand pounds? Yes! Fifteen thousand from the gentleman at the back. How about twenty thousand pounds?' The auctioneer glanced at the man at the front who shook his head and lowered his paddle. Caroline wanted to leap up and yell 'yes' but instead she calmly raised her number again.

'Twenty thousand pounds to the lady by the window.' The auctioneer paused for dramatic effect. 'How about twenty-five thousand pounds?' he said glancing towards the back of the room. There was a pause and the atmosphere in the room was electric. Richard held up his number.

'Yes! Twenty-five thousand pounds for the fantastic helicopter ride - the gentleman at the back. Do I see thirty thousand pounds? How about thirty thousand pounds to be divided between these two excellent charities... thirty thousand pounds?' Caroline held up her number to the sound of more gasps and whispers in the room.

'I've got thirty thousand pounds here. Do I see any more bids. Caroline turned round to see Richard shake his head.

'Going once ... Going twice. All done! Thirty thousand pounds from the lady by the window. Number 71. Thank you.' The gavel came down with a bang and the audience applauded. Caroline could feel her face colouring as everyone turned to look at her, but she stayed calm and tried to act like she did this sort of thing all the time.

'Thank you everybody for a wonderful auction. I will now pass you back to Clive.'

Clive returned to the platform, clearly thrilled by the amount of money that had been raised in the last hour or so. All his efforts to organise the event had been well worthwhile. He made a small speech, thanking everyone who had donated to the auction and to each person who had bought something. He again showed appreciation to The Grand Hotel for providing the ballroom for free and he encouraged people to go and use their bars and restaurant afterwards.

The audience got up and stretched their legs and were chatting loudly. Caroline was aware of people looking at her, but she kept herself to herself and discreetly went and filled her bank transfer form for the officials at the back of the room. She noticed Richard nearby, but she still didn't acknowledge him. She saw him slip out and leave. Just as she was about to do the same a familiar voice whispered over her shoulder,

'I see what you did there.' Caroline turned to see Carmen from the cafe with a conspiratorial grin on her face. They both burst out laughing and flung their arms around each other. The two ladies walked out into the corridor together, aware that everyone was staring at them. Caroline could hear people saying 'Who *was* that?'

Caroline and Carmen had a quick catch up in the corridor for five minutes, another big hug and then Caroline nipped out and jumped into the waiting car outside, slipping into the seat next to Richard. They both burst out laughing and kissed each other with tears in their eyes.

'Oh I had the *best* time!' Caroline said.

'Me too. I was so proud of you! Love you'.

'Love you too.'

Chapter 27

George turned up at the Beachcomber Cafe clutching his trusty metal detector and spade. He had some rather interesting bits and pieces in this pocket that he'd found today. He did wish Young George had come with him. He'd love to discuss those old coins and strange metal objects with him. They could have sat down at the table and Young George would have used the internet on his phone to look them up and they would have had a delightful lunch together. He realised that Young George was much more busy with his friends nowadays, which was normal for a lad his age, but he felt that he would have been thrilled with today's treasures. Nevermind – he would call in at Miriam's on the way home and see if Young George was there.

George was quite hooked on the metal detecting now. He didn't really know why. He'd managed quite well without it all his life but there was something addictive about it. And now that golf was proving rather too much for his dodgy shoulder, he found himself making trips to Sebleigh Bay almost every time the weather was good. Young George kept saying he couldn't wait to come again, but other things nearly always seemed to get in the way.

The Beachcomber Cafe was a delightful place. George smiled to himself as he remembered the time the huge dog crashed into his table, showering his newspaper with wet sand, before proceeding to cause mayhem throughout the café with his canine partner in crime. George had ended up feeling quite sorry for their handler, Poppy. She seemed such a pleasant young woman, and she was clearly mortified by the chaos the dogs had caused.

Whilst in the cafe he had also noticed the charming lady from the beach hut called Alice, to whom he and Young George had given the bracelet. She had been in the cafe a couple of times since. When he left after the commotion with the dogs, she was talking to Carmen the cafe owner, and she had given George such a lovely smile. She was good looking as well. After his wife Evelyn died, he'd never considered getting involved with anyone else – he was much too long in the tooth for that sort of thing. He'd had one or two single women at the golf club paying him rather more attention than he really wanted - but he was firmly against any sort of new attachment. But the beach hut lady had made quite an impression on him.

As he stood in the queue at the counter, he was rather pleased to notice the lady again through the window, arriving at the cafe. Perhaps he should say hello this time? He was aware of the door opening and her standing in the queue behind him. He wanted to turn round and find an excuse to talk to her but he suddenly became nervous and couldn't quite find the words. What an idiot he felt. He carried on standing with his back to her feeling quite ridiculous, and then to his surprise she suddenly said 'Hello'. He turned round with a big smile and opened his mouth to say hello when he realised that she had her mobile phone to her ear and wasn't talking to him at all. He quickly turned back, feeling such a fool. George felt himself blushing. As if a lovely lady like that would try and start up a conversation with him. She probably didn't even remember him from the beach hut. Now that he thought about it he had just heard a quiet buzzing noise which was obviously her phone ringing in her bag. Why hadn't he realised it was a phone ringing? She was speaking quietly.

'Caroline dear, I'm out at the moment ... Oh I hope you didn't worry about me ... yes the phone's out of order. Look it's a bit difficult to talk now ... can I call you when I get home? ... Love to you all. Bye.'

George was now at the front of the queue and Clive was serving. He looked over the counter at George's metal detector.

'Ah hello ... Any interesting finds today?'

'Well yes actually. Some very old coins. I'm wondering if they might be Roman?' George pulled a couple of tiny muddy coins out of his pocket and showed them to Clive.

'Interesting. You could try taking them to the Sebleigh Bay museum – they've got quite a few coins there. They might be able to identify them for you.'

'Oh where's that then?'

'Up in Pitching Street, by the library. Do you know it?'

'Oh yes I know. Thank you I might just pay them a visit. I'll just have a cup of tea today please,' George said, not wanting to hang around too long after making a fool of himself. As he walked away from the counter with his cup of tea, he heard the cafe owner saying,

'Nice to see you Rose. How are you today?'

Ah, so her name's Rose. George thought to himself. *The perfect name for her – a true English rose.* Having made a fool of himself he found a small table as far away as he could by the window and resolutely turned his back to the rest of the cafe. He looked out at the beach, and towards the families sitting at the tables on the forecourt. A couple of young children, a girl and a boy, were sitting just outside eating brightly coloured icecreams, and they kept looking at him through the window. George wondered if he was making them feel uncomfortable, so he got his old coins out of his pocket and put them on the table. He sat studying them intensely as he sipped his tea. He could see out of the corner of his eye that Rose was sitting at a table quite near to him – but he couldn't bring himself to look in her direction. As he had suspected, chatting up women was clearly something with which he was no longer comfortable. He left as soon as he'd had his tea, and set off for home – forgetting all about lunch and about the museum where he might get his coins identified. He looked straight ahead as he walked out of the cafe, but he thought he saw Rose looking up at him as he left.

Chapter 28

Once more Rose felt the disappointment of seeing George leaving the cafe without giving her a second glance. In fact he even looked pretty grumpy. For a brief moment when they were both queuing at the counter, she thought he was going to start talking to her. Did he think she was saying hello to him when she started talking to Caroline on her mobile? This thought amused Rose. Perhaps he felt silly when he realised she wasn't talking to him. Oh dear – that was most unfortunate. How was she ever going to start up a conversation with him now? She hoped he would come back again. Why was it proving so difficult just to say hello to him though? There was such a friendly atmosphere in the cafe – she often made small talk with other customers, why couldn't she do that with George? Perhaps it just wasn't meant to be? She didn't know anything about him anyway. He may well have a wife after all. Perhaps she'd been a little optimistic assuming he was single. Maybe he came metal detecting on the days that his wife was at bridge classes, or something similar?

Several people left the cafe at the same time and it suddenly seemed very quiet. Carmen came out of the kitchen and got talking to Rose while she was cleaning the tables.

'It's so quiet in here at the moment. I can't understand it for this time of year. We're normally much busier than this in the summer.'

'Perhaps if we get some more consistent weather you'll have more visitors?' said Rose.

'Maybe. But there's another cafe opened on the seafront just beyond the carpark – next to the funfair rides. It's a noisy place with slot machines. It doesn't compare to the Beachcomber, but I'm just wondering if people are going in there rather than bothering to walk along here?'

213

'Carmen,' Clive came wandering over. 'I've been meaning to tell you about that cafe ... I just found out this morning who owns it.'

'But it's the Fudge Shop people isn't it? They closed the shop and converted it to a cafe ...'

'No,' Clive interrupted, 'Apparently they were in the process of converting it when they ran out of money, or it was costing them more than they had planned, or something like that. Anyway Seamus Booth got wind of it and came along and made them an offer they couldn't refuse. It's his cafe!'

'Oh no! The slimy so and so! I knew he was up to something, coming in here and spying on us. He was obviously sussing out the competition.'

'Well it would certainly seem like it,' Clive said. Carmen was livid though.

'Bloody cheek. He'd better not come in here again. Crumbs! How much of the town does he own now? Oh sorry Rose. You came in here for a quiet cuppa, you didn't want to listen to us ranting.'

'That's alright. I can understand you being upset,' Rose said kindly.

'Oh Carmen,' Clive said with a brighter voice, 'David called in earlier and dropped off the posters for his photographic exhibition – there's some leaflets there to give out as well.'

'Oh good. I've been telling everyone about it of course, but the posters will help. Rose, do you know David? Brilliant photographer, looks like Harry Potter?'

'Oh yes, I know the lad you mean. He often comes in here doesn't he.'

'Yes, well he's like a son to me ... to us ... isn't he Clive? ... He's got his first major exhibition at The Grand Hotel next week featuring photos that he's taken of the beach huts. I've seen some of them – they're fantastic. We're going to buy one to put up in here.'

'Oh how lovely. I'll be sure to visit the exhibition.' Rose got up from her chair. 'Well take care, and I hope things improve for you soon.'

'Thanks Rose. That's sweet of you. We'll see you soon love.'

'Bye bye.'

'Lovely lady isn't she Clive ... Oh no! ...' Carmen exclaimed as she looked out of the window.

'What is it Carmen? What now? A Dog giving you an evil stare?'

'Very funny. No it's that blooming seagull sitting on our wall.'

'Blooming seagull indeed! ... It's what you get at the seaside you know ... '

'It's not funny. It's intimidating the customers. It nearly took a scone off an elderly woman the other day. Go and chase it away Clive.'

'You chase it away if you don't like it. I've got customers to serve.'

Over the next few weeks, Rose found it hard not to think about George, and every time she came down to the coast she would keep an eye out for him on the beach and in the cafe. She found herself taking a little extra care over her appearance just in case he turned up. He always looked very smart – even in casual clothes. There was an air of class about him.

Chapter 29

Carmen arrived at The Grand Hotel for David's Photographic Exhibition. She was so proud of him and wild horses wouldn't have kept her away. However, it was still a huge deal for her just to set foot in the hotel. This would be only the second time since she'd spent that beautiful evening here with Jem – just a few days before he died - the other time being for the Grand Charity Auction.

During the past few months she had repeatedly gone over that special evening with Jem, trying to make sense of everything. Jem was so passionate and tender. He was unusually quiet and thoughtful too, telling her 'whatever happens Carmen – remember I love you.' She wondered what had affected him so much. It was as if Jem knew he was going to die. But they said it was natural causes – no mention of suicide or some horrible disease which was waiting to claim his life. Surely no-one can predict that they're going to pass away in their sleep can they?

As she entered the building through the main entrance, she saw a large board with one of David's striking beach hut photographs on it advertising the exhibition. That made her smile. She spoke to the receptionist, who thankfully she didn't recognise from her days of visiting Jem here.

'Good morning – can I help you?' the receptionist said in a professional manner.

'Hello – I'm here for the David Hatchard exhibition.'

'Just follow the corridor down to the Garden Gallery at the end.'

'Thank you.'

Carmen walked slowly down the lavish corridor trying to compose herself and concentrate on David. *Deep breaths Carmen.* What joy he'd brought to her life, and Clive's too.

He was like the son they'd never had. His mother had been a good friend until she tragically passed away. It meant so much to Carmen that she and Clive had been able to look after him and encourage him back on his feet. How proud she was today to be visiting his first exhibition.

As she walked along the plush red carpet and past the huge paintings in heavy antique gold frames, she took in the beautiful chandeliers which were subtly lighting the corridor. The hotel was known for them. She was aware of the sounds of relaxed chatter coming from the Seafarers bar, and the scent of freshly ground coffee. She glimpsed into the room as she walked past the door and was reminded of that horrible moment when she'd been having a drink in there with Jem and she'd spotted Seamus Booth standing at the bar staring at them smugly. She felt he was smirking at her and purposely willing her to feel uncomfortable. Jem reassured her 'we're doing nothing wrong. I'm having a drink with a good friend. Clive knows we're here.'

'It's the way he's looking at us though. It's like he wants us to know that he's clocked us.'

'Ignore him.' Jem had insisted.

And now Seamus had opened a cafe on the Beachcomber's doorstep which explained why he'd been blatantly hanging out in the Beachcomber – sussing out the competition.

As she turned the corner at the end of the corridor she once again tried to dispel the negative thoughts from her mind, and concentrate on David's exhibition. She could hear David chattering – always a comforting sound. He was giving someone a leaflet and saying 'Enjoy the exhibition.' Carmen forced a smile on her face and stepped into the beautiful Garden Gallery. David's large photographs were on stands all down the left hand side of the long narrow room, with the sunlight pouring through the vast windows along the opposite side.

'Carmen!' David exclaimed.

'Oh David – come here you.' She gave him a big hug and tried to keep her emotions under control. David noticed she was looking a little watery eyed.

'Are you ... alright?'

'Yes of course,' she replied, trying not to burst into tears. 'This is wonderful David,' she said looking towards the photographs. How's it going?'

'Good thanks. Can't complain. Plenty of visitors. Lots of them Beachcomber customers no doubt. Thanks to you.'

'Oh I do my bit, but it's your talent – no-one else's. I love the way you've displayed the photos. I'll go and take a proper look. You've got more visitors, she said nodding towards the door.'

'Here Carmen – take one of my leaflets.'

'Thank you my love. I'm going to enjoy this.'

As David greeted the next visitors, Carmen took her time, studying each photograph. David had captured the pastel colours of the beach huts beautifully, and the different moods created by the changing weather and lighting conditions. There were stunning sunsets, and beach huts in the snow. Some of the photos were of single beach huts, and others were taken from a distance showing long rows of them and vast expanses of sand and pebbles. The last photograph, at the far end of the gallery, was the one of the pretty blue and white hut covered in snow. Jem's hut. Number eighteen. It was now called 'Alice'. Carmen was feeling so emotional she couldn't stay and look at it for too long. She turned to walk back and saw David coming towards her.

'It's popular that one – I've sold several prints already. The lighting was just perfect that day.'

'It belonged to my ... our friend Jem who died in January.'

'Oh yes ... I remember,' David said feeling awkward as he remembered Clive's unusual bitter outburst when he saw that photo in the Sunday magazine.

'Did your friend ... err ... name it Alice?'

218

'No he didn't. It was his nephew who inherited it. Anyway ...' Carmen said, trying to brighten up her voice and snap out of her serious mood, 'have you sold many pictures?'

'Yes, it's going well. I didn't expect to sell much – I just hoped I'd get back the money I had to pay for the gallery. Lots of people have been asking if it was me who took the photos in the Sunday supplement. I've mentioned that in the leaflet of course – but they don't tend to read that straight away. Actually you may find you get a few extra visitors to the cafe as I've heard lots of people saying, *I haven't been down to the beach huts for years,*' David continued in one of his funny voices, '*I forgot how lovely they are ... ooh aren't they pretty ... we must take a walk down there again sometime mustn't we Fred.*' Carmen laughed, and then looked serious again.

'Well we can do with all the customers we can get at the moment.'

'Oh actuallly, now you say that, it reminds me ... err one person said something about the Beachcomber having closed. I insisted it wasn't of course, but they said someone had told them it wasn't open any more.'

'Really? That's odd.'

'I know. Sorry – more visitors to see,' he said noticing some new arrivals entering the room.

'Yes, go on. I'll leave you to it David. Let me know how the rest of the day goes. Clive will be over later.'

'Thanks for coming.' He kissed her on the cheek.

'Bye love.'

Later on that day David sat quietly at his table near the door of the gallery looking through the orders he'd received. He was on quite a high. What a great day it had been, not just because of the sales he'd made, but because of the many great conversations he'd had with the visitors. They included locals, holiday makers and staff from The Grand Hotel. Most interestingly he'd been approached by the hotel's publicity manager about doing some work for them for their new website. A meeting was going to be arranged for David to show them his portfolio of commercial work.

David glimpsed up at the clock – only 45 minutes to go today. He may not get any more visitors at this time. He leaned back in the chair and relaxed just as a pretty young woman walked in the room.

'Hello. Are you still open?' she asked politely.

'Yes of course. Welcome.' He sat up straight and grabbed one of his leaflets to give to her. 'Plenty of time left – here, have a leaflet. It explains all about the exhibition.'

'Thank you,' she said giving David a beautiful smile. *Today just gets better and better.*

'Feel free to browse at your leisure.' *That was a really stupid thing to say. Pull yourself together David.* He carried on studying his paperwork, not wanting her to feel self conscious as she was the only person in the gallery. After she'd looked at a couple of photos she asked him,

'Are you the photographer?'

'Yes. Guilty.'

'These photos are lovely. Well done.'

'Thanks,' he said getting up from his chair.

'I love the beach huts – they make good subjects don't they.' David was flattered that she was bothering to talk to him. He got up and walked towards her.

'Err yes. They have a certain old fashioned charm about them don't they. These ones are well looked after too. When I did the photos for the Sunday Times magazine I visited others around the country and some of them were very dilapidated.'

'Oh I didn't see that. The Sunday Times did you say?'

'Yes, it was at the beginning of July.'

'Oh I missed that.' An elderly couple came into the gallery chatting to each other so David excused himself and went to greet them. He made his usual little welcoming speech which he had said countless times today, and then left them to walk down the gallery. He walked around slowly trying to think up an excuse to talk to the young woman

220

again. He stood by the windows and admired the well kept grounds of the hotel, and then heard a gasp.

'Oh!' he thought he heard the young woman say. He glanced over at her and saw her looking really shocked. Like she'd seen a ghost. She was staring at the last photograph in the gallery.

'Um, are you okay?' David asked quietly.

'Oh, yes, yes, of course ... your photos are lovely. I was just thinking I hadn't been down there for ages, I must pay the huts a visit sometime.' She quickly moved back to the previous photo. David could see that she was flustered so he backed off. He smiled at the elderly couple and decided to make conversation with them.

'Are you ... local?'

'Oh yes. Sebleigh Bay born and bred, the man said. 'Yes, my Aunt used to own one of the beach huts – a long time ago. Mind you, I wondered if we might recognise it, but I'm afraid I can't recall the number of it.' David chatted to the couple about old times in Sebleigh Bay but as he talked he noticed that the young woman had returned to look at the same photo which had startled her. Eventually the elderly couple left. He said goodbye to them and thanked them for coming. He then turned to the young woman who was slowly walking towards him studying the leaflet.

'Are you okay there?' David asked cheerfully.

'Yes, thank you. I was just looking at the price list. I'd like to order one please.'

'Yes of course ... I've got a form here if you'd like to come over to the table. Which picture is it?' he asked, although he already knew the answer.

'The one of the beach hut called Alice please.'

'Righty ho,' David said as he marked the form. 'And which size would you like?' He pointed to some samples on the wall behind his table. 'This is the large one, and this is the small one, and you can have them with frames or mounted on a block, or just a print.'

'I'll have the large one on a block please,' she said handing over the money.

'Thank you. Would you just fill in your name and contact number please, and I can let you know when it's ready.'

He glanced down at the form she was filling in and noticed her name.

'Oh! Your name's Alice! No wonder you like that photo. And there was me thinking it was my brilliant photography that had impressed you.' She laughed at David and said,

'Can I ask you, when did you take that photo? I was just wondering ... I haven't been down there for a while and I didn't know the hut had been named Alice.'

'I'm not sure. All I can say is that I took that picture in April this year when it snowed. I think possibly the name was put on there not long before that - month or two maybe?'

'Oh right. So you'll let me know when it's ready?'

'Yes. Do you know the art shop called Framed in Dooley Street? You can collect it from there, but I'll let you know. It will be about a fortnight.'

'Lovely. Thank you. Bye then, and good luck with your photography.'

'Thank you. Nice to meet you.'

David couldn't help thinking to himself what a pretty girl she was, but he also noticed her wedding ring and was pretty sure that she was pregnant as well.

Chapter 30

'Oh my God Clive, have you seen what's just about to come in the door?'

Clive looked out the window to the path outside.

'What are you talking about?'

'That scary looking dog there. It's one of those nasty ones isn't it. This is what I was worried about when we started letting dogs in.'

'Oh I think it's a Rottweiler,' Clive said smiling.

'Exactly.'

'Good morning,' Clive said loudly, making a big point in front of Carmen of giving the woman and her Rottweiler an extra friendly welcome, as they entered the cafe.

'Good morning. It is okay to bring Rosie in isn't it?'

'Yes of course – she's very welcome. Come on in Rosie.'

'Here we are Rosie.' The smartly dressed woman was in her 60s and was quite short which only served to emphasise the size of her large muscular looking Rottweiler.

'And what can I get you?' Clive asked with an extra big smile, as Carmen stood nervously next to him.

'Just a cup of tea please and a piece of Victoria sponge. Actually I don't know whether you can help me, but I really came here in search of some information. I understand there's a lady who comes in here a lot who works as a dog minder?'

'Yes ... I think I know who that is.'

'Well I've got to go into hospital soon for a hip replacement operation and I haven't got anyone to look after Rosie. I'm not keen on putting her into kennels – well not full time anyway – and even afterwards I'm not going to be able to walk her for quite a while, so I wondered if you know how I can get in touch with this lady?'

'That would be Poppy that you're looking for,' Clive said. 'Poppy Dancey. She may well be able to help you out.'

'If she's free?' Carmen piped up. 'She's very booked up these days, she ...'

'Well we can certainly put you in touch with her,' Clive interrupted. 'Actually, she's always in and out of here. If you're lucky she might even turn up while you're drinking your tea. If she does, I'll send her over to you for a chat, but I'll give you one of her business cards anyway. She comes highly recommended.'

'Oh good. I've heard she's very experienced.'

'She certainly is. Carmen – where are Poppy's cards?' Clive asked as he searched under the counter.

'Oh I think we've run out,' Carmen said quickly.

'Really? That's odd. We had loads of them.' Rosie's 'mum' paid and thanked Clive for his help and took a seat over by the window, with Rosie sitting down quietly beside her.

'Oh there they are,' Clive said to Carmen.

'What?'

'Poppy's cards - on the shelf over there.'

'Shh ...   Poppy might not want to look after that creature ...'

'Why? What's wrong with it?'

'Look at it with the huge evil grin it's got – it stretches from ear to ear.'

'It's a Rotty. That's what they're supposed to look like. My uncle had one when I was a child. Actually I think it looks like a really soppy old thing.'

'It looks really scary to me. You shouldn't inflict that on Poppy.'

'Poppy's a grown woman. She doesn't need us to vet her clients for her ... vet? ... haha ... Anyway, that could be a lucrative bit of business for her by the sounds of it. Oh look ... It's your dad. Is he at a loose end or something? I keep seeing him wandering about. Phone's ringing. I'll get it.'

224

'Yes, that's the second time he's been in here this week. Hello Dad!' Carmen addressed her dad warmly with an element of surprise in her voice. 'To what do we owe this pleasure?'

'Morning constitutional Carmen,' he said in his deep gravelly voice.

'Not driving today then?' Carmen came out from behind the counter.

'Nope. I wouldn't be doing my morning constitutional if I was driving would I? ... Anyway less of the interrogation please, and how about getting your old dad a cup of coffee?'

'Coming up Dad. Go and get yourself a nice window seat.' At that moment Clive stuck his head round from the kitchen door.

'Carmen – it's Ellie on the phone.'

'I'm just getting Dad's coffee,' Carmen replied.

'I'll see to Rumpelstiltskin,' Clive said quietly. 'Ellie particularly wants to talk to you Carmen.' Clive made a coffee and took it over to Carmen's dad. 'Oswald! Delightful to see you here again – this is becoming quite a habit.'

'Can't a bloke visit his daughter and enjoy a quiet cup of coffee without all the comments?' Clive laughed. He and his father-in-law had always enjoyed some good banter.

'You know you're welcome here any time Oswald.' They both watched as Carmen wandered over towards them. Clive was a bit concerned, knowing that Ellie ringing up so close to the start of her shift didn't bode well.

'Ellie not coming in?' He said to Carmen.

'No. She's got personal problems…'

'Oh I wondered why she didn't want to talk to me. We're in a bit of a fix then aren't we? It's due to be busy today and we are unlikely to get anyone at such short notice.'

'I know. Have the Harrises gone on holiday yet?'

'Err ... yes, they'll have gone already – the girls won't be available.'

'Hmm ...I'll go and make a couple of phone calls.'

'Nice Rottweiller over there Clive,' Oswald said looking at Rosie who was a couple of tables away.

'Oh that reminds me,' Clive said. 'I need to go and get Poppy's card while I think of it, before I get bogged down in working out how we're going to run the cafe with zero staff!'

'Well if you've got a problem I could lend a hand,' Oswald said.

'That's kind of you Oswald but I expect Carmen will find someone.' At that moment, Carmen came back from the kitchen.

'Unfortunately I can't Clive. What are we going to do? I think we might have to shut the cafe for the day. We can't run it with just the two of us in the summer holidays.'

'We can't shut it either – that will look really bad when people turn up and we're not here, and besides a lot of fresh food will get wasted. Actually you won't believe it but your Dad offered to help.' Carmen burst out laughing.

'I hope you're not laughing at my expense!' Oswald said gruffly as he got up and approached the kitchen.

'As if!' said Carmen, laughing some more.

'Look – it's obvious you're in a fix. Why don't you let me help you out.'

'Are you serious Dad?'

'Yes. I'm free all day.'

'How come you're free so much at the mo...'

'Never mind about that,' Oswald interrupted abruptly, 'you've got a crisis to sort out. Now where shall I start? I can be handy with a dish cloth and a tea towel for a start.'

'Well it's not like washing up at home you know ...'

'Don't be so patronising Carmen ... washing up's washing up! How hard can it be? I think I can handle some fancy dish washer and a sink. It's not rocket science!'

'Well that's telling me. Come on then Dad – let's get you an apron.'

Chapter 31

Oswald was now happily installed at the Beachcomber Cafe, and was enjoying keeping busy and being useful to his daughter. Having Carmen and Clive's company was a real bonus too. He admitted to them (begrudgingly) that his job driving people to hospital had come to an end because of the latest cut backs. He would make a point of visiting some of the more regular patients and might even try and bring them down to the cafe sometimes. However, in the meantime he was pleasantly surprised how well his latest little job here seemed to be working out. He was starting to get to know some of the regular customers. He already knew David – he was like family. He was in here now in fact, killing time between taking photos no doubt. He would enjoy seeing him more regularly.

'Ah, here comes Poppy,' Carmen said pointing over to the window. 'Dad, have you been introduced to her yet?'

'Poppy? Red head ... walks dogs?'

'Yes, that's right ... keep your voice down ...'

'Well she *has* got red hair and she *does* walk dogs. What's wrong with saying ...'

'Poppy, we were just talking about you? Have we introduced you to my Dad?'

'No not formally. Hello.' She said stretching her hand out to Oswald.

'Hello Poppy. I'm Oswald. You've just rescued me from a telling off from my daughter!'

'Hardly!' Carmen said with a laugh, 'Oh, Poppy my love, before I forget, I keep meaning to ask, would you like one of these?' Carmen pulled out a bright orange doggy ball thrower complete with yellow tennis ball, from under the counter. 'Someone left it behind a couple of weeks ago. No one's claimed it so you might as well have it.'

'Oh crumbs!' Poppy said. 'You really wouldn't want to trust me with one of those.'

'Why not?'

'I just don't do balls.' David, who had been sitting quietly in the corner reading his newspaper, intrigued by the conversation, burst out laughing.

'Be quiet you,' Poppy told him and then turned back to Carmen. 'Honestly I've got no coordination I've never been able to throw and catch balls.'

'Well surely you don't need to be very good at it to throw a ball for a dog to fetch?'

'Oh believe me I really am bad. I used to live in dread of PE lessons at school, I was such an embarrassment.'

'But what about your dogs?' asked Carmen, 'I thought everyone threw balls for their dogs.'

'Not me. Never have done.'

'Not even for Pluto?'

'No. Well I did used to kick a ball around the garden for him a bit. It was a large football so even I couldn't miss that.'

'Surely your coordination can't be that bad Poppy?'

'Well yes it is actually.'

'You should see her dancing!' David mumbled with a grin on his face, which quickly turned to a mock look of fear as Poppy glared at him and pretended to hit him. David pushed his foot out from under the table and started rubbing it with a pained expression on his face. 'Almost healed up from the latest dancing accident ....'

Clive came out of the kitchen wiping his hands on his apron.

'Ah the ball slinger. About time you gave it to Poppy.'

'She doesn't want it. She says her coordination is terrible.'

'Well I've never used one of those things,' Clive said, 'but surely anyone can fling a ball with it. Haven't you got a dog with you today Poppy?'

'Yes, I've got Bobby and Bounce. Do you remember? The two English sheepdogs who ransacked the cafe that time! Unsurprisingly I've left them outside today.' Clive wandered over to the window, and spotting the tethered dogs, a big smile spreading across his face,

'Aren't they fabulous creatures! They look very calm at the moment - its hard to believe they were so naughty isn't it.'

'It's not their fault,' Poppy whispered, 'Their owners are useless. They haven't trained them at all. I've suggested classes for them but they can't be bothered. They pay me to deal with them instead.'

'What they need is some exercise - a nice ball to chase after - why don't we try out that contraption?'

'We?! ' exclaimed Carmen.

'Yes. Why not? If Poppy doesn't fancy flinging the ball I could do it for her,' Clive suggested.

Carmen laughed, 'Boys and your toys! You can't resist can you Clive?'

'It's a plastic gadget from the pet shop Carmen, it isn't the latest games machine you know!'

'Oh go on then. You've been itching to use that thing haven't you. You might as well – seeing as it's so quiet in here again. We'll watch from the window.'

'This I must see,' David sniggered to himself as he got up, abandoning his newspaper and heading for the window. Clive and Poppy went outside and collected Bobby and Bounce and headed off onto the beach. David and Carmen watched from the window.

Oswald came over with a cloth and began cleaning the tables.

'Isn't anyone doing any work round here today?' he mumbled.

'Not much work to do it's so quiet,' Carmen complained. 'Anyway David, hark at him – he's only been working here five minutes and he thinks he's the boss.'

'Hmph!' said Oswald dismissively. 'What are you watching anyway? Is that seagull pestering the customers again?'

229

'No – Poppy and Clive are going to go and try out that ball throwing contraption.'

'Oh I've always wanted to have a go with one of those.'

'Not you as well! You men honestly! Shall we just close up the cafe and then we can all go and play ball.'

'Customers to serve. Don't you worry. I'll go,' Oswald muttered sarcastically, as a family came in the door.

'Look David, Clive's about to sling that thing,' Carmen said. They watched Clive successfully hurling the ball out towards the sea. Bobby and Bounce hurtled off at great speed to see who could reach the ball first.

'It went a surprisingly long way didn't it?' Carmen said.

'Yes – I must admit I didn't expect it to go that far,' David replied, 'Come on Poppy – I want to see you giving it a go.'

'You are naughty David. Mind you I can't really see how she can go wrong. Oh look, the dogs aren't bringing the ball back. Aren't they supposed to do that?'

'Poppy said they're not trained. Perhaps they don't know what to do with a ball.'

Clive and Poppy walked further out on the beach to join Bobby and Bounce who were playing with the ball. Carmen and David could see Clive in the distance handing the ball thrower to Poppy.

'Go on Poppy,' urged David mischievously from the cafe. 'Go for it.' Poppy turned to face back up the beach, and Clive was explaining to her how to use the ball slinger. After a bit of messing about Poppy eventually pulled her arm back and launched the tennis ball as far as she could ... so far in fact that it came hurtling towards the cafe, bounced on to the forecourt and banged loudly against the window, followed by Bobby and Bounce who sprinted towards the cafe as fast as lightening. The unfortunate family sitting on the cafe forecourt, nearly had the life frightened out of them by an unexpected ball banging loudly on the cafe window and then bouncing on their table, knocking one of their cups of tea flying. They braced themselves as they saw the two huge shaggy dogs speeding towards them. Carmen and David watched on in horror as Bobby crashed straight into the table knocking cups, plates, tea, scones, knives and spoons everywhere. The mum and dad stood up with looks of horror and disgust all over their faces. The little girl started crying and their older boy thought it extremely funny and was laughing his head off as he held on to his lolly. The two big dogs were bouncing around excitedly looking for the ball, totally oblivious to the havoc they had caused.

Carmen went rushing outside and put her arm around the shocked looking mother,

'Oh, I'm so sorry. Are you alright?'

'Well yes. It's not your fault. It's the irresponsible people with these dogs,' she said looking crossly at Clive and Poppy who were running towards the cafe, calling the dogs. The father was cuddling the little girl,

'Its alright Kylie ... it was a bit of a shock that's all ... the dogs are harmless, they're just looking for their ball.' Carmen turned and spoke to the children,

'Sorry about that my loves, are you alright? They're naughty dogs aren't they, but they won't hurt you.'

'That was so funny,' said the boy, 'Look what they've done!' he said pointing to the broken crockery on the ground. Clive and a very distraught looking Poppy had managed to catch the dogs and put their leads on. Poppy was about to launch into a huge apology, but Clive stepped in firmly, held up his hand to Poppy to signal to her not to speak, and he addressed the parents who were looking pretty hostile.

'I am so sorry about that. These dogs don't belong to Poppy, she walks them for someone else, and they're very badly trained. She didn't want to use this contraption, but I persuaded her to give it a go. It's totally my fault. We will of course give you another set of drinks and food – you can have whatever you want.'

'Yes of course we will,' added Carmen. 'If you just give us a few minutes to clear this up, we'll come and see what you'd like.' At that moment David came out holding a dustpan and brush and a cloth, and was clearly hiding his

231

face and trying not to laugh. Carmen grabbed the dustpan and cleared up the mess, while she chatted to the family – trying to lighten the mood and distract them from what had happened. David wandered over to Poppy.

'Naughty Bobby! Naughty Bounce!' he whispered jokingly before he fell about laughing with his back to the family.

'Stop it!' she whispered back. 'It's not funny. Stop laughing.'

'What's not to laugh about? Oh if only I'd filmed it! I could make a fortune if I shared it on social media.'

'Oh stop it! I think I'd better take these dogs away quickly then everyone can relax.' The boy came walking towards them.

'Can I stroke your dogs please?'

'Yes of course you can,' Poppy answered, relieved someone was being friendly to her! 'This is Bobby, and this is Bounce.'

'That was so funny what happened,' the boy said, with one hand stroking Bounce's head and other holding his lolly.
'They're very naughty aren't they?' As he stroked Bounce's head, Bobby was straining to grab the boy's lollie.

'Right!' said Poppy as she pulled hard on the lead, 'I really must take these boys home before they cause any more trouble.' Carmen brought out a tray of fresh tea and scones in addition to some very generous portions of cakes for the family. 'On the house obviously. Enjoy them in peace now, hopefully.'

'Oh wow!' said the little boy excitedly, 'Who's getting that whopping big piece of cake? Can I have it?'

As Carmen went back indoors she spoke quietly to David,

'Oh crumbs, I left Dad in charge! Is he behaving? He wasn't supposed to be serving the customers.'

'Not in his job description eh? Well no one seems to have complained.'

'I heard that!' Oswald said grumpily from behind the counter. 'I'm quite capable of making cups of tea, serving cakes and taking the money while you lot are swanning around outside.' Something caught Oswald's eye outside. 'Oh look – it's the posh bird.' Clive looked puzzled, and wondered who Oswald was talking about.

'Did you say posh bird?' he asked.

'Yes – the posh bird. She's talking to Poppy.' Carmen finished serving someone and said, 'What was that Dad? Were you talking about one of Poppy's dogs? The posh one did you say?'

'*No*, not the dog. The posh bird I said. She's talking to Poppy – oh Poppy's going now – taking those maniac dogs away, and the posh bird's coming in by the looks of it.'

'What *are* you talking about Dad?'

'Posh bird. Lived here all her life. There she is.' Carmen and Clive burst out laughing as they saw Rose outside heading towards the cafe. They couldn't keep a straight face as she came through the door.

'Someone's having fun,' said Rose.

'Hello Rose love. Rose you probably know my father Oswald don't you.'

'Oh yes,' she said smiling. 'Oswald and I go back donkies years but I didn't realise you were Carmen's father.'

'For my sins ... yes,' he winked. 'I remember you well Rose. Haven't seen you for a while though.'

'We were actually in the same class at school weren't we?'

'Yes that's right and I remember your friends Ivy and err whatsername? Doris wasn't it? I've seen them both around.'

'Yes. You've got a good memory. Funnily enough I met up with both of them recently. We had a good old reminiscing session at my niece's beach hut.'

'I heard Doris isn't so good these days. That's a shame isn't it.'

'Yes – you mean her dementia? It's very sad.' Rose paused and then said meaningfully. 'But occasionally she remembers things from the past in great detail.'

Carmen interrupted, 'Rose – go and sit yourself down and I'll bring your tea over. It's on the house today. The least I can do if you're going to be stuck entertaining my old Dad. Go on Dad – have a break and a chat with Rose.'

'Less of the old please, Carmen. No respect from the youngsters eh Rose?'

Clive had been watching with amusement the exchange between Rose and Oswald. He spoke quietly to Carmen,

'Good job Rose has turned up – I was just thinking we might as well close up it's so quiet.'

'I know. It's nearly empty. I'm not at all happy with how quiet it's been in here lately,' said Carmen, but right now I'm really glad hardly anyone was around for that incident!'

'Oh that's the least of our worries Carmen. A few pieces of broken crockery and some free cakes for the customers are irrelevant with the problems we've got.' He turned towards David, who was sipping his drink. 'Talking of it being quiet in here, David, Carmen mentioned that someone at your exhibition told you that we were closed. What was that about?'

'I don't know – I was quite busy at the time so I didn't really take it in, but I think it was an elderly couple who said something like *shame the Beachcomber Cafe has closed now – we enjoyed going there*. I did make a point of telling them that it definitely isn't closed, in fact we had quite an argument about it - well a friendly one - they were adamant, but I insisted it is open for business as usual and that I had been down here more than once in the last few days.'

'That's worrying,' Carmen said, 'Why would they think that? There must be some confusion. Is there any other cafe around here which has closed recently?'

'Well there's nothing else down here is there?' Clive stated. 'And along the seafront you've got that new Octopus place, and then there's The Hut, and The Diner just past the arcades, and you've got those takeaway places at the fairground. Actually I didn't want to say this, but I'm wondering if somebody is doing this maliciously?'

234

'I hope not! But then it's either that or it's that horrible Octopus place that is taking our customers?'

'We need to get to the bottom of this – it looks like there may be an explanation as to why we are so quiet at the moment. I keep meaning to ask you Carmen – have you checked that review website you signed up for?'

'No – not for a while. I'd forgotten all about it actually.'

'Oh Carmen! It's really important to keep an eye on it and see what people are saying about us.'

'Well I checked it a few times after we started letting the dogs in and everyone – well most people – were saying good things, and giving us full marks. It was only the occasional person who made a fuss – you know, like that cranky woman who complained about the grumpy looking St Bernard, or whatever it was, who was apparently giving her dodgy looks when she was trying to relax with her vanilla latte.'

David sniggered. 'Vanilla lattes?' he said in a funny posh voice. 'I didn't know you sold vanilla lattes.'

'We don't!' Clive and Carmen stated in unison.

'Classic!' David laughed.

'That was ages ago – haven't you looked since then?' said Clive with irritation in his voice.

'I can't remember.'

'I'll take that as a no then.'

'Don't have a go at me Clive – you could have kept an eye on it too.'

'Now now children,' David interrupted, 'Just give me a moment and I'll try and find it on my phone.'

'Oh, can you do that on there?' Carmen asked.

'Hilarious! Funnily enough we are in the 21st century Carmen... hang on a jiffy ... here we are ...' David said hesitantly as he started reading the reviews, the expression on his face dropping to one of concern.

'What does it say David?' Carmen asked anxiously.

'Aah ... this isn't too good actually ... err ... there's several bad ones I think ... oh dear ... mm ... the vanilla latte incident was the least of your worries I'm ....'

Carmen interrupted impatiently:

'Oh God! Read them out David.'

'Okay. First one. *This cafe has seriously gone downhill since it changed it's name from Pebbles to Beachcomber. The interior looks tired, and the staff even more so. Very few customers bother to walk this far down the promenade any ...*

'Bloody cheek!' yelled Carmen. 'Who wrote that? How can anyone say the interior's tired? We did it up beautifully.'

'You'd better continue David,' Clive said looking unhappy.

'*My cooked breakfast looked like it had been cooked, or should I say incinerated, the day before and reheated. It was so dried up I couldn't eat it. Rating ... one out of six.*'

'That's not true! What else is there David?' Carmen asked, 'You might as well read them all ...'

'Okey dokey ... next one ... *I walked all the way down to the Beachcomber at 3 o'clock on a Saturday and the cafe was closed ...*'

'That's rubbish!' Clive said, 'When have we ever closed that early on a Saturday. Not even in the winter. Carry on David.'

'*I shan't be bothering with the Beachcomber again. One out of six. Next one ... Very disappointing food and drinks. The chips were barely cooked and my coffee was cold by the time the staff stopped chatting and bothered to bring it over to me. I won't be returning. Two out of Six. ... What were they thinking allowing dogs in the cafe? There was a strong odour of damp dogs as I went in the door. I was going to have fish and chips but the smell put me off eating anything. Don't bother to go in here if you're not a dog owner. Rating: One out of six ...* oh here's a nice one! *I don't agree with any of the bad reviews. We visit the Beachcomber every year when we're on holiday in Sebleigh Bay and are never disappointed with the friendly staff, excellent meals and beautiful view of the beach. We were delighted to see that dogs are now allowed in the cafe and because of this will*

236

consider bringing Teddy on holiday with us next year. Rating: Six out of six.'

'That's brilliant!' Carmen said, 'That's more like the sort of reviews we used to get all the time. Where have all these complainers come from?'

'Are there more David?' Clive asked sternly.

'Yes unfortunately.' David scanned through them. ' ... *Slug looking up at me from my lettuce ... staff thought it was funny when I complained ...* Oh here's the most recent one – only about a week old ... *It wasn't worth the walk down to the Beachcomber, dried up pizzas, poor standards of hygiene, I'll be sticking to the new Octopus cafe in future. They know how to treat their customers.'*

'The Octopus! That lousy place?' Carmen fumed.

'Maybe that's a clue?' Clive suggested. 'Look we know those reviews aren't genuine. They're full of rubbish and lies, and its a hell of a coincidence we suddenly get loads of bad reviews just when the Octopus opens.'

'It must be them! Slimy Seamus living up to his reputation I bet.'

'Well let's not jump to conclusions shall we? But we do need to check that place out – see what's going on in there.'

'But how can we do that? I mean I know he comes in here spying on us but we're not going to find out anything if we go in there ourselves. Seamus Booth knows us.'

'If you mean you want somebody to spy on them,' said David. 'I could go. I could sit in there for ages with my newspaper and everlasting cup of coffee and see if I can pick up any gossip?'

'There's an idea. Mind you, he might recognise you. You know what he looks like don't you?'

'Yes. I don't know that he'd recognise me though. And anyway, he probably doesn't work in there much himself if he owns all these other businesses. Look, why don't I give it a go? And if I don't find out anything, we can try and think of something else.'

Chapter 32

'Evening!' David said to Poppy as she opened her front door with a hangdog expression on her face.

'Come in David,' Poppy said as she turned miserably away from the door.

'Oh dear, someone seriously needs cheering up. Is this about the Bobby and Bounce incident?' he said trying not to laugh.

'I know you think it's funny David, but I'm mortified by the damage we caused today.'

'Look, nobody blames you Poppy – Clive took full responsibility.'

'I hate to think what Carmen and Clive said after I left. They were very nice about it but they must be thoroughly fed up with me. That's the second time I've caused havoc in their cafe. They've been so good to me as well. I'll offer to pay for the damage.'

'Well actually, for your information Miss Poppykins, I was in there for ages this afternoon and they didn't mention you at all – in fact they've got far more serious things to deal with. Those dogs smashing up the cafe is the least of their worries at the moment. Believe me.'

'Oh? What's going on?'

'Well that's what I came to see you about. I need your help. Hopefully this will cheer you up a bit. I need to find a disguise!'

Chapter 33

'I can't believe I'm actually doing this,' David muttered to himself as he crossed the road outside Anchor House and started a slow jog along the sea front. 'Hey, maybe I'll get to like it?' he added sarcastically. He glanced up at Poppy's flat to give her a wave and an over-the-top smile and was horrified to see she was taking a photo of him.

'I'll get you later Miss Poppy!' *Crumbs! Talk about a good turn never goes unpunished.*

Poppy, as David expected, had fully embraced the task of finding him a suitable disguise for his surveillance mission to the Octopus cafe. As if traipsing round every charity shop in Sebleigh Bay wasn't tedious enough, she then made him stand there in front of strangers while she held up numerous items of clothing against him to check for size. This was beyond embarrassing, and seemed more the behaviour one would expect from a mother with a young child. After a while, David, a bit like a small child in fact, started playing up and saying in a babyish voice things like, 'Mummy, can we go to the toy shop now?' or 'Can I have some sweeties please?' Poppy as usual, went along with his silliness with great patience, and giggled endlessly inbetween raising her eyebrows many times. On their walk back to Anchor House laden with carrier bags of second hand clothes and hats, David said 'What do we do now – hold a jumble sale?'

'No. You provide a bottle of good wine and I come round tonight and help you decide on an outfit.' This sounded reasonable to David until Poppy turned up at his door that evening holding several wigs in her hands which Selina had lent her. David did an exaggerated double-take and gently closed the door on her. Then he opened the letter box and called through it, 'No pets allowed in here thank you,' before opening the door again and letting her in. David poured them each a glass of wine and kept trying to divert the attention to anything other than the matter of trying on clothes.

'I bumped into Mrs Carpenter this morning ... I've got an interesting commission to do for the Town Council ... How's Lucky the giant poodle? Haven't seen him recently...'

'Right!' Poppy said firmly, ignoring David's distraction attempts as she put down her glass of wine on the glass coffee table and emptied a whole bag of clothes on to the living room floor. 'Where shall we start?'

'More wine Poppy?' David said reaching for the bottle. Ignoring the question Poppy picked up a tie dye t-shirt.

'How about the hippy look? We've got the wig too.' She sent David off to the bedroom with a complete outfit to try on. He reluctantly called her in when he was ready to model it. On entering the bedroom she immediately collapsed into fits of laughter, so much so that she couldn't speak. David stood, straight faced, staring at himself in the mirror.

'Well ... what do you think?'

'Wait a minute ...' Poppy eventually managed to utter in-between laughing. She rushed out of the room and came back with her mobile phone and she took a photo of David. He posed for her, looking hilarious in his long floppy wig and oversized hippy clothes.

'I'm warning you – if that appears on social media you're in big, big trouble.'

'Mm, there's a thought! Actually, we need to try something else – those are too big.'

'Whose fault is that? You picked them and held them all up against me, humiliating me in front of half of the residents of Sebleigh Bay.'

Several bags of clothes and a bottle of wine later, Poppy and David came to the conclusion that the hippy look, hilarious as it was, just made David look very conspicuous, which wasn't the effect they were trying to achieve at all. But somehow, they hit upon the idea of a fitness fanatic.

'You can be a jogger!'

'You're joking – I'm not used to jogging – I might keel over.'

'Don't be silly. You're young and fit – you'll be okay.'

'You think I'm fit do you?' David looked at his reflection in the mirror with admiration, and he puffed out his chest, and clenched his muscles.

'Well, that wasn't quite what I meant ... but ... have you got a tracksuit?' As it happened David did have a tracksuit which he'd bought at university and never used, and he even had a bright red sweat band. As he tried to fix it round his head he took off his glasses.

'That's it!' yelled Poppy, making David jump, 'The glasses! You've got to take them off. You look so different.'

'No way! I can't see!'

'Oh you'll be okay. You can see enough to go in there and buy a cup of tea can't you?'

'I might fall down a hole on the beach when I'm jogging along. That's if I don't have a heart attack first. It's ages since I've exercised.'

'You can stick to the pavement. You simply have to take the glasses off – you're unrecognisable like that. Oh ... and a change of hairstyle ...'

'Whoa! Stop right there! If you think you're going to get me along to your friends, Mr and Mrs Short and Spiky from the purple poodle parlour, you've got another thing coming.'

'Poodle parlour?'

'It might as well be for poodles. Hey! There's an idea. I'm surprised they don't do dogs. How come Shortlegs and Longlegs or whatever they're called, haven't gone all purple and spiky yet ...'

'David!' Poppy interrupted, 'Crumbs! Talk about being over dramatic. I meant, we could use a bit of hair gel. Did I say anything about a complete makeover at Stardust? Honestly! Mind you ... come to think of it ... I'm sure Selina wouldn't mind doing us a little favour.' David put his hands on his head in despair and fell backwards on the bed. Poppy

241

was thoroughly enjoying winding him up ... about time the boot was on the other foot.

So, after several days of planning, David found himself jogging slowly towards the dreaded Octopus cafe wearing his unused track suit and headband, with a bit of gel on his hair making the fringe stand up for a change. He had planned on walking there, but Poppy insisted he needed to arrive looking hot and sweaty and out of breath to make it realistic. They decided that he could keep his glasses on until he approached the cafe, so when he was about fifty metres away he took them off and slid them into the pocket of his joggers. Everything was a blur. Once again David said to himself, 'I can't believe I'm doing this! Here goes ...' He jogged around the side of the cafe and slowed down as he entered through the door by the beach where the music was coming from.

A blurry male character stood behind the blurry counter and greeted David,

'Good morning. Nice day for a run.'

'Err yes.'

'What can I get you?'

'Err, I'll have a tea please.'

'Sure. Anything to eat?' David was just thinking that if he had some food as well it would give him an excuse to stay longer in the cafe and maybe have more chance of finding out what was going on. He looked up at the blurry menu on the wall behind the counter, and couldn't read a single word.

'Err ... I might have something to eat ... jogging making me hungry ... what do you recommend?' The young man turned towards the board and simply read the list of meals.

'There's Octopus burger and fries, Octopus cheese burger and fries, Octopus ...' David's brain was switching off to all these Octopus meals – he'd been thinking more in terms of a cake, but found himself saying,

'Okay. I'll have the first one on the list?'

'Octopus burger and fries?'

'Yes, go on then. Not, err ... made of Octopus is it?' The young man behind the counter laughed politely, presumably having heard that comment endless times. After paying for his meal David shuffled across the room to a table, crashing into a few blurry chairs on the way. He sat down at the back of the cafe and got his phone out – pretending to study it as he tried to observe what went on there. *This is ridiculous! I can't see a bloody thing. I can't even read my phone! Wonder if my hearing will improve to make up for it?* David heard talking – two young men. He looked up and now saw two blurry shapes behind the counter. He needed to see who they were. He waited until some more customers came in and then slipped his glasses on and caught a glimpse of the staff. *No sign of Seamus.* It seemed to be just the two youngsters working there. He quickly took the glasses off again.

David waited quite a while for his meal to be brought to him. *No prizes for speed here.* Finally, his burger and chips arrived . As he bit into his burger he realised that he wasn't at all hungry. *Hardly surprising at just 10.45. Oh no. What was I thinking ordering this? I've only just had breakfast.* There weren't many customers in the cafe. David listened to as much of the conversation as he could behind the counter, but there was nothing interesting to hear. Just a few comments about what one of the lads got up to in the pub last night, and some discussions about stocks of burgers and salad.

A couple of boys came in and started playing on the slot machines. David thought they looked like they should have been at school, but what did he know? He couldn't see properly anyway. After wondering how much of his burger and chips he was going to be able to consume, he remembered he had a folded local newspaper in his trouser pocket. He pulled it out and pretended to read it inbetween nibbling small bits of the unwanted burger. He considered ordering another cup of tea to wash down the excess food, but decided to give up and cut his losses. He wasn't going to learn anything from his trip. It had all been for nothing. In fact, the only thing he'd learnt was just how much he relied on his glasses!

He got up from the table feeling quite sick from the unwanted food, and checked that he had his phone and his glasses. As he walked towards the door, trying desperately hard not to bump into anyone, a blurry man entered the cafe. One of the young men addressed him.

'Morning Seamus.'

'Yeah. Get yourself down to the car park. It's quiet in here so Alex can manage on his own for a bit.' *Pretty rude,* David thought.

'Right you are. How long do you want me on car park duty?'

'Just get down there quickly. I'll let you know when you can come back.' *He's a charmer,* David thought as he walked out the door and along the path. *Oops! Forgotten my newspaper.* David turned round and walked back to the cafe. As he walked towards the door Seamus had his back to him and said,

'What was he doing here?'

'Who?'

'Him in the tracksuit. He's a friend of the Colliers at the Beachcomber.' One of the young men coughed to let Seamus know that David was just outside. David decided to leave the newspaper and continue walking along the path past the cafe.

'Usually wears glasses.' he heard Seamus saying.

244

Chapter 34

'Oh David! About time!' Carmen exclaimed as David came in through the Beachcomber door. 'We've been waiting all day for you. Poppy said you set off in your jogging outfit hours ago.' Carmen laughed as she remembered the photo of David which Poppy had showed them on her mobile phone.

'Well it's alright for you to laugh – you're not the one who had to dress up like an idiot and *run* to that vile Octopus place, *without* my glasses, risking life and limb. And talking of the glasses – I wouldn't have minded so much if it had worked! It might have worked for Superman, but it didn't work for me.'

'Oh! Did you get recognised then?' asked Clive, catching on quicker than Carmen about the Superman comment.

'Of course I bloody did!'

'Sit down David,' Carmen said laughing, 'And I'll get you whatever you want to eat and drink – I think I owe you!'

'No thanks, I'm not hungry. In fact I'm so not hungry I don't think I'll be eating for three days. Have you ever tried eating an Octopus bloody burger and bloody Octopus fries less than an hour after your breakfast?'

'So come on then,' asked Carmen eagerly, 'What happened?'

'Well, nothing happened – apart from me bumping into every chair and table in the place – I might as well have been blindfolded!'

'Oh ... so you didn't find out anything? No sign of them slagging us off?'

'I don't hear you saying "poor David are you okay?" or anything!'

Carmen laughed at David again, 'So you didn't find out anything at all then?'

'Well actually ... there was one thing ... which I was just coming to ...'

'Oh? What's that?'

'Well ... I don't understand what they were referring to exactly, but when Slimy came in, ordering his staff about, very rudely by the way ... he said ... now what was it?' David looked thoughtful and then turned directly to Carmen, 'Actually Carmen – could I have that cup of tea afterall?'

'*David*! Just tell us!'

'Okay okay. Slimy said to one of his staff something like, *As it's quiet you can go and do car park duty. QUICK!* I was trying to work out what that was about, I mean, which of Seamus's businesses has got a car park?'

'Oh that's strange,' Carmen said thoughtfully.

'Interesting,' Clive said. 'I'll get us all some tea and we can have a think about that.'

'And by the way,' David said. 'I've been meaning to ask - what's Oswald doing out there with that enormous water pistol? That's the second time I've seen him going stomping outside with it.' Clive raised his eyes in irritation and explained,

'You may well ask David. My dear wife and Oswald have got this obsession with a seagull out there who is apparently intimidating the customers! Oswald thinks he can squirt at it with the water pistol to frighten it away. Ridiculous!'

'It's alright for you to moan, Clive,' Carmen said, 'but it helped itself to that man's pizza yesterday! So we had to replace it for him at our cost. Your friend the seagull is hitting our profits.'

'Well that was his fault because he left it unattended outside and went to the loo. You shouldn't have given him another one. I wouldn't have done. I suppose we'd better put a sign up outside telling people not to leave their food unattended.' David was trying not to laugh too much as Carmen and Clive squabbled.

246

Over their cups of tea, they all discussed Seamus Booth's various businesses which they knew about in the town, but couldn't work out what 'car park duty' might be referring to. Clive said he would ring some friends who knew Seamus, and see if they had any ideas.

David walked back along the seafront and past the beach huts. As he walked into the Chalk Cliff Way car park he spotted a young man standing by the sea wall. As David walked through the car park, the young man started walking towards him. They looked at each other. David recognised him as one of the people who were working in the Octopus that morning, and the young man clearly recognised David and immediately turned away. David noticed he was holding some leaflets. *Bingo!* David thought. *So, **this** is the car park in question! They must be giving out leaflets advertising the Octopus.*

When David was out of earshot he rang Clive and explained what had happened. Clive said he would ask a friend of his who doesn't normally spend time on the seafront, to go and do a bit of spying in the carpark. David said he was only too willing to help, if they wanted to sort out some kind of campaign, and he was sure Poppy would too. So Clive suggested they all met up tomorrow after they'd closed the Beachcomber and discuss what they could do.

Chapter 35

David had a highly successful day taking photographs for the Lynchester Golf Club's new website. Clive, being a regular member, had heard that the club was looking for someone to take photographs and of course recommended David. He had been photographing the clubhouse interior in the morning, especially the bar and the reception areas, and had spent the rest of the day concentrating on the exterior of the building and general shots of the golf course itself. David was keen to get home and load them onto the computer, but he didn't have time as he was due at the Beachcomber for their meeting.

He drove straight to the cafe and parked round the back. He turned up just as Carmen was turning over the SORRY WE ARE CLOSED sign on the door. Carmen smiled and opened the door for him.

'How are you my love?'

'In good shape!'

'Very smart! Obviously been working?'

'Yes, I've come straight from the golf club.'

'Of course. I'd forgotten about that, with everything else that's been going on. Tea?'

'Please. '

'Good day?'

'Yes, I enjoyed it. Walked about a million miles - but all good.'

'Is Poppy coming?'

'Yes, she was very keen to help. I'm surprised she's not here yet.' Clive appeared from the kitchen removing his apron.

'Hello David. There's been so little business today that I've already cleared up. Ridiculous isn't it. Anyway, I got my friend Jasper to visit the car park this morning. He couldn't

248

stop long, but he had a quick look around and saw a lad approaching people as they arrived, having a friendly chat with them and handing out leaflets. He didn't get approached himself, but he did manage to find one of the leaflets on the ground and he brought it in for us.' Clive took the leaflet out of his pocket. He unfolded it and put it on a table. David sat down. Carmen came over with a tray carrying mugs of hot tea. She put the tray down and looked at the leaflet like it was something she'd just scraped off the bottom of her shoe.

'I'll give him bloody Octopus burgers ... I mean how naff can you get? And who wants to eat bleedin' Octopus anyway? I certainly wouldn't.'

'Well I don't think they're actually made of ...' They were all interrupted by the sound of rapid foot steps outside and as they looked up the door swung open and Poppy burst in breathless ....

'You're not going to like this ... but ... I've found out what's been going on! I think I've solved the mystery!'

'Sit down Poppy. Have a cup of tea,' Clive said wearily, pulling out a chair for her. Poppy was expecting a bit more of a reaction, but everyone was just sitting there looking pretty glum.

'I think we know what's going on Poppy,' Carmen said. 'They've been giving leaflets to everyone in the Chalk Cliff Way Car Park, so they all go to the Octopus cafe instead of here.'

'Oh that's not all!' Poppy said as she sat down.

'Really?' the others all said in unison as they looked up.

'They're telling everyone The Beachcomber's closed! They've been purposely spreading it around.'

Carmen gasped. 'They can't do that. It's a lie. It must be illegal!'

'That makes sense,' Clive added. 'David, someone told you at your exhibition that we had closed didn't they? How do you know this Poppy?'

249

'Well ...' Poppy said as she leant back in the chair, 'I went to visit my mum and dad today. I had Chip with me, and I thought I'd take him to see them as they've been feeling quite down lately since my Uncle's been ill. They love Chip and he enjoys having a good run round in their garden. Anyway, virtually the first thing my mum said to me was, 'Oh we heard about your favourite cafe closing. That's a real shame! Where are you going to go now?' Well obviously I told them that you certainly are not closed, and of course I asked them who told them that news. They argued a bit about where they first heard it and eventually recalled that it was their neighbour Mabel who told them.'

'But who told her?' Carmen asked impatiently.

'Well, they then said that she was getting on a bit and sometimes gets confused, so maybe she'd got it wrong. I was keen to find out how the news was being spread about so I persuaded them to introduce me to Mabel. We popped round to see her - she likes Chip too - and she was very definite that The Beachcomber had closed, and that it had been Mrs Townsend from The Corner Shop who had told her.'

'That's interesting,' Carmen said, 'because Jenny Townsend often used to come down here on her day off, but I was just thinking the other day that I hadn't seen her for a while.'

'Exactly! Well after I'd taken Chip home I decided to go down to The Corner Shop and see Jenny. She told me that she was going to come down here a few weeks ago. So she drove into Chalk Cliff Way Car Park, and as she got out of the car a young lad approached her, and struck up a friendly conversation mentioning in passing that the Beachcomber was closed – indefinitely! Jenny said she'd been meaning to contact you and see if you were alright.'

'Oh so that's what they're doing!' Clive said angrily, 'They're not just giving out leaflets, they're actually spreading it around that we're closed! Bloody Seamus! Right! I'm going to find him right now.' He pushed his chair back and started getting up.

250

'No Clive. Please. No!' Carmen begged, putting her hand on his arm. 'We need to think about this calmly. I don't want you getting into a fight.' Carmen was seething, but something else was worrying her. She'd always wondered if Seamus had suspected something was going on with her and Jem. She didn't want to risk Clive finding out now, after Jem had died and it was all over.

'It's too late. He's started this, and I'm going to give him what for.'

Poppy grabbed Clive's arm. 'Clive please. I understand how you feel, and I'm really angry too, but Carmen's right, we've got to think carefully how to deal with this.'

David chipped in too, 'The ladies are right Clive. At least we know now what's going on. You can easily sort this out. All you need to do is let everyone know you *are* open. Look, I've been in that lousy place. It's rubbish. It's no competition for the Beachcomber. Once people know you are open they'll be delighted, and they'll all come rushing back.

'David's right,' Carmen said. 'Let's all sit down calmly and think about this. We can come up with a plan and organise some publicity.'

'I'm surprised you're being so calm about this Carmen,' Clive said. 'It's not like you at all. Look how much business he's lost us over the last few weeks.'

'Believe me Clive I'm as livid as you are. But at least we know now what's been going on and we know it's not down to us that people haven't been coming in here so much. And of course … like David says… we can fix it!'

Chapter 36

Towards the end of yet another worryingly quiet morning in the cafe, Carmen looked up from wiping the counter to see Clive returning. He was deep in thought as he approached the cafe, but he looked up and smiled as he came in through the door.

'Someone looks pleased with himself?' she said smiling back at him.

'Yes – it's been a productive morning actually. I managed to have a long chat with Daniel Whitton, you know the DJ at Sebleigh Radio. I explained everything that's been going on. Oh, by the way, he can't stand him either – Seamus I mean – had a run in with him some time ago. He'd love to see the smirk wiped off his face too. Anyway, he recorded an interview with me. He told me not to name any names but I explained all about the lies that have been circulating about us being closed. He's going to try and air it today. That will be a good start.

'Oh great. Well done Clive. I'll turn the radio up and listen out for it - make sure I hear it. Do you think that will be enough?'

'Oh no – that's just the start. He recommended I go and see someone at the Sebleigh Free Press and hopefully they'll carry an article about us this Friday. So if you can manage without me I'll be off there shortly.'

'Well we're hardly snowed under are we?' Carmen said glancing around the cafe, 'unless of course the radio airs your interview straightaway and everyone comes pouring in?'

'Mmm… David been in?'

'Yes. He's been working on the leaflet for us – he's such a love isn't he? – Bought me a copy to look at – it's in the kitchen. Give him a ring if you're happy with it and he'll take it to the printer this afternoon. Oh that reminds me, Rose was here as well and she said she'd pay the WI a visit – hasn't been there for ages – and she'll give out the leaflets too and tell everyone about us.'

'Excellent – that's a good start. If word of mouth has nearly ruined our business, I don't see why it can't save it too. Oh, and another thing... I gave Peter Plaistow a ring – left a message telling him what's happened. Would like to get some friendly advice from him.'

'Good. Hopefully you being mates with a cop will encourage you to stay on the straight and narrow and not go and do anything stupid.'

'As if...?' Clive said with a smile.

'You wouldn't would you?'

'I don't know what you mean.'

'Yes you do.'

'Okay, I promise I'll behave. Scouts honour. Mind you I can't say that the thought of seeing Booth wandering around the town with two black eyes and a broken nose doesn't appeal to me.'

'Shhhh – keep your voice down.'

Despite Carmen listening carefully all day to the radio in the cafe, at close of play she still hadn't heard any mention of Clive and his interview about the cafe. That evening at home Clive told her not to worry, it would probably be aired the next day.

However, another day passed and in fact by the end of the week not only had the radio interview not been aired but on Friday the Sebleigh Free Press came out and despite Clive having supplied them with a good story there was nothing in the paper.

Clive went into the kitchen with his mobile and spent quite some time on the phone to the radio station and the newspaper. Carmen was serving their few customers and was rather embarrassed as she could hear Clive's raised voice in the kitchen in the background. When he came off the phone he called her into the kitchen away from the customers.

'God you won't believe this! Bloody Seamus! He's really got it coming to him now.'

'Why? What's happened?'

'Well... put it this way... because he advertises extensively on the radio *and* in the Sebleigh Free Press, neither of them are prepared to run my story. Bloody ridiculous! I didn't even mention his name in the interview! The people at the Free Press wouldn't even talk to me, but I eventually got hold of Daniel Whitton at the radio. He was very embarrassed about it but he kind of hinted as to what had happened – his boss obviously wouldn't let him go ahead with it. Can't upset a major advertiser!'

'That's ridiculous! So where does that leave us? I really thought that would be the answer to all our problems.'

'Right! That's it. I can't hang around here doing nothing. I'm off to the stupid Octopus right now to see if he's there.' Clive ripped off his apron, threw it on the counter and charged out the door, leaving Carmen standing there open mouthed.

'Oh no,' she said quietly to herself. But as she watched Clive charge off outside she was relieved to see the familiar figure of PC Plaistow approaching and Clive, in thunderous mood, almost bumped into him.

'Oh thank God,' Carmen said to herself. She watched as Clive and PC Plaistow stayed outside away from the customers to have a chat. She could see Clive ranting at the policeman who stood there calmly taking it all in. After a while they both came in the cafe.

'Carmen, would you get us some tea – it is tea you like isn't it Peter?' By the time Carmen had fetched some tea and cakes, their last remaining customers had left so she sat down and joined Clive and the policeman.

'Carmen,' PC Plaistow addressed her, 'I've just been telling Clive I don't want him going anywhere near Seamus Booth.'

'Good – but we can't just sit back and do nothing. He's

254

got us into a right mess here.'

'I didn't say anything about sitting back and doing nothing did I? Look, what I've been trying to say is, I've lived in this town all of my life and this isn't the first time something like this has happened. If you turn this into a big battle with Booth, it will just end up making both of you look pretty bad.'

'Why should it make us look bad? We haven't done anything wrong Peter...' Carmen interrupted.

'What I'm saying is that if it turns into a big slagging off situation people will just end up thinking it's six of one and half a dozen of the other. Believe me – I've seen it all before. The best thing for you to do is to completely ignore him and put all your energies into publicising your own business. Let everyone know you're open... get some publicity – positive publicity, instead of slagging off Seamus to the press or to anyone... Just hold a special event or two - like you did with the open day for the dogs. Or you could come up with an anniversary or a special date... I don't know – make something up if you have to. And as far as Seamus Booth's concerned the best way to get back at him is to hold your head high and show him how well you're doing.'

'Yes I know you're right Peter, but it's easier said than done' Clive said sulkily.

'I don't want you going anywhere near him okay? I hope I've got that message across.'

'Hmm ... Yes, okay.' Clive said begrudgingly.

'Oh another thing ... do you two belong to that local Facebook Group? Sebleigh Conversation Group or something like that?'

'You're joking,' Clive sneered, 'we're not great with all that stuff. We wouldn't know what Facebook was if it bit us on the bum.'

'We haven't managed to keep up with the review site let alone anything else,' added Carmen.

'Well you should join Facebook and follow that group. People advertise their businesses a lot on there, and you can write pretty well anything you like on it. I would advise you not to go slagging people off though – the rows that develop on there have been pretty horrendous – just stay professional and use it to let everyone know you're up and running, and tell them about what you do, special offers, that sort of thing. Don't mention anything negative. Just publicise yourself.'

'But I can't think that many locals bother to look at it Peter,' Carmen said.

'You're joking!' Peter laughed. 'At least half of Sebleigh is on it. You're missing out big time if you're not using it. And you need to set up your own Facebook page for the cafe. You could've sorted all this out ages ago if you'd used it.'

'I'm sure David could help us with that Carmen – all the youngsters are into it aren't they?'

'Changing the subject Peter,' Carmen said 'is there anything you can do to help us – with Slimy I mean? Surely it can't be legal him going around spreading those lies about us can it?'

'Well no, not officially… it would be virtually impossible to prove he's done anything wrong… so there is nothing really I can do.' But as he said that he turned to Carmen and gave her a very obvious wink.

Chapter 37

Carmen and Clive, painfully aware of the fact that they'd already lost a large chunk of their vital summer business, didn't waste any time in organising their comeback campaign, with much help and encouragement from their friends, especially Poppy and David.

Naturally they weren't only spurred on by a need to salvage their business, but also to wipe the grin from Seamus Booth's face. Clive talked to his friends at the golf club and the Rotary, many of whom had business connections in the town. They were keen to help if they could. One of his friends ran a sign making company and produced a magnificent, large, Beachcomber Cafe sign and Clive applied to the council for planning permission to erect it in the Chalk Cliff Way car park. He was infuriated to be told that it would be a month until the next planning meeting was going to take place and he'd have to wait until then before they would even discuss it. However, PC Peter Plaistow advised him on the quiet that if he put the sign up straight away, the worst that was likely to happen was that the council would ask him to take it down. So he might as well get on and do it anyway.

David took some photos and designed an attractive leaflet and poster, advertising the Beachcomber Cafe and Carmen got busy arranging some offers and special events for different groups. Particularly popular were the weekly cut priced OAP lunches. Rose was very keen to do her bit to help so she enthusiastically publicised them at the Sebleigh Bay W.I. Poppy did a wonderful job of delivering leaflets to Sebleigh Bay's businesses and houses during her dog walks. She also approached anyone she saw with a dog and reminded them of the delightful dog friendly cafe along past the beach huts. She was surprised how many people in

Sebleigh Bay didn't even know about the Beachcomber or hadn't been there for many years.

As Poppy entered the cafe at the end of a particularly busy lunchtime she came face to face with Carmen who was rushing around looking flushed.

'Gosh Carmen – you look like you've been rushed off your feet.'

'Yes. I'm not used to this – we haven't been this busy for ages. I'm not complaining mind. Today's big turnout is all thanks to our lovely Rose bringing her ladies from the WI along for lunch.'

'I passed a whole group of them walking back to the car park just now, and I heard one of them saying that she hadn't been to the cafe for 25 years, and how lovely it is now.'

'I know! We've had a lot of good feedback – several people said they'd come back again soon. It's surprising how many people in Sebleigh Bay don't even know about us, or haven't visited since we took it over. It's made me realise that we need to advertise regularly, and let people know what we do here. Oh and David's going to create a Facebook presence for us.'

'Talking of which I came to tell you I've completely run out of my leaflets now.'

'You've run out? What all of them?' Carmen was flabbergasted. 'Free cappuccinos for you for life!'

'Let me have some more and I'll carry on. Oh, and by the way ... there was a police car outside the Octopus just now.'

'Really? That's funny – Clive saw one there yesterday afternoon too. He thought it was Peter Plaistow. Wonder what's going on?'

Seamus Booth stormed in through the door of the Octopus cafe after receiving a text message from one of his staff there.

'Do you mind telling me what's going on?' he aggressively addressed the policeman who was talking to a bunch of teenagers who were playing on a slot machine.

'And … who might you be?' PC Plaistow slowly and calmly asked Seamus, knowing very well who he was.

'I'm Seamus Booth – Councillor Seamus Booth - I own this place and I'd like to know what you're doing here. I've been told you were here yesterday as well.' A family who were just about to enter the cafe, noted the policeman and the raised voices and changed their minds and decided to look for somewhere else to have their snack.

'I'm just carrying out random spot checks for drugs – that sort of thing.'

'Drugs!!? Well we don't have any trouble here so I'd thank you not to bother my customers.'

'It's alright,' Peter spoke calmly as he checked his police radio. 'I've spoken to everyone in here already. Everything's under control.'

'Well, unless there's anything else I can help you with, can I show you out then?'

'Actually ... seeing as you asked, there is something else. I think I'm due a tea break. I'll have a cup of tea please.'

'To take away?' Seamus asked hopefully.

'No. I'll drink it here thank you.'

Peter Plaistow sat down at the back of the cafe and leisurely sipped his cup of tea which Seamus had begrudgingly ordered one of his staff to make for him. Normally he didn't like his presence to make people feel uncomfortable, but on this occasion he was enjoying observing Seamus's agitated behaviour. He knew how much stress a vindictive person like Booth could cause his victims and he was determined to try and help the Colliers. They were thoroughly decent people and didn't deserve the lies that had been spread about their business. Booth had been a troublemaker for years. They had a file on him at the Police Station – lots of complaints of minor harassment and intimidating behaviour – even a suggestion of blackmail - but nothing concrete enough that the police could actually charge him.

259

Seamus was pacing up and down behind the counter, regularly glaring at the policeman and willing him to leave so as not to put off his customers. It was bad enough that his police car was parked outside on the road without him choosing to take his tea breaks in here too! Peter was just considering having a piece of cake in order to stretch out his visit further, when a family friend came in with her two boys providing him with the perfect excuse to hang around for a while.

'Oh hello Peter!' she said, delighted to see him. 'That's a coincidence – we saw Ingrid this morning in the supermarket. We were saying we must arrange a get together. A barbeque would be good if the weather holds out.'

'That would be excellent. How are you my dear?' Peter got up and kissed his wife's best friend Natalie on the cheek.

'I'm great thanks. Just bringing these two in for a burger – they've been nagging me for ages.'

'Leo look!' said the older boy. 'These burgers are made of octopus.'

'Eww ... I'd rather have a beef burger please. Can we sit with you Peter?'

'Yes of course you can. Look Natalie, let me buy these for you. You've treated us to so many wonderful barbeques in your beautiful garden. Ingrid and I were saying that it's our turn to reciprocate, and as we've never got round to building a barbeque let me at least buy you these.'

Natalie of course said that it wasn't necessary, but Peter was insistent and after all he did feel that he was using this family a little for his own agenda in order to have an excuse to keep an eye on Seamus. After he'd ordered food and drinks for them he approached another couple of teenagers who'd just come in, and he politely asked if he could search the bag that one of them was carrying. Peter could see Seamus's face going red and him clenching his fists in anger but being unable to complain in front of the customers. Sebleigh Bay police did have a policy of carrying out regular spot checks in certain areas, mainly to let the youngsters know that if they were tempted by drugs they stood a good chance of being caught out. It had proved to be an effective way in helping school kids in particular to stay clear of them.

After enjoying a delightful half hour with Natalie and the boys, Peter bought them all an ice-cream before leaving. At the counter Seamus muttered angrily to him,

'I trust it's not just my cafe that you're paying your visits to?'

'Oh no. Rest assured I'll be spending plenty of time all along the seafront today.'

Seamus breathed a sigh of relief as the policeman finally left the cafe, but it was short lived when he realised that the policeman had set off along the seafront on foot leaving his police car right outside the Octopus. And there it stayed all afternoon while Peter went about his duties in the town.

The following morning Poppy turned up at the Beachcomber with Rosie the Rotty. Carmen was petrified of her so Poppy tied her lead to the railing outside. She could see Carmen watching her through the window with a disapproving look on her face.

'I hope you get paid well for all that Rottweiler sitting you do?'

Poppy laughed. 'Same rates as usual.'

'You should get double for dangerous dogs. Anyway ...' she said changing to a lighter mood, 'I'm glad you're here. You said yesterday that you'd delivered all those leaflets, and I didn't get round to thanking you properly. Come here.' Carmen gave Poppy a big hug. 'You've been so good to us. We owe you big time. It's really starting to pay off too. We've got lots more people coming in again. This morning I've taken bookings for two different company staff lunches – good numbers too. That's all thanks to the leaflets you dropped in. Oh and Clive's got the sign up this morning in the car park.

'I know! It's huge! It looks fantastic. That will make all the difference.'

'Yes it should do. Trouble is we haven't got permission yet so no doubt that nasty creep will be telephoning the council today as soon as he sees it. Anyway – we'll just wait and see what happens. What can I get you my dear? It's on the house.'

'Cappucino please Carmen.'

'Have a cake as well. Here - I'll give you a lemon drizzle - I know it's your favourite. You know about the police car outside the Octopus don't you.' Carmen said quietly with a mischievous smile.

'Yes. Two days running !' Poppy laughed. 'Was there an incident?'

'I couldn't possibly say! It's not there again today is it?'

'No – or at least it wasn't when I walked by. Actually ... now you say that ... I did notice that there was a pest control van outside.' Carmen looked puzzled and then burst out laughing.

'Excuse me ...' she rushed into the kitchen and spoke to Clive and came out with a big grin on her face. Poppy leaned over and whispered to Carmen,

'He's not a friend of Clive's is he? The rat bloke.'

'I couldn't possibly comment. There's only one rat in that place and he'll need more than the pest control people to sort him out.'

'Mm.'

'Oh and talking of pest control, that bloody seagull has just had someone else's dinner. Dad keeps going after it with his water pistol!'

As Poppy walked back along the beach with Rosie she couldn't help veering towards the Octopus to see if anything was going on there. As she clipped Rosie's lead back on she laughed to herself remembering the way that Carmen always gave the soppy great dog such dirty looks. She tickled

Rosie's head and said 'Come on Gorgeous – let's go and see what they serve at the Octopus.'

Poppy spent some time reading the menu in the window of the cafe. She couldn't see Seamus Booth in there – just some young lads and a girl serving the customers. It was very much a young person's cafe – all burgers and slot machines. Totally different to The Beachcomber Cafe. She couldn't understand why they would bother to try and ruin things for Carmen and Clive. Surely there was room for both cafes in a town like this. After all there were already numerous other food outlets along the seafront.

Next time she saw Clive in The Beachcomber she asked him what Seamus Booth's problem was.

'Oh he's had it in for us for a long time, but like you say, it's all so pointless. He's a very arrogant type. It's probably just a case that the Octopus isn't going nearly as well as he thought so he's choosing to blame us and our business instead of admitting he can't run a cafe and make it work.'

'But why has he got it in for you?'

'How long have you got? Well he and Carmen go back a long way. I think she was at school with him. He comes from a wealthy family – that's the only reason he's got so many businesses – it's the family money he's used to set them up. Carmen said that when he was young he was quite a good looking and known to be well off, so he was popular and had his pick of the girls as well. I guess he was used to getting his own way a lot. Don't tell Carmen I told you this but I think he made a play for her very publicly and she rejected him. Knowing his ego I doubt he ever forgave her. Then I had some run-ins with him over council business. I was on the council some years back. Seamus and I both fought for the same seat and I won. It was very amusing because he never thought for a moment that he'd lose. He didn't put any effort into his election campaign, but I spent many hours canvassing and listening to people on their doorsteps to find out what they really wanted for the town.

263

You should have seen his face when the votes were counted. Priceless!'

'I think I'm starting to get the picture!'

'That's not all. Seamus soon got himself elected anyway – only because someone dropped out and he was the only person interested. I never agreed with any of his ridiculous schemes. It was so obvious they were all geared up to lining his own pockets and not for the good of the town and its residents, so I objected to pretty well everything he proposed. Another reason he hates me!'

'What a delightful bloke!'

'You could say that.' Clive said with a laugh. 'Anyway, that's far too much about him for one day. Let's change the subject. Have you heard about the fun run?'

'No? Fun run? Hey that wouldn't have anything to do with me seeing David sneaking off at the crack of dawn in his jogging suit would it?' Clive laughed again!

'Oh so he really is going to enter then? No it's really great news actually. My friend Gordon Bell who I play golf with is the Chairman of the Sebleigh Bay Events committee. To cut a long story short he's come up with a fantastic event which is going to be put into action very speedily to catch the end of the summer holidays. It's a fun run along the beach starting at the pier ruins and ending right outside here!'

'Oh that's brilliant!' Poppy said enthusiastically.

'Yes – the cafe will be open but we're also going to put on an extra barbeque outside, and Gordon is arranging all sorts of stalls on the beach – crafts, games, competitions, that sort of thing. The tide will be out of course. It's going in the local paper this Friday to let everyone know and you can download sponsor forms on line or pick them up in shops and cafes.'

'Who is the money being raised for?'

'Well most of it is going to the damaged pier fund and a donation will be made to a local children's charity.'

264

'Amazing! Have you thought of including a dog show at all? You know ... just a fun one with all sorts of categories, so that anyone with a dog can enter? I'm sure it would attract lots of dog owners and provide another opportunity for them to see the Beachcomber.'

'That's a very interesting idea Poppy. Let me think about that one and see what Gordon says.'

That evening, Clive phoned Poppy at home and asked her if she'd like to organise the dog show. She leapt in the air with excitement. It was going to be the most fun challenge she'd ever had in her life. She agreed immediately and Clive took steps to get it added to all the publicity.

As promised the Sebleigh Bay Beach Fun Run was publicised widely. The local paper had a large feature and Sebleigh Bay Radio mentioned it at every possible opportunity. They interviewed various people who were involved in the organisation of the event and Poppy was asked to talk on air about the dog show. The whole town got behind the event because everyone had been so angry to lose the pier and felt very strongly that somehow the vast amount of money required to fix it must be found. Everyone knew that this event alone wouldn't raise the millions needed, but it was a good starting point and might help to attract investors.

Local businesses were keen to get involved and the event soon turned into something much more significant than was originally envisaged, with all sorts of beach activities being arranged all the way along the race route. Carmen and Clive were thrilled that every poster and piece of publicity mentioned that the race would be finishing outside the Beachcomber Cafe.

A whole week had gone by and the large Beachcomber Cafe sign was still up in the Chalk Cliff Way car park. Carmen and Clive had heard nothing from the council.

Late one afternoon in the cafe when things were quietening down, David came jogging along in his shorts, t-shirt and trainers and entered the cafe with his mobile phone in his hand. He bent over with his hands on his knees and as he struggled to get his breath back, he gasped,

'Poppy's just texted me. She's about to be interviewed on the radio.'

'Clive quick,' Carmen shouted. 'Turn the radio up – Poppy's on.' David and Carmen sat down just in time to hear Dan Whitton introducing her.

'... and today's Sebleigh Bay Beach Fun Run guest is Poppy Dancey. Welcome to the show Poppy.'

'Thank you Dan.'

'So Poppy, perhaps you would explain to our listeners exactly what it is you're organising for the event of the year in Sebleigh Bay?'

'Yes of course. I'm organising a Dog Show which will take place straight after the fun run, in an arena just outside the Beachcomber Cafe where the run finishes.'

'So just to remind everyone – the Beachcomber Cafe is at the far east end of the promenade, beyond the long row of beach huts.'

'Yes that's right – and of course it's one of the most dog friendly cafes in Sebleigh Bay. Water bowls are always provided and you can even take your dogs into the cafe with you. It's open all year round as well.'

'That's great. So Poppy ... what kind of dogs will be able to enter the show?'

'Absolutely any dogs at all Dan. Anything from pedigrees to mongrels, big dogs, small dogs. There's going to be lots of different categories fun categories – with prizes and rosettes for the winners. Nothing too serious.'

'So, I'm really intrigued to know what the fun categories might be. Can you give us some examples?'

'Yes of course, well there will be things like, dog with the most waggiest tail, most appealing expression, shiniest coat, dog that looks like its owner, best trick, cuddliest looking dog. People can enter their pet for as many categories as

266

they like. We're being sponsored by Sebleigh Bay Pets, and Pets-on-Sea. They're providing some fabulous prizes.....

'She's doing well isn't she?' Carmen said excitedly.

'She ought to be, she's practised enough,' David joked.

'Shhh!' Carmen said with a laugh.

As Poppy reached the end of her interview Dan asked her,

'So Poppy, I can tell you're obviously dog mad. Presumably you have a dog or two of your own?'

'No I don't actually,' she said sadly. 'Not since I lost my lovely dog a couple of years ago. I still miss him so much. He was a red setter cross called Pluto ...'

Ten days had passed since Clive erected the large Beachcomber sign in the carpark, and they hadn't yet heard anything from the council about it. David and Poppy had walked past the Octopus Cafe numerous times and hadn't seen Seamus for a while.

'Maybe he's on holiday?' Clive suggested to Carmen. 'You can bet that if he'd seen the sign he would have been straight on to the council to report us.'

'What about the council workers who maintain the payment machines in the car park? They would have seen it too.'

'They probably wouldn't take any notice. One department doesn't have a clue what the other's doing – I doubt anyone would bat an eyelid unless they're actually in the planning department. Of course, because we've applied to Planning you would think that they would have sent someone down there to have a look at the car park by now. They obviously haven't done that yet or they would have seen it.'

'Well whatever happens, it's done wonders for our business already – that and the leaflets – we're totally back on track. It's been our busiest week ever, and at least everyone knows we're open now.'

Funnily enough later on that day a group of officials, looking very out of place in their suits, turned up outside the Beachcomber Cafe. Carmen and Clive watched as they walked around outside with clipboards and pens. They were making marks in the sand and were measuring out areas. Carmen and Clive guessed they must be from the Sebleigh Bay Events Committee, making plans for the Fun Run day.

After a while they came into the cafe. All seven of them came up to the counter.

'Hello ladies and gentlemen,' Carmen said, pouring out all her usual charm.

'Hello,' said a very smart looking business woman of about 40, who was wearing a black trouser suit. She glanced down at her clipboard and said, 'Are you Mrs Collier by any chance?'

'Yes that's right. Carmen Collier, and this is my husband Clive.' She turned to Clive as he came out of the kitchen. The woman smiled.

'Ah excellent. I'm Amanda Borling from the Planning Department at Sebleigh Bay Town Council, and two of my colleagues here are also from the council and the others belong to the Sebleigh Bay Events Committee.'

Clive said, 'Oh you'll know my friend Gordon Bell then who's the Chairman?'

'Yes,' said a man standing at the back of the group. 'He can't be here today I'm afraid but I'm standing in for him and we're just making a few plans for the Fun Run.'

'Oh we guessed that's what you must be doing.'

After some polite chat about the Fun Run event and how exciting it was going to be for everyone, Amanda said they'd like to order tea and cakes all round. She gestured to the others to go and sit down and spoke to Carmen and Clive,

'I need to have a talk with you about the large Beachcomber Cafe sign which has been erected in the Chalk Cliff Way car park.' A family entered the cafe, so Clive steered Amanda over to a small table while Carmen served the customers, whilst desperately trying to listen to Clive's conversation.

'Right ... the sign ...' Clive said as he sat down. ' I don't know if you're aware of the circumstances at all...' Amanda held her hand up...

'Can I just interrupt you Mr Collier?'

'Well I'd like to explain if I can ...'

'We've received your planning application – a retrospective application as it happens,' she continued, ignoring Clive, 'which is due to be discussed at our next meeting. It was drawn to our attention last week that you had already erected the sign ...'. Clive raised his eyebrows.

'Seamus Booth no doubt.'

'Let me continue please Mr Collier. The Sebleigh Bay Events Committee has pointed out to me that it is vital that we have good signage in place for the Sebleigh Bay Beach Fun Run event, of which the Beachcomber Cafe plays such a significant part. We have however carried out an inspection of the sign and we need it to conform to health and safety standards.'

'Well I didn't make it as solid as I would have liked to because I thought I might have to...'

'My proposal is that the Sebleigh Bay Events Committee will organise for someone to carry out the work on the sign, at no cost to yourselves, to bring it up to the normal Council car park standards. But we would like your permission to attach some temporary signs to it – above it - which will advertise the event – which we will remove the day after the Fun Run leaving your sign in good order.'

Carmen was watching from the counter. She thought Clive seemed a little agitated trying to put his point across, and then she observed him visibly relaxing as the discussion seemed to be over and finally he signed some paperwork for Amanda.

When Amanda had joined her colleagues over by the window for their tea and cakes, Clive rushed back towards the kitchen and quickly whispered to Carmen 'Up yours Seamus!' and Carmen knew all was well.

Chapter 38

Poppy was woken up by the buzz of her alarm clock and immediately threw back the duvet and leapt out of bed in a state of excitement. The day of the Sebleigh Bay Fun Run day had finally arrived! And more importantly for Poppy, her very own dog show which had been on her mind every second of every day since she'd been asked to organise it.

She knew David was bored from hearing each last detail of her plans, but she just couldn't help herself. He did seem to be thoroughly amused though by the increasing collection of equipment that had been building up in her living room for the dogs' obstacle course. They had even set up one of the jumps and practised leaping over it whilst pretending to be various different breeds of dogs.

David was keen to record the events of the day so he set off down to the pier with his camera quite early on, to do some photography before the races started.

He couldn't remember ever seeing the beach as full of activity as it was today. Groups of people were standing around chatting as they watched the sea … willing it to recede far enough so that they could start setting up their stands and tables. David felt quite emotional seeing the whole town pulling together, and he thought of his mum.

*You'd have loved all this Mum... There's such a buzz about the place today ... It feels special ... Today's going to be brilliant... I wish you could have known my mad neighbour too. She's talked of nothing ... and I mean **nothing**, other than her dog show, ever since she dreamt up the idea. 'David, what do you think of this idea? David I've thought up another category of dogs.... How about dog with the pointiest ears? ... dog with the ugliest face? ... dog with the saggiest tummy?' Okay so I made those up, but you know what I mean Mum. And then there's her obstacle course!*

Do you know, she actually sets it up in her flat!! I keep hearing her crashing about in there trying out the jumps! Wouldn't be so bad if she wasn't so blooming clumsy! Okay, so if I'm honest, I did have a go too! But she's nuts Mum. She must have got through about a hundred notebooks full of plans for the little pooches. And she's gone through every idea at least six times each with me.

David was smiling as he thought about Poppy. *I'm going to make sure I photograph every second of that dog show for her. I don't think her own wedding, or the birth of her child could mean much more to her than this!*

David had photographed the pier (or what was left of it after the boat had crashed through the middle of it) on countless occasions in the past, and from almost every angle possible. But it was thrilling to see it come alive today with huge coloured banners stretched across the imposing black metal structure. David got busy with his camera, recording these unique images. There was even a large hoarding attached to one of the girders advertising the events at the other end of the beach with the Beachcomber Cafe and Poppy's dog show prominently mentioned. He would be able to show the photos to Poppy, Carmen and Clive as they wouldn't have time to come down to the pier this morning and see it for themselves.

Carmen and Clive had employed lots of extra staff for the day. Friends and their teenage offspring had been called in to help with the expected crowds. Some of them had offered as a favour, but Carmen and Clive insisted on paying them. Mind you, as they arrived at the cafe at the crack of dawn, Carmen was mumbling to Clive, 'I bloody well hope today is as busy as predicted and the expected hoards arrive or it will have bankrupted us paying all the staff and buying so much extra food.'

'Don't be so negative Carmen. I'm sure it will be fine, and even if it isn't, the amount of free publicity we'll get through this event will be more than worth it.'

'Yes I expect you're right Clive.'

'Oh that's a first!' Clive said sounding surprised. 'You admitting I'm right. What time's your Dad getting here with all the barbeque stuff?'

'Soon,' Carmen said glancing at the clock.

'Are you sure he knows what he's doing on the barbeque?'

'Well he says he does. As you know, he's a good cook.' Carmen put on a deep gruff voice that always made Clive laugh. 'No ready meals or takeaways for me Carmen ... none of that microwave nonsense...' Then Clive joined in and they said in unison, 'I'm not having my food *nuked* thank you very much ...'

Sebleigh's multi-storey car parks were filling up fast and every residential road was chockablock with parked cars. People were pouring through the streets on foot and heading towards the pier. Serious runners dressed in skimpy shorts and sports tops, showing well toned muscles, were mingling with the fun runners in the wackiest of costumes – anything from super heroes to toddlers' tv characters.

As David headed back towards his flat to get changed he spotted Wonderwoman and Spiderman nonchalantly strolling down the steps onto the beach. Spiderman saw David with his large professional looking camera and called out,

'Hey, Harry Potter, do you want to take our photo?' David laughed.

'Sure. Why not? Err ... why don't you pose just there and I'll photograph you with the pier in the background.' Without further ado, Wonderwoman leapt into Spiderman's arms and pouted her lips in an exaggerated way.

'Are you from the press?' she asked, as David composed the view.

'Well err no, not exactly, but I may well send my photos into the local rag.'

As David fired off some pictures Spiderman called out to someone behind David. 'Oi, Tinkywinky, come here quickly – we're being photographed for the newspaper. Come and have your picture taken.' Before David knew it he was organising groups of characters including the four teletubbies, some doctors and nurses complete with a hospital bed, and a large group of children dressed as pirates. He had no idea if Sebleigh News would actually use any of his photos, but he thought on his feet and gave out his business cards to everyone, telling them to check his website after the event.

Poppy parked in the space Clive had reserved for her at the back of the cafe. She couldn't fit all the dog show gear into her car, so her parents were collecting the rest of it in a while, along with David's camera bag. She rushed into the cafe calling out to Carmen and Clive with excitement in her voice,

'You won't believe how many people are heading towards the pier. The Fun Run's going to be *massive*! Half of Sebleigh must be entering. I hope they've printed out plenty of numbers for the runners. You're going to be busy here I can tell you.'

'That's brilliant Poppy.' Carmen said as she was rushing around getting the cafe ready. 'Any sign of Dad? He needs to get that barbeque underway soon I should think.' Funnily enough at that moment Oswald appeared outside along with three mature glamorous ladies laden down with bagfuls of food and barbeque gear. The four of them started setting up just beyond the finishing line. Carmen went out to greet her dad with a hug.

'So who are these lovely ladies?' She smiled at the women who were busy putting on their white aprons and chefs' hats.

'Carmen, May I introduce Judith, Helen and Catherine? They're all here to help produce the best barbeque you could wish for. Now, just go and get on with your job and leave us to get things going out here. No need to worry about us.'

'Yes Sir!' Carmen said with amusement. 'Ladies – what would you like to drink? The least I can do is get you a cup of tea or coffee. And what's with the super soaker Dad?' Carmen asked, noticing Oswald's giant machine gun sized water pistol leaning up against the table?'

274

'Never you mind. You just get on with your tasks and leave me to mine.'

'I assume it's for pest control.'

'You could say that.'

The beach outside the cafe was the busiest Carmen and Clive had ever seen it. As well as the finishing line which was marked out with large hoardings, there was a Punch and Judy show and numerous stalls which were going up all over the place. Clive's friend Gordon from the Sebleigh Events Committee was adding the finishing touches to the official looking stand which had been set up on the beach just outside the cafe, complete with large speakers and sound system. He picked up a microphone, switched it on and tried it out.

'Testing, testing, one, two, three ...'

'Hello Gordon, how's it going?'

'All up and ready I think Clive.'

'I must say I don't know how you've managed to organise such a big event in such a short time. It's incredible. When I was on the council it took months just to get permission for the most trivial of things.'

'Well we didn't have a clue how big this whole thing would turn out to be. If we had done it probably wouldn't have happened. But once it started it's just snowballed into something huge – everyone has wanted to be a part of it.'

'Everyone wants to get the pier back that's why.'

'Exactly. Every organisation in the town seems to have got behind us – and all the schools and local groups. There's a huge number of runners coming down to the beach – I can tell you now they haven't printed off nearly enough numbers for them.'

'Oh dear – does that matter?'

'No. We're not going to stop anyone from entering. Anyway – we've got someone working on it right now. Between you and me there's talk of this becoming a yearly event and we'll know what we're doing next time.'

'Well it looks to me like you're doing a pretty good job this time.'

'Oh I must tell you this ... Seamus Booth has been pestering us relentlessly to use the area outside *his* cafe. He's come up with all sorts of nonsense about the main events needing to be near the car park. When that didn't work he offered to have a special children's run starting there, claiming its too far for kids to run from the pier.'

'Half a mile?' Clive laughed.

'I know. That's only the half of it. He's tried to make out that we're not conforming with health and safety standards. He's been a right pest. He's even stooped as low as pretending to be concerned about the disabled and elderly, but we've got all that covered.'

'Oh yes, Oswald was telling me about the land rover shuttling people backwards and forwards on the back road?'

'Yes and it's free of charge as well. The Grand Hotel has put up the money. It will be operating all day and Chalk Cliff Way is being swept of pebbles as we speak so the mobility scooters and wheelchairs can use it – and the parents with prams.'

'Marvellous Gordon. I'm most impressed.' Clive's mobile phone pinged in his pocket with an incoming text message. 'Excuse me a moment Gordon – better check this.'

> *Clive, just to give you a heads up. Heard a rumour that Seamus wanted to enter the fun run - you know how competitive the old bastard is - but he doesn't want anyone to recognise him so he's wearing a Darth Vader costume!! Don't know for definite it's him but someone thought they spotted him putting the helmet on. Probably wants to spy on you all too. Have a brilliant day! May the force be with you ... hahaha ...*

Down at the pier huge crowds of runners were gathering while their families headed down towards the Beachcomber to see their loved ones complete the race. A large replica cannon was being positioned by the Sebleigh Battle Re-enactment Association to mark the start of each race.

Outside the Beachcomber a tape was stretched across the finishing line for the races and finally the cannon was heard in the distance! Everyone cheered and waited for the first winners to arrive. It didn't take long for the serious male runners who were in the first group to complete their race and arrive at the finish to enormous cheers from the crowds. The winners from each group were presented with medals to mark the event.

There was another loud bang from the cannon and the next group arrived soon afterwards - this time the group of the fastest ladies came powering through the finish line in their coloured Lycra with the names of local running clubs on their tops. The cheers from the crowds continued for every single race. The cafe and the barbecue area outside were chockablock with visitors buying coffees and snacks. Carmen and Clive and their band of helpers were rushed off their feet all morning. The races continued and David suddenly appeared over the finish line amongst a group of young men. Luckily, Poppy was there to see him and take some snaps of him on her phone. David was puffing and blowing and when Poppy asked him if he was alright, he acted up a bit and pretended to collapse in a really 'over the top' way. Poppy knew him too well by this point and wasn't fooled by his antics but a first aider rushed over to check that he was okay. Poppy reprimanded David for wasting the paramedic's time and explained that he was fine.

Next were the children's races in various different age groups, receiving extra loud applause and encouragement from their parents and relatives.

Finally, it was time for the groups of people in fancy dress. The crowds were ready with their cameras to photograph the hilarious looking characters lumbering towards the finish line in their crazy costumes. Up in the lead was none other than Darth Vader. He stormed towards the finishing line with his black cape blowing behind him.

277

But at the very last minute he seemed to trip and his feet somehow got caught up in the cape and he flew through the air at speed, crashing on the ground a few yards before the finish line.

The paramedics were alerted and came rushing over accompanied by a runner dressed as a gorilla. They all bent over him asking if he was okay as the other runners in costume finished their race, with Superman winning the medal for being first, and the very beefy looking men in nurses costumes carrying the hospital bed bringing up the rear. The 'patient' covered in masses of bandages hopped off the bed and offered it to Darth Vader who was being attended to by the paramedics. With the help of the gorilla and Superman, he was lifted onto the bed. A paramedic insisted that he took off his helmet so they could check he was alright. He resisted as long as possible, but eventually the helmet came off revealing a very sheepish looking Seamus Booth who was trying to cover his face because he didn't want to be recognised, particularly as he had made such a fool of himself.

Fortunately, David had filmed the incident and word soon got round to Carmen and Clive of Seamus's accident! Unsurprisingly they weren't exactly sorry for him. Seamus had injured his leg and was carted off by the paramedics leaving everyone else to enjoy themselves.

Now that the races had finally over, the finishing post was taken away and Poppy was able to assemble her doggy obstacle course in a cordoned off area on the sand, with David and her parents helping her. Numerous families and their dogs turned up and entered the many categories of the competition which Poppy had planned so meticulously. Unsurprisingly, her dog show was a huge success. It went on for some time, with regular announcements over the tannoy giving out the names of the dogs and their owners who had won each of Poppy's carefully thought out categories. Many dogs of different shapes and sizes could be seen wandering around with coloured rosettes attached to their collars showing off their achievements.

There were plenty of stalls for the people of Sebleigh Bay to visit, including sideshows, local farm produce and crafts. The Beachcomber Cafe was busy throughout the day with most of their stocks of food running out long before the close of play. Oswald's barbecue was a great success too and he managed to get a friend to organise another delivery of burgers and sausages during the afternoon to keep up with demand.

Carmen had never been so relieved when 5 o'clock arrived and an announcement was made over the tannoy that the event was now officially closed. Exhaustion had well and truly set in as she and Clive and their helpers finished clearing up the cafe.

The events organisers cleared the beach of all their paraphernalia in double quick time, while volunteers efficiently cleared the beach of litter before the incoming tide swept in. Everyone said their goodbyes and drifted off home.

Carmen, Clive, Oswald, Poppy and David sat around a table in the Beachcomber drinking wine as they watched a stunning sunset play out before them, with the beautiful pink light pouring in through the expansive cafe windows. Virtually everything in the cafe was sold out, but Carmen remembered she had a couple of bottles of wine in her car which she put in the freezer to chill while they were clearing up the cafe. They were all tired but extremely happy with the incredible success of the day. While David was showing a smiling Poppy some of the dog show pictures on his camera, Clive was checking messages from friends on his phone.

'Update on you-know-who,' he said. 'Apparently he *didn't* break anything … apart from his ego that is.' David sniggered and reached for his phone and said,

'Oh that reminds me - I might just have been filming when Darth Vader was heading for the finish line.'

'Really?' Clive said. 'Let's see.'

'Aha … here we are...' David held his phone out, turned it round so that they could all see, and started the video. Darth Vader was seen running towards the camera at speed before he somehow seemed to trip and launch himself into the air landing on the ground with a big thud and a loud yell of pain. They all laughed but the film stopped at that point.

'Oh David,' said Carmen looking surprised. 'You didn't stop there did you?'

'Of course I did. Darth Vader had nose dived and I didn't know it was Seamus.'

'Didn't you?'

'No. I didn't get the memo.'

'Play it again David,' Clive said enthusiastically. David replayed the video. They all roared with laughter again and then Clive said,

'Oswald, what were you doing there in the background with your water pistol? I didn't spot you on the first viewing.'

'Let's see,' Carmen said. 'Play it again David.' As David filmed Darth Vader and panned the phone round towards the finish line, Oswald could be seen standing next to the barbecue with an aggressive look on his face, pointing his large water pistol directly at Darth Vader as he approached the finish line.

'Dad!' Carmen said looking shocked … 'Did you put him off or distract him? Is that why he tripped?' Everyone turned to Oswald who was looking distinctly sheepish.

'I didn't squirt him. Honest. But I was tempted. He tripped up all by himself.'

'But you didn't know it was Seamus did you?' asked David. The silence that followed from Oswald showed that he did know. Clive sniggered.

'Oh come on,' Carmen said still amused by her Dad. 'Let's not focus on that scumbag right now. I don't even want to think about him. Let's just remember the truly wonderful day we've had. It's been a massive success, and I'm sure it will continue to be for the cafe. Poppy - so many people said how much they loved your dog show. Dad, you deserve a medal for what you did out there on your barbecue with your nice ladies. Where did you get them from by the way?'

'Don't sound so surprised, Carmen. I told you I would do a good job, and I have got friends you know.'

'Well, you certainly did an amazing job Oswald,' Clive said with a grin. 'Let's raise a glass to the huge effort that everyone put in. I think today will be remembered forever in the history of Sebleigh Bay.'

'Cheers!' they all said.

'Bottoms up!' added David. Clive then jumped to his feet holding out his glass and announced,

'May the force be with you!' They all roared with laughter.

Chapter 39

A few months had passed since the wonderful Sebleigh Bay Fun Run. Carmen and Clive were still reaping the rewards of their publicity campaign as Christmas approached. The Beachcomber Cafe continued to be really busy even as the weather got colder and increasingly windy. Having appreciated that regular events were vital to keep the cafe in the minds of the people of Sebleigh Bay, they had recently hosted another Special Dog Day event complete with treats and awards for the furry friends and their owners.

Poppy, whose dog walking business was now a roaring success, enjoyed a lie in one morning after one of her regular walks had been cancelled. Still wearing her pink floral pyjamas, she switched the kettle on and then wandered sleepily into the lounge and pulled open the curtains. She never grew tired of the view and today she particularly enjoyed watching the gentle swell of the blue-green sea with the sun sparkling beautifully on the water. What better way to start the day?

As Poppy admired the view she noticed the paper boy turning into the forecourt of Anchor House. *Friday! Local paper!* She waited until the lad had pushed the papers through the main front door of the building and left, then opened her own front door. She paused for a second considering the pyjamas she was wearing but then thought, *Oh well, no one's likely to see me,* and continued on to the landing and ran quietly down the stairs. She picked up the pile of newspapers from the floor and placed them on the table where the post was usually left. She took a copy for herself.

'Yes! Front page no less!' she said out loud. 'Brilliant!' The headline item was entitled *Possible new pier for Sebleigh Bay* and showed an artist's impression of what the pier might look like. It was a strange and modern looking structure – certainly not Poppy's idea of an old fashioned pier. However underneath it there was a small but noticeable article about the Beachcomber Cafe, with a photograph of Lucky the giant poodle posing obediently next to Clive and Carmen who was managing to smile convincingly at the camera whilst holding Chip the dachshund. The title was 'Beachcomber Cafe celebrates nine months of canine visitors and welcomed everyone to a special event.' Poppy had helped to organise the line up with the dogs she had been walking that day and David had taken the photos, which Clive had sent into the paper with a press release.

Poppy was reading the article enthusiastically until she was interrupted by a noise coming from upstairs. She looked up to see David at the top of the stairs sniggering at her.

'Morning,' he said as he walked down the stairs. 'You beat me to it. Nice pyjamas by the way,'

'Oh stop it. Trust me to get caught out.'

'No really ... they *are* nice ... why do I get told off for complimenting you?'

'Yeah right ...' Poppy mumbled as she continued to read the paper. David put on one of his silly voices,

'You look sweet.' Poppy chose to ignore him.

'Look, we've made it to the front page.'

'Really?' David sounded impressed. 'That should bring a smile to Carmen's face. Fancy a coffee?' he said glancing up towards his flat.

'Yeah, thanks. I'd better put some clothes on first though.'

'Oh don't bother – you look fine as you are – just bring the papers.'

'Oh David! There's a parcel here for you as well.'

'Aha! Brilliant! I know what that is.'

As they started climbing the stairs they heard the front door of one of the downstairs flats open. Poppy and David giggled as they rushed upstairs into David's flat. After they shut the door Poppy said,

283

'You do realise what she'll be thinking don't you?'

'Who?'

'Mrs Woolford of course.'

'What will she think?'

'That we're ... well you know ... '

'No? That we're what?'

Poppy raised her eyebrows and playfully hit David's arm.

'Just put the kettle on and make my coffee.'

'Oooo bossy ... I do like a bossy woman ... especially in winceyette pyjamas ... milk no sugar?'

David made the drinks and they both sat down in the armchairs in the lounge.

'Actually Miss Poppy … I might have a little present for you.'

'Really? Oh I expect this is some sort of joke!'

'As if! No it's not actually. Well, I was going to give it to you for Christmas but as you're going away with your parents, I think I'll give it to you now because I would like to see you open it. Just give me a moment.' David got up and disappeared into the bedroom. Poppy could hear some paper rustling about. David came back in the room with a smart square black box.

'Here you are,' he said, placing it on her lap and taking her coffee away. Poppy was almost expecting it to be some sort of prank, knowing what David was like, but she was absolutely thrilled to find a substantial photo book inside the box with a stunning picture of Poppy on the front presenting a rosette to the winning 'Dog the judge would most like to take home' at Poppy's Dog Show during the Sebleigh Fun Run day. Poppy's eyes lit up and she gasped with excitement. She took the book out and glanced over at David and slowly opened it to discover page after page after page of beautiful photographs of pretty well every dog that had entered her dog show. Dogs posing with their rosettes, dogs lined up and being judged, dogs jumping over the little fences of her assault course, dogs being cuddled by their owners, dogs being made a fuss of by small children. They were all in there for Poppy to look at again and again, and to relive those memories whenever she wanted.

Poppy put the book down and with tears in her eyes she got up and gave David a big hug and kissed him on the cheek.

'Oh David … I can't believe you did this for me. It's incredible! It's the best gift ever. Thank you *so* much.' Returning to her armchair Poppy continued to browse her incredible book.

'You are welcome. I thought you would like it.'

'Like it?' she said as she continued to turn the pages of the book. ' I love it. You're the best David!'

Chapter 40

Rose hadn't seen George for a while - not since the day she'd been standing behind him in the queue at the Beachcomber Cafe when she took a call on her mobile from Caroline. She thought maybe George had turned round – with a big smile on his face she remembered – thinking that she was saying hello to him. She suspected he may have felt a little embarrassed when he realised she wasn't talking to him. He needn't have done though as she would loved to have chatted to him. Oh dear ... he didn't seem to be coming to the cafe anymore. She had even asked Clive one day, in as casual a manner as she could muster, if he'd seen the gentleman with the metal detector lately, and he said he couldn't remember having seen him for some time.

Anyway, George or no George, she had become very fond of her walks down to the Beachcomber Cafe. They were keeping her fit, and she did so enjoy the chats with Carmen and Clive and some of the other customers. What a delightful find the cafe had turned out to be. Rose kept herself busy with her regular activities such as her Spanish conversation class, her yoga group and there were always plenty of old friends to see. But any time she was at a loose end she would pop down to the beach hut and the Beachcomber Cafe.

On one such occasion, she had been browsing through the dress shops in the town, but having failed to find anything of interest she had set off in the direction of the beach huts. She was walking along the busy high street when she spotted a familiar figure up ahead, coming out of the Sebleigh Bay Museum. *Oh goodness, it's George,* she thought. Her heart skipped a beat with excitement, but then she saw that he was accompanied by a woman – quite a bit younger than him. As they walked down the steps, Rose noticed George putting his hand on her back as he directed her along the pavement. Rose found herself walking some yards behind them, and watched them chattering with great familiarity. They stopped by a restaurant and studied a menu in the window. Rose walked unnoticed briskly past them.

She felt very upset indeed. She berated herself for feeling so emotional over a man who she didn't really know.

Lucky, lucky woman, being taken to that lovely restaurant by such a man who obviously cares very much for her. She's young too – much younger than me – as if he would be interested in me when he can choose someone like her.

Rose changed her mind about going to the Beachcomber. She didn't feel like talking to anyone. She walked home instead, feeling a little tearful, telling herself she had to accept now that George was taken. *Me and my silly dreams!*

Chapter 41

George returned home from another tedious shopping trip at his local supermarket. It wouldn't be so bad, he thought, if he didn't have to spend more time queuing up at the check out than he did selecting his purchases in the first place.

They never had enough cashiers on duty. And as for the supervisor who stood there directing customers to the least busy till – why didn't she just sit down at one of those empty tills instead and start serving people? As George put his shopping away in the kitchen, he recognised that he was in a bad mood because he didn't have anything interesting planned for this weekend. Young George didn't call round for model train sessions as often as he used to, and he couldn't come this evening because he was doing a detention. This was apparently as a result of his enthusiasm to prove to the year nine girls, unsuccessfully as it turned out, that it was possible to balance on the wall of the school pond without falling in!

However, despite George's initial pessimism and grumpiness, this actually turned out to be a weekend full of surprises. The first one being when, at a quarter past four, Young George turned up on the doorstep unexpectedly.

'Hello Grandad ... detention was cancelled ... teacher didn't turn up ... can we make a start on the railway extension?'

'Well yes, of course. That would be delightful. I've just been shopping as it happens. Come and choose a snack.' Young George dropped his school bag, kicked off his shoes, and strode into the kitchen. Before he had chance to go to the crisp cupboard, he spotted an oven ready meal on the side which George had left out for his dinner.

'Yum! Macaroni cheese! I love that. Mum never makes macaroni cheese for me.'

'I've got another one in the freezer – you can stay for dinner if you like.'

'Can I? I'll ring Mum.'

George and Young George spent an absorbing evening together expertly building a new extension to the model railway, and the evening was rounded off with Young George's favourite meal for dinner. As they sat down in front of the TV with their macaroni cheeses, Young George surprised his Grandad again.

'By the way Grandad, I was wondering ... if you're free tomorrow, shall we go treasure hunting at Sebleigh Bay again?'

'Well yes, I'd very much like to take you down to the coast again.'

'Great.'

'It might be a bit chilly but I don't think any rain is forecast. The only downside is that the Beachcomber cafe has gone unfortunately. We'll have to find somewhere else to go for ice creams.'

'No problem.'

The following morning George was feeling very positive after his splendid evening with Young George last night, and was just about to go and get the car out of the garage for their trip to Sebleigh Bay, when the phone rang. His heart sank. He knew things seemed too good to be true. Was that Young George cancelling? Teenagers could be so unreliable. As he picked the phone up he recognised the number but pretended not to know it was George though.

'Hello,' he said flatly.

'Hello Grandad,' Young George said cheerfully in his half broken voice which George still hadn't quite got used to – especially on the telephone.

'Hello Young George,' he said a little sulkily, waiting for the inevitable.

'Grandad. Can you do me a favour? I was wondering ... would it be okay if my friend came with us today? We could pick her up on the way?'

George was thrown. That wasn't what he expected. Did Young George say 'her'? He was so relieved that he wasn't cancelling though.

'Well yes – of course – that would be fine. *Who* is your friend?'

'It's Amy. I've been telling her all about the day we went down to Sebleigh Bay with the metal detector and she said she's always fancied having a go. I thought you wouldn't mind if she came along.'

'That's excellent. The more the merrier. I'll be with you in few minutes then.'

'Okay see you soon. Bye Grandad.'

Fifteen minutes later, the two Georges were in the car on the way to Amy's house.

'Grandad,' Young George said hesitantly. 'Could you do me a favour? Will you call me just George, instead of Young George? I mean I don't mind normally, but I'll never hear the last of it at school if Amy tells my mates.' George laughed.

'I'll do my best to remember.' When they drove into Amy's road, Young George was texting her to say they were there. Then he pointed at the houses.

'It's just there Grandad. You can pull over by that tree.'

George stopped the car and Young George jumped out. George watched as the front door opened and a very slim teenage girl appeared full of smiles for Young George. They gave each other a big hug. She was wearing a denim jacket, a tiny black skirt, black tights and big Doc Martin type boots. She had a mass of dark frizzy long hair, and huge eyes. George thought she looked like a little doll. She spotted George in the car and gave him a friendly wave. As Young George opened the back door for Amy he introduced her to George.

'Grandad, this is Amy.'

'Hello Amy. Coming for a spot of treasure hunting then?'

'Hello. Yes I can't wait. I'm really excited.'

290

Amy sat in the back of the car and kept leaning forwards to enthusiastically ask questions.

'Do you think we might find anything interesting today?'

'Well that depends what you consider to be interesting,' George replied.

'I'd love to find some ancient jewellery. Oh and George told me about the bracelet you found with the name Alice engraved on it, not far from the beach hut called Alice – that is so romantic. There must be a story there.'

'Yes it was rather intriguing I must say. I can't promise we'll find anything like that today though.'

George was impressed with Amy's confident and friendly personality. Some of his grandchildren had become very surly and monosyllabic in their teenage years, but Young George and Amy looked like being excellent company for this trip.

The three of them chatted happily all the way to the coast. George discovered that the two youngsters had got to know each other from being in the same science class at school, and that they often 'hung out' together. When they reached the coast and drove into the Chalk Cliff Way Car Park, George got his third surprise of the weekend when Young George called out excitedly,

'Look Grandad – there's a big sign saying that the Beachcomber Cafe *is* open. Amy, it's a lovely cafe right on the beach – we can go there afterwards.'

'Well I never!' George said. *This puts a whole different slant on things. So we will be visiting the Beachcomber again.*

They all got out of the car, and while George fetched a parking ticket from the machine, Young George and Amy rushed over to the sea wall.

'Oh look at the beach huts!' Amy squealed with delight, 'They're so cute. Oh I'm loving this. I've never visited this end of Sebleigh Bay before. Hey, let's give your grandad a hand.'

291

After collecting the metal detector and spade from the boot of the car, the enthusiastic trio made their way down on to the beach. Before they started any serious treasure hunting, Young George offered to show Amy the beach hut called Alice.

'Let's go and see if we can see the bracelet that Grandad and I found.' As Young George and Amy rushed off ahead, George was thinking of the day they first met Rose there, and how they'd just chatted so naturally – two strangers happy to share a few friendly words. Why had it become so utterly impossible to talk to her again? Amy was very impressed with the pretty blue and white striped hut. She even got her phone out and took a selfie of the three of them standing in front of it.

'It's the nicest one of all, and I love the name Alice,' she said.

'There's a window round the side,' said Young George. 'Let's see if they've still got the bracelet we found.' The two youngsters walked around the hut and peered in through the window.

'Look Ames. There is is. I can't quite see the engraving properly from here but it's definitely the one.'

'Cool. Oh I'd love to find something like that. Something with some meaning or some mystery attached to it.'

'Come on then. Let's get started.' George let the youngsters take it in turns to use the metal detector. He was just happy to have their company and amused to be observing Young George with this bubbly young lady who he'd never mentioned before. He couldn't help thinking about Rose as well and kept glancing around in case he saw her on her way to or from the cafe. He hoped it was still the same people running it as they'd always been friendly and interesting to talk to. Meanwhile Young George and Amy had dug up some modern coins and a fishing weight.

'Got something!' Young George said once again as the machine started beeping.

'Let's get digging,' said Amy, who, despite her delicate appearance, was very handy with the spade. Her enthusiasm to find some treasure was very endearing.

'It's a long way down,' said Young George, 'shall I do a bit?'

'No I'm okay,' she said as she thrust the spade into the sand again. A couple in their thirties came walking by and asked if they'd found anything interesting.

'I've always fancied having a go with one of those,' the man said to Young George, 'do you find much?'

'My Grandad's found some old Roman coins and we found a bracelet last time.'

'Do you mind if we watch?'

'No of course not. Come on Ames, I'll take over for a bit,' Young George said, taking the spade off Amy. George noticed a familiar face approaching with a small brown dachshund running around nearby, surprisingly quickly given the length of it's tiny legs, George thought.

'Hello young lady,' he said with a smile.

'Oh hello,' said Poppy cheerfully.

'Different companion today then?'

'Oh yes. Well I'm glad you're still talking to me after Bobby and Bounce nearly destroyed the cafe last time.'

'You know I didn't mind. It was quite amusing actually. Do you still walk those two?'

'Yes. For my sins. Someone has to do it. Actually I had another chaotic incident with them, but I can't bear to even think about that now! So how are you? I haven't see you for sometime?'

'No, well last time I came here I was told that the Beachcomber Cafe had closed down, so I didn't think I'd be coming any more.'

'Oh no, they got you as well did they?'

'Sorry?' said George not understanding.

'Why did you think the cafe was closed?'

'Well a lad approached me in the car park and told me it was closed.'

'Mm,' Poppy said with a frown, 'a lad who was working for a competitor and was doing his best to ruin Carmen and Clive's business. The cafe was never closed at all.'

'Really? I say! That's dreadful.'

'Yes. For ages we were all wondering why it was so quiet in there and then we found out what was going on. The horrible people who'd just opened up the Octopus cafe were spreading stories that the Beachcomber was closed.'

'Oh yes – the lad directed me to the Octopus – told me how great it was – but it certainly wasn't my cup of tea.'

'No it wouldn't be. There's no way the Beachcomber regulars would go there anyway.'

'Well I never! All this time I haven't been here and the cafe's been open all along. It's scandalous! I only visited today because my grandson, Young George over there, asked me to bring him and his friend metal detecting. We were pleased to see the big sign in the car park.'

'That's an extremely big hole they're digging,' Poppy said. George glanced over and saw that there were now another three people watching to see what Young George and Amy would find.

'Chip! Here sweety,' Poppy called to the dog. George and Poppy watched as the little brown shiny dog came hurtling over obediently. Poppy picked her up.

'She's a rather jolly little thing isn't she.'

'She's lovely. Do you mind if Chip and I join the audience over there and see what they find?'

'No of course not. I'm quite intrigued myself actually – I've never dug that deep before.'

'*Look*!' shrieked Amy.

'What is it?' asked Young George. Amy jumped down into the hole with Young George and crouched down and picked up something very small.

'It's a ring!' she said rubbing the sand off. 'Crumbs it's gold – it looks like a wedding ring.'

'Oh I say!' George said approaching the group, 'You found what you were looking for then.' Everyone gathered round to see Amy's ring. Someone said they thought it was 24 carat, and someone else was heard to say, 'I must get one of those detectors – we could make money finding things like that.' Amy and George hugged each other and then Amy jumped up and down with excitement.

'This is so cool. What are we going to find next?' she asked. George stepped forward and suggested that they all went for a cuppa.

'You must need it after all that digging. You can search some more afterwards.'

'Yes, good idea,' Young George said. 'You'll like the cafe Amy, it's just along there.'

George turned to Poppy again,

'So was the cafe affected badly by the rumours then?'

'Yes it was. Things got really bad … it was so quiet in there. It went on for quite a while during the summer until we worked out what was going on.' Young George and Amy were already walking towards the cafe carrying the metal detector and the spade. George and Poppy carried on chatting for a while, Poppy explaining all about Seamus Booth and his plot to get rid of the competition. George was quite upset that he'd been duped into not going to the Beachcomber.

'Oh well, I'd better go and join the youngsters. It's been nice talking to you again, and thanks for filling me in on the cafe.'

'Yes, we'll see you more often hopefully, now that you know that the Beachcomber is open.' George made his way over to the cafe. He was expecting to see Amy and Young George huddled over a table studying the ring, but as he entered the cafe he had his fourth and biggest surprise of the weekend. Young George and Amy were sitting at a table, not on their own, but with none other than the lovely Rose!

'Grandad! Over here!' called Young George as he caught sight of George coming through the door. 'Look who we've found. It's the lady from the beach hut called Alice. Remember? We gave her the bracelet. Her name's Rose.

295

Come and sit down, we've already got you a cup of tea.'
George was almost speechless.

'Oh ... I say, how nice ... err ... hello Rose, I'm George.'
He stretched out his hand to her and she shook it and gave
him her beautiful smile once again.

'Hello George. I hear it's been a very successful day of
treasure hunting.'

'Yes ... a gold ring no less ... well, it looks like it ... we
can't be sure.' George sat down opposite Rose.

'Oh it's definitely gold,' Rose said, 'I used to work in a
jeweller's a long time ago. What a splendid find.' Young
George addressed his granddad,

'We told Rose how we went and looked in the window of
Alice and saw the bracelet we found.'

'Oh,' George said, a little embarrassed, 'I hope you didn't
mind.'

'No of course not. I was delighted to hear that you were
all interested. We've told many people about that bracelet
and the engraving. It was so intriguing.'

'I'd love to know the story behind that,' Amy said, 'and
this lovely ring of course. Actually I was just thinking,' she
said looking puzzled, 'how can someone lose something so
valuable? I mean if someone gave me a precious gold ring
... a token of their love,' she said dramatically slipping the
ring on to her finger and stretching out her hand to see how
it looked. 'I wouldn't lose it.'

'Maybe,' said Young George, 'they had a blazing row on
the beach and she threw it at him and said 'I've *had* it with
you!' Everyone laughed, and George said,

'That's very cynical Young George... err George ... not
very romantic.' He hoped he hadn't blushed as he mentioned
romance. He'd forgotten what blushing was until he met
Rose.

'I've got an idea,' said Amy, 'Why don't we all try and
think of a story about how this ring might have ended up
buried on the beach? Shall I start?' Everyone listened as
Amy told a tale about a couple on honeymoon in Sebleigh

Bay. The lady's wedding ring was a little too big and she was going to get it adjusted after the holiday, but in the meantime she insisted on wearing it as it was so special to her. She was swimming in the sea and it slipped off and she lost it. She and her new husband spent the whole honeymoon trying to find it on the beach but they never did.'

'Very good,' said Rose. 'That could well have happened.'

'Your turn George,' Amy said to Young George. He refused to take this game seriously but under Amy's insistence he agreed to have a go.

'Okay … got it …' he said as an idea came to mind. 'This married lady was on the beach here with her dog. She took her wedding ring off when she applied her sun tan lotion. She needed somewhere safe to put the ring so she opened her lunch box and placed it on top of her sandwiches. She was so busy rubbing in her sun cream that she didn't notice her dog come along and stick his nose in the lunchbox and eat the sandwich and the ring! Realising what had happened the lady thought she'd wait 24 hours and then come back down to the beach with the dog to do his …'

'Okay George!' Amy interrupted, 'That's enough. We get the picture. Honestly! Boys! Why does it always have to be something revolting? Rose, I bet you could tell a good story.' Rose knew she'd be able to come up with something. She'd spent her whole life spinning romantic tales in her mind. She felt pretty self-conscious in front of George though, but she noticed that he seemed quite nervous around her which led her to think that just maybe he did like her after all. But what about the younger woman he saw her with at the museum?

'Alright … ' Rose said thoughtfully, 'My story is about a young teenage couple who lived long ago in Sebleigh Bay and who were very much in love with each other. They badly wanted to get married but the boy wouldn't propose because he was very poor indeed and he couldn't afford to buy a wedding ring, let alone anything else. He had just left school and he didn't have a job yet.

297

'But, as it happened, the girl already owned a beautiful gold wedding ring which had been left to her by her grandmother, and she would like nothing more than to use that as her wedding ring. She decided that she would propose to her boyfriend and tell him she'd like to wear her grandmother's ring when they were married.

'So, she took the ring and she set off to visit her boyfriend to surprise him. She walked through the town to get to his home, but as she passed Sebleigh Bay Museum she saw him coming out of the building with a glamorous young lady who he was laughing and joking with. She was devastated, so she turned round and ran all the way to the beach. She would always take a long walk on the beach whenever she was upset. She walked down to the sea's edge and paddled in the sea. She put the ring on her finger and imagined that she was walking in the waves with a lovely handsome man who she'd just married. The ring was much too big, as it was her grandmother's, and she didn't realise how easily it would slip off. She was so distracted by her thoughts and dreams that she didn't notice a big wave heading towards her which knocked her off balance. She put out her hand to steady herself as the wave splashed into her. When she looked at her hand the ring had gone.'

'Oh no,' Amy said. 'That's so sad. How about a happy ending? I wonder if there could be one? Could you come up with one Rose?'

'Well ...' Rose said ... desperately trying to think of something. 'The girl went home from the beach feeling very upset. But later on there was a knock on her door and her boyfriend turned up telling her that he had brilliant news. He'd been to the museum and had managed to get himself a job there which started today. It turned out that the glamorous girl at the museum was just someone who he'd been asked to show to a waiting car. Anyway ... because he now had a job, he proposed, and it all ended happily every after.'

'Very good Rose.' Amy said. She then turned to George with a smile. 'Now it's your turn George.'

'Oh dear. Us chaps just aren't any good at this sort of thing - I couldn't possibly make up a story. But there is something else I must tell you, while we're on the subject of the museum ... the last time I came down to Sebleigh Bay, I brought my daughter Miriam, Young George's mother. She wanted to do some dress shopping, and I wanted to take my Roman coins to the museum. I found them on the beach here on my previous metal detecting trip, and I was rather intrigued to see if they were of interest to anyone. So Miriam, and I showed them to the coin expert in the museum. It turned out they weren't of any particular value, but they didn't have any similar examples in there, so I donated them to the museum so that they could display them and everyone would get the benefit of them.'

While George was explaining about his museum trip, Young George quickly finished his drink and he had his mobile phone on his lap and was writing a text message to Amy.

> *have u noticed the way my Grandad and Rose r looking @ each other. He's got the hots for her!!! He even blushed! OMG let's make an excuse to leave the oldies on their own. I can't watch any more of this!*

Just as George was coming to the end of his story, a beep came from Amy's phone. She looked at it discreetly and nudged Young George with her elbow, and then when George finished speaking, she addressed Rose and George politely,

'Would you two mind if George and I go and do some more hunting? It's a bit cloudy out there and I think it might rain soon.'

'No of course not,' said Rose.

299

'That's fine,' George said. 'Go ahead. Good luck finding treasure.'

Amy and Young George picked up the metal detector and the spade and left the cafe quickly with poker straight faces. The minute they were out the door they both burst into laughter.

'You are so right George!' giggled Amy.

'I know! They really fancy each other, don't they?'

'Yes. It was all blushing and dopey smiles wasn't it.'

'Grandad actually seemed quite tongue-tied when he arrived and saw Rose there. I've never seen him like that before.'

'So, *Young* George, where shall we search this time?'

'Oh *no*! I told him not to say that. But he couldn't help himself. He's always called me that.'

'Aah. That's sweet. There's nothing wrong with that. No need to be embarrassed. Come on *Young* George – let's go this way. I want to find some more jewellery to go with the ring.'

'I can't get over Grandad. I thought he was too old for that sort of thing! It's weird!'

'Maybe Rose will take him back to her beach hut for some ...'

'*Don't*! Don't even go there Ames! This is my Grandad we're talking about. Anyway,' said Young George looking up at the blue cloudless sky, 'Where are these rain clouds you were talking about?'

'Err ... oops ... that was the best I could come up with on the spur of the moment. Do you think they would have seen through my lies?'

'Naaa. I don't think they would have noticed anything. They only had eyes for each other,' Young George said pulling a pained expression.

Chapter 42

'What the bloody hell is that Clive?' asked Carmen, with a tone of disgust in her voice, as she looked out the window.

Clive put down his tea towel and strolled over to the window with a smile on his face.

'Ah! The donkeys! I heard they were starting up rides at Easter – I didn't think they'd come down this far though. Well I never!' He said looking thoroughly intrigued.

'It's getting like a bleeding farmyard down here! First my cafe's overrun with dogs, and now we've got horses outside!'

'Donkeys Carmen.'

'Horses, donkeys, whatever. They'd better not leave great big piles of dung outside!'

'Oh I expect they'd clean it up if they did.'

'What? In little plastic bags like the dog owners carry around? They'd need bin liners more like.'

'Typical Carmen – always thinking the worst. You see a pair of donkeys go past the window with straw hats on, and the first thing that comes to mind is a huge mountain of dung being deposited on our forecourt!'

Carmen laughed. 'You do exaggerate Clive. I don't remember mentioning a huge mountain.'

'Actually it might bring more business in here. People who don't normally venture down this far will spot us for the first time.'

'Only the kids though – their parents will be lounging on the beach half a mile away enjoying their twenty minutes of peace and quiet.'

'Mm. Maybe. Well perhaps we should sell a few lilos and buckets and spades – have them on display outside the cafe so that kids on donkeys will see them and tell their parents.'

'That's hardly the image I've worked so hard to create here.'

'Image, image, image Carmen – so typical of you! I'm more interested in what makes us money, money, money.'

'Yeah – and don't I know it! Anyway – we've been rushed off our feet since the Fun Run Day – it's certainly done marvels for our business.' Carmen watched as the donkeys walked past the cafe. 'So we don't need to resort to silly gimmicks to get more customers in.'

'We should never be complacent though. Hey! Perhaps we could get together with the donkey ride people and organise some sort of joint venture with the cafe?'

Carmen nearly spat out the tea she was drinking.

'Look! I gave into the dog idea, and yes it *has* been good for business – I admit that – but I'm not having a donkey drop off point at the Beachcomber. If I'd wanted a farmyard I'd be living in the countryside, not at Sebleigh Bay!'

'Oh – I love winding you up. It's so easy.'

'Yeah well, it's alright for you to say that, but I thought the dog thing was a wind up, and before I knew it we had a cafe full of them.'

'Oh don't worry – I don't think the donkeys will fit through the door. Let's see.' Clive wandered over to the door and pretended to measure it up!'

'Oh, I'm sorry – do come in,' he said to a young woman who was just entering the cafe.

'Thank you', she smiled.

Carmen walked towards her and joked, 'You didn't arrive on a donkey did you?'

'No.' She laughed, 'I walked. They're lovely aren't they. I might bring my children down here for a ride at the weekend.'

While Carmen returned to clearing the tables, Clive went over to the counter to serve the young woman. Carmen was sure that she recognised her, but couldn't think where from. She was bound to be a customer she'd seen before. She'd ask her if she got the chance. Clive was having a laugh with her while he got her a hot chocolate 'with all the works', while telling her about how he'd been winding his wife up about the donkeys. Several more customers came in and Clive and Carmen were kept busy serving them for a while. Every now and then Carmen surreptitiously glanced over at the young woman who had sat down at the window. She was small with long dark straight shiny hair. She stayed in the cafe for quite a while. She looked as if she was killing time because usually left after they'd had their drink – especially if they were on their own.

A little later Carmen noticed that the young woman kept looking over at her – almost as if she was watching her. She started to feel a little suspicious. She wasn't a health and safety inspector was she? Maybe Seamus was up to his tricks again and had reported them for something. But Carmen had definitely seen her before. They wouldn't send someone familiar surely.   Carmen wanted to get to the bottom of this so she went over and asked her if she enjoyed her hot chocolate?

'Yes thanks. I love the chocolate buttons. It's a nice touch.' She seemed pleased to talk to Carmen.

'They all come from Lyncombe Chocolates – the hot chocolate powder and the buttons and meringues. We try our best to support local companies. They're good quality too.'   Carmen noticed the woman glancing over at the counter. She looked a little nervous.

'Actually, Carmen ... there's something I wanted to ask you.'

'Oh yes, of course.' Carmen was intrigued now. 'Fire away.'

'Well this might sound a bit odd, but, I came in here some time back with a friend. His name was James. We lost touch, but ... I really need to contact him again. It's ... important. And it's just that ...' she hesitated, 'I'm not sure, but I think I might have remembered him saying that he gave you his phone number?'

The penny dropped. Carmen remembered where she'd seen this woman before.

'Oh I remember you! I *knew* I'd seen you before. Yes of course. Did you mean James Glanville? You came here with him a few times.'

'Yes, well sort of ... I know this sounds daft, but I never knew his surname. We only met up a few times, and I only knew him as James. When we stopped seeing each other I deleted his phone number. I had to.' She paused, glancing down at her lap. 'Did you say his name is Granville?'

'No Glanville – with an L. We knew his Uncle who was also James Glanville.' Carmen felt the old stab of pain, and she wondered if this young woman knew about her and Jem – was that why she was being so cautious - only wanting to speak to Carmen when Clive was out of the way? Carmen was now glancing over at the kitchen as well to make sure Clive wasn't within earshot. It was fine though. The cafe was busy and quite noisy with chatter.

'So ... do you have his phone number by any chance?'

'Oh yes, of course. Look I'll write it down for you and let you have it in a minute okay?'

'Brilliant. Thanks,' she said looking relieved, and then a little scared, Carmen observed.

'I'll have to get on – customers to serve. No peace for the wicked. I'll be back in a minute.' Carmen smiled kindly and rushed off to clear tables.

Chapter 43

James trudged wearily up the garden path after a long stressful day at work. As he rummaged in his pocket for his front door key, he noted that even good old Tom, his dear grey and white cat, wasn't on the doorstep to greet him today. He let himself in the door, threw his jacket on the banisters and headed straight for the kitchen cupboard where he kept his bottle of whiskey, only to be greeted by Tom who'd just come bounding in through the cat flap with a loud clatter.

'Hello mate,' James said, bending down to stroke him. 'I don't really need a drink do I? Becoming a habit. I'll put the kettle on instead. After I've fed you of course.'

As James took a cat food pouch out of the cupboard he noticed the light flashing on the answerphone. He'd listen in a minute. Bound to be his parents. He fed Tom and then filled the kettle and switched it on. As he waited for it to boil he once again picked up the Sunday magazine which had been lying on the work top ever since last summer. The one with the beach hut article. He'd often wondered how many beach huts there might be in the whole country – hundreds? No thousands surely? The article didn't provide that fact. He wondered what would be the odds of there being a photo of not just the Sebleigh Bay beach huts, but of his very own hut, the beach hut he had named 'Alice', photographed in the snow no less? Well it used to be his very own hut - just for a few months. Sometimes he would imagine Alice buying a Sunday paper – flicking through the magazine – and seeing the beach hut.

He often wondered how Alice felt? Was she still affected by things like he was. Did she still walk along the beach past the huts? How did she react when she first saw the name – her name – which he had put on the hut. It seemed to still be there – or at least it was when the beach hut photographs had been taken. Maybe she didn't walk along there any more? Perhaps she'd kept away, tried to forget him and the hut, and get on with her life with her husband and kids. Maybe she never even knew he'd named the hut after her.

She'd chosen to stay with her husband. Was she happy? How could she be? She said she'd never loved him. Did she still think about James?

So many unanswered questions. He still missed her. She was special. He had considered turning up at the garden centre where she worked, and trying to talk to her. That would have been so awkward and embarrassing though. She could have contacted him any time – she had his mobile number – but she'd chosen not to. He had to respect her wishes, but he'd clung on to the hope that she would change her mind one day and phone him. She hadn't though.

On this occasion, as he flicked through the well thumbed pages of the magazine, he told himself that it was about time he put it away, or maybe even put it in the bin and moved on ... or tried to at least.

He pushed the magazine to the back of the worktop and poured his cup of tea. As he reached for the fridge door to get the milk out he pressed the button on the answerphone and heard a woman's voice, talking slowly and nervously. Strange.

'Hello James ... This is Alice ... I'm so sorry to bother you ... and for phoning you out of the blue like this, ... but ... please would you call me. I know I've no right to ask anything of you, but ... it's important. *Really* important. There's something I must talk to you about. My number is ....
'

James grabbed a pen and frantically scribbled down the number – almost as if he only had one chance and it might disappear if he didn't write it down straight away.

'Thank you James. I hope all is well with you. Bye.' The message ended.

Having taken down the number, he listened to the message again ... and again. It was incredible to hear her voice again. She sounded as he remembered her, but very nervous. What had happened? He could tell it was a big deal for her to phone him.

His hands were shaking as he picked up the phone and dialled her number.

Two days later James drove in through the entrance to the Chalk Cliff Way car park. It all looked pretty much the same except for a new and very large sign advertising the Beachcomber Cafe. He was ten minutes early. It was a windy but bright spring day. He walked over to the sea wall and looked out at the waves breaking dramatically in front of him. Then he glanced to the left at the row of pretty beach huts which he hadn't seen since 'that' winter. He recalled the conversation he'd had with Alice on the phone two days ago.

She was very grateful to him for returning her call and apologised for calling him out of the blue. She didn't like to interfere with his life – he was probably with someone else now. He told her he wasn't. Would he do her a favour and meet up with her? Even if it was just the once. She needed to tell him something – explain things. He got the impression she was no longer with Tim. He hoped he was right. She'd said something like 'it's just me and the kids now ... can I see you when they're at school?'

He expected to see Alice arriving by car but he hadn't heard one turning up, so he was surprised to have his thoughts interrupted by her voice coming from behind him.

'Hello James'. That nervous voice again. He turned round to see Alice standing just a few yards from him. She had a completely different hairstyle – her dark hair was long and straight – but the beautiful smile appeared when he looked at her and she became the same Alice he remembered. They both stepped forward and hugged each other.

'It's good to see you Alice,' he found himself saying to her.

'And you. Thank you for coming.'

'Where do you want to go? Along to Carmen's cafe?'

'Actually ... can we just go somewhere quiet? Sit on the beach perhaps?'

'Yes, of course.'

As they walked down to the beach they made polite conversation, asking each other how they were, and saying how lovely the sea looked.

'Shall we sit by the waves?' Alice asked, 'The tide's going out.'

James assumed that Alice was about to explain to him what had happened after they last met – why she had decided not to see him again, or maybe to explain that she and Tim had split up, so he didn't say much and waited for her to talk. He could sense she was anxious and that this was a very big deal for her. They both sat down on the pebbles.

'James ... I've thought about this moment over and over again in my mind, wondering what I would say to you ... if I got the chance ...' she looked out at the distant horizon as she spoke and then paused and picked up a smooth pebble. His mind flashed back to the first time they'd met and sat on the beach together outside the hut.

'There is no easy way to say this ...' she said, turning to look at him with a serious expression. 'I'll just have to come straight out with it.' The serious tone of her voice surprised him. What was going on here? He began to suspect that it was something more significant than he'd originally expected.

'In December ... I had a baby boy... His name is Jacob ...'

'Oh ...'

'And ... he's your son.' Alice just about got the words out before she burst into tears. 'I'm sorry ...I ...'

'Are you serious? ... Yes ... of course you are ... but ... I thought ... that I probably couldn't ...' His voice trailed off. He wanted to comfort her but was stunned by what she said. He reached over and put his hand on hers and she took it and held on to it. She wiped her eyes with her other hand as she tried to compose herself.

'James ... he's definitely yours.'

'But what about your husband?'

'He's not the father. Jacob can only be yours. Look I'm sorry – I know this is a lot to take in, but can I explain to you what's happened over the last year or so?'

'Yes ... of course...' James said ... He let go of her hand and listened carefully to Alice's story. 'Take your time,' he said quietly.

Alice took a deep breath ...

'Well, going back to the day that we last arranged to meet, when I panicked and decided I couldn't see you anymore ... believe me, when I sent you that text message ... it was horrible ... it wasn't what I wanted at all. Honestly, I couldn't have had stronger feelings. But ... I was just really scared ... I didn't know what to do. After bumping into my mother-in-law's friend at the golf club I became so paranoid about the family finding out. I suppose it just brought the reality of the situation to a head. My imagination ran away with itself ... imagining nasty custody battles over Mollie and Sam and other horrible scenarios. I didn't realise at the time, but I think the pregnancy hormones were driving me a bit mad. Anyway, after I texted you I immediately deleted your phone number from my mobile, and regretted it straight away. You've no idea how many times I wished I hadn't done that. It was soon after this that I found out I was pregnant. I'm ashamed to say I genuinely didn't know who the father was – you or Tim. You said you didn't think you were fertile, and I'd insisted on Tim taking precautions – even though he didn't want to. I didn't even do a test for a

309

while because I didn't think it could be possible. When I did ... I was totally shocked as you can imagine. But then... just the next day... when I was still in a state of shock ... my mum was diagnosed with cancer.'

'Oh ... I'm sorry ...'

'Thanks. It looked really bad – in fact we were all told to prepare ourselves for the worst – she may not live long. I tried to spend as much time with her as possible ... I took lots of time off work ... went to all her hospital appointments with her. She had an operation, and lots of treatment. I visited her every day in hospital and at home. I tried not to think too much about the pregnancy, but I had a lot of morning sickness so I couldn't hide it. My Mum guessed, and I told Tim. He was delighted initially, but he soon realised that I just didn't want to talk about it and that something was wrong. I think to begin with he just put it down to my Mum's situation, and he knew I hadn't wanted another baby at this time.

'Anyway, one evening after I'd spent a particularly worrying time with my Mum at one of her hospital appointments, I was feeling so awful with the morning sickness, and the children were playing up ... I just lost my rag ... big time! The pressure had got to me, and I couldn't cope. I stormed off upstairs and shut myself away in the bedroom. I couldn't think straight... I felt like my brain was caving in. Tim came to talk to me and said he understood that things were really difficult at the moment, but what had got into me this evening? Something inside me just snapped, and without thinking I just blurted out, "My Mum might die and I don't know if you're the father of my baby."

'Poor Tim. I told him about us – none of the details though – he doesn't know about the beach hut or anything. I told him I wasn't in touch with you any more. I think he just assumed I had a fling with a holidaymaker so I let him carry on believing that. Things drifted on for a while. We were all in a daze – just surviving from one day to the next. Tim and I hardly spoke to each other for ages, but one day we managed to have a serious talk about things, and we agreed not to make any decisions for a while, as Mum was in a critical state and I was pregnant. That was enough to cope with.

'Thankfully just a few weeks before Jacob was due, Mum's situation started improving. She had responded amazingly well to the treatment, and we were told that there was real hope of a recovery. It turned out that things hadn't been quite as bad as they first thought. She improved so much that she was able to be with me at the birth. Tim was away at the time, and it all happened very quickly - Jacob came a bit early. But we both knew that if things had been okay between us he would never have risked going away on business around that time.

'Anyway, baby Jacob arrived safely, and as soon as I saw him I felt sure he was yours. He looked different to Mollie and Sam and I thought he looked like you.

When Tim came home he said he needed to know if the baby was his - he wanted DNA tests done. We did the tests and they showed that Jacob wasn't his. He didn't seem surprised.

'And ... how did *you* feel Alice?' James asked nervously.

'I was actually pleased. Even though life might have been simpler all round if he was Tim's. I couldn't explain it, but I really wanted him to be yours ... and I kind of felt deep down that he was anyway.'

'So what happened next?'

'Well, we didn't really talk about it to start with. I think we were both just trying to get used to the news, but a few days later, Tim came home very late from work, which was unlike him. He didn't apologise. Didn't explain. Just said he'd been to see a solicitor and he wanted a divorce. He said he couldn't live with what I'd done.

'It was sad but to be honest, I was relieved. *Hugely* relieved in fact. I couldn't stand living a lie anymore. I didn't want to spend my life being married to someone I didn't love, even though I couldn't fault him as a husband

311

and dad. It all happened very quickly. As soon as he could find somewhere to live, he moved out. Don't get me wrong though – I *was* upset. Tim is a really decent person and a great dad, and I was very upset that my marriage had failed, and of course I didn't want to shatter my children's lives.

'How have they taken it?'

'Well, it's not been easy. They were very shocked. I don't think they can understand why we split up. They kept expecting their dad to move back home again. And it's been very hard to explain to them that Tim isn't the father of their baby brother – they don't even know about the birds and bees yet. It's been difficult.

'The good thing though is that Tim met someone else quite quickly - I'm not sure but I have a feeling he already knew her quite well through his work. Since then things have improved between us. The children say that he and his girlfriend are all loved up which kind of helps me too because I don't feel quite so guilty! Also I think it must have made Tim realise that things were never as they should have been between us, so he seems kind of okay, maybe relieved like I was. He lives nearby so the children see him a lot. We found it hard to organise things to start with but we're getting into a good routine now, and we've been communicating well about the children. We're really working as a team to make things as stable as possible for them. I couldn't ask for more in that respect - I'm grateful for the way things are now.'

'That is good. I know several families where the parents are divorced and there is so much anger and bitterness – it's really horrible. When I split up with my wife I was genuinely relieved that we hadn't had children because of that.'

'I know. I remember you saying that. Anyway ... now that things have settled down a bit I just knew that I had to try and get in touch with you somehow. I hadn't kept your phone number, and I didn't even know your surname! How mad is that? I remembered you said you worked in St Giles

House so I kept ringing up different companies in the building, asking for James. I got laughed at more than once because I didn't have any more details.'

'Yes you would do – there must be loads of us in that huge place.'

'I felt really stupid. How had I got myself into this mess? If only I'd kept your phone number. Honestly I felt such an idiot. I also thought about getting on the train and standing outside the building all evening waiting for you to come out, but I did some research and discovered there were several different buildings that you could be working in. I might have resorted to that though if Carmen hadn't been able to give me your number.

'I let it go for a while,' continued Alice. 'I haven't had much time to myself. Then one day I woke up in the night and was remembering the times we spent together and you telling me about your Uncle having an affair with Carmen in the cafe, and I vaguely thought you might have said that you gave her your phone number. I honestly wasn't sure though – I thought I might have dreamt it. As the time has gone on I've just felt more and more that whatever your circumstances were, you had a right to know about Jacob, so I decided that I just had to go and speak to Carmen, in case she was able to help.

'The first time I went she wasn't there – I think she'd left early. The second time was a busy day and she was working in there, but her husband was there too and I didn't want him to hear our conversation because of the connection with your Uncle and the affair she'd had. Anyway, she actually recognised me and said she remembered me coming in with you, and yes she was more than happy to give me your phone number.'

'Oh – I wondered how come you had my landline number – we used the mobiles before didn't we.'

'Yes, I must admit, I thought she might have told you that I'd been in and asked you for her number.'

'No – I haven't heard from her for a while.'

313

'Anyway ... you know the rest!'

'Wow! This is quite something. I guess I've wondered from time to time if you might get in touch with me one day ... but I didn't expect this.'

'I know.'

They both sat silently with the waves breaking in front of them.

'He looks like you...' Alice broke the silence. 'He really does.'

'So ... I have a son,' James said. As if saying the words out loud might help them to sink in. 'I bet he's dead handsome!'

'Of course he is.' They both laughed nervously.

'Oh my God ... is this for real? It's hard to believe.'

'I know. It must be. Look, I've brought something for you. This might help a little bit.' Alice opened her bag and got out a photo of a smiling baby. James took the photo ... his hands were shaking.

'Oh God, he looks just like my nephew Jack did when he was little.' James smiled at the photo.

'Are you starting to believe me then?'

'Maybe. Where is he now?'

'He's with my Mum.'

'Oh. How is she now?'

'She's really great. She's so much better and the prognosis is very good. And she just loves her new grandson. I really think that having Jacob has given her so much pleasure – something to live for.'

'That's amazing,' James said thoughtfully.

Alice paused ...

'Would you like to meet your son?'

'Of course. When can I see him?'

'Mum lives five minutes from here.'

'Really? This is a lot to take in. Are you saying I can meet him today?'

'Do you want to sit here for a while and let things sink in?'

'I think I'd better.   Actually, can we walk along the beach?'

'Yes, whatever you like. It will take about 20 minutes to get to Mum's on foot – when you're ready we can always walk there if you like. I can fill you in some more on the way.'

'Okay,' James said anxiously as he stood up. 'Are you going to let your mum know we'll be coming?'

'No – we'll surprise her. She knows all about you. We've become very close since she got ill and since Jacob was born. She was there at the birth, and she has a very strong bond with him.'

'Crumbs, what will she think of me?'

'You don't need to worry about that. She was fond of Tim but she knew it was never right between us. When we split up she encouraged me to try and find you.'

'Really?' said James with surprise.

'I thought you might be with someone else by now, but I had to tell you about Jacob whatever your circumstances were. You had a right to know.'

'Thank you. There hasn't been anyone else significant.'

'I'm sorry you didn't know from the beginning. I really am.   I hope you understand ... I just couldn't cope with facing up to all this on top of my Mum's situation ... I thought I was going to lose her, and I didn't know how to find you anyway.'

'It's okay,' James said quietly.

'If I hadn't found you through Carmen, I would have found another way eventually. Honestly, I wouldn't have given up.   You probably would have found me hanging around outside your office one day!' James smiled at that thought.

'I'm glad,' James said. He was very quiet though. He kept looking at the photo of smiling baby Jacob. He noticed how much his hands were shaking.

'Gosh, I think I'm in a state of shock.'

'I'm not surprised ... I'm so sorry.'

'No ... I *think* it's a good shock.' They stopped walking and James continued to stare at the photo. Alice put her hand on his arm reassuringly.

'He's a wonderful little boy. Everyone says so. I think you'll be very proud.'

'To be honest I just can't take this in.'

'I think maybe you need more time to get used to the idea.'

'I don't know. I think I just want to see him. So, he's just four months old?'

'Yes. Look James ... I'm just thinking ... It was silly of me to suggest taking you round to my mum's place. That's not fair on you. This is such a big deal. Look, if you're sure you want to see him now, I'll go and get him, and bring him here. I've got the car. I'll drive there.'

'O... kay ... '

'Are you sure you want me to get him now? We can wait a bit.'

'No. I feel like I won't believe this until I meet him. No time like the present.'

'Alright. If you're sure.' Alice kissed James on the cheek and said 'I won't be long,' and she left him staring at the photograph.

Without thinking, James headed slowly towards the beach hut. He had wondered if he and Alice would go and see it ... but he hadn't expected any of this. In some ways he had thought he didn't want to see the hut with other people's things in it – he wanted to remember it exactly as it was. He had wondered if the 'Alice' sign was still there – it had been in the newspaper supplement. But his thoughts of the beach hut had slipped into total insignificance compared to the news he'd just been given.

Unsurprisingly as he walked up the pebbles he could hardly concentrate on the hut as he approached it. He noticed the name sign though – it was still there, but slightly weathered. He went straight to the window round the side and looked in. He was barely concentrating, but he vaguely

316

noticed that everything looked the same. The collection of stones and beach glass, the framed photo of Jem ... oh and there was another photo. He couldn't quite see the picture. The settee and the deckchairs were still there. Nothing had changed. It was just the same as the day that he and Alice ... *This is where ... the baby ... my son ... I've got a son ... was conceived. How am I going to feel about the baby? ... Jacob ... nice name. How do I feel about Alice? Is there a future for us?*

Something shiny on the windowsill caught his eye. Draped across the driftwood. A scratched silver bracelet. *That looks like the one I bought for Alice – and threw in the sea? I'm pretty sure it has the inscription on it.* James's mind was buzzing. He couldn't think straight. None of this was what he expected at all. He had hoped that Alice would be free ... that there might be a chance for their relationship again ... but this ... this was something else altogether.

317

Chapter 44

As Rose left the Beachcomber Cafe and walked along the path past the beach huts, she was remembering with amusement how Carmen had just commented on how well and happy she looked today. 'Sparkling' was the word she used. Goodness! – did it really show that much? All she could think of was her date tomorrow with George. He was going to collect her from her home and take her to lunch at The Grand Hotel. She'd felt like an excited teenager ever since he'd phoned her to arrange it. She'd been trying on endless outfits at home, but decided that the smarter clothes she had weren't very up-to-date. George always seemed to look naturally classy, and of course it was The Grand Hotel they were going to, so she ended up buying a new elegant blue dress for the occasion, which the shop assistant said brought out the pretty blue colour of her eyes. This time tomorrow she'd be getting ready to meet George. She could hardly believe this was actually happening.

As she walked along Chalk Cliff Way she noticed a young woman approaching in the distance, chatting to her baby in a pram. Rose watched the young woman turn towards the beach as she spotted someone on the beach and waved, and Rose thought she heard her call out, 'I guessed you might be here.' Rose was intrigued to see who she was talking to and could tell that it was someone special by the way her face lit up. As Rose got nearer the girl bent over the pram and lifted the baby out and gave it a big smile. Sure enough a handsome man stepped out on to the pathway from between the beach huts. With a huge smile the girl announced very proudly,

'This … is Jacob!' and then she burst into tears. The man put his arms around the girl and the baby and they all stood in a tight huddle.   As Rose discreetly walked past she noticed the man was crying too.

Chapter 45

James was bowled over by baby Jacob, his gorgeous happy little son. Every morning he would wake up thinking about this extraordinary change that had happened in his life. The first thing he said to himself on waking was 'I've got a son. His name's Jacob. I'm a dad!' Then he would get out of bed with a huge smile on his face.

James and Alice agreed to take things slowly and not rush into anything. Alice thought it best not to introduce James to her children Mollie and Sam yet as they were still having a few ups and downs getting used to Tim and his new girlfriend being together. Tim had Mollie and Sam to stay with him most weekends though, so James came down to Sebleigh Bay on those occasions to spend time with Alice and Jacob, often enjoying long walks together on the beach and around the town. Sometimes Alice's mum looked after Jacob so that James and Alice were able to spend some quality time together and go out on some dates. The first time Alice had taken James to meet her mum, James was greeted with the words 'Well there's no doubt who you are!! – You're the spitting image of Jacob!' James loved the fact that there was such a strong resemblance between him and his little son.

James's parents however were unsurprisingly stunned to learn of the existence of their unexpected grandson. James broke the news to them over one of his mother's delicious Sunday lunches, although very little roast dinner was actually eaten once James had made the surprise announcement. His mother did all she could to try and hold herself together emotionally while his father gave him a thorough grilling about 'this Alice', with questions such as 'Why didn't she tell you before? ... How can you be sure the baby's yours? ... Have you had a DNA test done? ... Does she know you're wealthy? ... '

James managed to reply calmly to the barrage of questions as he would have expected nothing less from his father. However his parents' minds were put to rest as soon as James brought Alice and Jacob to meet them. The adorable little Jacob was a spitting image of James and other members of the Glanville family and it was clear that Alice and James were very much in love with each other. James's sister Maria, and her family lived in New Zealand so his parents missed their grandchildren very much and had to rely on video chats with the family, and rare trips to the other side of the world. After the initial shock, James' parents began to feel extremely happy that they had such a beautiful little grandson so much closer to home.

Alice and James and often took walks together along the beach with baby Jacob and they were always drawn to the beach hut called Alice. Alice told James how she nearly died of shock when she went to the photographic exhibition at The Grand Hotel and saw the photograph of the beach hut with the name sign 'Alice' on it.

'The photographer even came up to me and asked me if I was alright!' James saw the impressive picture she'd purchased and had displayed in her house in pride of place. 'Everyone says what a lovely picture it is, but they don't know just how much it means to me.' James explained how he had seen the article in the Sunday magazine and simply couldn't believe that his own beach was featured in it.

When they were on the beach looking at the beach hut called Alice, James pointed out the scratched silver bracelet through the window. It had been draped across a piece of driftwood. James explained to Alice that he'd bought it for her and had it engraved with her name, and that when she texted that she wasn't going to see him anymore, he threw it into the sea.

'I've no idea how it made it's way back here. I guess someone must have found it.' he said. Alice was overcome with emotion, to think that he'd done all that for her and she hadn't turned up. They agreed it must have been fate that the bracelet managed to find its way back to the beach hut again. They had a good look through the window and they loved the fact that everything inside the hut was exactly the same as they'd left it. The old settee, the rug on the floor, and the striped deckchairs leaning against the walls. And of course the interesting collection of bits and pieces on the windowsill was exactly the same as when they last saw it – except of course for the addition of the bracelet.

'It looks like there's another photo there,' James commented.

'There are two frames but you can't see the pictures from this angle.'

'There was only one before wasn't there? The one of Jem with his glass of wine.'

'That's a point. There's definitely another one.' Alice agreed. 'It's a shame we can't have the bracelet,' Alice said thoughtfully. 'I wonder if the owners of the hut might let us have it if they knew the history behind it.'

'Mm. I was thinking that as well. You never know.'

'Would you be able to contact the people you sold it to?'

'Well the sale was handled through the agent so it would probably be easier to ask Carmen if she has any information about the current owners. I'll see what I can find out.'

Chapter 46

David and Poppy were sitting on some large rocks on the beach, just across the road from their flats at Anchor House. They were wrapped up warm and chatting quietly as they sipped cool white wine from large glasses and watched the sun setting over Sebleigh Bay. Half an hour ago David had turned up at Poppy's front door asking,

'Do you fancy a drink?' as he held out a glass of cold wine for her.

'Wow! Look at the size of it! How can I refuse? Your place or mine?'

'Well, it's a lovely evening, and the tide's almost in ... I thought we'd take it over to the beach.'

'Oh?' Poppy was thrown by the suggestion. 'Great idea actually. I'll grab my keys, and put my coat on.'

Halfway through her large glass of wine, Poppy paused and said thoughtfully,

'How lucky are we? I mean how many people can just walk out of their home and cross the road to the beach?'

'I know. And how many people have got such a lovely neighbour ... as me?' Poppy's eyes rolled upwards.

'For one moment there I thought you were going to give me such a nice compliment. Should have known!' Poppy tried not to laugh.

'Oh come on ... you do find me funny though don't you?' David said, nudging her with his elbow.

'Yeah right!' she replied sarcastically.

'Actually I meant to say ... I saw you earlier on the beach in the distance down near the carpark – couldn't quite make out which of your hounds you were being pulled along by.'

'Oh, that would have been Rosie, my last walk of the day.'

'Ah ha! Rosie the cutesie, softy, cuddly little old Rottweiller.'

'Who Carmen is such a great fan of.' They both laughed. 'She is a big softy really. Funny how everyone keeps away though.'

'I just can't think why! Nothing to do with the massive muscular shoulders which Mike Tyson would be proud of, or the huge mouthful of gnashers stretching from ear to ear by any chance? I trust you take her for regular walks past the Octopus?'

'Oh I so do! I make a point of it every time so that she can give them one of her extra special Rosie smiles.'

'That's my girl! You do realise Carmen's terrified of her don't you?'

'Yes, she laughed. 'Must admit I don't take her in the Beachcomber too often because I know she makes people feel uncomfortable. But sometimes sit outside sometimes if it's quiet, and if I haven't already had three coffees that day. Shame they don't allow dogs in the Octopus – I'd go in there with her otherwise.'

'Really?' David sniggered.

'No, not really. Nothing would make me support that scummy place.'

'I know,' David agreed. 'Let's change the subject. This is too nice for all that. Do you know? Last night I was lying awake at about three in the morning and guess what I was thinking about?'

'I don't know David,' Poppy answered suspiciously, 'what were you thinking about?'

'I was considering how funny it is that your surname is Dancey.' Poppy hit David playfully.

'Oh here we go!' she said.

'I can't believe I hadn't made the connection before, I mean between your, ahem ... nimble dancing skills, and your name.'

'Yes David, I know exactly what you mean! Is it possible for you to get through more than 10 minutes without poking fun at me?'

'Well you must admit it is funny.'

'Yeah sure.'

'Come on, you've got to laugh. I mean if I can laugh about it when my left foot still bears a deep and angry scar, I'm sure you can.'

'I'm glad you're not the sort of person who bears grudges or lays guilt trips or anything.'

'No of course not, but come on, you've got to admit, I do make you laugh don't I? ... don't I? ... Come on, I can see the corners of your mouth twitching.'

Poppy laughed.

'Well where you're concerned David, it's a case of either laughing or crying really isn't it?'

'Oh come on, you love me really?'

'Do I?'

'Go on admit it ... you do really.'

'I'll tell you what. I did like the way you turned up on my doorstep with a *ginormous* glass of wine.'

'And whisked you off to the beach to watch the sunset.'

'Yes – that as well. Nice idea. You can do that more often if you like. These are huge glasses by the way – I'm starting to feel a bit drunk.'

'Yes they're good aren't they. Saves bringing the bottle over.' Poppy held up the glass and looked at the view of the sea, distorted through the glass of wine.

'Mm, look at that,' she said. 'It would make a nice photo. Stunning ... in an abstract sort of way.' David leaned over to have a look too.

'You're right. I like that. Hold it there a moment.' David got his phone out of his pocket and used it to take a photo of the view through the wine glass.

'Let's have a look.' David accessed the photo he'd just taken.

'Hey, that's really great,' Poppy said. 'I like that. Good idea of mine wasn't it.'

'Mm, shame it's only on the phone. I can't be bothered to go and get my camera.'

'You could do an exhibition called 'Through a glass of wine.'

David turned to Poppy and smiled at her.

'Yes? What now?' asked Poppy. 'You're about to make fun of me again. I can tell.'

'No. I was just thinking – you're really ... sweet ... when you're tipsy.'

'I'm not tipsy.'

'Yes you are. You said you were starting to feel drunk.'

'I'm not slurring my words or staggering about or anything.'

'You might be if you stand up.'

'No I won't. Anyway, I don't normally drink – well not in public anyway – I'm frightened of making a fool or myself or doing something clumsy.'

'Surely not!' David said, trying to stifle a laugh.

'I can't be bothered to get annoyed with you,' she said laughing.

'You see ... you do find me funny.'

'Well ... I can't believe I'm saying this ... must be the wine talking ... but I am lucky having you as my next door neighbour – I'll give you that.' She put her arm round him and hugged him.

'And ... erm ... I'm lucky too.' *That felt nice*, David thought.

Chapter 47

James walked through the front door of his house enthusiastically. He couldn't wait to take a shower and drive off down to Sebleigh Bay to spend the weekend with Alice and Jacob. He went through his usual routine of throwing his jacket over the banisters and strode into the kitchen to feed his cat. He bent over and made a big fuss of Tom knowing that his kind neighbour would be calling in many times over the weekend to feed and make a fuss of him. He must remember to buy her a thank you present while he was away. As he straightened up from stroking Tom he noticed the red light flashing on his answer machine. He pressed the button.

Hello James. Father here. Question for you James. During your visits to Sebleigh Bay, you haven't come across a lady called Carmen Collier have you? At the ... Beachcomber Cafe? Funnily enough I was just looking at a magazine of Jem's which I kept when we cleared out his house, and I found a letter in it. It's in an envelope with a stamp on it and everything - looks like he was going to post it. It's addressed to Carmen Collier. If my memory serves me correctly I think the magazine was beside Jem when he was found ... err when he passed away, which is kind of why I kept it, if you know what I mean... for ... well ...sentimental reasons. So, I'm wondering if he wrote the letter just before he died. Your mother told me not to open it, and she said you're going down there this evening to see Alice. Perhaps you would pick it up from us on the way and take it to this Carmen if she's still at the Beachcomber Cafe? Cheers James.

Chapter 48

James, Alice and baby Jacob had spent a lovely Friday evening together last night, but James had explained to Alice that today he had some business to attend to and he asked her to meet him at 2 o'clock on the beach close to where they first met.

Naturally Alice was intrigued and a little puzzled but suspected that James had maybe arranged to see the beach hut owner to ask about the bracelet. As it turned out she didn't have too much opportunity to think any more about it. Tim had messaged to say that Mollie was unwell, probably suffering from a bug, and he felt that she might be happier to be with her mum. Alice realised that if Mollie did come home she would obviously have to introduce her to James. She'd already told Mollie and Sam about her special friend, but she still had a fair bit of explaining to do and was taking things one step at a time. As it happened, Mollie felt better by lunch time and decided that she would remain with Daddy for the weekend. Alice's mum had offered to take Jacob out in the afternoon to see a friend of hers and their grandchildren, and so Alice was free for a couple of hours to go and meet James.

The weather was warm and sunny when Alice turned up at Chalk Cliff Way and walked along the path to meet James near the beach hut called Alice. She couldn't stop smiling as she was recalling the earlier date with James last year when they ended up shutting themselves in the beach hut, and of course Jacob was the result of that beautiful encounter.

When Alice arrived, James was waiting for her on the beach just in front of that special blue and white beach hut.

She ran up to him and they had a cuddle and then kissed passionately.

'I hope you didn't mind me not bringing Jacob?' Alice asked when she had the chance, 'My Mum wanted to take him to meet some little friends – we can pick him up in a while – I just thought it would give us a little bit of time on our own.'

'That's alright. Actually ... I've got a present for him. I wanted to give him something ... something special ... but, he's a bit young at the moment – obviously!   So you probably won't want to hand it over to him just yet,' he said with amusement in his eyes.

'Oh? I'm intrigued.'

'So ... I'll give it to you. When he's old enough you can explain to him.' James rummaged in his jacket pocket and brought out a small and beautifully wrapped present in gold foil wrapping paper with a gold bow, and he handed it to Alice. She read the label aloud:

'*To my dear son Jacob, love Dad, kiss kiss kiss.* So this is for him when he's older?'

'Yes, but you can open it now, and you can use it ... the present I mean ... until Jacob's old enough to take responsibility.'

'Curiouser and curiouser.'   Alice looking puzzled carefully pulled the ribbon undone and opened the gift.

'A key?' she looked puzzled. James glanced behind him. Alice looked over at the beach hut called Alice. She gasped.

'You're joking! Not the beach hut?'

'Go and try it.'

'Seriously? How come?'

'I bought it back! You know how we were saying we'd like to get the bracelet back, well, a few weeks ago I rang Carmen and asked her if she knew anything about the people who own the hut now, and it turns out she knows them quite well.   Carmen said she wasn't sure they'd want to keep it because they'd only had one holiday here which didn't go very well. But that's another story.   Anyway – there's an older lady called Rose who's the Aunt of the owners, and she lives in Sebleigh and keeps an eye on it for them.   Carmen arranged for me to meet her. I called in at the Beachcomber Cafe two weeks ago before I arrived at your house and had a great chat with Rose. Lovely lady! You must meet her sometime. I asked her if there was any chance they'd want to sell it back to me. She said she thought they might as they were in the process of buying a villa in France where she thought they would be more likely to spend their holidays.'

'Oh! Not much difference.' They both laughed.

'As soon as you and I met up again, I obviously regretted selling it. And the fact that everything inside is exactly the same – the furniture, the jars of glass, the driftwood and everything – it just felt like we were meant to have it back. Anyway, I was sorting it all out legally this morning, and I've put it in Jacob's name, but I thought you could all enjoy it. You're in charge and I'll pay for any maintenance that's needed. I hope that's alright? I just wanted to do something special for Jacob ... and for you of course.'

'Alright? It's a lot more than alright . Oh James!' She flung her arms round him and kissed him again. 'I love you so much. I'm so happy. Wow! You'll certainly win Mollie and Sam over with this.'

'Love you too. Come on, let's go inside.'

Alice unlocked the door. They went inside and she flung her arms round James and kissed him again.

'I just can't believe this. You're amazing James.'

'You too.'

'The bracelet!' Alice turned to the windowsill and picked it up from the piece of driftwood it was draped over and looked at it. When you said to me to meet you here today, I thought you had maybe managed to obtain the bracelet. It never occurred to me that you would've bought the beach hut. Oh it's such a lovely piece of jewellery. I can't believe you bought this for me and got it engraved. It's beautiful. I'm going to put it on and treasure it forever. I wonder how it got back here?' James helped Alice to fasten the bracelet.

'You won't believe it, but I found out all about that from Rose. A man was down here with his grandson and a metal detector and they found it on the beach down there and dug it up. I think his name is George. The grandson had noticed the name Alice on this hut. Rose was here at the time with her friends and the man and his grandson came and introduced themselves to her and told her to keep it to put in the hut.'

'That's an amazing story!'

'It is. And I also got the impression that Rose and the metal detecting guy have become close as a result of meeting here.'

'Wow! The power of this little beach hut … and you naming her Alice of course! Oh look … the pictures in the frames …'

'Ah yes … the other one …'

Alice picked up the silver frame and they looked at the new picture which had been left in the hut. It showed a little girl dressed as a fairy with beautiful iridescent wings and incredible make-up swirling and sparkling all over her happy face. She was sitting in front of a campfire with lots of other fairies twirling around in the background dancing.

'I wonder who she is?' Alice said. 'What a magical picture! Mollie will be fascinated by this.'

James carefully took the picture from Alice and placed it down on the windowsill next to the one of Jem. Then he closed the door.

'Now … how much time did you say we have before we collect Jacob?'

Chapter 49

As Carmen went about her various duties at the Beachcomber, she kept touching her trouser pocket which contained the precious envelope that James had brought into the cafe for her that morning. She was desperate to open it but she had to wait for the right moment. She couldn't just sneak off to the ladies for a minute's privacy – that wouldn't do. She needed to go somewhere peaceful and have time on her own to compose herself, and take in its contents when she was ready.

James had been very discreet as always. He sat as far away from the counter as possible and waited until she came over to his table for a chat, and he explained quietly about the letter his father had found addressed to her with Jem's handwriting on it, and how it had been found inside the pages of a magazine which was close to Jem's body.

James handed the letter over to Carmen quickly and discreetly. She had wanted to talk more to him but he told her apologetically that he had an appointment in half an hour to do some business, before meeting Alice.

Carmen was thrilled that James was making regular visits to Sebleigh Bay again. It was as if he was her connection to Jem. Although James was younger and slimmer than his Uncle had been, he reminded her very much of him. He had a similar look in his eyes. Carmen had managed to have a few discreet conversations with him. He remained the only person who she'd ever confided in about her affair with Jem, and that alone made James special to her. Alice seemed nice as well. Carmen was so glad she'd been able to be some help in reuniting them. They made a good couple, and as for that gorgeous baby, Jacob – she could clearly see the Glanville genes in him as well. It was as if that little family were keeping a small part of Jem alive for her.

Clive had just left the cafe for the afternoon to get some supplies, so when she closed up later on she would take a walk along the beach by the cliffs, and settle herself down on the rocks where she and Jem had visited a couple of times. She would take a few deep breaths and prepare herself for whatever was in Jem's letter. He'd never written her a letter before. Would it give any clues to his death? Would it explain his unusual behaviour on their last beautiful evening together at The Grand Hotel? Then again, maybe it was just something trivial? A newspaper cutting perhaps? It might be disappointing. It may not bring her any closer to him after all? On the other hand …

Chapter 50

My Darling Carmen,

As you know I'm not good with the written word, but I will try and express myself the best I can. Bear with me my love.

You probably wondered why I was so emotional when we said goodbye on Monday. Well let me try and explain.

When Clive and I went for our whiskies at lunch time on Monday, he hit me with some somewhat shocking information. In fact talking of "hitting me", I'm extremely surprised that he didn't do just that!! He said that he'd known of our affair for some weeks. I tried to deny it of course but he told me not to insult his intelligence and I knew he meant business. There was no point in trying to bluff my way out. I've no idea how he found out – I didn't get chance to ask. He just told me to shut up and listen. I was so shocked I just did what he said.

At this point I need to go back in time and explain something further. Rather stupidly – some years back, my judgement severely compromised by the several glasses of Bells I'd drunk, I admitted to Clive that I had once made some bad decisions and carried out, shall we say, a less than honest deal on the stock exchange. It was a major deal in fact which accounts for a large percentage of my current assets.

Anyway – Clive told me on Monday that unless I keep away from you and never contact you again – he will report me to the police for insider trading. I have to say Carmen that he really loves you. I could see the determination in his eyes. He genuinely wasn't prepared to share you or indeed lose you under any circumstances, and he knew he'd got me over a barrel.

When I said goodbye to you at the Grand, I really meant "goodbye". I didn't intend to see you ever again. I had no choice – or so I thought at the time. I've lain awake for the last three nights – hardly slept a wink - looking for another way, because faced with the possibility of losing you, it's made me see that I can't give you up. I've realised that you mean absolutely everything to me my darling.

I love you Carmen, with all my heart.

By the time you get this letter I will be on the other side of the world in my favourite pad – you know where I mean. I'm untouchable there because they can't extradite me. I want you to join me my love. Permanently. We'll be happy together – you know we will. You are aware that there have been other women in the past, but this will be different. It will be just you and I. That's a promise.

As soon as I arrive there I'm going to make arrangements for you. Call in at Chapman's Travel Agent in Lynchester on the first of next month and there'll be a package for you. All very discreet I promise. If you don't collect it, they'll cancel it within a week.

Please join me. Forever yours
Jem

Epilogue

Carmen and Clive trudged wearily through their bungalow each carrying several heavy bags of supermarket shopping into the kitchen, and dumped them all on the table.

'Careful,' Carmen said, 'I think that one's got the eggs in.'

'I *was* careful. Anyway, I should think the eggs are the least of our worries. By the time we've filled the fridge with that huge turkey I don't know where we're going to put everything else.'

'We'll manage. A lot of it's going in the freezer anyway.'

After a long day in the cafe they had spent some time cleaning up the kitchen and closing the place up for the Christmas break. Then they hit the supermarket on the way home for their big Christmas shop.

As they silently unpacked everything and put it away Carmen was trying to pluck up the courage to talk to Clive about Jem. She'd been in a daze ever since she read his letter all those months ago. She found herself feeling surprised that it wasn't actually Jem's declaration of love that he made just before he died which had affected her so much, but it was Clive and the fact that he knew about their affair and had kept it to himself. She was truly shocked about that. She always assumed that he would have dropped her like a stone if he'd found out. But he'd stayed with her and kept quiet. Carmen just couldn't get over that. Jem said in his letter that Clive really loved her. She knew he did, but had never realised just how much. How long had he known? What did he know? How did he find out? Carmen had been torturing herself laying awake late every night trying to get her head round everything and remember if Clive's mood had changed at any particular time.

Just lately Clive had said to her several times that she was looking pale and maybe she should go to the doctor. What for? She'd thought. To get a pill to relieve her of her guilt?

She couldn't bear to think that Clive knew. What had she done to him? How was he feeling? How did he feel about Jem's death? Was he glad? Did he feel responsible at all? He would know that Jem died soon after Clive threatened him. How would that affect him? Was *she* in any way responsible? She'd never know.

The more she thought about things from Clive's point of view, the more she regretted what she'd done. She loved Clive. They had a good marriage. She was so lucky to have him. Why had she allowed herself to be swept off her feet by Jem? If only things had been different. How strange was it that less than a year ago she was completely obsessed with Jem - he was always on her mind. But now she wished she'd never got involved with him. How she wished she had appreciated Clive in the past as much as she did now.

The guilt was eating away at her and affecting her behaviour ... and her health. She couldn't carry on like this. She had to bring it all out into the open and let Clive know she loved him and regretted everything. Let him know it was him she was fretting over, and not Jem anymore. It never seemed to be the right time to bring it up though. She knew the conversation could have devastating consequences, but she had to tell him how she felt ... letting Clive know that it was him that mattered most to her. .. let him know that she regretted what she did and would *never* do anything like that again.

'Shall I open the bottle of red wine?' Clive asked when the table was finally cleared of the shopping.

'Yes, that's a good idea. Clive ... we need to talk ...' she blurted out.

The phone in the hall started ringing.

'I'll get it,' Clive said. 'You can get the glasses out.'

Carmen was feeling more nervous than she'd ever felt before. As she took two glasses out of the cupboard her hands shook and the glasses jangled together. *This is going to be awful ... but it's got to be done. We can't move on until it's out in the open.* Carmen was only very vaguely aware of

337

Clive laughing and joking in the background as he chatted on the phone. There was obviously some good news. She uncorked the wine and carried the opened bottle and glasses through to the lounge.

Kicking off her shoes she collapsed on to the settee and waited for Clive to finish his phonecall. Clive walked into the room laughing.

'Ha ha ... wait till you hear this. Have you opened the bottle? We've got something to celebrate.'

'Oh?'

'Cheer up! Its the best news we could ask for – just in time for Christmas.' Clive sat down next to Carmen. He poured the wine into the two glasses and took a sip. 'Cheers. Well ... Seamus Booth has closed down the Octopus and it's up for sale! It didn't work out. Apparently it lost him a lot of money. I told you he didn't have a clue how to run a cafe.'

'Couldn't have happened to a nicer person,' Carmen said quietly.

'What's the matter? I thought you'd be ecstatic.'

'Oh I am ... I am Clive ... it's great news ... obviously.'

'Have you got a headache coming on again?'

'No. I just think we ought to talk about things ...'

'Hey! What are the youngsters doing tonight? Shall we phone them?'

'Youngsters?'

'David and Poppy – they were so supportive with our campaign – I think we should tell them the good news – they'll be thrilled. Shall I phone them?'

'Err ... no ... they're out this evening. It's the Christmas Ball ... you know ...   at the dancing classes at The Grand Hotel.'

'Oh yes. Of course.'

'Clive ... look ...'

'Well we can enjoy our wine, and relax and get into the mood for Christmas, and it's being made all the more sweet knowing that the greasy spoon and its slimy excuse for an owner has well and truly failed.'

338

As Clive continued to chatter on about how Seamus had actually done them a favour as it had given them a kick up the backside and made them up their game with the cafe, Carmen began to suspect that Clive knew she wanted to talk about Jem but he was purposely avoiding it. He didn't want it to happen. As she sipped her wine it dawned on her that if it didn't come out into the open and they acted like it had never happened, then Clive could carry on and they could stay together. But if he admitted he knew all about it, his pride would take over and it would be the end of their marriage. She owed it to Clive to respect his wishes and to let him have it his way. What mattered most was that she didn't want to lose him and would do anything to keep him. But somehow she had to let him know how she felt and hopefully gradually rebuild his trust again.

'Clive. It's brilliant news, it really is. We have got a lot to celebrate. But I want you to know that the only thing that really matters is that I've got you. I love you Clive – more than you'll ever know.' She took his glass from him and put it down on the table and started kissing him.

He stopped and looked at her. He seemed surprised by this sudden outpouring of feelings and show of affection, but it was obvious that she really meant what she was saying. He picked up the bottle of wine, pretended to look at the label and said,

'Crumbs – what do they put in this stuff?'

'Put it down and come here,' she laughed.

She started kissing him again and then said,

'Actually, on second thoughts, pick it up again and bring it upstairs.'

George drove his car carefully between the huge pillars at the entrance of The Grand Hotel, with the lovely Rose smiling contentedly beside him. She put her hand on her tummy and said,

'Goodness me – I'm not sure about dancing – I can hardly walk after that delicious meal.'

George laughed.

'Well we don't have to dance straight away – we can always go to the bar for a quiet drink first, or we could just sit and watch everyone else dancing.' George parked the car and turned off the engine.

'Oh don't worry,' Rose said. 'We've only learnt a slow waltz so far – I think I can manage that.'

'You're being awfully tactful – you mean I've only learnt the waltz so far in my two classes. I think you could manage a lot more.'

'It was surprising how much I remembered from my younger days.'

'Well I'm so glad you liked the restaurant anyway. We'll have to go there again soon if you'd like to.'

'Try keeping me away,' she laughed.

'Actually, Rose, before we go and trip the light fantastic … I've got a little present for you.' George turned and leant backwards picking a gift bag up from the back seat. 'If I can just explain? You were saying how you felt a little sad about Caroline selling the beach hut … and … well I was doing some shopping in the town after I saw you last week, and I saw something in the window of the photographic shop which I thought you might like as a little keepsake. It means a lot to me too because of course it was at the beach hut called Alice where we first met. Here you are…'

'Well this is exciting,' Rose said opening the bag and taking out a photo in a silver frame. 'Oh how lovely … what a beautiful photograph of Alice …'

'And if you turn it over… you will see it was taken by David …'

'Oh yes of course. I went to his exhibition. He is so talented. Oh thank you, George. This is a marvellous gift. So thoughtful.' Rose gave George a beautiful smile and a kiss. She looked at her framed photo again.

'It is lovely that the beach hut called Alice is now owned by the original Alice and her family isn't it.'

George was suddenly aware of flashing blue lights and glanced up at the mirror.

'Goodness, there's an ambulance arriving.'

'Oh dear, I wonder what's happened?' Rose said as she turned round to look behind.

'Probably some old chap like me overdoing it on the dance floor.'

'Don't be silly,' Rose giggled. 'You're in very good shape.'

'Hardly! Shall we go in then?'

George quickly got out of the car and went round and opened Rose's door for her. She got out of the car and they paused and stepped back as they saw two paramedics leave the ambulance and walk briskly through the side entrance of The Grand Hotel.

'They look like they mean business don't they,' Rose said. 'I do hope it's nothing serious.'

As Rose and George entered the building a male member of staff greeted them.

'Good evening. You're here for the Christmas Ball?'

'Yes, that's right,' George replied. 'Here are our tickets.'

'Thank you. Could I ask you to take your coats down to the cloakroom along the corridor. It's free of charge tonight, if you just show your tickets.'

They walked down to the cloakroom listening to the dance music coming from the Ballroom. George helped Rose off with her coat. She loved every second of George's company. He was such a gentleman in every sense of the word. Once their coats had been taken from them, and George tucked the numbered tickets into his inside jacket pocket, he took Rose's hand and led her towards the Ballroom.

There seemed to be something going on. The man who had greeted them at the door was addressing a few people in the corridor.

'Could I ask you all to just stand aside quickly please, and let the paramedics through. Thank you,' he added, looking at George and Rose.

341

The paramedics were pulling along a stretcher trolley and to Rose and George's surprise there was David lying on it holding something against his head, and he was followed by a very distraught looking Poppy.

'David!' Rose gasped. 'What happened? Poppy!'

When Poppy saw Rose she burst into tears. Rose rushed over and put her arms around her.

'Oh Poppy – what's happened?' Poppy couldn't talk she was so upset, but the three of them followed the paramedics out to the ambulance. As they were getting David into the ambulance, one of the paramedics turned to Rose.

'It's alright – we think he'll be fine but he took quite a knock to the head. He was unconscious briefly so we're taking him in to get him checked out.

'Rose ... Rose ...' David groaned loudly. 'The pillar tried to kill me.'

'It was my fault,' Poppy sobbed. 'I did the wrong step and turned left instead of right and I tripped him up and he crashed headlong into the pillar.'

George tried to comfort her.

'Don't blame yourself Poppy – it could have happened to anyone – I'm sure it wasn't your fault.' The paramedic turned to Poppy.

'Right he's all in, are you coming with us?'

'Yes, if that's alright?'

Rose stood there feeling helpless and badly wanted to be of some assistance. Just as they were about to shut the door she called out,

'Poppy – you've got my mobile number haven't you. Call me. We can come and collect you if it will help?'

'Rose...' David called out. 'Rose, I need a crash helmet for next time.'

As the door was closing Rose and George heard the paramedic say,

'Don't worry, concussion often causes a bit of confusion.'

Rose turned to George.

'If I know David that wasn't confusion, but his sense of humour!' They waited outside until the ambulance had driven away, and then George took Rose's hand again.

'Are you alright?' he asked her. 'That was a bit of a surprise wasn't it.'

'It certainly was! I couldn't believe it when I realised it was David on there.'

'He should be okay. They didn't seem too worried, and it's only a few minutes to the hospital isn't it. They'll look after him.'

'I know. Actually I think I was more concerned about Poppy – she was so upset. Do you know I believe they had an accident here once before – she trod on his foot with a high heel. He's never stopped teasing her about it.'

'He's a lad isn't he! I'll tell you what - how about you give it say ... an hour ... and then if you haven't heard from Poppy you could phone her and ask her how things are?'

'Yes, I'll do that.'

'In the meantime – I think I can hear a nice Waltz playing. Would you like to dance?'

'I would love to.' Rose smiled serenely at George as he led her to the ballroom.

Alice was sitting on the settee with her legs tucked under her, admiring the precious silver bracelet on her wrist once again. Even though she'd been wearing it for several months now, she still couldn't believe that she was lucky enough to actually have it after it's interesting journey. It consisted of a delicate thin chain with a small silver shape in the middle on which her name was engraved. The piece with Alice on it was scratched and dented from its time in the sea but she wouldn't hear of having it replaced, which James had offered to organise for her. She loved it just as it was and wore it every day. Without moving from the settee she called up the stairs,

'Have you cleaned your teeth yet you two? Mollie? ... Sam? ... I said ... have you cleaned your teeth yet?' No reply. She raised her eyebrows in frustration and then turned to James and sighed. She then gave a big over-exaggerated smile to the little pyjama-clad Jacob who was bouncing on James' knee giggling.

'Come on Jacob. Let's go up anyway. Bedibyes.'

'Bebibi ...' gurgled little Jacob. James carried him and followed Alice upstairs. Mollie and Sam were in the bathroom arguing over how many sleeps there were left until Christmas. As Alice walked in they turned to her.

'Muumm, Mollie says it's only ...'

'Not now Sam. You can both stop arguing thank you. It's ridiculously late. For the hundredth time, have you both cleaned your teeth? ... Oh yes I can see you have by all the mess you've left in the sink. Now come on, time for bed for all of you.'

'Really?' James whispered. 'Sounds good to me.' He winked at Alice.

'Okay then,' called Sam, 'but first I need to choose a book for you to read to us.'

'Not tonight Sam,' said Alice. 'We stayed up late tonight as a special treat...'

'But Mum ...' moaned Mollie. 'you promised us yesterday. You said we could all sit on my bed – all of us including James, because he'd be here tomorrow – which is today – and we'd have a story together.'

'Yes you did,' added Sam. 'I'll go and look for a book ...'

'Alright,' Alice said with a sigh. 'Mollie's bed it is then.' Sam rushed off into his room to look for a book while Mollie got into her bed and Alice, James and baby Jacob settled down on the side of the bed.

'Jacob can come in with me can't he?' said Mollie. 'Come on Jacob, let's have a cuddle while we listen to a story.'

'Okay,' James said. 'Are you ready Jacob?' James held Jacob up and flew him like an aeroplane into the bed saying

'Coming to land in between Mollie and Mr Bunnie.' They all fell about laughing, but then Mollie said indignantly,

'He's called Floppy – not Mr Bunny.'

'We'd better do it again then!' James picked up Jacob and held him up in the air and once more zoomed him into bed, 'Coming to land Jacob ... in between Mollie and Mr Floppy.'

'Not *Mr* Floppy ... just Floppy,' Mollie shouted! Alice couldn't stop laughing either but said,

'Nothing like having a nice calm relaxing time before bedtime!'

'Once more ...' James said as he picked up Jacob again. 'Here we go Jacob... last time ... in between Mollie and *just* Floppy.'

'No!!' Mollie squealed. 'Not *just* Floppy! It's Floppy!' Everyone was now in fits of laughter.

'Where's Sam with the book?' Alice giggled.

'I'll go and help him,' James said as he tucked Jacob into the bed cozily next to Mollie. At that moment Sam walked into the room.

'I can't decide which book to choose. I mean, we've already done most of them and the others would be too scary for Jacob. Mollie doesn't like them either.'

'Oh Sam ...' said Alice, who was getting a little impatient as she could see the likelihood of her and James getting any time alone tonight disappearing rapidly. 'Just pick something.'

'I'll tell you what,' James stated decisively, 'How about I tell a story? Then you'll know it definitely won't be one you'll have ever heard before?'

'How do you know we won't know it already?' asked Mollie.

'Because no-one's written it yet!' Mollie and Sam looked confused.

'Right!' Alice said. 'Sam, get yourself into bed with Mollie and Jacob and then James can start.'

As Sam climbed in, Alice said, 'Oh you all look so sweet together – I'm going to have to take a photo.' Alice rushed off to the bedroom to get her phone.

'James,' said Sam. 'What's your story about?'

'Well ...' James said slowly – desperately hoping that he hadn't forgotten how to use his imagination. 'It's about three very clever children, called ... Mollie ...Sam ... and Jacob. And ... they all have amazing superpowers!'

'Cool!' said Sam.

'James ...' Mollie asked, 'will you tell me what the little girl called Mollie's superpowers are?'

'Well let's just wait and see shall we?'

'Go on,' said Alice, returning with her phone, 'I'll take a photo while James is telling the story.'

'Okay ... are you all ready then?' James said looking at each of the three children individually, and giving little Jacob a tickle under the chin.

'Once upon a time, there were three very lucky children called Mollie, Sam and Jacob. The reason they were so lucky was that their family owned a little blue and white beach hut with magic powers ... and the beach hut was called Alice ... and lots of very special things happened there ...'

If you enjoyed reading The Beach Hut called Alice, please leave a review and keep an eye out for the next Sebleigh Bay novel. Thank you.

Acknowledgements

I want to thank my lovely husband for his help with editing, my son for being awesome, and my friends who encouraged and inspired me to write this book.

Printed in Dunstable, United Kingdom